FIRE

Chewbacca saw it first. The ship, aerodynamically perfect, slid through Kessel's atmosphere like a vibroblade. The ship fired surgical strikes of turbolasers at the *Falcon's* maneuvering jets, disabling them further.

"We're already crashing!" Han bellowed. "What more do they want? But he knew: they wanted the *Falcon* to be destroyed on impact, all occupants erased.

When the Hornet tried to outflank them, Han swept the ship aside as a towering plume of atmosphere boiled into the sky. The Hornet Interceptor tried to second-guess his move, but Han lurched sideways again, driving the Hornet into the roaring upward flow of wind.

Han gave a cry of triumph. . . .

Then the surface of the planet Kessel rushed up at them like a gigantic hammer.

STAR WARS®

The Jedi Academy Trilogy

Volume I

JEDI SEARCH

Kevin J. Anderson

BANTAM BOOKS
TORONTO · NEW YORK · LONDON · SYDNEY · AUCKLAND

Jedi Academy Trilogy Vol. I: JEDI SEARCH
A BANTAM BOOK : 0 553 40808 9

First publication in Great Britain

PRINTING HISTORY
Bantam edition published 1994
Bantam edition reprinted 1994 (three times)
Bantam edition reprinted 1995 (twice)
Bantam edition reprinted 1997
Bantam edition reprinted 1999

Bantam Books are published by Transworld Publishers,
61–63 Uxbridge Road, London W5 5SA,
a division of The Random House Group Ltd,
in Australia by Random House Australia (Pty) Ltd,
20 Alfred Street, Milsons Point, Sydney, NSW 2061, Australia,
in New Zealand by Random House New Zealand Ltd;
18 Poland Road, Glenfield, Auckland 10, New Zealand
and in South Africa by Random House (Pty) Ltd,
Endulini, 5a Jubilee Road, Parktown 2193, South Africa.

Printed and bound in Great Britain by
Cox & Wyman Ltd, Reading, Berkshire.

Dedication

To my editor
BETSY MITCHELL,
for giving me the opportunity to play
in such a vast and entertaining universe
and for helping shape my work into
the best it could be.

Acknowledgments

Lucy Autrey Wilson of Lucasfilm Licensing for keeping watch over a million things at once and for suggesting new things faster than I could possibly implement the old ones; my wife Rebecca for all her brainstorming and her sharp editing skills—and her love; Bill Smith for his suggestions and the invaluable STAR WARS source material available from West End Games; Ralph McQuarrie for his wild ideas and imagination that sparked more than one avalanche of possibilities; Dave Willoughby for his help in alien geology and the other STAR WARS authors Tom Veitch, Dave Wolverton, Timothy Zahn, and Kathy Tyers for helping my story fit in with theirs.

1

The black hole cluster near Kessel reached out for the *Millennium Falcon* with jaws of gravity, drawing it close. Even in the mottled blur of hyperspace, Han Solo could see the huge distortion as a bruised whirlpool, trying to suck them down to infinity.

"Hey, Chewie! Don't you think that's too close?" He stared at the *Falcon*'s navicomputer, wishing they had chosen a course that would take them a safer distance from the Maw. "What do you think this is, an old smuggling mission? We got nothing to hide this time."

Beside him, Chewbacca looked disappointed and grunted an excuse, waving his hairy paws in the stifling air of the cockpit.

"Yeah, well we're on an official mission this time. No more skulking about. Try to act dignified, okay?"

Chewbacca groaned a skeptical reply, then turned to his navigational screens.

Han felt a pang at returning to his old haunts, reminded of when he had been just on the other side of the law, running spice, being chased by Imperial scout ships. When his life had been free and easy.

On one of those frantic missions, he and Chewbacca had practically shaved the bottom plating off the *Falcon*, taking a shortcut and skimming closer to the Maw cluster of black holes than had ever before been recorded. Sensible pilots avoided the area, using longer paths that kept them clear of the black holes, but the *Falcon*'s speed had carried them to safety on the other side, making the Kessel run in under twelve parsecs. But that "guaranteed sure thing" mission had ended in disaster anyway; Han had dumped his load of spice just before being boarded by Imperials.

This time, though, Han was returning to Kessel under different circumstances. His wife Leia had appointed him an official representative of the New Republic, an ambassador of sorts, though the title seemed somewhat honorary.

But even an honorary title had its advantages. Han and Chewbacca no longer had to dodge scout ships, or duck under planetary sensor nets, or use the secret compartments under the deck plates. Han Solo found himself in the unlikely, and uncomfortable, position of being *respectable*. There was no other word for it.

But Han's new responsibilities weren't just quaint annoyances. He was married to Leia—who could have imagined *that*?—and he had three children.

Han leaned back in his flight chair and locked his hands behind his head. He allowed a wistful smile to cross his face. He had visited the kids as often as he could, in their protective isolation on a secret planet, and the twins were due to come home to Coruscant in a week. Anakin, the third little baby, had filled him with wonder as he tickled the tiny ribs, watching an expression of amusement cross the infant's face.

Han Solo, a father figure? Leia had said a long time ago that she liked "nice men"—and that was exactly what Han was turning into!

He caught Chewbacca looking at him out of the corner of his eye. Embarrassed, Han sat up straight and frowned down at the controls. "Where are we? Shouldn't it be about time to end this jump?"

Chewie growled an affirmative, then reached out with a furry paw to grasp the hyperspace controls. The Wookiee watched the numbers tick away on his control panel; at the appropriate moment he hauled backward on the lever that dropped them back into normal space. The mottled coloring of hyperspace fanned into starlines with a roar that Han felt more than heard; then they were surrounded by the expected tapestry of stars.

Behind them the spectacle of the Maw looked like a garish finger painting as ionized gas plunged into multiple black holes. Directly in front of the *Falcon*, Han saw the blue-white glare of Kessel's sun. As the ship rotated to align them with the ecliptic, Kessel itself came into view, potato-shaped and maned with the tendrils of escaping atmosphere, orbited by a large moon that had once housed a garrison of Imperial troopers.

"Right on target, Chewie," Han said. "Now let me have the controls."

Kessel looked like a wraith coasting along its orbit, too small to hold on to its own atmosphere. Huge generating factories constantly processed the raw rocks to release oxygen and carbon dioxide, making it possible for people to survive outside with simple breath masks instead of total environment suits. A good portion of the newly manufactured atmosphere escaped into space, wisping behind the small planet like the tail of a giant comet.

Chewbacca barked a short, nasal comment. Han nodded. "Yeah, it looks great from up here. Too bad it's so different when you get a closer look. I never liked the place."

Kessel was a major planet for spice production and seat of heavy smuggling activities, as well as the site for one of the toughest prisons in the galaxy. The Empire had controlled spice production except for what smugglers managed to steal from under Imperial noses. But with the fall of the Emperor, the smugglers and the prisoners in the Imperial Correction Facility took over the planet. Kessel had laid low during the depredations of Grand Admiral Thrawn and the recent resurrection of the Emperor, keeping quiet and trying hard not to be noticed, answering no one's request for help.

A low growl rumbled in Chewie's throat. Han sighed and shook his head, "Look, I'm not happy about going back there either, buddy. But things are different now, and we're the best people to do it."

With the civil war ended and the New Republic once again firmly seated on Coruscant, leaving scattered groups of Imperial warships to fight each other, it was time to reopen negotiations. *Better to get them on our side than to let them sell out wherever they can,* Han thought, *which is what they'll probably do anyway.* As representative of the new unified smugglers, Luke's old nemesis Mara Jade had tried to contact Kessel and been flatly rebuffed.

The *Millennium Falcon* approached Kessel, firing aft thrusters to help them catch up with the planet's motion, preparing for insertion into orbit. On the helm's scanner screens, Han checked their approach. "Vectoring in," he said.

Chewie made a quick comment and pointed at the screens. Han looked down to see blips already in orbit around the planet, emerging from the blanketing clouds of the atmosphere. "I see 'em. Looks like about a half dozen ships. Too far away to determine the types."

Han brushed aside Chewie's uneasy growl. "Well, then we'll just tell them who we are. Don't worry. Why do you think Leia made such a fuss about getting us proper diplomatic ID signals and everything?"

He switched on the New Republic beacon that automatically pinged out their identification in Basic and several other languages. To his surprise, the orbiting ships changed their vector in unison and increased speed to intercept the *Falcon*.

"Hey!" Han shouted, then realized he had not switched on the audio pickup. Chewie roared. Han toggled the switch on. "This is Han Solo of the New Republic ship *Millennium Falcon*. We are on a diplomatic mission." His mind raced, wondering what words a real diplomat would use. "Uh, please state your intentions."

The two closest ships raced in, first growing into distinct points of light, then taking on shapes. "Chewie, I think you'd better get our forward deflector shields up. I've got a bad feeling about this."

He reached for the communications switch as Chewbacca brought up the shields, but then he looked through the front viewport. The two incoming ships roared toward him at unbelievable speed, spreading out on either side. The sight of their squared-off solar panels and central pilot compartments turned Han's blood to ice water.

TIE fighters.

"Chewie, get over here. I'm taking the laser cannon."

Before the Wookiee could reply, Han hauled himself up the access tube into the gun well. He grabbed on to the gunner's chair, trying to reorient himself in the new gravity field.

The TIE fighters came in for a two-pronged attack, spreading above and below the *Falcon* and firing their lasers. As the ship lurched from the impact, Han managed to throw himself into the gunner's chair, grabbing for the harness buckle and strapping himself in. One of the attacking ships swooped overhead, and the *Falcon*'s sensor panels howled with the sound of Twin Ion Engines, from which the TIE fighter took its name. The enemy vessel fired again, but the beams streaked harmlessly through space.

"Chewie, take evasive action! Don't just fly straight!"

The Wookiee shouted something from below, and Han yelled back. "I don't know—you're piloting, *you* figure it out!" Obviously Kessel had not rolled out the welcome mat for them. Had some vestige of the Empire taken over the planet? If so, Han needed to get that information back to Coruscant.

Other ships were approaching now, and somehow Han didn't think they were coming to help. Up ahead, the two TIE fighters swooped up in a tight arc, executing a complete one-eighty and roaring back for a second attack on the *Falcon*.

But this time Han had managed to strap himself in and power up the laser batteries. On his scope the TIE fighter made a digitized target, growing larger. The enemy ship came closer and closer. Han tightened his grip around the firing levers, knowing the TIE pilot would be doing the same. He waited, feeling sweat build up on his neck. He realized he was holding his breath. One more second. One more second. The targeting cross showed dead center on the starboard wing of the fighter.

The instant Han pressed the firing button, Chewbacca threw the *Falcon* into an evasive roll. The laser blasts went wide, spraying toward the distant stars. The TIE fighter's shot also missed, streaking in the opposite direction and coming perilously close to striking the second TIE fighter.

The second fighter managed to readjust his aim quickly enough that his two shots scored the *Falcon*'s shields. Han heard sparks spraying from the control panels. Chewie bellowed a preliminary damage report. Aft shields gone. Forward shields still holding well. That meant they had to take the TIE fighters head-on.

As the first fighter swung around for a third pass, Han swiveled his gun turret as far as it would go and stared at the targeting screen again. This time he would forget about finesse and perfect accuracy. He just wanted to blast the sucker. His lasers were fully charged, and he could afford to waste a few shots, as long as this wasn't going to be a prolonged battle.

As soon as the targeting cross touched the image of the fighter, Han squeezed his firing buttons at full power, strafing his deadly laser across the path of the incoming ship. The Imperial fighter swooped in but could not change its course quickly enough, plowing through the shower of laser bolts.

The ship erupted into a flame-flower of exploding fuel tanks and expanding atmosphere. Han and Chewbacca shouted their triumph in unison. Even euphoric, Han didn't sit around patting himself on the back.

"Let's go after the other one, Chewie." The second TIE fighter swerved outward in a long trajectory, then headed back toward Kessel. "Hurry, before those reinforcements can get here."

He wondered if perhaps he and Chewbacca shouldn't turn and flee immediately. But part of him refused to let anybody take pot-shots at the *Millennium Falcon* and just walk away from it.

Chewbacca increased speed, closing the gap between the *Falcon* and the TIE fighter. "Just get me one good shot, Chewie. One good shot."

He was in an unmarked modified light freighter—why would the TIE fighters come out shooting at them in the first place? Was it the New Republic ID beacon? What was going on at Kessel? Leia sat around thinking about details like that, analyzing the possibilities, and coming up with scenarios. With her tremendous load of diplomatic duties, she was becoming more and more of a thinker each day, trying to solve things by committee and negotiation. But a political solution wouldn't work if an Imperial TIE fighter came in shooting at you.

Another ship soared up from behind as they chased the TIE fighter toward Kessel. Han shot off a few bursts from his laser, but they all missed; then he turned his attention to the ship tailing them. The *Falcon* had no operational shields back there.

Chewbacca called out again from below; then Han got his second surprise for the day. "I see it, I see it!"

An X-wing fighter approached from the rear, slowly gaining on the *Falcon* as they neared Kessel. Han took another potshot at the TIE fighter. Even from this distance the X-wing fighter seemed old and battered, as if it had been repaired many times.

"Chewie, contact the X-wing and tell him we'd appreciate whatever help he can give us." Han pressed his back against the firing chair and focused his attention on his target.

The fleeing TIE fighter soared into the wispy tail of atmosphere behind the planet. Han could see a bright pathway as the speed of the ship ionized the gas.

Then the X-wing fired on the *Falcon* from behind. The lasers scored a direct hit, incinerating the protruding sensor dish mounted on the top of the ship.

Han and Chewie shouted at each other, scrambling to figure what to do. Chewbacca took the *Falcon* into a tight dive closer to the atmosphere of Kessel.

"Turn us around! Turn us around!" They had to get their unprotected aft section out of the X-wing's line of fire.

The X-wing shot again, burning metal on the hull of the

Falcon. All the lights went out inside the ship. From the lurch of the cabin Han knew the hit had been a bad one. He could already smell something burning below decks. Emergency lights clicked on.

"We've got to get out of here!"

Chewbacca barked the Wookiee equivalent of "no kidding."

They ducked into the atmospheric tail, buffeted by the suddenly dense gas particles pelting the ship. Around them streamers of heated gas glowed orange and blue. The X-wing came in from behind, still firing.

Han's mind raced. They could skim around Kessel in a tight orbit, then slingshot back out of the system. With the black hole cluster so close at hand, no one would risk jumping into hyperspace without intensive prior calculations, and neither he nor Chewie could spare the time to do them.

With the *Falcon*'s sensor dish slagged, Han couldn't even send out a distress call or try to sweet-talk the traitorous commander of the X-wing. He couldn't even surrender! Talk about being stuck. "Chewie, if you have any suggestions—"

He stopped talking as his mouth dropped open. As they swept around Kessel, Han detected wave after wave of fighter ships launching from the garrison moon, raising a defensive curtain the *Millennium Falcon* would never be able to cross.

He saw hundreds of ships of every size and make imaginable, salvaged warships and stolen pleasure cruisers. Reaching the safety of numbers, the second TIE fighter did another tight loop to join the rest of the group. And they all came in shooting with a blur of turbolaser bolts that looked like a fireworks display. Despite the motley appearance of the Kessel fleet, Han's sensors showed that their weapons worked just fine.

The attacking X-wing scored a direct hit. The cabin shook.

The *Falcon* took a turn upward as Chewbacca tried to flee the oncoming wave of ships. Han sent a barrage of laser fire into the cluster and was gratified to see the engine pod of a small Z-95 Headhunter fighter burst into flames. The snub fighter dropped out of the attacking fleet and wobbled toward Kessel's atmosphere. Han hoped it would crash.

Seeing that it would serve no purpose to keep firing against overwhelming odds, Han dropped back down the access shaft of the gun turret to the cockpit to see what he could do to assist Chewbacca.

Then the fleet of ships began pummeling them. The X-wing fired again, scoring a second direct hit. A firestorm of laser blasts struck their forward deflector shields. Chewie slewed the *Falcon* from side to side in a futile evasive maneuver.

Han settled himself into the other pilot's chair just in time to see the indicator lights for the forward shields wink out. They were now unprotected from the front and from behind.

Another hit rocked them, and Han's chest smacked against the control panel. "There goes the main drive unit. We're space-meat in the next barrage. Take us down, Chewie. Get us into the atmosphere. It's the only thing we can do."

Chewbacca started to express his disbelief, but Han grabbed the controls and sent them lurching down toward Kessel. "It's gonna be a bumpy ride. Hold on to your fur."

The swarm of attacking ships whirled in space as the *Falcon* plowed into the white atmosphere of Kessel. Han grabbed his seat as the ship struck the clouds. He suddenly felt the buffeting winds caused by gouts of air escaping into space. From his control panels and the stench leaking from the back compartments, Han knew that his maneuvering capabilities would be minimal. By the groaning sounds from his copilot, he knew the Wookiee had realized the same thing.

"Think of it this way, Chewie. If we land this thing in one piece, our skill as pilots will be legendary from one end of the galaxy to the other!" Han said with a humor he did not feel. *I knew I shouldn't have come back to Kessel.*

The *Falcon* was going down. Both Han and Chewbacca fought to keep a steady downward course that would not burn them up in the insubstantial atmosphere.

Kessel's main defensive fleet swept into orbit and prepared for an orderly descent. One sleek, insectile ship, which Han recognized as a black-market-built Hornet Interceptor, peeled off, streaking downward in the *Falcon*'s backdraft.

Chewbacca saw it first. The ship, aerodynamically perfect, slid through the atmosphere like a vibroblade, ignoring the heat generated on its hull. The ship fired surgical strikes of turbolasers at the *Falcon*'s maneuvering jets, disabling them further.

"We're already crashing!" Han bellowed. "What more do they want?" But he knew: they wanted the *Falcon* to be destroyed on impact, all occupants erased. Han suspected he didn't need any help from the Hornet Interceptor.

As they plunged downward, the *Falcon* approached one of the giant atmosphere factories, a huge smokestack mounted on the surface of Kessel, where immense engines catalyzed the rock and cooked out gases into a cyclone of breathable air.

The Hornet Interceptor fired again. The *Falcon* lurched from a near miss. Chewbacca's face was grim. His fangs showed as he concentrated on keeping them alive.

"Chewie, pull as close to the plume as you can. I've got an idea." Chewbacca yowled, but Han cut him off. "Just do it, buddy!"

When the Hornet tried to outflank them, Han swept the ship aside as the towering plume of atmosphere boiled into the sky. The Hornet Interceptor tried to second-guess his move, but Han lurched sideways again, driving the Hornet into the roaring upward flow of wind.

An aileron strut in the delicate insectile wing snapped off, and the Hornet spun into the cyclone. Other parts of its hull broke apart as the ship tried to escape but lurched deeper into the danger zone. Han gave a cry of triumph as the ship exploded into flames that were pulled to tatters by the atmosphere factory's vortex.

Then the surface of Kessel rushed up at them like a gigantic hammer.

Han fought with the controls. "At least we'll have a soft landing with the new repulsorlifts we installed," he said.

He grabbed at the panel, priming the controls. Chewbacca barked at him to hurry. Han activated the repulsorlifts as he simultaneously heaved a sigh of relief.

Nothing.

"What?" He slammed his fingers on the switch again and again, but the repulsorlifts refused to operate. "I just had those fixed!"

Han yelled above the noise of screaming wind as he fought to bring the *Falcon* under some semblance of control. "Okay, Chewie, I am definitely open for suggestions!"

But Chewbacca had no time to answer before the ship crashed into the rugged surface of Kessel.

2

The towers of Imperial City rose to the sky, high above the shadowed surface of the planet Coruscant. The cornerstones of the towers had been in place for more than a thousand generations, dating back to the formative days of the Old Republic. Over the millennia higher and higher structures had been built on top of the ruined foundations.

Luke Skywalker stepped onto a shuttle-landing platform that jutted out from the scarred, monolithic face of the former Imperial Palace. Gusts of wind whipped around him, and he pulled back the hood of his Jedi robe.

He looked into the sky, pondering the thin layer of atmosphere that protected Coruscant from space beyond. Wrecked ships still rode in haphazard orbits, debris from the vicious battles when the Alliance had recently recaptured the planet from Imperial control during civil war in the remnants of the Empire.

Higher than the tops of the towers, kitelike hawk-bats

rode thermal currents rising from the canyons of the city. As he watched, one hawk-bat swooped down, down, into the dark crevasses between ancient buildings, finally emerging a moment later with something cylindrical and dripping— a granite slug, perhaps—in its claws.

Luke bided his time, using a Jedi meditation technique to quell the anxiety inside him. As a younger man he had been fidgety and impatient, filled with uncertainty. But Yoda had taught him patience, along with so many other things. A true Jedi Knight could wait as long as necessary.

The New Republic Senate had been in session for only an hour, and they would still be working on mundane issues. Luke wanted to startle them after they had been talking for a while.

The immense metropolis of Imperial City bustled around him, little changed now that it was the seat of the New Republic instead of the Empire; prior to that it had been capital of the Old Republic. The capitol building, formerly Emperor Palpatine's palace, was made of polished gray-green rock and mirrored crystals, sparkling in the hazy sunlight of Coruscant as it towered over all other structures, even the adjoining Senate building.

Much of Imperial City had been laid waste during the months of civil war following the downfall of Grand Admiral Thrawn. The various factions of the old Empire had fought over the Emperor's home world, turning vast districts into graveyards of crashed ships and exploded buildings.

But the tide of battle had turned, and the New Republic had driven back the vestiges of the Empire. Many Alliance soldiers now turned their efforts to repairing the damage, his friend Wedge Antilles among them. Top priority had been given to rebuilding the former Imperial Palace and the Senate chambers. The Emperor's own construction droids ranged through the battle-scarred wastelands, automatically scraping up raw materials from the wreckage for conversion into new buildings.

In the distance Luke could see one of the enormous droids, forty stories tall, wrecking a half-collapsed building shell and plowing a path where its programming had deemed a new elevated transport path should be routed. Its girder arms toppled the stone face of the building, pulling free metal support structures and feeding the debris into a processing mouth where the materials would be separated and new components extruded.

During the previous year of violent strife, Luke had been whisked away to the resurrected Emperor's stronghold in the galactic core, and there he had allowed himself to learn the dark side. He had become the Emperor's chief lieutenant, just like his father, Darth Vader. The struggle had been great within him, and only with the help, and the friendship, and the *love* of Leia and Han had he been able to break free. . . .

Luke saw a diplomatic shuttle dropping down from orbit with its locator lights rippling in a complex sequence. Its jets turned off with a whining sound as it coasted toward a landing pad on the far side of the palace.

Luke Skywalker had been through the fire now. Inside, his heart seemed a diamond-hard lump. He wasn't merely another Jedi Knight—he was the only remaining Jedi *Master*. He had survived tests and rigors more potent than routine Jedi training prepared him for. Luke understood more about the Force now than he had ever dreamed possible. Sometimes it terrified him.

He thought of the days when he had been idealistic and adventuresome, riding the *Millennium Falcon* and dueling blindly with a practice remote as Ben Kenobi watched. Luke remembered also the skepticism he had felt as he swooped down upon the first Death Star during the Battle of Yavin, trying to locate a tiny thermal-exhaust port; Ben's voice had spoken to him then, telling him to trust in the Force. Luke understood much more now, especially why the old man's eyes had held such a haunted look.

Another hawk-bat swooped down into the dark maze of the lower levels of buildings, flapping its wings as it climbed back up, holding a squirming prize in its claws. As Luke watched, a second hawk-bat dove in on an intercept course, grabbing the prey out of the first's grasp. Far away, he could hear their cawing sounds as they slashed and tore at each other. The squirming prey, no longer heeded, fell through the air, buffeted by rising currents, until it struck ground somewhere in the alley dimness. The two hawk-bats, locked in mortal combat, also fell as they struggled with each other, until they too smashed into an outcropping of the abandoned lower levels.

A troubled expression crossed Luke's face. An omen? He was about to address the New Republic Senate. The time had come. He turned and walked back inside the cool corridors, pulling his robe tightly around himself.

Luke stood at the entrance to the Senate assembly chamber. The room swept down to a giant amphitheater in which sat the inner circle of appointed senators and outer rows of representatives from different planets, different alien races. Realtime holos of the proceedings would be broadcast around Imperial City and recorded for transmission to other planets.

Sunlight filtered through the fragmented crystal segments in the ceiling high overhead, fanning out the spectrum in a rainbow effect over the most important people at the center of the room, scintillating around them as they moved—designed, Luke knew, by the Emperor himself to strike awe into those observing him.

As she spoke now on the central dais, Mon Mothma, the New Republic's Chief of State, seemed uncomfortable in the grandeur of the assembly chamber. Luke allowed a smile to cross his face as he remembered the first time he had seen Mon Mothma describing the plans of the second Death Star as the Rebels approached Endor.

With her short reddish hair and soft voice, Mon Mothma did not look like a tough-as-nails military commander. As a former member of the Imperial Senate, Mon Mothma seemed to be more in her element now, trying to forge the pieces of the New Republic into a strong, unified government.

Beside Mon Mothma sat Luke's sister Leia Organa Solo, straight-backed and listening to every moment of the proceedings. Leia had been performing more and more important diplomatic activities with each passing month.

Around the dais sat the members of the Alliance High Command, important figures in the Rebellion given roles in the new government: General Jan Dodonna, who had led the Battle of Yavin against the first Death Star; General Carlist Rieekan, former commander of Echo Base on the ice planet Hoth; General Crix Madine, an Imperial defector who had been invaluable in planning the destruction of the second Death Star; Admiral Ackbar, who had led the rebel fleet in the Battle of Endor; Senator Garm Bel Iblis, who had brought his Dreadnaught ships against Grand Admiral Thrawn.

Battlefield credentials did not necessarily imply that these brave leaders would be gifted politicians as well, but since the hold of the New Republic was still shaky, as the recent devastating civil war had shown, it made good sense to keep military commanders in positions of power.

Finishing her speech, Mon Mothma raised her hands.

For a moment it looked as if she were about to give a benediction. "I call for any new business. Does anyone wish to speak?"

Luke's timing had been perfect. He stepped into the light at the entrance archway and drew back his hood. He spoke softly, but used his Jedi powers to project with sufficient strength that everyone in the entire amphitheater heard him.

"I would address the assembly, Mon Mothma. If I may?"

He walked down the steps with a gliding stride, quickly enough that the others would not lose patience, but with enough grace to imply his own strength of character. Appearances could deceive, Yoda had said, but sometimes appearances could be very important.

As he descended the long ramp, Luke felt all eyes turn toward him. A hush fell over the assembly. Luke Skywalker, the lone remaining Jedi Master, almost never took part in governmental proceedings.

"I have an important matter to address," he said. For a moment he was reminded of when he had walked alone into the dank corridors of Jabba the Hutt's palace—but this time there were no piglike Gamorrean guards that he could manipulate with a twist of his fingers and a touch of the Force.

Mon Mothma gave him a soft, mysterious smile and gestured for him to take a central position. "The words of a Jedi Knight are always welcome to the New Republic," she said.

Luke tried not to look pleased. She had provided the perfect opening for him. "In the Old Republic," he said, "Jedi Knights were the protectors and guardians of all. For a thousand generations the Jedi used the powers of the Force to guide, defend, and provide support for the rightful government of worlds—before the dark days of the Empire came, and the Jedi Knights were killed."

He let his words hang, then took another breath. "Now we have a New Republic. The Empire appears to be defeated. We have founded a new government based upon the old, but let us hope we learn from our mistakes. Before, an entire order of Jedi watched over the Republic, offering strength. Now I am the only Jedi Master who remains.

"Without that order of protectors to provide a backbone of strength for the New Republic, can we survive? Will we be able to weather the storms and the difficulties of forging a new union? Until now we have suffered severe struggles—but in the future they will be seen as nothing more than birth pangs."

Before the other senators could disagree with that, Luke continued. "Our people had a common foe in the Empire, and we must not let our defenses lapse just because we have internal problems. More to the point, what will happen when we begin squabbling among ourselves over petty matters? The old Jedi helped to mediate many types of disputes. What if there are no Jedi Knights to protect us in the difficult times ahead?"

Luke moved under the diffracting rainbow colors from the crystal light overhead. He took his time to fix his gaze on all the senators present; he turned his attention to Leia last. Her eyes were wide but supportive. He had not discussed his idea with her beforehand.

"My sister is undergoing Jedi training. She has a great deal of skill in the Force. Her three children are also likely candidates to be trained as young Jedi. In recent years I have come to know a woman named Mara Jade, who is now unifying the smugglers—the former smugglers," he amended, "into an organization that can support the needs of the New Republic. She also has a talent for the Force. I have encountered others in my travels."

Another pause. The audience was listening so far. "But

are these the only ones? We already know that the ability to use the Force is passed from generation to generation. Most of the Jedi were killed in the Emperor's purge—but could he possibly have eradicated all of the descendants of those Knights? I myself was unaware of the potential power within me until Obi-Wan Kenobi taught me how to use it. My sister Leia was similarly unaware.

"How many people are abroad in this galaxy who have a comparable strength in the Force, who are potential members of a new order of Jedi Knights, but are unaware of who they are?"

Luke looked at them again. "In my brief search I have already discovered that there are indeed some descendants of former Jedi. I have come here to ask"—he turned to gesture toward Mon Mothma, swept his hand across the people gathered there in the chamber—"for two things.

"First, that the New Republic officially sanction my search for those with a hidden talent for the Force, to seek them out and try to bring them to our service. For this I will need some help."

Admiral Ackbar interrupted, blinking his huge fish eyes and turning his head. "But if you yourself did not know your power when you were young, how will these other people know? How will you find them, Jedi Skywalker?"

Luke folded his hands in front of him. "Several ways. First, with the help of two dedicated droids who will spend their days searching through the Imperial City databases, we may find likely candidates, people who have experienced miraculous strokes of luck, whose lives seem filled with incredible coincidences. We could look for people who seem unusually charismatic or those whom legend credits with working miracles. These could all be unconscious manifestations of a skill with the Force."

Luke held up another finger. "As well, the droids could search the database for forgotten descendants of known

Jedi Knights from the Old Republic days. We should turn up a few leads."

"And what will you yourself be doing?" Mon Mothma asked, shifting in her robes.

"I've already found several candidates I wish to investigate. All I ask right now is that you agree this is something we should pursue, that the search for Jedi be conducted by others and not just myself."

Mon Mothma sat up straighter in her central seat. "I think we can agree to that without further discussion." She looked around to the other senators, seeing them nod agreement. "Tell us your second request."

Luke stood taller. This was most important to him. He saw Leia stiffen.

"If sufficient candidates are found who have potential for using the Force, I wish to be allowed—with the New Republic's blessing—to establish in some appropriate place an intensive training center, a Jedi academy, if you will. Under my direction we can help these students discover their abilities, to focus and strengthen their power. Ultimately, this academy would provide a core group that could allow us to restore the Jedi Knights as protectors of the New Republic."

He drew in a deep breath and waited.

Senator Bel Iblis raised himself slowly to his feet. "A comment, if I may? I'm sorry, Luke, but I have to raise the question—we've already seen the terrible damage a Jedi can cause if he allows himself to be swayed by the dark side. We just recently fought against Joruus C'baoth, and of course Darth Vader nearly caused the death of us all. If a teacher as great as Obi-Wan Kenobi could fail and let his student fall to evil, how can we take the risk of training an entire new order of Jedi Knights? How many will turn to the dark side? How many new enemies will we make for ourselves?"

Luke nodded somberly. The question had been working at the back of his own mind, and he had pondered it deeply. "I can only say that we have seen these terrible examples, and we must learn from them. I myself have touched the dark side and come through stronger and more wary of its powers than ever before. I agree there is a risk, but I cannot believe the New Republic will be safer *without* a new force of Jedi."

A murmur rippled through the chamber. Bel Iblis stood a moment longer, as if he meant to say something else, but instead he sat down, looking satisfied.

Admiral Ackbar got to his feet and applauded with his flipperlike hands. "I agree that the Jedi's request is in the best interests of the New Republic," he said.

Jan Dodonna also stood. After narrowly surviving the Battle of Yavin, Dodonna had treated Luke with complete trust. "I agree as well!"

Soon all the senators were standing. Luke saw a broad grin on Leia's face as she too stood. He felt the rainbows around him from the crystal ceiling, seemingly full of power, and he felt warm inside.

Mon Mothma sat, nodding gravely. She was the last to stand up, and she raised her hand for silence. "I give you my hopes for the rebirth of the Jedi Knights. We will offer whatever help we can. May the Force be with you."

Before Luke could turn, applause from the audience rolled like a storm through the chamber.

3

Leia's quarters were among
the most spacious and accommodating in the Emperor's
abandoned palace—and the room echoed with emptiness.
Leia Organa Solo, formerly a princess, currently the New
Republic's Minister of State—felt tired and worn as she
returned to her rooms at the end of a long day.

The high point had been Luke's triumphant address
before the assembly, but that was merely one detail in
a day filled with problems. Confusing contradictions in
multilingual treaties that even Threepio couldn't fathom,
alien cultural restrictions that made diplomacy nearly
impossible—it made her head spin!

As Leia looked around her quarters, a frown etched
her face. "Illumination up two points," she said, and the
room grew brighter, driving some of the quiet shadows
farther away.

Han and Chewbacca were gone, ostensibly to reestablish
contact with the planet Kessel, although she believed it was

more of a vacation for him, a way to relive the "good old days" of gallivanting across the galaxy.

Sometimes she wondered if Han ever regretted marrying someone so different from himself, settling down with diplomatic entanglements on Coruscant. He tolerated endless receptions during which he had to dress nicely in clothes that obviously made him uncomfortable. In conversations he had to speak with a measured tact that was completely foreign to him.

But Han was off having fun at the moment, leaving her stuck in Imperial City.

The New Republic's Chief of State, Mon Mothma, gave Leia more and more assignments, letting the fate of planets hang on how well she accomplished her tasks. So far Leia *had* performed well, but the seven years since the Battle of Endor had been filled with many setbacks: the war against the alien Ssi-ruuk Imperium, the resurgence of Grand Admiral Thrawn and his bid to reassemble the Empire, not to mention the resurrected Emperor and his gigantic World Devastator machines. Though they seemed to be enjoying a time of relative peace at last, the constant warfare had left the New Republic on shaky ground.

In a way it had been easier when they had the Empire to fight against, to unify all the factions of the Alliance. But now the enemy was not so clearly defined. Now Leia and the others had to reforge links between all the planets that had once been crushed under the Imperial boot. Some of those worlds, though, had suffered so much that now they wanted to be left alone, given time to lick their wounds and heal. Many wanted no part of a galaxywide federation of planets. They wanted their independence.

But independent worlds could be picked off one by one if other powerful forces ever allied themselves against them.

Leia walked into her bedchamber and stripped off the

diplomatic clothing she had worn all day. This morning it had been crisp and bright, but the fabric lost its vigor after too much time under the rainbow lights of the grand audience chamber.

Within the next week or so, Leia would have to arrange meetings with ambassadors from six different worlds in an effort to convince them to join the New Republic. Four seemed amenable, but two insisted on complete neutrality until their planets' specific issues were addressed.

Her most difficult task would be two weeks hence, when the Caridan ambassador would arrive. Carida was deep in territory still held by vestiges of the Empire, home of one of the primary Imperial military training bases. Even though Emperor Palpatine was dead and Grand Admiral Thrawn overthrown, Carida refused to face reality. It had been a major victory that the ambassador agreed to come to Coruscant at all—and Leia would have to entertain him, no doubt smiling pleasantly the entire time.

Leia turned on the controls of the sonic bath and set it for a gentle massage. She eased herself into the chamber, letting out a long sigh, wanting just to blank out the troubles from her head.

Around her, fresh-cut flowers from the Skydome Botanical Gardens brightened the room with their faint perfume. Mounted on the wall were nostalgic scenes from the planet Alderaan, pictures of the planet where she had grown up, the planet Grand Moff Tarkin had destroyed to demonstrate the power of his Death Star: the peaceful, sweeping grasslands that whispered in the wind, the soaring kite creatures that ferried people from one smooth tower city to another, the industry and deep settlements built into the walls of wide cracks plunging into Alderaan's crust . . . her home city rising from the center of a lake.

Han had procured those pictures for her just last year; he wouldn't say where he had found them. For months the images wrenched her heart every time she looked at them. She thought of her foster father, Senator Bail Organa, and her childhood as a princess, never suspecting her true heritage.

Now Leia looked on those pictures with bittersweet fondness, as an indication of Han's love for her. He had, after all, once won a whole planet in a card game and had given it to her for the other survivors of Alderaan. He did love her.

Even though he wasn't here now.

After only a few minutes the sonic bath unknotted her muscles, revitalizing and refreshing her. Leia dressed again, this time in something more comfortable.

In the mirror she looked at herself. Leia no longer spent the meticulous time with her hair that she had when she was a princess on Alderaan. Since then she had borne three children, the twins, who were now two years old, and recently a third baby. She was able to see them only a few times a year, and she missed them terribly.

Because of the potential power carried by the grand-children of Anakin Skywalker, the twins and the baby boy had been taken to a carefully guarded planet, Anoth. All other knowledge of the planet had been blocked from her mind, to prevent anyone from prying it out of her thoughts.

During their first two years, Luke said, Jedi children were most vulnerable. Any contact with the dark side could warp their minds and abilities for life.

She activated the small holodais that projected recent images of her children. The two-year-old twins, Jacen and Jaina, played inside a colorful sculptured playground artifact. In another image Leia's personal servant Winter held the new baby, Anakin, smiling at something out of view. Leia smiled back, though the static images couldn't see her.

Part of that long loneliness would soon be over. Jacen and Jaina could now use some of the Jedi powers to protect themselves, and Leia could shield the twins as well. Within little more than a week—no, it was exactly eight days—her little boy and girl would be returning home.

Knowing that the twins were coming to stay lightened her mood. Leia eased back into the self-conforming chair as she turned on the entertainment synthesizers, playing a pastorale melody written by a famous composer from Alderaan.

The door chime sounded, startling her from her reverie. She glanced down to make certain she had remembered to dress herself, then went to the entryway.

Her brother Luke stood in the shadows, cowled in his brown hood and cloak. "Hello, Luke!" she said, then gasped. "Oh, I forgot completely!"

"Developing your Jedi powers is nothing to take lightly, Leia." He frowned, as if scolding her.

She gestured him to come inside. "I'm sure you'll have me make it up with extra practice sessions."

When seen from a distance, the huge construction droid moved at a plodding pace, lifting its immense support pods only once every half hour to shuffle a step forward. But standing right beneath it, General Wedge Antilles and his demolition teams saw the construction droid as a blur of motion, its thousands of articulated arms working on structures to be disassembled. The walking factory plowed deeper into the morass of collapsing and half-destroyed buildings in an old sector of Imperial City.

Some of the droid's limbs ended with implosion wrecking balls or plasma cutters that sent explosive jolts into the walls. Collector arms sorted through the rubble, yanking out girders, shoveling boulders and steelcrete into dispensing receptacles. Other raw wreckage was scooped directly into the churning mandibles and conveyor belts that brought the resources down to elemental separators, which in turn pulled out the useful substances and processed them into new building components. The heat rising from its internal factories rippled in miragelike waves, making the immense machine glow in Coruscant's star-filled night.

The construction droid continued to work its way through the buildings damaged from the devastating firefights during the recent civil warfare. With so much to repair or destroy, sometimes the droid's collector arms and debris nets were not sufficient.

Wedge Antilles looked up just in time to see a packed receptacle split from its moorings. "Hey, keep back, everybody! Under cover!" The demolition team scrambled under the protection of an outcropping of wall as the debris fell twenty stories.

A rain of boulders, transparisteel, and twisted rebars crashed with explosive force into the street below. Someone yelped into the comlink, then promptly silenced himself.

"Looks like this main building is going to go any minute," Wedge said. "Team Orange, I want you to keep at least half a block away from that thing. There's no telling what that droid's going to do, and I don't want to shut it down. It takes three days to reinitialize and get it working again." Wedge had not been thrilled with using the outdated and unpredictable technology of the construction droids, but they did seem to be the fastest way to clear the wreckage.

"I copy, Wedge," the Orange Team Leader said, "But if we see any more of those feral refugees, we're going to have to try and rescue them—even if they are faster and hide better." Then the comlink channel broke into chatter as he ordered other team members to move.

Wedge smiled. Even though he, like Lando Calrissian and Han Solo, had been promoted to the rank of general, Wedge still felt like "one of the guys." He was a fighter pilot at heart, and he liked it that way. He had spent the last four months in space with the salvage crews there, hauling wrecked fighters into higher orbits where they would pose no risk to the incoming ships. He had salvaged the vessels not too badly damaged and self-destructed those that posed too great a hazard in the orbital traffic lanes.

Last month Wedge had requested a ground assignment for a change, though he loved to fly in space. Now he was in charge of almost two hundred people, supervising the four construction droids that churned through this section of the city, restoring it and erasing battle scars from the war against the Empire.

The construction droids each had a master plan deep in their computer cores. As they repaired Imperial City in swaths, the droids checked the buildings in front of them, fixing those that needed minor repairs, demolishing those that didn't fit into the new plan.

Most of the sentient life forms had been evacuated from the deep underworld of the ancient metropolis, although some creatures living in the darkest alleys could no longer be classified as fully human. Shabby and naked, with pallid skin and sunken eyes, they were the descendants of those who had long ago fled to Coruscant's darkest alleys to escape political retribution; some looked as though they had not seen the sun their entire lives. When the New Republic returned to Coruscant, an effort spearheaded by the old veteran of Yavin 4, General Jan Dodonna, had been to help these poor souls, but they were wild and smart, and eluded capture every time.

The streets—or what had been streets centuries ago—were covered with dank moss and a lush growth of fungus. The smells of decaying garbage and stagnant water swirled around them anytime Wedge's team moved. Microclimates of rising air and condensing moisture created tiny rainstorms in the alleys, but the dripping water smelled no fresher than the standing pools or gutters. Wedge's teams deployed floating repulsor-lights, but clouds of settling dust from the demolition work filled the air with thick murk.

The construction droid paused in its work for a moment, and the relative silence sounded like a thud in Wedge's ears. He looked up to see the droid extending two of its big wrecking-ball arms. It swung the balls with mammoth force, toppling the wall in front of it. Then the droid levered its support-pod legs forward to take a step into the collapsing building.

But the side of the wall did not slough inward quite as Wedge expected; something inside had been reinforced more than the rest of the building. The construction droid tried to step down, but the wall would not yield.

The titanic droid began making loud, hydraulic sounds as it attempted to regain its balance. The forty-story-tall mechanical factory tilted sideways and hung poised on the verge of toppling. Wedge jerked out his comlink. If the construction droid fell, it would take out half a block of buildings with it, including the area where he had just sent Team Orange to take refuge.

But then a dozen of its arms locked together and extended to the adjacent wall of buildings, splaying out, breaking through in places, but steadying the droid's weight just long enough for it to regain its balance. A rustling noise came over the comlink as Wedge's teams let out a collective sigh of relief.

Wedge tried to see by the light of the shimmering aurora overhead and the floating lights they had strung. Hidden behind an edifice indistinguishable from the rest of the buildings stood solid metal walls, heavily reinforced but buckled and ruptured by the enormous foot of the construction droid.

Wedge frowned. The demolition teams had encountered a lot of ancient artifacts in the ruined buildings, but nothing that had been so powerfully shielded and hidden. Something told him this was important.

He looked up with a start to see that the construction droid had reoriented itself and returned to the reinforced building that stood in its way. Bending down its scanner-dome head, the droid inspected the tough walls of the shielded room, as if analyzing how best to rip it to shreds. Two of the explosive electrical claws extended downward.

The construction droid knew nothing about what secrets these buildings might contain. The droid merely followed the blueprint in its computer mind and carried out its programmed modifications.

Wedge felt an agonized moment of indecision. If he shut the droid down to inspect the mysterious building, it would take three days to reset all the systems and power it up again. But if the droid had indeed uncovered something important, something the Cabinet should know about, what would a few days matter?

Blue-white lightning flickered on the ends of the construction droid's explosive claws as it reached toward the shielded walls.

Wedge picked up his comlink and made ready to shut down the droid—and then his mind blanked. What was the code?

Beside him Lieutenant Deegan saw his moment of panicked confusion and snapped the answer. "SGW zero-zero-two-seven!" Wedge instantly keyed it into the comlink.

The droid froze just as it was about to discharge its electrical claws. Wedge heard the hissing rumble as the factories inside went into standby mode, powering down and cooling off. Wedge hoped he had made the right decision.

"Okay, Purple and Silver Teams come on in with me. We're going to do a little exploring here."

Summoning a cluster of floating lights to follow them, the teams converged at the foot of the construction droid and then moved into the wreckage. Loose dust flickered down.

They scrambled over the rubble, careful not to cut themselves on shattered transparisteel and protruding metal. Wedge heard the skittering sounds of small life-forms hiding in the new cracks. The patter of falling stones continued to fall as the collapsing walls shifted and reshifted. "Watch your backs—this place is still falling apart," Wedge said.

Ahead a wide cavelike gash had opened in the heavily shielded room, showing only a lightless interior.

"Let's go in. Nice and easy." Wedge narrowed his eyes at the shadows around them. "Be ready to retreat at a moment's notice. We don't know what's in there."

A deafening screech sounded far above, reverberating in the night. The demolition teams jumped, then forced themselves to relax when they found it was only the cooling construction droid venting waste heat.

Wedge stepped to the edge of the darkened hole. The buckled crack in the wall was completely dark, showing nothing.

The moment he poked his head into the darkness, the monster lunged forward, all fangs and spewing saliva.

Wedge cried out and stumbled back, bouncing against the jagged edge of the opening as the locomotive of claws and fur and armored body plating charged at him.

Before he could straighten his thoughts—before he could even imagine shouting an order to his troops—a spiderweb of crisscrossed blaster fire erupted into the night. Most of the beams struck home with a smoking hiss into the creature's body. A second round of blaster fire lanced out.

The monster roared in explosive surprise and pain before collapsing with enough force to start a small avalanche in the debris. Its death sigh sounded like steam escaping from a furnace.

Wedge slumped to the ground and suddenly felt his heart begin beating again. "Thanks, guys!"

The rest of them stood, frozen in surprise and terror, gawking at their own reflexively drawn blasters and at the heaving, dying hulk of the monster that had dwelled within the shielded building.

The thing looked like a huge armored rat with spines along its back and tusks coming out of its mouth. It had the tail of a krayt dragon, flicking in its final convulsions as black-purple blood oozed around burned craters of blaster wounds in its hide.

"Guess it got hungry waiting in there," Wedge said. "Your fearless leader needs to be a little more careful from now on."

He sent the bobbing lights through the opening to illuminate the chamber ahead. Nothing else seemed to be moving inside. Behind them the giant armored rat shuddered with a last groaning sigh, then sagged.

In pairs they pushed through the opening into the isolated chamber. The metal-plated floor was strewn with cracked bones and skulls from the subhumans that lived in the city's lower levels. "I guess it found something to eat after all," Wedge said.

On the far side of the dark room, they found another tunnel from deeper underground where a grate had been peeled aside. The grate was rusted, but bright score marks from large claws showed where the rat-thing had torn its way through.

"Not it—a *she*," Lieutenant Deegan said. "And now you can see why she was so upset." He pointed to the corner where the worst damage had occurred.

Broken blocks of building material lay piled on the rat-thing's nest. Bright smears of blood showed where three of the creature's young—each one the size of an Endorian pony—had been crushed by the boulders.

Wedge stared for a moment before he looked around the rest of the gloomy room. Adjusting the light-enhancers on his visor, he could see dark gadgets, consoles, bed-platforms with manacles and chains. Parked and dormant on two stands were glossy black Imperial interrogation droids; secret computer ports stared gray and dead like amphibious eyes.

"Some sort of torture center?" Lieutenant Deegan asked.

"Looks like it," Wedge answered. "Interrogation. This could yield a lot of information the Emperor didn't want us to have."

"Good thing you shut down the construction droid, Wedge," Deegan said. "It's worth the delay."

Wedge pursed his lips. "Yeah, good thing." He looked at the cruel interrogation droids and the torture equipment. A part of him wished he had never found this place.

The sculpture on Leia's crystal table jittered forward, stopped, then rose into the air.

The figure was a fat man with spread palms and a grin wide enough to swallow an X-wing fighter. The dealer had assured Leia that it was a genuine Corellian sculpture, that it would make Han think fond memories of his own world just as Han's images of Alderaan did for her. Upon receiving the anniversary gift, Han had thanked her profusely, but could barely control his laughter. He finally explained that the statue was a trademarked figurine stolen from a chain of cheap Corellian eating establishments. . . .

"Keep concentrating, Leia," Luke whispered into the silence, leaning closer. He watched her intently. Her eyes were focused in the far distance, not seeing the sculpture at all.

The statue continued to levitate, rising higher off the table; then suddenly it bumped forward to topple onto the floor.

Leia heaved a sigh and slumped back in the self-conforming chair. Luke tried to cover his disappointment as he remembered his own training. Yoda had made him stand on his head while balancing rocks and other heavy objects. Luke had received other training from the twisted Joruus C'baoth, and he had learned the depths of the dark side from the resurrected Emperor himself.

His sister's training had been much less rigorous, and more haphazard as she continually rescheduled lessons to accommodate her increasing diplomatic duties. But Leia concerned him: he had been working with her for more than seven years now, and she seemed to be blocked, having reached the limit of the powers she could master. Given her heritage as the daughter of Anakin Skywalker, Leia should have been easy to train. Luke wondered how he would manage to instruct a large group of students at his proposed Jedi academy if he could not succeed with his own sister.

Leia stood and picked up the fallen statue from the floor, setting it back on the table. Luke watched her, keeping his face free of any downcast expression. "Leia, what is it?" he asked.

She looked at him with her dark eyes and hesitated before answering. "Just feeling sorry for myself, I guess. Han should have arrived on Kessel two days ago, but he hasn't bothered to send a message. That's no big surprise, considering him!" But Luke saw more wistfulness than sarcasm in her eyes.

"Sometimes it wears on me not to have my own children here. I've been with the twins for only a fraction of their lives. I can count on one hand the number of times I've visited the baby. I haven't had time to feel like a mother. The diplomatic chores won't give me a rest." Then she looked directly at him. "And you're about to go off on your great Jedi hunt. I feel like I'm missing out on life."

Luke reached out to touch her arm. "You could become a very powerful Jedi if you would only devote some concentration to your work. To follow the Force, you must let your training be the focus of your life and not become distracted by other things."

Leia reacted more strongly than he had anticipated, drawing away. "Maybe I'm afraid of that, Luke. When I look at you, I see a haunted expression in your eyes, as if a vital part of you has been burned away by the personal hells you've walked through. Trying to kill your own father, dueling with a clone of yourself, serving the Dark Side for the Emperor. If that's what it takes to be a powerful Jedi, maybe I don't *want* the job!"

She held up her hand to stop him from saying anything until she had finished. "I am doing important work for the Council. I'm helping to rebuild a whole republic of a thousand star systems. Maybe that is my life's work, not being a Jedi. And maybe, just maybe, I might want to fit being a mother in there, too."

Luke looked at her, unmoved. No one could read his expressions anymore; he was no longer innocent. "If that is your destiny, Leia, it's a good thing I'll start training other Jedi soon." They stared at each other in an uncomfortable silence for a few moments. Luke looked away first, retreating from that line of conversation.

"But you still need to protect yourself from the Dark Side. Let's work a little more with shielding and your inner defenses, and then we'll call it a night." Leia nodded, but he could sense that her spirits had sunk further.

He reached out with his fingers to touch her dark hair, drifting over the contours of her head. "I'm going to try to probe your mind. I'll use different techniques, different touches. Try to resist me, or at least pinpoint where I am."

Luke let his eyes fall half-closed, then sent faint tendrils of thoughts into her mind, deftly touching the topography of her memory. At first she didn't react, but then he could feel her concentrating, building an invisible wall around his probe. Though slow, she succeeded in blocking him off.

"Good, now I'm going to try different places." He moved his touch to a different center. "Resist me if you can."

As he kept probing deeper, Leia became better at fending him off. She parried his attempts with greater speed and stronger force as he guided her to put up barriers. He grew more pleased as he worked with her, touching random spots in her mind, trying to take her by surprise. He could feel her own delight with her improving abilities.

Luke reached to the back of her mind, an area of deep primal memories but little conscious thought. He doubted he could get any defensive reaction there, but no attacker would be likely to strike at such places. Her thoughts were like a map laid out in front of him, and Luke touched inward to an isolated nub in her mind. He pushed—

And suddenly felt as if a giant invisible palm had planted itself on his chest and shoved backward. Luke stumbled to keep his balance, taking two steps away from her. Leia's eyes went wide, and her mouth dropped open in surprise.

Luke said, "What did you do?" in the same moment Leia said, "What did I do?"; then both answered, "I don't know!" simultaneously.

Luke tried to reconstruct what he had done. "Let me try that again. Just relax."

She seemed anything but relaxed as he probed her again, reaching to the back of her mind, finding the isolated nub among her instinctive centers. Touching it, he found himself knocked away again with physical force.

"But I didn't do anything!" Leia insisted.

Luke allowed himself to smile. "Your reflexes did, Leia. When a medical droid taps your knee, your leg jerks whether you want it to or not. We may have just stumbled upon something a potential Jedi has that others don't. I want you to try it on me. Here, close your eyes and I'll give you an image of what I did to you."

"Do you think I'll be able to?" Leia asked.

"If it truly is instinctive, all you need to do is find the right spot."

"I'll try." Her face wore a skeptical expression.

"Do, or do not. There is no try. That's what Yoda always said."

"Oh, stop quoting him. You don't need to impress me!"

Leia touched her brother's temples, and he took a deep breath, using Jedi relaxation techniques to drop his guard. He had erected so much mental armor in the past seven years that he hoped he could still let her inside. He felt the touch of her thoughts, delicate mental fingers tracing the contours of his brain. He directed her search toward the back, where primitive thoughts slept. "Can you—"

Before he could finish his question, Leia stumbled backward into the self-conforming seat. "Wow! I found the nub, but when I touched it, you knocked me off my feet."

Luke felt wonder tingle through him. "And it was completely unconscious on my part. I wasn't aware of doing anything."

Luke touched his lips as new thoughts raced through his mind. "I need to try this on other people. If it's completely a reflex reaction, this could be a very useful test for finding people who have latent Jedi powers."

Next morning, the metropolitan shuttle skimmed over the rooftops of Imperial City, like a bus on the thermals rising from chasms between the tall buildings. The strip of buildings newly erected by the construction droids looked like a gleaming stripe through the ancient city.

Admiral Ackbar piloted the shuttle himself, holding the controls in his articulated fin-hands as he watched the skies with his widely set fish eyes. Behind him, strapped into their seats, rode Luke Skywalker and Leia Organa Solo. The bright dawn spread long shadows in the lower levels of the city.

Ackbar leaned forward to the comlink. "General Antilles, we are on approach. I can see the construction droid up ahead. Is everything cleared for our landing?"

"Yes, sir," Wedge's voice sounded clearly from the speaker. "There's a good spot just to the right of the droid that should be perfect for landing."

Ackbar cocked his head to peer through the curved viewplate, then brought the metropolitan shuttle in, aligning it with gaps in the buildings, descending to the unexplored street levels.

Wedge came out to meet them after Ackbar had settled the shuttle beside the powered-down construction droid. Ackbar emerged first into the rubble-strewn clearing, tilting his domed head up to look at the strip of sunlight coming from high above. Luke and Leia stepped out side by side as the vehicle hummed into its standby/cooldown mode.

"Hi, Wedge!" Luke called. "Or should I say, General Antilles?"

Wedge grinned. "Wait until you see what the demolition crew found. I just might get promoted again."

"I'm not sure you'd want to," Leia said. "Then you'd be stuck with diplomatic duties."

Wedge motioned for them to follow. The construction droid blocked out the sun. Luke could hear teams scrambling up access ladders and automated lifts on the outer shell of the droid. Maintenance crews were taking advantage of the shutdown time to check the internal factories and resource processors, to modify some of the programming inside the droid's computer blueprint.

The stripped carcass of a large beast lay in the rubble just outside the opening of the shielded room. Wedge gestured to it. "That thing attacked us last night, and my team killed it. Sometime when we were up in the construction droid's pilot lounge, napping and cleaning up, other scavengers came out and stripped the meat off its bones. Too bad. The xenobiologists might have wanted to classify it, but now there's not much left."

Wedge ducked inside the breached metal walls of the shielded room. Luke could hear people shuffling and banging inside. He saw Leia wrinkle her nose at the strange smells wafting out.

Luke's eyes took a moment to adjust to the glowing yellow illumination of the floating lights posted around the chamber. Something powerful had gone berserk in here. At first he saw broken equipment scattered on the floor, wires torn out, smashed computer terminals. Long claw marks gashed the walls. A black spherical Imperial interrogation droid lay split open in one corner. He saw Leia's eyes fix on it, and he sensed a wave of revulsion pass through her.

Several people from Wedge's team had wrestled a heavy metal grate back into place against one wall and were now laser-welding it into its channel. The grate had been horribly bent.

"More excitement last night," Wedge said. The welders looked up from their work, waved to Wedge, then bent back to their beams. "The mate of that rat-creature came back up through the tunnels, found its companion killed, and smashed everything it could." He frowned. "Ruined most of the old equipment here, but we still might be able to salvage something. The Emperor kept the place under tight security. Seems to be some kind of deep interrogation facility."

"Yes, indeed," Ackbar said, striding through the wreckage. Broken circuit boards crunched under his wide feet. "We wouldn't want any of this to fall into the wrong hands."

Luke's attention drifted over to a tangle of wires and flat sheet-crystal readers on the floor. His forehead furrowed with concentration as he went to look more closely. "Is that what I think it is?" he mumbled.

"What did you say, Luke?" Leia asked, following him.

He didn't answer her as he bent over the equipment, pulling wires and cables and trying to sort through the mess. "It looks like there were three separate units here. They're probably all destroyed." But he felt a growing excitement within him. Maybe they would be able to piece the components together.

"What is it?" Leia asked again.

Luke uncoiled one of the cables and found an intact sheet-crystal reader at the end. It looked like a glassy silver paddle longer than his hand. "I've read about this in my research on the old Jedi Knights. The Emperor's hunter teams used it to seek out Jedi who were hiding during his great purge."

He found a second intact sheet-crystal paddle, then picked the control pack that looked the least damaged. With his cyborg hand, Luke brushed aside some of the dust, then jacked the cables into either side of the pack, holding the paddles, one in each hand. He flipped the power switch on the control pack and was gratified to see a warm flurry of lights as the unit went through its initialization diagnostics.

"The Emperor's teams used equipment like this as sort of a Force detector, for his henchmen to read the auras of people they suspected of having Jedi talent. According to the records, the remnants of the Jedi Knights held this thing in great fear—but maybe we can use it to restore the Jedi."

He grinned, and for a moment he felt like the fresh, excited farm boy he had been back on Tatooine. "Hold still, Leia. Let me test this on you."

She stood back, alarmed. "But what does it do?" Both Wedge and Ackbar had stepped over to watch.

"Trust me," Luke said. He held the sheet-crystal paddles at arm's length, bracketing Leia. When he tripped the scan switch, a thin slice of coppery light traced down Leia's body from head to toe. Suspended in air above the control pack, a smaller echo of the copper scan-line reappeared in reverse motion, assimilating the data and constructing a tiny hologram of Leia.

It looked different from the small holo of Leia that Artoo Detoo had projected for Ben Kenobi. Instead, it was a wire-frame silhouette of her body, with color-coded lines tagged to readings that projected a column of numbers in the air. Surrounding the outline was a corona of flickering blue, faint but definite.

"Can you understand anything from that, Luke?" Admiral Ackbar said, peering closer.

"Let's get another one for comparison." This time Luke pointed the paddles at Wedge, who flinched as the coppery scan line ran up and down his uniform. When his wire-frame holo appeared beside Leia's, most of the color-coded details were similar—-but his image showed no blue corona.

"Now let's try you, Admiral." He extended the paddles toward the Mon Calamarian, adjusting the control pack to take Ackbar's alien physiology into account. When his scanned image appeared, it too lacked the blue aura.

"Leia, would you do it to me, just so we can be more sure?"

Leia handled the equipment reluctantly, as if uneasy to touch a device that had been used by those who had designed the interrogation droid. But she operated the scanner easily, holding the sheet-crystal paddles on either side of Luke.

His image bore the bright corona.

"This is very valuable," Luke said. "You don't need any particular skill with the Force to use this equipment. We can find people with Jedi potential just by scanning them. It will be a great help in finding candidates for my academy. Maybe some good will come of this device after all these years."

"Very good, Luke," Ackbar said.

Luke pursed his lips. "Wedge, I want to try something. Would you relax for a minute and let me do a mind touch on you?"

"Uh," Wedge said, then saw his team members looking at him. He straightened. "Whatever you say, Luke."

Luke wasted no time, reaching out to touch Wedge's temples, running a mental probe over the surface of his mind, back to the primitive area, the surprising nub in the contour of thoughts—

But when Luke touched it, nothing happened. Wedge probably didn't even know he was being probed. Luke pushed harder, but he triggered no reflexive counteraction, no uncontrolled push as Leia had given him.

"What was that all about?" Wedge asked. "Did you do anything?"

Luke smiled. "I just strengthened a theory of mine. We have gotten a lot closer to bringing back the Jedi Knights."

4

At least **the ship didn't explode**
on impact.

That was the first thing Han Solo thought as painful
consciousness returned. He blinked his eyes, listened to
the hissing of atmosphere streaming through breaches in
the *Millennium Falcon*'s hull. Somehow they had survived
a crash landing. He wondered what planet he was on.

Kessel!

His eyes widened as he saw red splashes across the
control panels. His own blood. His leg felt as if it were on
fire, and he tasted liquid tin in his mouth. As he coughed,
more blood splashed out. Han had not managed to strap
himself in before the crash. It was a good thing he had
not stayed up in the gun well. From his skewed vantage
he could see that the ship had spun on impact, with the
top gun well crushed beneath them.

He hoped Chewbacca had fared better. Turning his
head, Han felt as if shards of ground glass were rubbing his spine. In the copilot's chair, the Wookiee lay

motionless, his pelt matted with discolored blood oozing from wounds hidden by his shaggy fur.

"Chewie!" he managed to croak. "Say something, okay?"

Han heard the thud of a small explosive charge on the primary hatch; then someone from outside managed to hot-wire the ramp. The rest of the *Falcon*'s air spurted into Kessel's thin atmosphere. "Great," he mumbled. With the shattering pain in his ribs, it had already been hard enough to breathe.

Heavy footsteps marched up the ramp. Han wanted to pull out his blaster or at least knock a few enemies down in a fistfight. But he could barely raise his eyes, expecting to see an orderly column of white-armored stormtroopers. That would be an appropriate end to a day like this.

Instead, the intruders wore a hodgepodge of armor, some parts modified from prison-guard uniforms, other plates adapted from stormtrooper equipment. None of it made any sense to Han, but his mind had already maxed out with things that should never have happened. A TIE fighter and an X-wing fighting side by side? Against him?

The boarding party wore oxygen masks fitted over their faces to let them breathe the thin atmosphere of Kessel. Their voices were muffled as they shouted orders to each other.

One man, looking scarecrowish with impossibly long arms and neck, strode into the *Falcon*'s cockpit. Han felt recognition stir inside him, but he couldn't pinpoint a name. The scarecrow wore armbands from an Imperial prison, but at his side he carried a modified double-blaster that was patently illegal on most planets. The scarecrow turned wide-set, flinty eyes on Han.

"Han Solo," he said. Though the breath mask covered his lower face, Han could tell the man was grinning widely. "You're going to wish you never survived landing on Kessel."

With a flash of memory, the scarecrow's name came to Han. *Skynxnex*. That was it! But Skynxnex had been locked up in the Imperial Correction Facility, barely avoiding a death sentence. Questions had just begun forming in his mouth when Skynxnex brought an armored fist down on Han's head, sending him back into unconsciousness. . . .

Kessel. Spice. His thoughts mixed into nightmares as he fought to come back to himself.

Han had always been proud to boast that the *Falcon* had made the Kessel run in record time, but he rarely recounted the whole tale, that he had actually been fleeing Kessel with a full load of spice in his secret belowdecks compartments, when Imperial tariff ships had tagged him.

Han got the shipment, as always, from Moruth Doole, the froglike man in charge of skimming black-market spice from Imperial production quotas. Doole was some sort of official in the gigantic Imperial prison complex, from which came most of the spice-mine laborers. The Empire maintained strict control over the spice output, but Doole managed to keep quite a little side market of his own. Han Solo and Chewbacca had run spice for him, whisking it past Imperial patrols and putting it into distribution channels run by gangsters such as Jabba the Hutt.

But Moruth Doole had a habit of stringing along his helpers until he decided he could gain bigger favor by turning them over to the authorities. Han had never been able to prove it, but he suspected that Doole himself had tipped off the tariff ships on the *Falcon*'s flight away from Kessel, providing the exact coordinates where Han planned to enter hyperspace.

Han had been forced to jettison his entire cargo of glitterstim spice, worth a fortune, just before being boarded. When Han tried to circle back later and retrieve the floating cargo, the Imperials had given pursuit. During the chase he had desperately skimmed closer to the gravity influence of the immense black hole cluster than the navcharts claimed was possible. One of the tariff ships had been lost in the swirling maelstrom of hot gases plunging into a bottomless singularity. But the *Falcon* had survived, breaking into hyperspace and fleeing to safety.

Temporary safety. The lost cargo of spice alone had been worth 12,400 credits and Jabba the Hutt had already paid for it in full. Jabba had not been pleased. . . .

The thought of all those months frozen in carbonite, motionless, hanging on Jabba's wall, made him shiver. The cold was black around him, and he couldn't see. His teeth chattered together—

"Cease your thermal convulsions!" a raspy metallic voice snapped. It sounded like a plasma saw cutting through rock. "The temperature in the medical center has been lowered to minimize surgical shock to your metabolism."

Opening his eyes, Han stared up into the bulletlike face of a medical droid. Most of the metal was a primary green, but a black hooded attachment extended over its optical sensors. Segmented mechanical arms reached toward him, displaying a wide variety of out-of-date medical implements, all of them sharp.

"I am the prison medical droid. I have not been programmed for anesthetics or the niceties of making you comfortable. If you fail to cooperate, your treatment will only be more unpleasant."

Han rolled his eyes back. This was a far cry from traditional medical droids who were programmed specifically with the patient's comfort in mind.

Han tried to move. Around him the prison medical center was white and cold, with gleaming medical appliances and empty bacta tanks mounted on the wall. Han vaguely sensed several guards standing near the doors.

When he turned his head, the medical droid reached out with cold metal hands to clamp against his temples. "You must remain motionless. This will hurt. A great deal. Now relax—immediately!"

Out of sight on the other side of the room, Chewbacca let out a great roar of pain. Han was relieved to know the Wookiee was still alive. *Before* treatment, at least.

Han winced as the medical droid began to work on him.

Chewbacca shook him awake with a hairy, enthusiastic, and grateful hug. Han groaned and blinked his eyes, but the room was so dim he had to stare for a few minutes before anything came into focus. His entire body felt as if it had been beaten instead of healed.

Chewbacca groaned and hugged him again. "Take it easy, Chewie! You'll send me back to that medical droid!" Han said. Instantly, the Wookiee released his grip.

Han mentally assessed how he felt. He sat up, flexed his arms, then got to his feet. Two, no *three* of his ribs, as well as his left leg, tingled with the maddening bee stings that indicated where bone knitters had repaired the fractures. Han remained weak, but replacement/nutrient solutions had probably brought him back up to nominal levels.

Chewbacca also looked scruffy and haggard. Patches of fur had been shaved from his body, and Han could discern lumpy scars where medical droids had made quick patchwork with no finesse. After treatment the two of them had been tossed into this dank place.

Finally, Han took a deep whiff of the air inside the chamber. "What died in here?" He suddenly realized that wasn't just a joking comment.

Chewbacca answered by pointing to the hulking form that occupied a third of the space in the cell. Han blinked again to be sure his vision was adjusting properly.

The thing was huge and hideous—part crustacean, part arachnid, and judging from the rows of dagger teeth, entirely carnivorous. Its claw hands were as big as a human was tall, and its jointed body armor was covered with scablike bumps. The only good thing about it was that it was dead. The carcass reeked.

The first time Han had been near a rancor, he had been blind from hibernation sickness after being thawed in Jabba's palace. Jabba fed the monster below his throne room with his enemies—or anyone else at random. Han had seen many more rancors on the planet Dathomir during his courtship of Princess Leia. One of the beasts had somehow died here in the Imperial Correction Facility. The rancor had decayed as far as it was going to, and then mummified the rest of the way.

The prison itself, from what Han knew of it, was a cross between a zoo and a correctional facility, because the different life-forms had different degrees of sentience. The only factor in common was that they were all violent.

Their cell was gigantic, as far as cells went—large enough to hold the rancor and give it room to maneuver. Brittle, moldy bones lay scattered around the floor, many of which had been gnawed and pulverized, as if in a desperate attempt by the starving rancor to find more food. Green and blue smears of slime oozed down the walls. Tiny dripping sounds were the only noises Han could hear.

"How long have we been here, Chewie? Do you know?"

Chewbacca didn't know.

Han ran it over again in his mind. They had come to Kessel, they had identified themselves both by name and with a New Republic call sign. A fleet of ships had come out to attack them—TIE fighters and X-wings and a motley bunch of other ships. Obviously, the people in charge of Kessel were up to something, and they didn't want the New Republic to know about it.

Then he remembered scarecrow-like Skynxnex, who had boarded the crashed *Falcon*. Skynxnex had been a thief and an assassin, the primary point of contact between Moruth Doole and the spice smugglers. Skynxnex had wrangled a nominal post as a prison guard in the correction facility, but now he seemed to have changed jobs . . .

Han heard the click and hum of the deactivation field around the cell doors, and then a grating whirr as hydraulic lifts hauled the huge door upward. As the door raised, garish white light flooded into the room. Han clapped a hand over his eyes. He hadn't realized the cell was so dim.

"Get ready, Chewie!" Han whispered. If there weren't too many guards, they could rush them, slug their way out, and escape. But then he felt a twinge of pain from his recently broken ribs, and dizziness washed over him. Chewbacca leaned weakly against one of the damp walls of the rancor's cell and groaned.

Well, maybe if there's only one guard, who has poor eyesight and is recovering from weeks' worth of dysentery . . .

"Never mind, Chewie. Let's see what they have to say."

The skeletal figure standing in the door was obviously Skynxnex. As Han's eyes adjusted to the light, he could see four other guards behind Skynxnex, wearing not-quite prison uniforms, patches of body armor to protect sensitive areas but showing no rank or insignia.

"So, Han Solo, I trust you appreciate our . . . hospitality?" Skynxnex asked.

Han smirked and looked behind him at the dank cell, the dead rancor. "Yeah, you guys are really turning Kessel into a resort world. Just like the planet Ithor."

Skynxnex followed his gaze to the mummified monster. "Ah yes, during the turmoil when we took over the prison, someone forgot to feed the rancor. It was a pity. Months passed before we remembered him. A double pity, too, because by the time we thought of him, we had plenty of Imperial prisoners we needed to dispose of. That would have been fun to watch. Instead, we had to send them all into the spice mines."

Skynxnex smiled for just an instant; then his face took on its flat, mechanical composure again. "I hope the medical droids helped you recover from your crash injuries. It's important that you both are healthy enough to withstand interrogation. We want to learn exactly why you came to spy on Kessel."

It occurred to Han that for once he could actually tell the truth and be completely open about his mission. "Ready when you are, Skynxnex." Somehow he was afraid the truth wouldn't be good enough in this case.

The gangly man allowed another flash of a smile. "So you do remember me, Solo? Good. Moruth Doole will want to talk to you immediately."

Han raised his eyebrows. That meant Doole was still alive, still running things—but Han had no idea how the pieces fit together. "I'd love to talk to old Moruth. It's been a long time. He was a good buddy of mine!"

Skynxnex snickered at that, then stopped. The other guards behind him also chuckled. "Yes," Skynxnex said, "I do believe I've heard him mention your name. Several times."

The lift took them out of the main cell-block areas, along a tube to the outer corners of the correctional facility. They rocketed skyward along the angled metal tracks.

Looking through the scratched transparent walls of the elevator, Han could see that the prison itself was a massive tan-and-gray edifice made of plasteel and synthetic rock. The flat front face sloped backward at about a forty-five-degree angle; elevator turrets glided along each of the corners. A glassed and mirrored substructure protruded from the slanted face, housing the administrative offices and prison personnel.

In the racing elevator car Skynxnex watched both of them with flickers of amusement, keeping his modified double-blaster trained on them. The two guards, armed with more conventional weapons, also stood tense and ready.

Seeing this, Han felt ironically impressed. He didn't know what he had done to instill such fear in these people.

Both Han and Chewbacca had been strapped into stun-cuffs, a restraining fixture across the wrists that sent paralyzing jolts of electricity directly into the nervous system, proportional in strength to the amount of struggle a prisoner exerted. Han controlled himself well enough and received only an unpleasant tingle along his forearms. As usual, Chewbacca could not keep his temper in check and managed to stun himself into a stupor.

When the elevator doors opened, Skynxnex prodded the two prisoners forward. Han complied and walked easily ahead, trying to put a self-confident spring in his step. He'd had his troubles with Moruth Doole, and he did not trust the man a bit—but as far as he knew, there was no powerful grudge between them.

Skynxnex escorted them through administrative offices, many of which had been ransacked or burned. They went past a broad anteroom to a huge office faced by giant windows that looked out upon the barrens of Kessel. In the distance Han could see the crumbled salt flats. Great jets from the atmosphere factories sent gouts of oxygen, nitrogen, and carbon dioxide into the pinkish sky, keeping the planet barely habitable. Powerful radiation shields in orbit filtered out a large percentage of the deadly X rays and gamma rays pouring from the nearby Maw. If not for the precious spice, no one would bother trying to live on Kessel.

The original sign on the desk-unit announced this to be the warden's headquarters, but someone had crossed out the previous ID tag and mounted a hand-lettered sign in Basic: DOOLE'S PLACE. On the wall to the right of the desk-unit hung a man captured in final throes of agony, frozen in carbonite. Doole had taken a lesson from Jabba, displaying some old nemesis for all to see. Han shivered just to look at the trophy.

Next to the window a barrel-shaped form stood silhouetted by the garish light. Han recognized Moruth Doole immediately.

Doole was a Rybet, squat and soft-skinned. His bright-green coloring and tan highlights looked like worm stripes up and down his cheeks, arms, and shoulders. His skin was dry, but so smooth it looked slimy. As always Doole dressed in the skins of less-fortunate reptiles. His waistcoat looked like something from an ancient history vid. Doole sported a bright-yellow cravat, which meant he was in mating readiness, though Han couldn't imagine where on the planet Doole would ever find a willing female of his own species.

Doole turned around, displaying a much-changed face, jittered with nervous tics and paranoia. His Rybet eyes were overlarge, lanternlike, with vertical slits—but one of his eyes was now milky white, like a half-cooked egg. He wore a mechanical focusing device over his other eye, strapped onto his smooth head with brown leather straps.

Doole fiddled with his mechanical eye, and the lenses clicked and whirred into place, like a camera unit. His Rybet fingers were long and wide at the end, showing signs of vestigial suction cups as he adjusted the focus and pressed his face close to Han's. The blind eye stared milkily off in another direction. After a long inspection he finally hissed in recognition. "It *is* you, Han Solo!"

Han frowned. "Been hitting the spice too heavily, I see, Moruth. Always gets the eyesight first."

"It wasn't spice that did this," Doole snapped, tapping the contraption on his eye. He drew in another long sputtering breath that sounded like a carbonated drink spilled on hot coals. "Why are you here, Solo? I want you to tell me, but maybe I want you to resist just a little bit so I can make this *hurt*."

Chewbacca roared in anger. Han tried to spread out his hands, but the stun-cuffs zapped him. "Wait a minute, Moruth! You'd better explain a few things to me. I don't quite know—"

Doole didn't hear him, rubbing his splayed hands together and smiling with his squishy lips. "The hardest part is going to be restraining myself from having you dismembered right here where I can watch."

Han felt his heart pound. "Can we be reasonable for just a minute? We were business partners, Moruth, and I never crossed you." Han didn't mention his suspicions that Doole had crossed *him* in that last spice run. "I apologize if I did something to upset you. Can we work it out?"

He remembered his conversation with the hit man Greedo in the Mos Eisley cantina. Once offended, Jabba the Hutt had never been interested in working anything out. He hoped Doole would be more reasonable.

Moruth Doole stepped backward, fluttering his long-fingered hands. "Work it out? What are you going to do, buy me a droid replacement for my eye? I hate droids! Because of you, Jabba tried to have me killed. I had to beg them to take only my eye. I had to *beg* them to take my *eye*!" He jabbed at his boiled-egg blind side.

Skynxnex shambled closer to Doole, lowering his voice. "I think you're confusing him, rather than frightening him, Moruth. Maybe he really doesn't know what happened."

Doole sat down at his desk and straightened his lizard-skin waistcoat, regaining his composure. "When you dumped your load of spice, Jabba blamed it on me! He put out a contract on my life. All because of your cowardice."

Chewbacca roared in outrage. Han barely kept his anger in check. "Jabba put out a contract on me too, Doole. Greedo tried to assassinate me on Tatooine. Boba Fett captured me on Bespin and I was trapped in carbonite, just like your friend there"—he gestured to the gruesome trophy on the wall—"and I got sent to Jabba anyway."

Doole waved a hand in dismissal. "Jabba's men had already infiltrated the spice-mining operations, and he wanted to expose me, so his own people could procure the glitterstim directly. One of his hit men fried my eye and half blinded the other. He was about to do more, but Skynxnex killed him."

At the doorway the scarecrow smiled with pride.

"Jabba forced my hand, and I had to act. We staged the prison revolt. The warden himself was Jabba's man, but half of the guards were on my side. I paid them well, you see. Luckily, the Empire was thrown into chaos right about the same time. We took Kessel for ourselves. There were a few other upstart slave lords on the other side of the planet, but they didn't last long. I've been stockpiling spice supplies and building up a massive defense fleet with everything I can scrape together. Nobody—and I mean *nobody*!—is going to come here and take things away from me."

Doole grabbed his head with his long fingers in a gesture of weariness. "Everything was going just fine before you had to get Jabba angry at me! Everything was safe.

I knew just how to play the game. Now I'm jumping at shadows, afraid every moment."

Doole stared at Han with his mechanical eye. "But ruining my life once isn't good enough for you, is it? You come back here broadcasting a message from the New Republic. Somehow I thought remnants of the Empire would try to grab the spice mines back first, but big governments are all the same. You are a spy, a particularly inept one. Did you think you could just fly into our space, look around, and go back to your Republic with all the information they need to come take us over?" He slapped his palm on the desktop with a damp splat. "We'll strike the first blow by killing their spy, and we will be ready to blast them out of the sky the moment your attack ships come out of hyperspace!"

"You haven't got a chance!" Skynxnex sneered.

Han allowed himself to smile, then actually chuckled. "You boys have it all wrong. Absolutely wrong." Chewbacca grunted his agreement.

Skynxnex scowled. Doole stared at Han in silence for a moment. "We'll see about that."

Doole reached into the pocket of his waistcoat and withdrew a small ancient-looking key, which he inserted into one of the drawers of the former warden's desk. He fumbled with the lock, then opened the drawer. Reaching in, he pulled out an armored strongbox. He hefted the strongbox to the table, then dug in another pocket of his waistcoat to extract a second key.

Han watched, his curiosity piqued, as Doole opened the strongbox and withdrew a smaller sealed container. Doole meticulously slipped both his keys back into his pockets before looking at Han.

"I'd like to spend time interrogating you thoroughly, but I want to know exactly when the New Republic plans to come in and take over, how many ships they are sending, what type of forces they will use. I'll get the information now, but I may have time to enjoy interrogating you later, just on general principle."

Doole placed his webbed Rybet palm on the top of the sealed container. With a slight hum a beam of light curled around his fingers in an ID scan; the small container burped as the airtight seal was broken. The lid slid away to reveal a padded interior compartment.

The box was filled with slender, black-wrapped cylinders about half as long as a finger. Han recognized them immediately. "Glitterstim," he said.

Doole looked at him. "The most potent form of spice. With it I'll be able to read the truth of what you say. Your errant thoughts will betray you."

Han felt a sudden sense of relief. "But what if I don't have any hidden thoughts to betray?"

Skynxnex struck Han's head with the back of his hand, sending him reeling. Chewbacca tried to stagger forward, but the stun-cuffs silenced his bellows and made him sway dizzily, barely able to keep his balance.

Doole selected one of the slim black cylinders and held it in his fingers. With a deft motion he peeled off the opaque outer wrapper and withdrew a thin bundle of transparent glassy fibers. As Doole held the inert glitterstim up to the light pouring through the broad viewing window, the light-sensitive spice began to scintillate and glow from within, ripening.

Han watched until it was ready for Doole to consume. He swallowed a dry lump in his throat.

Doole opened his mouth when the segment of glitterstim glowed a pearlescent blue. He extended his sharp purplish tongue to wrap around the crystalline fibers, which he drew back into his mouth. The glitterstim crackled and fizzed; as Doole flexed his lips, tiny sparks seeped out the corners.

Han stared as Doole closed his blind eye and breathed deep, watery breaths. The spice would act on Doole's mind, pump up his latent powers. The automatic focusing gears of Doole's mechanical eye clicked and whirred, spinning around as it tried to make sense of the visions pouring through the Rybet's mind. Then Doole turned to face Han and Chewbacca.

Han winced as he felt tiny fingers clawing around in his brain, picking through the lobes of memory, images he had stored in his thoughts . . . searching, searching. He tried to shrink away but knew he could keep no secrets from anyone pumped on glitterstim.

Skynxnex chuckled, then immediately fell silent, as if afraid of directing Doole's attention to himself, where his own brain could be picked.

Han felt anger growing, outrage that Moruth Doole could dissect the private moments he had with Leia, could observe the births of Han's three children. But the spice effects lasted only a few moments, and Doole would be concerned mainly with learning why Han and Chewbacca had come to Kessel.

"I really was telling you the truth, Doole," Han said quietly. "We are on a peaceful mission to reestablish diplomatic contact with Kessel. The New Republic is trying to open up trade and welcome you. We came in peace, but you just declared war on yourself by shooting down their first ambassadors."

Chewbacca growled.

Skynxnex stiffened, then took a few awkward steps forward. "What is he talking about?"

Han raised his voice. "Read the truth in my mind, Moruth."

The Rybet's mouth hung slack, and Han could see glitterstim sparks sputtering around his cheeks. He felt the tiny probing fingers crawl deeper and deeper into his mind, scrabbling around. Doole was frantically trying to find some proof of his suspicions as the spice enhancement faded away.

But Doole could find nothing; there was nothing to find. The only thing he did learn was the power of the Alliance forces that would be arrayed against him. A fleet that had succeeded in overthrowing the entire Empire would certainly be sufficient to destroy a ragtag outlaw operation on Kessel.

"No!" Doole wailed. He whirled to glare at Skynxnex. "What are we going to do? He's telling the truth!"

"He can't be!" Skynxnex said. "He's a—he's—"

"The spice doesn't lie. He's here for exactly the reasons he said. And we shot him down. We took him prisoner. The New Republic is going to come after us, and they'll wipe us out."

"Kill the two of them now," Skynxnex said. "If we work fast, we can cover everything up."

Han felt sudden fear return. "Now, wait a minute! I'm sure we can fix this with a few careful messages. I *am* the ambassador, after all! Diplomatic credentials and everything. I wouldn't want a simple misunderstanding—"

"No!" Skynxnex said, keeping his attention fixed on Doole. "We can't risk that. You know what Solo has done before. He knows you tipped off the Imperial tariff ships to go after him."

Actually, Han hadn't been certain until that very moment. "Now, there's no need to panic," he said again. "I can talk to the New Republic Senate. I know Mon Mothma personally, and my wife Leia is a cabinet member, and—" His mind whirled, trying to think of how Leia would handle this. Many times he had watched her smooth diplomatic problems. She had a finesse with words, a way of approaching other people's concerns and stroking them, delicately maneuvering opposing sides into a compromise. But right now Leia wasn't with him.

"Yes, I think I agree," Doole said, tapping a finger against his swollen lips. Han let out a sigh of relief. "I agree with *Skynxnex*. I'll review the battle tapes, but I don't believe you transmitted any messages after coming out of hyperspace. One of our fighters shot off your subspace antenna dish. The New Republic has no way of knowing you arrived safely. With no evidence they will conclude you got swallowed up by the Maw."

Doole began to pace in front of the large viewing window. "We'll delete any mention of you from our records. Instruct all my mercenaries to forget about the attack. Yes, that'll be the safest alternative!"

"You're making a big mistake!" Han said. He could barely restrain his urge to yank at the stun-cuffs.

"No," Doole replied, tapping his squishy-tipped fingers together. "I don't think so."

Chewbacca bellowed a loud string of guttural words.

"My best bet would be to kill you right away," Doole answered; then he rubbed his fingers against his blind eye. "But you still owe me for this, Solo. Even if you worked every day for a hundred years, it would never repay me for the loss of my eye. You both are going down into the spice mines, the deepest and most distant tunnels. They've been needing quite a few replacements lately."

Doole grinned with his wide froglike mouth. A final flicker of blue sparks rippled at the corner of his lips.

"No one will ever find you down there."

5

The former Imperial Information Center lay buried deep beneath the old palace, covered by layers of shielding walls and guarded by tight security at every entrance. To keep the temperatures within tolerable limits for the great data archive machines, vast heat-exchanger systems and powerful cooling units filled the room with a background roar.

Hunched over fourteen consoles were lumpy dull-gray slicer droids, hardwired into the terminals as they meticulously hacked at the security encryption codes and backup viruses set up in the Emperor's mainframes. The slicer droids had been working for a full year, ferreting out vital tidbits from the labyrinthine databases. Already they had exposed twenty-three Imperial spies in deep cover trying to sabotage the burgeoning New Republic.

The hum of the cooling units and the motionlessness of the slicer droids blanketed the Center with an echoing emptiness. Lonely and fidgety, the protocol droid See-Threepio paced back and forth, his servomotors whirring, as he viewed the room with his optical sensors for the hundredth time.

"Haven't you found anything yet, Artoo?" he said.

Jacked into one of the information ports, Artoo-Detoo bleeped an impatient negative and continued whirring as he tunneled through the overwhelming amounts of information.

"Don't forget to double-check everything," Threepio said, and began pacing again. "And don't be afraid to follow unlikely leads. Master Luke would call them hunches. This is very important, Artoo."

Artoo hooted indignantly.

"And remember to check every planet from the Old Republic. The Empire didn't necessarily have time to update its information on all of them."

This time Artoo did not bother to reply but continued to work.

A moment later Threepio heard the outer doors open, and a shadowy figure moved toward them with silent grace. As always, Luke Skywalker wore his Jedi cloak, but this time the hood was draped casually over his shoulders. Luke walked with an eagerness in his step.

Threepio was glad to see a resurgence of the excited boyishness that had so characterized young Luke when the droids first met him after they had been purchased from the Jawas on Tatooine. Of late Luke's eyes had not been able to hide the haunted look and the barely contained power of a Jedi Master.

"Master Luke! How good of you to check on us!"

"How's it going, Threepio? Found anything yet?"

Artoo beeped an answer, which Threepio translated. "Artoo says he's going as fast as he can, but he wishes me to remind you of the enormous amount of data he must inspect."

"Well, I'll be leaving in a few hours to follow up on

some earlier leads I uncovered by myself. I just wanted to make sure you two have everything you need before I take off."

Threepio straightened in a gesture of surprise. "Might I ask where you are going, Master Luke?"

Artoo chittered and Luke turned to him. "Not this time, Artoo. It's more important that you stay here and continue the search. I can fly by myself."

Luke turned to answer Threepio's question. "I'm going to Bespin to check on somebody there, but first I want to go to an old outpost called Eol Sha. I've got reason to believe that at least one lost Jedi descendant might be there." With a swish of his cloak, Luke turned to depart from the Information Center. "I'll check back with you when I come home." The door slid shut behind him.

Threepio spoke immediately to Artoo. "Punch up the data on Eol Sha—let's see where Master Luke is going."

Artoo obliged, as if the idea had been in his own circuits. When the planetary statistics came up on the screen accompanied by ancient two-dimensional images, Threepio raised his golden mechanical arms in horror. "Earthquakes! Geysers! Volcanoes and lava! Oh my!"

When Luke emerged from hyperspace, the starlines in the viewport funneled into points. Suddenly brilliant pastel colors splashed across the universe—magentas, oranges, and icicle-blues of ionized gas in a vast galactic ocean known as the Cauldron Nebula. The automatic dimmers in the pilot's compartment muted the glare. Luke looked at the spectacle and smiled.

Leaving the hyperspace node, he punched in the coordinates for Eol Sha. His modified passenger shuttle arced through the wispy gas, leaving the nebula above him as the engines kicked in. The double wedge-shaped craft descended toward Eol Sha.

He had wanted to take his trusty old X-wing, but that ship was a single-person craft, with room for only an astromech droid in the back. If Luke's hunches about Jedi descendants proved correct, he would be bringing two candidates back to Coruscant with him. . . .

According to outdated records, the settlement on Eol Sha was established a century before by entrepreneurs who intended to use ramjet mining ships to plow through the Cauldron Nebula and scoop up valuable gases. The mineship pilots would distill the gaseous harvest into pure, rare elements for sale to other outposts.

Eol Sha was the only habitable world close enough to support the commercial venture, but its days were numbered. A tandem moon orbited very close to the planet, spiraling in on a death plunge as gravity dragged it down. Within another hundred years the moon would crash into the planet, smashing both into rubble.

The nebula mining scheme had never paid off. The incompetent entrepreneurs had not counted on the true costs of ramjet ships and the unremarkable composition of the Cauldron's gases. The outpost on Eol Sha had been left to fend for itself. At about that time the Emperor's New Order had begun, and the Old Republic had crumbled to pieces. The few survivors on Eol Sha had been forgotten in the chaos.

The outpost had been rediscovered two years ago by a New Republic sociologist who had visited them briefly, recorded his insights, and filed a report recommending immediate evacuation of the doomed colony—all of which was promptly forgotten in the already blossoming bureaucracy of the New Republic and the depredations of Grand Admiral Thrawn.

The item that had attracted Luke's attention, though, was that a woman named Ta'ania—an illegitimate descendant of a Jedi—had been one of the original colonists on Eol Sha. Luke would have suspected the Jedi's bloodline had ended there, except for one small detail.

According to the sociologist's report, the leader of the ragtag colonists, a man named Gantoris, was said to be able to sense impending earthquakes, and he had miraculously survived as a child when his playmates were killed in an avalanche. Somehow Gantoris escaped injury while the others, a mere arm's length away on either side of him, had been crushed.

Luke attributed many of these stories to exaggeration in retelling, for even someone with a great deal of Jedi potential could not control such things without training—as he himself knew. But still the clues and the circumstantial evidence led him to Eol Sha. He had to follow every lead if he was to find enough candidates for his Jedi training center.

Luke took the modified shuttle on a figure-eight trajectory around the looming moon and vectored in on the remnants of the outpost on Eol Sha. After crossing the terminator where the planet's night fell into day, Luke looked out the viewport at the scabbed and uninviting surface of the planet.

His hands worked the controls automatically. As he swooped low, he could see the decrepit and shored-up habitation modules that had been battered by natural disasters for decades. In the near distance hardened mounds of lava sprawled around a volcanic cone from old eruptions. Curling smoke rose from the heart of the volcano, and glowing orange smudges showed where fresh lava seeped through cracks in its side.

Luke took the shuttle past the battered settlement and beyond a stretch of cratered, jumbled terrain. The shuttle settled onto the rocky hardpan, and Luke exited through flip-up doors behind the passenger seats.

The air of Eol Sha smoldered in his nostrils, filled with acrid sulfurous smoke and chemical vapors. The gigantic moon hulked on the horizon like a platter of beaten brass, casting its own shadows even in daylight. Murky clouds and volcanic ash hovered in the air like a hazy blanket.

When Luke stepped away from the passenger shuttle, he could feel the ground hum beneath his boots. With senses heightened from the Force, he could touch the incredible strain the close moon placed on Eol Sha, squeezing and tearing it with tidal forces that grew worse each passing year as the moon spiraled closer. A hissing white noise permeated the air, as if the innumerable steam vents and fumaroles breathed out gasps of pain from the world.

Pulling the dark cloak about him and securing the lightsaber at his belt, Luke strode across the rough terrain toward the settlement. Around him small craters and deep pits dotted the ground, encircled by white and tan mineral deposits. Sounds of gurgling steam came from deep beneath them.

Halfway to the settlement Luke fell to his knees when a jolt went through the ground. The rocks bounced and the earth rumbled. Luke spread his arms to keep his balance. The tremors rose, then fell, then increased again before stopping abruptly.

Suddenly, the random craters around him crackled, then belched towers of steam and scalding droplets of water. Geysers, all of them—he had walked into a field of geysers, triggered by the earthquake to erupt simultaneously. Steam rolled over the ground like a dense fog.

Luke pulled the hood over his head for protection and took shallow breaths as he trudged forward. The settlement was not far away. On all sides of him the geyser field continued to gasp and howl, gradually lessening as the spumes declined in intensity.

When Luke finally emerged from the steam, he saw two men staring at him from the doorway of a rusted and ancient prefab shelter. The outpost on Eol Sha had been built from modified cargo containers and modular self-erecting shelters. By the looks of the hovels, though, the maintenance subsystems had failed decades before, leaving the forgotten people to eke out a crude existence. The rest of the settlement seemed deserted and quiet.

The two men stopped their work shoring up a collapsed entranceway, but they didn't seem to know how to react to the presence of a stranger. Luke was probably the first new person they had seen since the sociologist had visited them two years earlier.

"I have come to speak with Gantoris," Luke said. They looked at him with bleak expressions. Their clothes appeared worn and patched, sewn together from pieces of other garments. Luke's gaze held one of the two men. The other shied back into the shadows. "Are you Gantoris?" Luke asked softly.

"No. My name is Warton." He fumbled for words; then they came out in a rush. "Everyone is gone. There's been a rock slide in one of the crevasses. It buried two of our youngest, who went out to spear bugdillos. Gantoris and the others are there, trying to dig them out."

Luke felt a stab of urgency and grasped Warton's arm. "Take me there. Maybe I can help."

Warton allowed himself to be nudged into motion, and he took Luke along a winding path through jagged rocks. The second man remained behind among the collapsing shelters. Luke and Warton descended through switchbacks down the steep wall of a crack in the ground, a split wrenched apart by tidal forces. Down here the air seemed thicker, smellier, more claustrophobic.

Warton knew exactly where to find the other survivors in the maze of side channels and partial landslides. Luke saw them shoulder to shoulder in an elbow of the crevasse, scrambling over newly fallen rock, working to haul boulders aside. Every one of the thirty people there wore the same implacable expression, as if their optimism had burned away but they could not allow themselves to give up their duties. Two of the women bent over the rubble, calling into the cracks.

One man worked with twice the effort of the others. His long black hair hung in a braid on the left side of his face. His eyebrows and eyelashes had been plucked away, leaving his broad face smooth and angular and flushed with his exertion. He shoved rocks aside, which the other people hauled away. They had already managed to clear some of the debris, but they had not yet uncovered the two victims. The dark-haired man paused to glance at Luke, failed to recognize him or understand his presence, then returned to his efforts. By the way Warton and the others looked to him, Luke guessed the man must be Gantoris himself.

Before Warton had taken him to the base of the rockfall, Luke stopped and, with a quick glance, took in the positioning of the boulders. He let his arms fall to his sides, rolled his eyes back in concentration, and reached out through the Force, using the strength he found there to feel the boulders, to move them, and to keep other rocks from doing further damage. When Yoda had trained him to lift large stones, it had been merely a game, a training exercise; now two lives depended on it.

He paid no attention to the astonished sounds as the colonists stepped back, ducking out of the way as Luke mentally hurled boulder after boulder from the top of the rock pile, tossing them into other parts of the crevasse. He could feel life down in the shadowy depths, somewhere.

When the rocks began to show splashes of blood, and he exposed a pale arm, part of a shoulder hunched in the secret shadows of the avalanche, several people rushed forward. Luke made an extra effort to keep the unstable pile of rocks steady enough for the rescue operations. He continued to remove fallen boulders.

"She's alive!" someone shouted, and several helpers rushed into the debris, brushing away stones and hauling free a young girl. Her face and legs were battered and bloody, one arm was obviously broken; she began weeping with pain and relief as the rescuers pulled her out. Luke knew she would be all right.

Near the girl, however, the young boy had not been so lucky. The avalanche had crushed him instantly. The boy had been dead long before Luke arrived.

Luke continued to work grimly, until they had excavated the body. Amid sobs of grief, he released himself from his semitrance and opened his eyes.

Gantoris stood directly in front of him. Barely suppressed anger seethed beneath his controlled expression.

"Why are you here?" Gantoris asked. "Who are you?"

Warton stepped up beside Luke. "I saw him walk out of the geyser field. All the geysers went off at once, and he just strode out of the steam." Warton blinked in awe as he looked at Luke. "He says he has come for you, Gantoris."

"Yes—I know," Gantoris muttered to himself.

Luke met the other man's eyes. "I am Luke Skywalker, a Jedi Knight. The Empire has fallen, and a New Republic has taken its place." He drew a deep breath. "If you are Gantoris and if you have the ability, I have come to teach you how to use the Force."

Several of the others walked up, bearing the broken, rag-doll body of the dead boy. The man carrying the boy let his stony expression flicker for just an instant.

The look on Gantoris's face seemed a frightening mixture of horror and eagerness. "I have dreamed of you. A dark man who offers me incredible secrets, then destroys me. I am lost if I go with you." Gantoris straightened. "You are a demon."

Surprised, especially after his efforts to save the two children, Luke tried to placate him. "No, that isn't it."

Other colonists gathered around the confrontation, finding a focus for their anger and suspicion. They looked at Luke, at this stranger who had arrived in time to usher in the death of one of their dwindling number.

Luke glanced at the people around him and decided to gamble. He stared directly into Gantoris's eyes. "What can I do to prove my intentions to you? I am your guest, or your prisoner. What I want is your cooperation. Please listen to what I have to say."

Gantoris reached out to take the body of the boy in his own arms. The man who had been carrying him looked forlorn and lost as he stared at the bloodstains on his sleeves. Gantoris nodded back to Luke. "Take the dark man."

Several people reached forward to grasp Luke's arms. He did not struggle.

Bearing the dead boy, Gantoris led a slow procession out of the chasm. He turned once briefly to glare at Luke. "We will learn why you are here."

6

Leia stood in the private communications chamber, heaving a sigh as she glanced again at the chronometer. The Caridan ambassador was late. He was probably doing it just to spite her.

Out of deference to the ambassador, she had reset her clock to Caridan local time. Though Ambassador Furgan had suggested the transmission time himself, it seemed he couldn't be bothered to abide by it.

Two-way mirrors displayed empty corridors outside the communications chamber. At this late hour most sensible people were deeply asleep in their own quarters—but no one had ever promised Leia Organa Solo that diplomatic duties kept regular hours.

When such obligations crept into her schedule, Han usually grumbled at being awakened in the depths of the night, complaining that even pirates and smugglers kept their activities to more civilized time slots. But this evening Leia's alarm had awakened her to empty and silent rooms. Han still had not called.

A cleaning droid puttered along the corridor, polishing the walls and scouring the two-way mirrors; Leia watched its lampreylike scrubbers do their work.

With a burst of static from poorly tuned holonet transmitters, the image of Ambassador Furgan of Carida formed in the center of the receiving dais. Maybe the poor transmission quality was deliberate—yet another rude reaction. The chronometer told Leia that the ambassador had made his transmission a full six minutes past the time he himself had insisted on. Furgan made no attempt to apologize for his tardiness, and Leia studiously avoided calling attention to it.

Furgan was a barrel-chested humanoid with spindly arms and legs. The eyebrows on his squarish face flared upward like birds' wings. Despite the Emperor's known prejudice against nonhuman species, apparently the Caridans had been acceptable enough to secure the Emperor's business, since Palpatine had built his most important Imperial military training center on Carida.

"Princess Leia," Furgan said, "you needed to discuss certain planning details with me? Please be brief." He crossed his arms over his broad chest in clearly hostile body language.

Leia tried not to let her exasperation show. "As a matter of protocol I would prefer if you could address me as minister rather than princess. The planet on which I was a princess no longer exists." Leia worked hard to keep the scowl off her face.

Furgan waved her comment aside as if it were of no consequence. "Very well then, Minister, what did you wish to discuss?"

Leia took a deep breath, quelling the hot temper rising behind her cool expression. "I wanted to inform you that Mon Mothma and the other Cabinet members of the New

Republic will be hosting a formal reception in your honor when you reach Coruscant."

Furgan bristled. "A frivolous reception? Am I supposed to give a warm and glowing speech? Make no mistake, I am coming to Coruscant on a pilgrimage to visit the home of the late Emperor Palpatine—not to be pampered by an upstart, illegitimate band of terrorists. Our loyalty remains with the Empire."

"Ambassador Furgan, there *is* no centralized Empire." It took all her effort not to rise to the bait. Her dark eyes burned with obsidian fires, but she smiled instead at the ambassador. "Nevertheless, we will extend to you every courtesy in the confidence that your planet will find a way to adapt to political reality in the galaxy."

The Caridan's holographic image shimmered. "Political realities change," he said. "It remains to be seen just how long your rebellion will last."

Furgan's image fizzled into static as he cut the transmission. Leia sighed and rubbed her temples, trying to massage away the headache lurking behind her eyes. She left the communications chamber discouraged.

What a way to end the day.

Deep underground in the Imperial Information Center, all hours looked the same, but See-Threepio's internal chronometer told him it was the middle of Coruscant's night. A pair of repair droids worked at dismantling one of the great air-exchange systems that had burned out. The repair droids dropped tools and discarded pieces of metal shielding with reckless abandon, making the echoing chamber sound like a war zone. Threepio much preferred the humming loneliness of the previous day.

Buried in their own universe of data networks, the hunched slicer droids worked undisturbed. Artoo-Detoo slavishly continued his days-long search without pause.

With a loud clatter the repair droids dropped an entire three-bladed fan assembly. "I'm going to give those droids a piece of my mind!" Threepio said.

Before Threepio could march off, Artoo jacked out of the data port and began chittering and whistling. In his excitement the little astromech droid rocked back and forth, bleeping.

"Oh!" Threepio said. "You'd better let *me* check that, Artoo. It's probably another one of your false alarms."

When data scrolled up on the screen, Threepio could see nothing that would have captured Artoo's interest—until the other droid recompiled the information to emphasize his point. A name popped up beside every entry—TYMMO.

"Oh, my! It does appear suspicious when you look at it that way. This Tymmo person seems a likely candidate indeed." Threepio straightened, suddenly at a loss. "But Master Luke isn't here, and he gave us no further instructions. Whom can we tell?"

Artoo bleeped, then whistled a question. Threepio turned to him with offended dignity. "I will not wake Mistress Leia in the middle of the night! I am a protocol droid, and there is a proper way to go about these things." He nodded in affirmation of his decision. "We will inform her first thing in the morning."

The levitating breakfast tray brought itself to Leia's table on the park balcony high in the Imperial towers. The sun gleamed on the city that stretched across the entire landmass of Coruscant. High in the air flying creatures rode the morning thermals.

Leia scowled down at the food the breakfast tray presented to her. None of it looked appetizing, but she knew she had to eat. She selected a small plate of assorted pastries and sent the breakfast tray on its way. Before it departed, the tray told her to have a pleasant day.

She sighed and picked at her breakfast. She felt exhausted mentally as well as physically. She hated to feel so dependent, even on her own husband, but she never slept well while he was away. Han should have arrived on Kessel three days ago, and he was due back in two days. She didn't want to cling, but it disappointed her that he had not yet transmitted so much as a greeting. With diplomatic duties that kept her busy at all hours, they saw too little of each other even when they were both on the same planet.

Well, the twins would be coming home in another six days. Han and Chewbacca would be back by then, and their entire lifestyle would change. A pair of two-year-olds running around the palace would force Han and Leia to look differently at many of the things they took for granted.

But why hadn't Han gotten in touch? It shouldn't have been so difficult to send a holonet communiqué from the *Falcon*'s cockpit. She wasn't quite ready yet to admit she was worried about him.

With a greeting signal from the archway of the park balcony, an older-model protocol droid marched into view. "Excuse me, Minister Organa Solo. Someone wishes to see you. Are you accepting visitors?"

Leia set down her breakfast pastry. "Why not?" It was probably some lobbyist wanting to complain to her in private, or a panicked minor functionary who needed her to make a decision on some uninteresting detail, or one of the other senators trying to hand off some of his own duties.

Instead, with a flourish of his vermillion cape, Lando Calrissian walked through the arch.

"Good morning, Madame Minister. I hope I'm not disturbing your breakfast?" He flashed a broad, disarming smile.

Seeing him, Leia felt her mood immediately lighten. She stood up and met him near the archway. He gallantly kissed her hand, but she was not satisfied until she had given him a friendly hug. "Lando, you're the last person I expected this morning!"

He followed her back to the table overlooking the skyline of Imperial City and pulled up a chair, sweeping his cape over its back. Without asking, Lando took one of her untouched pastries and began to munch on it.

"So what brings you to Coruscant?" she asked. She realized how eager she was just to have a normal conversation without diplomatic entanglements and hidden agendas.

Lando brushed crumbs from his mustache. "I just came to see how you all are doing in the big city. Where's Han?"

She grumbled. "That seems to be a sore subject this morning. He and Chewie went off to Kessel, but I think they just used it as an excuse to go joyriding and remembering their glory years."

"Kessel can be a pretty rough place."

Leia avoided his eyes. "Han hasn't bothered to call in six days."

"That's not like him," Lando said.

"Oh, yes, it is—and you know it! I suppose we'll have words when he comes back day after tomorrow." Then she forced an artificial air of brightness. "But let's not talk about that right now. How can you find time to trot around visiting people? A respectable man like yourself has so many responsibilities."

Lando averted her gaze this time and began fidgeting. He stared at the expanses of gleaming new buildings visible through the metropolis. For the first time Leia noticed a slight scruffiness to his appearance. His clothes seemed a bit ragged around the edges, the colors faded as if from too much wear.

He spread his hands, then took another breakfast pastry. "To tell you the truth, I'm . . . um, in between engagements right now." He gave her a lopsided grin, but she frowned back at him.

"What happened to your big mining operation on Nkllon? Didn't the New Republic replace most of your destroyed machinery?"

"Well, it was still a lot of work, and not paying off—bad publicity after the Sluis Van attack, you know. And Nkllon is a hellish place—you were there. I just needed a change."

Leia crossed her arms and looked at him skeptically. "All right, Lando. The appropriate excuses are logged and recorded. Now, what really happened to Nkllon?"

He squirmed. "Well, I lost it in a sabacc game."

She couldn't keep herself from laughing. "So you're out of work?" His expression of wounded pride was obviously faked. Leia considered for a moment. "We could always reactivate your commission as a general in the New Republic. You and Wedge were a great team on Calamari."

His eyes widened. "Are you offering me a job? I can't imagine what you would want me to do."

"Formal receptions, state dinners . . . plenty of wealthy backers wandering around," Leia said. "The possibilities are endless."

Just then the old protocol droid shuffled through the arch again, but before he could announce his business, See-Threepio and Artoo-Detoo bustled around him, making a direct path to Leia. "Princess Leia!" Threepio could not contain his excitement. "We've found one. Artoo, tell the princess. Oh, General Calrissian! What are you doing here?"

Artoo launched into a series of electronic sounds, which Threepio dutifully translated. "Artoo was checking the records of various winners in different gambling establishments throughout the galaxy. We seem to have encountered a man who has extraordinary luck at the Umgullian blob races."

Threepio handed a hardcopy printout of the winning statistics to Leia, but she passed it on to Lando. "You're better trained to understand this than I am." Lando took the page of figures and stared at them. He didn't appear to know what he was looking for.

Threepio added his own commentary. "If it is displayed only as wins and losses, Mr. Tymmo's record shows nothing out of the ordinary. But when I had Artoo plot the magnitude of wins, you will note that while Mr. Tymmo loses quite often in minor races, in every instance when he bets more than a hundred credits on a particular blob, that blob wins the race!"

Lando tapped the sheet of numbers. "He's right. This is pretty unusual. I've never seen the Umgullian blob races myself, and I'm no expert in the nuances, but I'm inclined to say that these odds are next to impossible."

"This is exactly the sort of thing Master Luke asked us to look for." Threepio moved his arms up and down, whirring the servomotors until they whined in protest. "Do you think Mr. Tymmo could be a potential Jedi for Master Luke's academy?"

Lando looked at Leia with questions in his eyes. He had obviously not heard of Luke's recent speech. But Leia's eyes sparkled. "Someone needs to check this out. If it's just a scam, we need a person who knows his way around gambling establishments, Lando, isn't that a job you could do?"

She knew his answer before she even asked the question.

7

The cracked and gasping waste- lands of Kessel always made Moruth Doole hungry. Staring out the landscape window, Doole's mechanical eye focused to the far distance.

Kessel's surface was whitish and powdery, with a few hardy transplanted weeds trying to survive in the crevices. Great plumes from the atmosphere factories gushed into the pinkish sky in a losing battle against the weak gravity. Unseen radiation from the Maw crackled against the atmospheric shields. The garrison moon housing Kessel's defense fleet was just setting on the horizon.

Doole turned from the window and went to an alcove in the former warden's office. Time for a snack.

He withdrew a cage of fat and juicy flying insects, pressing his face close to the mesh so he could see better with his dim eyesight. The insects had ten legs, iridescent body cases, and succulent abdomens. They panicked the moment he moved the cage.

Doole rapped spongy fingers on the mesh, stirring them

up. The insects flew around the confined space in a frenzy. Somehow terror released a hormone that made their meat sweeter. He licked his swollen Rybet lips.

Opening the mesh door, Doole thrust his entire head into the cage. The insects fluttered around his eyes, his ears, his cheeks. Doole's sharp tongue shot out again and again, spearing the insects and slurping them into his mouth. He snapped up three more, then paused to swallow. Their squirming legs tickled the inside of his mouth. Giving a sigh of pleasure, Doole lapped up another pair. One insect flew directly into his open mouth, and Doole swallowed it whole.

Someone knocked on his door and marched in before he could respond. Wearing the insect cage over his head, Doole turned around to see Skynxnex, his gangly arms and legs jittering. "I have a report, Moruth."

Doole extricated his head from the insect cage, then sealed the opening. Three bugs managed to escape and flew to the wide picture window, flinging themselves against the transparisteel. Doole decided to catch them later. "Yes? What is it?"

"We have finished overhauling the *Millennium Falcon*. All identifying marks are removed, replaced with fake serial numbers. We made a few other modifications in addition to the regular repairs it needed. With your permission I'll have it flown up to the garrison moon where it can be incorporated into our space navy. Light freighters aren't the best warships, but with a good pilot they can still cause plenty of damage—and the *Falcon* is closer to a fighter than a freighter."

Doole nodded. "Good, good. What about our work on the energy shield generators? I want them functional as soon as possible, just in case the New Republic comes after us."

"Our engineers on the moonbase think they can reroute

the circuits so we won't need all the parts we're missing. Kessel will be impregnable before long."

Doole's single eye lit up with eagerness. "Have Han Solo and his Wookiee gone into the mines yet?"

Skynxnex tapped his fingertips together. "I've reserved an armored personnel transport and will make the delivery personally within the hour." He fingered his double-blaster. "If they try anything, *I* want to be the one to deal with it."

Doole smiled. "I look forward to them rotting in the dark." He waved his splayed hands. "Well, what are you waiting for?" Moving with his jerky walk, Skynxnex left the warden's chambers.

Doole smiled at the thought of his revenge on Solo, but uneasiness tugged at him. The New Republic seemed far away and insignificant, but from his scan of Han's mind, he knew the magnitude of firepower that could be directed against him. Not since Doole had taken over the prison facilities from Kessel's upstart slave lords had he felt such impending doom.

Under the old system it had been so much simpler. By blackmailing or paying off prison guards, Doole had managed to set himself up as a kingpin of spice smuggling right under the Empire's nose. He sold maps and access codes for Kessel's energy shield, fostering small-time spice operations on other parts of the planet. Hapless entrepreneurs would work their new mines, then sell the product in secret to Doole. Once the spice veins began to play out, Doole (acting as a loyal prison official) would "discover" the illicit operation and report it to his Imperial contact. When Imperial troops raided those illegal mines, Doole's handpicked guards made certain that anyone who could point a finger at Doole never survived capture. The other helpless lackeys would be put to work in the primary mines. It was a win-win situation for Doole.

During the prison revolt Doole targeted his primary rivals and made the toughest guards go after the worst smugglers until they slaughtered each other. This left Moruth Doole in charge, with Skynxnex as his right-hand man.

Doole had captured the warden, sending him to work in the spice mines until he was broken. Then, for the entertainment value, Doole had planted spice grubs in his body. As the grubs chewed up his insides, the warden had gone through marvelously theatrical convulsions, in the middle of which Doole encased him in carbonite, using freezing equipment that had once been used to prepare violent and dangerous prisoners for transport.

Reminiscing always aroused him. Reaching into a drawer of his desk, Doole withdrew the bright-yellow cravat that signified his readiness to mate. He secured it in place, then drew in a long hissing breath as he refocused his mechanical eye and glanced at his reflection. Irresistible!

Doole rubbed his palms along his ribs to straighten the lizard-skin waistcoat, then strutted out of his office, down the corridor. He entered the secure wing, keying in the access code that only he knew; then he sucked in a deep breath. Flicking his tongue in and out, he could pick up the pheromones from the air.

Inside their cubicle-cells, the captive Rybet females huddled in the corners, trying to hide in the shadows. Doole's yellow cravat seemed very bright in the dimness.

Alone on Kessel, Moruth Doole had been frustrated for many years. But now that he ran the planet, he could afford to have dozens of female slaves shipped from his homeworld. Sometimes the females did not cooperate, but after years of working in the correctional facility, Doole had plenty of experience in dealing with unruly prisoners.

Lately, his only difficulty had been in *choosing* among the females. As he sauntered down the narrow corridor, setting his mechanical eye to high focus and peering into the cells, Moruth Doole's writhing lips formed a huge, lustful smile.

Kessel's landscape rushed beneath the armored prisoner transport. Han Solo could see only a narrow strip through the window slits in the prisoners' compartment. He and Chewie had been strapped into their seats and linked to resistance-feedback electrodes that would knock them unconscious if they struggled too much. Chewbacca had even more trouble with the full-body restraint than he had with the stun-cuffs.

Skynxnex hunched over the pilot controls, circling the transport away from the battlements of the Imperial Correction Facility. An armored guard sat in the copilot's seat, directing his blaster rifle toward Han and Chewie.

"Hey, how about pointing out some of the landmarks, Skynxnex?" Han said. "What kind of tour is this, anyway?"

"Shut up, Solo!" Skynxnex said.

"Why should I? I bought a full-price ticket."

Skynxnex sent a painful jolt through the restraining electrodes. Chewbacca roared. Han muttered, "There goes your tip, Skynxnex."

The scarecrow guided the transport around a huge open pit that plunged deep into the ground. Rusted girders and support structures stood like skeletal fingers propped up in the whitish barrens. It took Han a moment to realize this was a shaft bored into the crust by the giant atmosphere factories, chewing through the rocks and dissolving out oxygen and carbon dioxide to replenish the constantly fading air. After the huge factory had sucked out the viable breathing gases, it had left access to an entire network of underground tunnels for spice mining.

Skynxnex set the prisoner transport down on the rocky ground and fitted a breath mask over his nose and mouth; he gave another mask to the guard.

"What about us?" Han said.

"You won't be out very long," Skynxnex said. "A little light-headedness will do you good."

Punching a button on the control panel, Skynxnex released their restraints. Han stretched his sore arms. Instantly, the guard snapped up his rifle, and Skynxnex whipped out his modified double-blaster, both pointing the deadly barrels directly at Han.

Han froze. "Just . . . stretching. It's okay. Calm down!"

When Skynxnex opened the side door to the transport vehicle, Han felt his ears pop. Moist air flashed into white vapor, wafting in the rarefied atmosphere next to the open pit.

Han felt oxygen being stolen from his lungs. Instinctively, he drew in a deep breath, but that helped little. He and Chewbacca stumbled out of the craft as Skynxnex and the guard prodded them.

At the rim of the crater they found an elevator cage on tracks that plunged deep into the pit. Skynxnex seemed to be moving with deliberate slowness. Unable to breathe, Han tried to hurry, stumbling into the elevator cage and gesturing Chewbacca after him. He gasped and wheezed. Black spots began to appear in front of his eyes. When he did manage to breathe an entire lungful of the thin air, the cold of Kessel bit into his chest.

"A few years ago we had the atmosphere factories running full tilt," Skynxnex said, his words muffled behind the facemask. "Doole figured it was a frivolous waste of energy."

The guard shut the wire mesh door, and Skynxnex oper-

ated the elevator controls. The cage descended at a rapid
clip until the window of sky shrank to a small spot of blue
light high above.

They saw openings into the rock wall sealed off with
steel doors. At each level a ring of light encircled the
pit, but many of the illuminators had either burned out
or been broken.

Chewbacca hung on to the bars of the elevator with
his long hairy arms, panting for air. His pink tongue
protruded, turning purplish from lack of oxygen. Han,
shivering and dizzy and starved for breath, slumped to
the bottom of the elevator.

When the elevator abruptly stopped, the jolt slammed
Han's head into the mesh. As he looked down through the
open cage floor, he saw the pit continuing immeasurably
far below them.

"Get up!" Skynxnex said, kicking him. "No time to
sleep. Come on, you'll get a breath of fresh air inside."

With some help from Skynxnex, Han managed to haul
himself to his feet. The smaller guard had much more
difficulty manhandling Chewbacca forward.

Opening the gate of the elevator, they had access to one
of the sealed metal doors. Skynxnex cranked the hatch,
and all four of them staggered into a small tiled chamber.

Han could barely see anymore. His ears buzzed. His
eyesight was a mixture of black specks, roaring blood,
and dim shadows of the objects around him. But as soon
as Skynxnex sealed the door, glorious oxygen flooded the
chamber.

Before the captives could recover, the guard shoved
the barrel of his blaster rifle under Chewbacca's chin,
and Skynxnex held his own weapon against Han's head.
"Almost there," Skynxnex said. "No funny stuff now."

Han, happy just to be breathing again, couldn't dream
of doing anything. At least not yet.

On the other side of the airlock was a large muster room filled with lethargic-looking workers ready to begin their shift in the spice mines. The muster room had been blasted out of solid rock, and a tall bank of bunks ran along one side of the room. An empty eating section with long tables took up the central area.

Cameras stared down at the activity from perches on the walls. Guards in hodgepodge stormtrooper uniforms waited behind screens in the control rooms. Other guards kept an eye on the people moving about in the muster area. All the workers looked pale and haggard, as if they had been underground and underfed for years.

A burly man strode up to meet them, keeping his eyes fixed on Skynxnex. The man had a lumpy face, a lumpy chin covered with bristly black stubble, and lumpy arms as if his massive muscles had all been attached at the wrong places.

"You brought me two more?" the man said. "Only two? That's not enough." He reached out to grab Chewbacca's hairy arm. Chewbacca roared and flinched away, but the lumpy man didn't notice. "Well, the Wookiee's worth three men, but I don't know about the other one. This doesn't take care of half the people I've lost."

Skynxnex glowered at him. "So stop losing people," he said with a voice of ice, then nudged Han. "This is Boss Roke. He's in charge of breaking you. He gets extra points with Moruth Doole to make your life miserable."

"He doesn't seem to be doing a very good job of keeping track of his workers," Han said.

Roke flashed him a withering glare. "Something's taking my men down in the deep tunnels. I've had two more missing since yesterday. They vanish without a trace—no locators, nothing."

Han shrugged. "It's hard to get good help these days."

Skynxnex pulled out his double-blaster and shoved it in

Han's face again, but he spoke to Boss Roke. "Get thermal suits for these two. We'll watch them while they get into uniform."

Roke snapped his fingers, and two guards went rummaging through some cubicles. "The human won't be difficult, but the Wookiee—we don't carry much in that size."

In the end the guard found a large misshapen suit that had once been worn by some alien creature that had three arms, but it fit Chewbacca well enough after they sealed off the third arm; the empty sleeve and glove dangled down his chest.

A heater-pack between the shoulder blades powered the whole thing to keep them warm down in the frigid mine tunnels. Han was relieved to see a small breath mask attached to the suit.

Skynxnex backed toward the elevator. The guard had already entered the airlock chamber. One last time, as if he felt he hadn't used enough tiresome threats for one afternoon, Skynxnex pointed the double-blaster at Han. "Next time maybe Moruth will let me use this."

"If you clean up your room without being told, and if you eat all your vegetables," Han taunted, "then he might let you have a special treat."

"Shift alpha, ready for work detail!" Boss Roke bellowed into the muster room, and dozens of weary people shuffled to squares painted on the floor. Roke pointed to two empty squares. "You two, positions eighteen and nineteen. Now!"

"What, no new-employee orientation?" Han asked.

With a sadistic grin on his face, Boss Roke shoved him toward the squares. "It's on-the-job training."

At some unspoken signal the workers mounted breath masks on their faces. Seeing this, Han and Chewbacca followed suit. A big metal door on the far side of the wall slid open to reveal an illuminated chamber a hundred meters long, in which floated a centipedelike mine transport of little cars linked together by magnetic attractors.

A high-pitched tone *pinged* through hidden speakers, and the workers took their seats on one of the floating mine cars. As people climbed aboard, the separate sections of the cars swayed back and forth.

Chewbacca grunted a question. Han looked around, blinking. "I don't know any more about this than you do, buddy." Now that Skynxnex had departed, he no longer needed to continue his blustering. Fear started to trickle into his limbs.

Boss Roke took a seat in the pilot car; other guards were stationed evenly throughout the open tram. All the guards wore infrared goggles. Every one of the prisoners sat motionless. Behind them the metal door slammed shut. Everyone seemed to be waiting for something.

"Now what?" Han mumbled to himself.

All the lights went out. Han and Chewbacca plunged into an absolute suffocating blackness like a blanket of tar.

"What the—" Han drew a sudden deep breath. The blackness was palpable. He couldn't see a thing. Beside him Chewbacca groaned in alarm. He heard the other workers moving, shuffling. Han's ears strained as his imagination tried to understand what was going on. He heard a clunking, sliding sound. "Hold on, Chewie," he said.

A metal door at the opposite side of the chamber opened up. The sound of its movement along rough metal tracks echoed in the enclosed space. Wind rushed around their ears as the air spilled outward into the mine tunnels of Kessel.

In a sudden panic Han pushed his breath mask tighter against his face just as he felt the atmosphere grow thin. The fleeing air took with it whatever heat had remained, making his exposed skin tingle with cold.

The mine cars lurched on their repulsorlifts, picking up speed. Acceleration slammed Han into his hard, uncomfortable seat. He could hear the air roaring past his head, feel the tunnel walls around him. The transport whipped around a curve, and Han grabbed the cold metal railing to keep himself from flying out of his seat. The mine cars whisked along, tilting downward, then lurching sideways. He had no idea how Boss Roke could possibly see where he was going unless the whole system was computer controlled.

Behind them, just after they had passed under an echoing archway, a heavy metal door slammed shut with a sound like an avalanche of scrap metal.

Han couldn't understand why the spice miners didn't string up at least some cheap illuminators as guideposts along the tunnels. But then it came to him like a slap in the face: the realization that since glitterstim spice was *photoactive*—made potent in the presence of light—it obviously had to be mined in total darkness or else it would be ruined.

Total darkness.

Han and Chewbacca would spend their days at hard labor in the mines without ever being able to see each other, or where they were, or what they were doing. Han had to blink his eyes just to make sure they were open instead of closed—not that it made any difference.

A shiver went down his back. Boss Roke had said that some unknown thing deep in the mines was preying on helpless workers, snatching them unawares. How could anybody run from a carnivorous attacker while surrounded by complete darkness?

The quality of the sound changed off and on. As Han's mind grew accustomed to processing information through his ears, it became obvious whenever the rushing mine car passed side tunnels, because of the sudden hole in the wind. Breathing through the mask, he could smell nothing other than flat recycled air.

The mine car wobbled from side to side, rocking as somebody moved about in the seats, climbing over the individual cars. The person slowly clambered over one seat back, then another, approaching their position. Han thought he heard someone breathing, straining, growing nearer.

"You there! Number fourteen! Sit down!" a guard shouted.

Number fourteen? Han thought. How could the guard possibly see which one had been moving about? Then he remembered the infrared goggles. The guards could probably see everyone, bright silhouettes against the backdrop of blackness.

The car stopped jostling for a few moments, but then the rocking started again. The mysterious person kept moving toward them. Somebody heaved himself over the seat to the empty spot right behind Han and Chewbacca.

"Hey, I told you to sit down!" the guard shouted.

"This is my new seat," a voice said.

"That's your new seat!" the guard said, strangely repeating the words before he fell silent.

Han forced himself not to speak. Since he couldn't see anything himself, the intruder must be just shifting about, unable to tell where he was going. Or could he have his own set of infrared goggles? Had Skynxnex or Moruth Doole hired some assassin to get rid of Han and Chewbacca while no one was watching?

A quick slash from a vibrator knife? A shove that knocked him off the floating transport, abandoning him down in the empty labyrinth of tunnels? In the darkness Han would never be able to find his way back. He wondered if he would starve, freeze, or suffocate first. He didn't want to find out.

He heard the faint, echoed breathing of someone speaking behind a breath mask, leaning closer. Beside him Chewbacca bristled in anticipation.

"Are you really from the outside?" the voice said. "I haven't been above ground for years." It seemed hopeful, soft, and tenor, but muffled behind the breath mask and the rushing wind. Han couldn't tell if it was the voice of an aged man, a deep-voiced woman, or a quiet and meek clerk from the former Imperial prison.

Han's mind pictured a skeletal old man with long scraggly hair, tattered beard, and ragged clothes. "Yeah, we're from out there. A lot of things have changed."

"I'm Kyp. Kyp Durron."

After a moment's hesitation Han introduced himself and Chewbacca. Suspecting some kind of trap, he decided not to give too much information. Kyp Durron seemed to sense this and talked about himself without asking too many prying questions.

"You'll get to know everybody here. That's just the way of it. I've lived most of my life on Kessel. My parents were political prisoners, exiled on this planet when the Emperor started cracking down on civil unrest. My brother Zeth was taken off to the Imperial military training center on Carida, and we never heard another word from him. I got stuck here in the spice mines. I always thought they'd come back and haul me to Carida too, but I guess they forgot."

Han tried to imagine Kyp's life going from bad to worse. "How come you're still down in the mines?"

"During the prison revolt they didn't much care who ended up here. Now most of the workers are the old Imperial prison guards. Nobody thought to let me out when they changed everything up top. I've never been important enough."

Kyp made a sound that must have been a bitter laugh. "People say I have good luck in all sorts of things, but my luck has never been good enough to let me have a normal life." He paused, as if gathering hope. In that moment Han wished he could see the stranger's face. "Is it really true the Empire has fallen?"

"Seven years ago, Kyp," Han said. "The Emperor was blown up with his Death Star. We've been fighting battles ever since, but the New Republic is trying to keep everything together. Chewie and I came here as ambassadors to reestablish contact with Kessel." He paused. "Obviously the people of Kessel weren't interested."

Han snapped his attention to the front as he heard something happen to the cars ahead. The front car split off; he could hear it echo with a diminishing *swoosh* down one of the side tunnels. A few moments later another two cars separated themselves and went down another side tunnel as their sounds diminished in the hollow distance. The rest of the floating mine car continued down the main tunnel.

"They're separating the mining teams," Kyp said. "I wanted to be with you. Tell me everything."

"Kyp," Han said with a sigh, "it looks like we'll have plenty of time to give you the details."

The audio hum of the mine cars' repulsorlifts deepened. Han felt the breeze on his face dwindle as they slowed. His hands and face were numb; his ears tingled with the cold, but the rest of his body seemed comfortably warm in the heated thermal suit.

The guard who had shouted at Kyp spoke when the floating cars stopped. "Everybody out. Link up. March to the work area."

The remaining cars swayed as the prisoners climbed off and stood in silence on the crumbled ground. Their equipment grated against each other in the darkness, and their boots scuffed the dirt. A pandemonium of little sounds echoed in the claustrophobic tunnel, making the blackness press in even more heavily.

"Where are we going?" Han said.

Kyp grabbed a loop on Han's belt. "Just hold the person in front of you. Believe me, you don't want to get lost down here."

"I believe you," Han said. Chewbacca made his own noise of agreement.

When the work detail had lined up, the front guard began to march them along. Han took small shuffling steps to keep from stumbling over rubble on the floor, but he still tripped into Chewbacca several times.

They turned to pass through another tunnel entrance. Han heard a faint thump and a yowl of pain from the Wookiee. "Watch your head there, buddy," he said. He heard the rustle of fur inside a thermal suit as Chewbacca bent down to pass through the arch.

"Here's the rail," the guard said. "Stop here, take your time, and go down."

"What's a rail?" Han asked.

"Once you touch it, you'll figure it out," Kyp answered.

The noises he heard made no sense to Han. He couldn't determine what was actually happening. He discerned sliding sounds of fabric, bitten-back outcries of surprise or fear. When Chewbacca shuffled up, he voiced a guttural complaint, shaking his entire body in refusal.

The guard lashed out with something hard that struck Chewbacca. The Wookiee roared in pain and swung his arm trying to hit the guard, but apparently smacked only the rock wall instead. Chewbacca grew more upset, flailing right and left. Han had to duck to keep from being battered.

"Chewie! Calm down! Stop it!" The Wookiee slowly regained control of himself at the sound of Han's voice.

"Do what I tell you!" the guard shouted.

"It's okay," Kyp added his own encouragement. "We do this every day."

"I'll go first, Chewie," Han said, "whatever it is."

"Down there," the guard snapped.

Han bent over, fumbled with his hands, and felt a big hole in the floor like a trapdoor to lower tunnels, with piled rubble all around it. His fingers found a cold metal railing about the size of a typical steel girder, polished smooth and plunging downward, like a slide or a metal banister.

"You want me to ride that?" Han asked. "Where does it go?"

"Don't worry," Kyp said again. "It's the best way down."

"You've got to be kidding!"

Then he heard Chewbacca laughing, a nasal, chuffing sound. That made up Han's mind for him. He sat down on the metal rail and wrapped his legs around it, placing his hands behind his hips and gripping the rail as best he could. The slippery fabric of the thermal suit immediately started him sliding. The darkness grabbed at him as he picked up speed. Han imagined sharp stalactites just centimeters above his head, waiting to take off the top of his skull if he sat up at the wrong moment. He continued to accelerate. "I don't like this!" he said.

Suddenly the rail disappeared beneath him, and he tumbled onto a mound of powdery sand. Another two workers scrambled forward to yank him clear of the end of the rail. He brushed dust off his thermal suit, though he couldn't see the dirt anyway.

A few moments later Chewbacca came down with a long, echoing howl, and shortly after that came Kyp Durron and the guard. "Line up again!" the guard said.

Chewbacca grunted and huffed a few words. Han snorted. "Don't tell *me* it was fun!"

The guard marched them ahead. When the ground dropped out from under them, they splashed into a shallow lake. The pressure of the water pushed against the legs of Han's suit. The captive miners sloshed ahead, holding on to each other in their blindness.

The water had a sour, brackish smell, and Han's stomach clenched, anticipating a drop-off that would plunge him in over his head. Chewbacca whined but kept his comments to himself.

Under the water something soft and fingerlike poked against Han's legs. Other contacts nudged at his feet, prodding and coiling around his calves. "Hey!" He thrashed about with his feet. The ghostly, touching things swarmed about him. Han pictured soft blind grubs, hungry in the darkness; their mouths would be filled with fangs, waiting for something to eat, something helpless in the dark—as he was. He splashed again to drive them away.

"Don't call attention to yourself," Kyp Durron said in a low voice. "That will only bring more of them."

Han forced himself not to overreact, to walk with gliding, even strides. None of the other prisoners cried out; apparently, no one had been eaten alive yet, though the small probing fingers or suckers or mouths continued to play around his legs. His throat felt very dry.

He wanted to drop to his knees when they finally reached the tunnel on the other side of the subterranean lake. Behind them dripping water and tiny splashing sounds echoed in the grotto.

An unknown time later they arrived at the actual spice-mining area. The guard withdrew an apparatus from his pack, making shuffling and clinking noises as he did so. Unseen, he set it up along the walls of the tunnel.

"We have to go deep to get the good spice deposits," Kyp said. "Down here the glitterstim is fresh and fibrous, instead of old and powdery like in the higher mines. The spice veins are laid in crisscross patterns along the walls of the tunnel, never going much below the surface of the rock."

Before Han could say anything else, a high-pitched, teeth-jarring hum pounded against the tunnel. Chewbacca roared in pain. Then a skin of rock along the inner tunnel sloughed off. The guard had used an acoustic disruptor that penetrated only a few inches into the rock, crumbling it down. "Get to it!" he said.

Kneeling on the rubble-strewn floor, Kyp showed Han and Chewbacca how to sort through the crushed rock, feeling with cold-numbed fingers through the broken pebbles and debris to pluck out strands of glitterstim, like tufts of hair or asbestos fiber.

Han's hands felt raw from the work and the biting cold, but none of the other prisoners complained. They all seemed beaten. He could hear them breathing and gasping as they continued to exert themselves. Han stuffed fragments of glitterstim into the gathering pouch at his hip. He felt a sinking feeling, like a knife twisting inside him. He could be at this job for a long, long time.

After the team finished sifting through the rubble, the guard moved them farther down the tunnel, then activated his acoustic disruptor to bring down another section of the wall.

As they huddled in the tunnel, picking at broken rock, Han could think only of his aching knees, his burning fingers. Of how nice it would be to be back with Leia again. No one had told him how long a shift was—not that he had any way of telling time in the darkness. He grew hungry. He grew thirsty. He kept working.

During a lull Han felt a tingle go up his spine. He looked, knowing he could see nothing in the dark. But his ears, now attuned as his primary sense, picked up a distant rustling, a thousand whispering voices growing louder, picking up speed like a hydrolocomotive bulleting down a tube. A pearly glow seemed to seep out of the air.

"What—?"

"Shhh!" Kyp answered. The prisoners had stopped working. A faint glittering dazzle like a dense cloud of faint fireflies shot through the tunnel, humming and chittering.

Han ducked. Around him he heard the others also falling flat on the debris-covered floor.

The glowing thing shot down the hollow tube, rolling and roiling. Once it passed them and went beyond the point where they had mined spice from the walls, the glowing thing suddenly curved right and plunged straight into the solid rock, vanishing like a fish falling back into a dark pool.

Behind them, along the curving lengths of the tunnel, tiny blue sparks flickered from the exposed spice that had been activated by the light source whizzing past. The blue sparks sputtered and flickered, and quickly faded.

Han's eyes ached from the sudden barrage of light—a light that was probably too dim for him to have seen under normal circumstances, but his eyes had been yearning in blackness for hours now. "What was that?" he shouted.

He heard Kyp panting beside him. "Nobody knows. It's about the fifteenth one I've seen over the years. We call them bogeys. They've never hurt anybody, or so we think, but nobody knows what's grabbing those people down in the deep mines."

The guard himself seemed shaken, and Han could hear a quaver in his voice. "That's enough. End of shift. Let's make our way back to the cars."

That sounded like a good idea to Han.

When the string of mine cars returned to the long holding grotto and the metal door closed behind them, Han heard the sound of weapons being drawn. All workers were ordered to strip out of their thermal suits. Han could understand the precautions—with a brief mental boost from stolen glitterstim, a prisoner might be able to stage an escape . . . although Han had been to the barren surface of Kessel and wondered where an escapee might go.

When the standard lights finally came back on, the blinding glare was enough to make Han crouch over, as if someone had punched him in the gut. He shielded his eyes.

He felt a hand take him and lead him into the muster room. "It's okay, Han. Just follow me. Let your eyes get used to it. There's no hurry."

But Han was in a hurry to see what Kyp Durron looked like. He kept blinking away tears and forcing his pupils to contract enough that he could make sense out of the brilliant images showering around him. But when he finally discerned Kyp's form, he blinked again—this time in surprise.

"You're just a kid!" Han saw a dark, tousle-headed teen who looked as if he cropped his own hair with a blunt object. He had wide eyes surrounded by dark rims, and his skin was pale from years of living in the darkness of the spice mines. Kyp was wiry and tough looking. He stared at Han with hope and a little intimidation.

"Don't worry," Kyp said. "I do the best I can."

Kyp reminded him of the brash and wide-eyed young Luke Skywalker Han had first met in the Mos Eisley cantina. But Kyp seemed tougher than Luke had been, not quite so naive. With the rough life Kyp had had, growing up on Kessel and locked in the spice mines without anyone to watch over him, it was no wonder the kid had a hard streak in him.

At the moment Han couldn't decide which he hated more—the Empire, for inflicting such hardships on Kyp and his family, or Moruth Doole for perpetuating them . . . or himself, for getting Chewie and him into this mess in the first place.

8

Night on Eol Sha offered little rest. Falling darkness fought against the simmering orange glow from the nearby volcano, the pastel blaze of the Cauldron Nebula, and the looming spotlight of the too-close moon. Hissing blasts from the geyser field broke the quiet at irregular intervals.

Luke sat alone in the cramped storage module Gantoris had given him for sleeping accommodations. Never intended as a living area, the module had few comforts: a basin of filmy water and a cloth-covered mound of dirt for a bed. Gantoris took a perverse pleasure in telling Luke that it had been one of the dead boy's favorite places to play. Either the refugees blamed Luke for not being able to save both children, or perhaps Gantoris just wanted to keep him off balance.

Luke had his lightsaber and all the powers he had learned from Jedi training, should he decide to escape. But that was not the reason he had come to Eol Sha. Cupping his chin in his hands, he stared out at the hostile night. He needed to convince Gantoris to listen to him, to see the need for rebuilding the Jedi Knights—but why would someone from an isolated colony, with no conception of galactic politics, bother to care?

If Gantoris was indeed a descendant of the long-ago Ta'ania, Luke had to make him care.

When the other people drifted to their quarters for the evening, Warton brought him a steamed bugdillo to eat. Luke poked at the glossy black shell of the crustacean, splitting open the cracks in its multiply segmented body to get at the pinkish meat. That afternoon a boy had been killed trying to spear these small creatures. . . .

At any time Luke could leave the battered module, walk to the passenger shuttle on the far side of the geyser field, and retrieve his own rations; but he didn't want to leave, not until Gantoris agreed to come with him. Luke ate the sour-tasting meat, chewing in silence.

"Come with me." Gantoris stood silhouetted in the square doorway of Luke's quarters.

Luke blinked and came out of his trance, refreshed and surprised to see the gray morning light shining through cracks in the module. Without a word, he stood up and stepped outside.

Gantoris wore the faded uniform of a trader captain. It fit him poorly, but he carried himself with pride. The uniform must have been passed down from generation to generation as the hopeful colonists waited for the ramjet gas miners to return and make their settlement a booming town.

"Where are we going?" Luke asked.

Gantoris handed him a woven pouch, then slung a similar one over his own shoulder. "To get food." Tossing his thick black braid behind him, he marched toward the geyser field.

Luke followed across the rugged terrain, sidestepping the lime-encrusted network of geysers and steam vents. The planet of Eol Sha hummed with the tidal strain, like fading vibrations from a struck gong.

Gantoris moved with outward confidence, but Luke sensed trepidation, an uncertainty in him. Luke decided this might be a good time to talk about the Force and its powers.

"You must have learned something about the order of Jedi Knights," he began. "For a thousand generations they served the Old Republic as guardians and keepers of order. I believe one of your own ancestors—Ta'ania— was the daughter of a Jedi. That is why I've come to you. She was among the people who established this colony on Eol Sha.

"The Emperor hunted down and killed all the Jedi Knights his assassins could find, but I don't believe he could have traced every descendant, every bloodline. Now the Empire has fallen and the New Republic needs to reestablish the Jedi Knights." He paused. "I want you to be one of them."

He gripped Gantoris's shoulder. The other man flinched, and pushed Luke's hand away. Luke's voice took on a more pleading tone. "I want to show you the powers of the Force, the infinite doors it can open. With this new strength you'll be able to help hold the entire galaxy together. I promise we'll take your people and move them to a safe planet, one that will seem like a paradise after Eol Sha."

Luke realized he was proselytizing. Gantoris looked at him with dark, unfathomable eyes. "Empires and republics mean nothing to me. What have they cared for us before? My universe is here, on this world."

He stopped in front of the wide opening to a geyser and peered into its depths. The creeping stink of rotten eggs wafted into the morning air. From his hip pouch Gantoris withdrew a battered old datapad and consulted a column of numbers that looked to be some sort of timetable. "Here. We will go inside the geyser and harvest."

Luke blinked. "Harvest what?"

Without answering Gantoris lowered himself over the lip of the geyser hole. Luke shrugged off his Jedi cloak and left it beside the geyser rim, then followed the other man underground. Was Gantoris just trying to see if Luke would follow him down into the belly of the geyser?

The shaft was a narrow, winding chimney through porous rock, a pipeline to gush superheated water. Colorful mineral deposits sparkled white and tan and blue, powdery in his hand. Luke found plenty of footholds as he followed Gantoris into the honeycombed passages. The rock felt warm and slimy. Acrid vapors rising from below stung his eyes.

Gantoris worked his way into a side crevice. Luke asked, "What do you want me to do?"

In answer Gantoris wedged himself deeper into a crack and shrugged the woven pouch off his shoulder. "Look in the dark pockets, the ones protected from the scalding water." Gantoris dug his fingers into a crevice, felt around, and pulled out a handful of rubbery tendrils. "With the heat and the mineral deposits, the lichens have a rich growing ground. It takes a great deal of processing, but we can make something edible out of this. On our world we don't have many choices. My people must take what we can find."

Luke likewise removed his pouch and began to search in the cracks, probing with his prosthetic hand. What if something poisonous lurked in the crevices to sting him? He could read ominous intentions from Gantoris but couldn't pinpoint them. Was Gantoris looking for a simple way to kill the "dark man" from his dreams? On his third try Luke found a mass of spongy growth and yanked it out.

Gantoris looked over his shoulder at Luke. "It would be better if we split up. If you stay by me, you will find only my leavings. I can never feed our people that way." Gantoris's voice changed to a mocking tone, and his forehead crinkled, raising his shaven eyebrows. "Unless your Force can miraculously create a banquet?"

Keeping his handholds, Luke edged over to another crack as Gantoris worked deeper into his own fissure, turning a jagged corner. A flurry of uneasiness shot through him, but Luke began to search among the crevices.

The lichen wasn't difficult to find, and Luke quickly filled his pouch, crawling through narrow openings. Perhaps Gantoris had expected him to get lost among the fissures. But even disoriented underground, Luke could always retrace his path. He had heard nothing from the other man, and, deciding that he had fulfilled his obligation, Luke began to work his way back to where they had split up.

When he reached the joined passage, Luke saw that Gantoris was no longer there. He crawled deeper into the fissure, looking for the other man, all the while expecting a trap but confident he could deal with it. He would have to impress Gantoris with his Jedi abilities.

The passage ended in a blocked wall of eroded stone. The smells of sulfurous smoke grew stronger, engendering a deep sense of claustrophobia in him. Luke recalled the two children buried under the avalanche, bright blood splashed on the bottoms of the fallen rocks. The ground around him hummed with barely contained murderous energy—what if another earthquake happened while he was wedged in the narrow cracks underground?

Gantoris was nowhere in sight. "Gantoris!" he called, but heard no answer. Looking up the shaft of daylight poking through from the surface, Luke finally saw the man's silhouette nearly at the top. Gantoris scrambled up the jagged walls, climbing as fast as he could manage, leaving Luke behind.

He was fleeing something.

Luke sensed rather than heard the buildup of pressure deep within the planet, the water table heated against magma crouching near the surface, coming to a boil, rising up, finding the most direct way to escape.

Gantoris had carried his own timetable. The geysers must erupt at regular intervals. He intended to trap Luke underground, where he would be cooked to the bone by curtains of superheated steam.

Luke grabbed for a handhold and hauled himself up, scrabbling with his boot for a place to rest his foot. He clambered up the bumps and corners of the chimney leading up. The heat increased around him, making it difficult to breathe. He gasped and blinked burning tears out of his eyes. Steam curled upward, as if seeping out of the very rocks.

His foot slipped and he nearly plunged downward, but his prosthetic hand flashed out, grabbing on to an outcropping and refusing to let go. When he finally regained his balance, the outcropping crumbled to pieces.

Luke had lost precious seconds. The light above shone brighter, urging him on. He held on to another corner, crawled up another few feet, reached out again.

Briefly he saw a shadowed head peer down into the geyser chimney, watching him. Gantoris. But he offered no help.

Luke clawed his way up, ignoring his torn flightsuit, climbing as fast as his limbs could carry him. Then he ran out of time.

He heard the explosion deep beneath him, the rumbling roar of a plume of boiling water rushing to the surface. Luke braced himself and knew he had one chance.

He had done this in Cloud City on Bespin, and during his training with Yoda, and other times. As the jet of steam and deadly water blasted toward him, Luke gathered his strength, his concentration, and sprang straight *up*, hurling his body out of the geyser shaft. He used the Force as a springboard to throw himself high and free, just as if he were lifting an inanimate object.

Luke shot out of the geyser chimney, flailing his arms as he dropped to the rugged ground. He tucked his shoulder and rolled, striking with enough force to knock the breath from him.

A second after he hit the ground, a wall of steam and superheated water belched from the geyser. Luke shielded his exposed flesh from the scalding droplets and waited for the blast to dwindle.

The geyser eruption lasted several minutes. When Luke finally crawled to his knees, he saw Gantoris and the other people of Eol Sha walking toward him, their faces grim, as usual. They had set him up, trapped him, tried to kill him.

But the anger faded quickly. Hadn't Luke challenged Gantoris to test him, to let him prove his intentions? Luke gathered his drenched Jedi cloak from the geyser rim and waited for them.

Gantoris crossed his arms over his chest and nodded. His face looked wide and bleak without eyebrows or eyelashes. "You passed my first test, dark man." Luke sensed both eagerness and terror from the man. "Now come and face your last trial."

As the people stepped forward to take him again, Luke did not resist. He had decided to take whatever risks proved necessary to rebuild the Jedi Knights.

He hoped the risks would be worth it.

• • •

It was like a religious procession. With Gantoris in the lead, the people of Eol Sha began a long march up the slope to the cracks of lava. Luke walked straight and proud, determined not to show fear, though the people had already proved their murderous intentions. Despite his Jedi training, he was in very real danger. The oppressive moon hung overhead like a gigantic fist.

Spires of lava rock jutted out of the hillside like rotten teeth. Gantoris did not slow his pace when the slope took a steep turn, but he stopped when they reached a sheltered opening in the volcano wall. Overhead a pall of smoke and ash hung in the air.

"Follow me inside," Gantoris told Luke. The others filed past, continuing along the rugged path. Luke stepped after him. He needed to earn Gantoris's respect, if not trust. In this circumstance Gantoris was making all the rules.

Gantoris strode confidently down the narrow passage into the dense shadows, a lava tube blasted through the side of the cone to ease pressure from an ancient eruption. Up ahead a fiery orange glow lit their way. Luke felt growing anticipation mixed with dread with each step they took.

The lava tube spread out, revealing a boiling lake of fire. Though the fissure opened to the sky, and other openings let in gusting cross-drafts, the chamber felt like the blast of an oven. Luke ducked his head, trying to shield his face with the damp Jedi hood, but Gantoris seemed unaffected.

Squinting through noxious gases belching from the lava, Luke watched the other people arrive on the far side of the chamber, lining up and waiting. All faces turned toward him.

Gantoris had to raise his voice over the growling sounds of the churning magma. "Walk across the fire, dark man.

If you reach the other side safely, I will allow you to teach me whatever you wish." Without waiting for a reply Gantoris disappeared back into the darkness of the lava tube.

Luke stared after him for a moment, wondering if Gantoris could be serious—but then he noticed dark objects in the blaze of bright lava. Hard stepping stones of denser rock that did not melt but made a precarious path across the lake of fire.

Was Gantoris testing his courage? What did the man want, and what did his dreams of a demonic "dark man" portend?

Luke swallowed, but his throat was dry as parchment. He stepped to the edge of the simmering lava. The stones beckoned, but common sense warned him to go back, to return to his shuttle and fly away. He could find other candidates for his Jedi academy. Threepio and Artoo must have uncovered some leads by now, and he himself had another possibility on Bespin. Luke hadn't even tested Gantoris yet; why should he risk his life for someone who might or might not actually have Jedi potential?

Because he had to. Forming a new order of Jedi Knights would be difficult, and if he flinched from the first test of his own powers, how could he consider himself worthy of attempting such a task?

Impossible heat swirled around him. Stepping to the edge of the fire, Luke looked at the broken sky above him. Then he set his foot down on the first stepping stone.

It supported his weight. Luke looked ahead, fixing his gaze on the opposite side. The gathered people kept watching.

Lava bubbled around him, belching noxious gases into the air. He tried to breathe in shallow gasps. He took another step. The other side seemed very far away.

Blinking irritated tears from his eyes, he counted the stones ahead of him. Fourteen more. Luke stepped to the next one.

Gantoris appeared on the far side, joining the other refugees of Eol Sha. Luke didn't expect them to cheer him on, but they remained too eerily silent.

Another step. Around him the lava gurgled like the belly of a giant beast, a hungry beast.

Luke moved to another step, then another. A tendril of euphoria began to rise within him. This wasn't as difficult as he had feared. He would be able to pass this test. With reckless courage and speed, he strode to the halfway point.

Then the lava began to bubble and hiss more forcefully, gushing as something stirred below. The volcanic chamber throbbed with a sound that drummed from just below his range of hearing, but enough to vibrate his teeth. He felt his stomach plunge with apprehension. He tensed, waiting to see what horror awaited him.

Something lived within the lake of lava. Something moved.

Suddenly a serpentlike creature burst above the surface, hissing like rocket fuel caught on fire.

The fireworm had a triangular head and pointed ear tufts. Crystalline scales armored every inch of its body. Its wide eyes were jewels glowing with a fire of their own. Insulated air intakes sucked in the hot atmosphere, filling bladders deep within the creature's core and making it rise to the surface of the lava pool, huge and fierce. The silicon armor plates glittered like mirrors in the firelight.

Luke kept his precarious balance on the stepping stone, avoiding sudden death in the molten rock, then leaped to the next rock. As the fireworm rose and coiled above him, he knew he could never outrun the monster. He stopped and found secure footing. Instinctively, he drew his lightsaber, igniting it with a snap-hiss. The green glow of his blade fought against the fiery orange of the lava chamber.

On the far side of the lava lake, the gathered people of Eol Sha watched in silence, unmoving.

The fireworm glared down at Luke with its viper's head. It opened a vast metallic mouth and spewed congealing lava at the wall. Armored intakes continued to suck air, raising coils of the behemoth's body to the surface. Luke held up his lightsaber, but it seemed pitifully small to fight a lava dragon.

With an ultrasonic bellow the fireworm dove beneath the magma again, splashing molten rock into the air. Luke danced from stepping stone to stepping stone, trying to avoid the deadly firefall. Globs of lava set his Jedi cloak on fire, but Luke managed to yank it over his shoulders and toss it into the bubbling pool, where it burst into bright flames.

He held his lightsaber in front of him. His eyes widened. He reached out with his Jedi senses, trying to second-guess the creature. His every nerve was tuned, ready to respond, but he saw only the restless surface of the lava.

"Where are you?" he whispered.

The fireworm's head exploded out of the lava on the other side, rearing up to strike. It plunged down, opening its huge mouth to reveal fangs like stalactites. Luke whirled, bringing up his lightsaber and dancing back to the previous stepping stone.

As the fireworm struck, Luke slashed with his humming green blade. But when the lightsaber smashed against the mirrored armor plates, the glowing green edge refracted into a thousand components, splitting and ricocheting around the chamber. Sparks showered all around him. The energy blade that could supposedly slice through anything broke only one small silicon armor plate.

On the other side of the chamber, the people of Eol Sha ducked to escape the flying shards of green power. Splintered rock fell into the magma lake. Luke knew he could not use the lightsaber against the monster again.

The fireworm yowled in surprise more than pain, then dove for refuge under the lava. Luke crouched, desperately trying to figure out what he should do next. He turned, ready to run to the other side where the people waited for him.

The fireworm would return any minute. He didn't know how much time he would have.

Suddenly, the creature launched itself out of the lava, roaring and hissing and making sounds too horrible for Luke to describe. He turned, lightsaber in hand and ready to die in battle—but now the monster had no interest in him at all.

Gouts of acrid smoke poured from the chink in the silicon armor, where lava ate its way into the fireworm's body core. The creature writhed and tossed, spewing lava into the air. Molten rock devoured the fireworm's internal organs like acid, killing it from the inside out. Burning within, the fireworm thrashed in agony, spraying lava as flames and foul smoke boiled out of the tiny breach in its armor. When the fiery rock burned through to the fireworm's inflated air bladders, the creature exploded.

Splatters of hardening lava rained down. Luke managed to deflect most of the burning chunks with the Force, but some scorched his back and shoulder. The fireworm's death throes churned waves in the molten rock, then gradually subsided.

Luke raised his eyes, blinking in disbelief. The people of Eol Sha still waited for him.

Most of the stepping stones had been washed away

in the turmoil. Nothing but impassable lava remained between him and Gantoris. He could not finish his journey. Giddy with terror and a backwash of possibilities from the Force, Luke stared at the impassable river of flames between him and his goal.

He thought of the potential for his proposed academy, for the return of the Jedi Knights. The New Republic needed him. He had to complete his promise. He would gather candidates to teach the ways of the Force. He *would*. Without a doubt in his mind, still throbbing with the Force after his battle against the fireworm, he closed his eyes.

Luke walked across the lake of fire.

He did not think about it. The lava refused to touch his feet. Only the Force burned bright around him. One step after another, he strode across the flaming rock, letting himself see nothing but his goal until he stood again on solid ground on the far side of the lake of fire, with Gantoris and his people.

When he reached safety, he nearly collapsed with relief, but he could not allow himself to show a change of expression. He tried not to think about what he had just done.

Gantoris stood before him, an expression of awe on his broad face. The others backed away, but Gantoris remained motionless. He swallowed as he met Luke's gaze. "I will abide by my promise." He drew a deep breath. "Teach me how to use this mysterious power within me."

Without a thought Luke reached forward with trembling hands and touched Gantoris's head. He sent mental fingers inward, probing to the back of the other man's mind, searching until he found the mysterious nub in Gantoris's subconscious, and pushed—

The strength of his reflexive reaction knocked Luke backward so that he had to catch his balance before tumbling into the lava. Gantoris did indeed have the Jedi potential, enough to make him a formidable candidate for the Jedi academy.

Luke allowed himself a sigh of relief. The terror and the testing had been worth it. He took Gantoris's hand, then looked at the gathered survivors of the abandoned colony.

"We will find a new home for your people. But first you will come with me to Coruscant."

ando Calrissian's ship, the *Lady*

Luck, received clearance from a bored-sounding traffic controller to land in the spaceport of Umgul. As the ship coasted through the misty atmosphere, Lando was amazed at the number of private ships, space yachts, and luxurious ground skimmers bustling around the landing center.

Lando cruised with the other traffic over flatlands surrounding a broad river on his way to Umgul City. Fleets of sail barges drifted over the sluggish river. Looking down, he could see flashing lights and gyrating bodies that spoke of wild parties on the barge decks.

A moist planet, but cool, Umgul was frequently blanketed by dense fog and low-hanging clouds; even now, in the middle of the day, wisps of mist drifted up from the river and spread across the lowlands. Though unremarkable in resources and strategic importance, Umgul had earned galactic fame as a sports center, home of the renowned Umgullian blob races.

The *Lady Luck* followed her designated vector to a spaceport carved into limestone bluffs rising above the river. Accompanied on either side by tiny two-person pleasure skimmers, Lando brought his ship through the cavern mouth. He barely managed to avoid hitting a blue zeppelin full of tourists. Inside, hairy attendants wearing bright-orange vests directed the *Lady Luck* into her parking stall by waving handheld laser beacons.

Lando turned to the two droids next to him in the pilot's compartment. "Are you boys about ready to have fun?"

Artoo beeped something Lando could not understand, but Threepio straightened in indignation. "We are not here to have fun, General Calrissian. We are here to assist Master Luke!"

"*I'm* here as a private citizen going to the blob races." Lando jabbed a finger at him. Being in close quarters with Threepio for only a day had already been enough for the prissy droid to get on his nerves. "*You* are my protocol droid, and you'd better play the part—or I'll have you run a complete diagnostic of all the sewage-control systems on Umgul City."

"I . . . understand clearly, sir."

As the *Lady Luck*'s ramp tongued out, Lando stepped into the chaos of the Umgullian reception center. Voices blurred by background noise made perpetual announcements over the intercom systems. Roars from departing vehicles echoed in the grotto. Acrid smells of exhaust fumes and engine-fueling ports stung Lando's nostrils.

Nonetheless, he held his head high and strode down the ramp, swirling his cape and beckoning the two droids to follow. "Threepio, can you understand any of those announcements? Figure out where we're supposed to go."

Threepio scanned the data walls that listed services offered by Umgul City. Text scrolled out in several languages.

Four stubby vendors rushed over to the new visitor, pushing trinkets and souvenirs at Lando. The scruffy-looking hucksters were Ugnaughts, the ugly little maintenance creatures that filled the lower levels of Cloud City. "Why not bring a baby blob home for the kids, sir?" The Ugnaught thrust out a greenish, oozing mass that looked like a fist-sized wad of phlegm.

"How about some blob candy, sir? Best in the city! My secondary mate makes it at home." The gelatinous blob candy looked identical to the baby blob the first Ugnaught had offered.

"Good-luck charm?" said a third Ugnaught. "Works for all religions!"

Lando waved them away. "Threepio, where are we going?"

"Adjusting for local time, sir, I believe there is an important blob race beginning in less than one standard hour. The Umgullian mass-transit systems will take us directly to the blob arena. I believe the mass-transit access is—"

The four Ugnaught souvenir vendors began falling over each other offering to guide the fine gentleman to the arena.

"—immediately to our left." Threepio gestured to a brightly painted tunnel entrance.

"Come on," Lando said and, without looking back, walked over to the mass-transit entrance. The disappointed Ugnaughts hurried off to hunt for other customers.

The mass-transit trip was like a roller-coaster ride without wheels. A slim tubelike car shot through the tunnel up to the top of the bluff, splashing through high-rising fog and rushing over woodlands where trees crammed into notches in the weathered limestone. The ground was a crazy quilt of bright signs describing tourist attractions, eating establishments, pawnshops, and high-interest, no-questions-asked gambling loans.

At the great entry kiosks to the blob arena, streams of people and other creatures pushed in, paying their credits and obtaining seat assignments. Lando paid for himself but argued with the ticket-taking computer over whether his two droids were companions (and thus needed to buy tickets) or subservient information-processing attendants; Lando won the argument, though Threepio seemed insulted at being classed as little more than an appliance.

The blob-racing stadium was a vast sinkhole that had collapsed into the top of the bluff, a circular pit in the rocky ground. The Umgullian stadium management had carved thousands of seats, stalls, pits, and sockets out of the sloping rocky walls to accommodate all manner of bodily configurations.

Giant whirring fans had been mounted around the rim of the sinkhole, generating a hefty breeze to shove back the encroaching fog that pushed in from all sides, driving it into the open air, where it dissipated.

After pushing his way along the crowded halls, Lando found his seat, pleased to see that it had a good view of the entire "blobstacle course" below. The odds panel in front of his seat listed information about the fourteen blob challengers for the day's first heat and also counted down the twenty minutes remaining before the next race would begin.

A grin spread across Lando's face as he took in the smells of treats and condiments, saw whirring robotic drink dispensers drifting through the stands. He was enjoying this already. It brought back plenty of old memories.

As baron-administrator of Bespin's Cloud City, Lando had spent much of his time in the high-class casinos, watching the tourists and high rollers. He had never seen blob racing before, but the excitement in the air made his heart beat faster.

Threepio fidgeted, looking at the crowd. A white ursine creature nearly knocked him over as it pushed its way to a seat farther down the mezzanine.

Lando couldn't forget the primary reason why he was here, though. Mounted to Artoo's body core was the power pack of the Imperial Jedi-detecting device, and Lando kept the sheet-crystal detector paddles secured to his own side.

"Okay, Artoo. Let's see if we can find our friend Tymmo. Jack into the stadium computer and see if he's bought a ticket or placed a bet. If so, let's find out where he's seated."

The announcer's voice echoed around the arena. "Sentient beings of all genders—welcome to the galaxy-renowned blob races of Umgul! Before we begin this afternoon's first heat, we'd like to call your attention to next week's special gala blob derby to be hosted in honor of a visiting dignitary, the Duchess Mistal from our sister planet Dargul. We hope you'll all attend."

The apathetic reaction from the crowd told Lando just how many visiting dignitaries Umgul must host throughout the year.

"For this afternoon's event we'll be running fourteen thoroughbred racing blobs through a twelve-point blobstacle course that has been thoroughly inspected and certified by the galactic racing commission. All data on the age, mass, and viscosity of our racing blobs is available at the terminal in front of your seat."

Lando smiled grimly at that. Umgul City claimed to run clean blob races, and cheating was a capital offense. "What does he mean by 'thoroughbred racing blobs'?" he asked.

Threepio heard him. "This species of blob has several

variants that are used for different purposes throughout
the system. Some upper-class people actually keep them
as pets. Others have seen certain medicinal value in blob
treatment, such as letting a blob ooze across one's back
for massage therapy or soaking one's aching feet in the
warm gelatinous mass."

"But these are racers?"

"Yes, sir, bred for speed and fluidity."

The announcer finished reading several standard dis-
claimers. "At this point we officially declare all betting
substations to be closed. The odds computer will post final
probability tables, which are now available at your terminals. We shall begin the race in just a moment. Please
enjoy a refreshment compatible with your biochemistry
while you wait!"

Hearing a ratcheting sound, Lando directed his attention to the rear of the playing field. Conveyor mechanisms
raised the blob platforms to a high ramp, stopping in
front of a gate that held the oozing blobs back from the
launching slide. The fourteen separate chutes in the steep,
lubricated ramp were designed to boost a blob's momen-
tum at the starting signal.

"On your mark!" the announcer said.

Lando could sense a blanketing hush through the stadium as the spectators craned forward, staring at the chutes
and waiting for the blobs to emerge.

A loud electronic tone reverberated through the air, like
a bullet hitting a brass bell, and suddenly the gates flew
open. The ramps tilted forward, spilling the multicolored
blobs down the lubricated chutes.

Fourteen syrupy masses tumbled and oozed pell-mell
down the slides, striking the low walls and slithering as
fast as they could to the bottom of the ramp. The blobs
showed a range of colors, primarily grayish green but
laced with bright hues. Variegated strands of vermillion

stood out on one, turquoise on another, lime-green on a third. Each blob had a holographic number imprinted in its protoplasm; the number somehow stayed upright no matter which way the blob oriented itself.

With the chutes equally lubricated, all fourteen blobs struck the bottom of the ramp at about the same time. When the low walls no longer separated the tracks, the frantic blobs began to make their way helter-skelter around each other, gushing forward into the blobstacle course.

One contender, Blob 11—a dark-green specimen laced with a striking amethyst pattern—burst onto the flat of the track with pseudopods already extended, as if trying to scramble away the moment it hit the bottom of the ramp. It squirted forward, clenching itself together and oozing its body core ahead.

The amethyst blob had pulled a small lead by the time it hit the first obstacle, a tall metal screen with a wide mesh. Blob 11 hurled itself onto the mesh grid with its full body and began to push its entire self through, dribbling in a hundred tiny segments out the other side, where it flowed its gelatinous mass back together again. It managed to push itself halfway through before the next blob struck a different part of the screen. Lando decided to cheer for the amethyst blob, though he had no money riding on the race. He still liked to root for winners.

The second blob took a different tactic, concentrating its body into a narrow streamer that spouted through one of the mesh holes, pouring its mass to the other side.

The amethyst blob finished reassembling itself on the bottom of the grid, took no time to rest, and pushed onward.

By this time all the other blobs were struggling to get through the first obstacle. The amethyst blob frantically mushed ahead, increasing its lead as if fleeing in terror.

"Go!" Lando shouted.

The second major obstacle proved more formidable. A tall ratline made of chain links led up to another steep, lubricated slide that dropped into a sharp, banked curve.

Blob 11 reached the bottom of the ratline and extended a pseudopod up to the first loop of chain, wrapping the jellylike tendril onto the flexible rung and extending another pseudopod again and again until it flowed like a tentacled amoeba, desperately hauling its amorphous form upward faster than gravity could slurp it back down.

The amethyst blob slipped, and a large segment of its body mass drooled downward, barely connected to the main core by a thin stream of mucus. According to the official rules posted in front of Lando's seat, the entire body mass of a blob had to get to the finishing circle; it could not leave portions of itself behind.

The second and third blobs reached the bottom of the ratline, also trying to scramble up.

The amethyst blob hovered on the ratline, sagging as it worked to siphon its precariously balanced appendage back into the main core. The chain links began to work through the soft organic material, but the blob moved faster, finally drawing itself up, and hooked over another loop of chain.

Behind it the next two blobs managed to ascend to the second level of chain loops.

Back at the first blobstacle, the last of the blobs squeezed through the mesh and began creeping at top speed toward the ratline.

Blob 11 reached the top of the ratlines and, coiling its mass, shot onto the steep, greased slide, rolling and spinning and tumbling. Its holographic number remained upright all the while. The blob reached the high banked curve at the bottom of the slide, rebounded, and gushed toward the next blobstacle.

The crowd was roaring and shouting now. Lando felt

exhilaration burst through him. He decided he'd have to return to Umgul when he had more time to relax, to make a few real bets.

"Excuse me, sir, but are we expressing enthusiasm for Blob Eleven?"

"Yes, Threepio!"

"Thank you, sir. I just wanted to be certain." The droid paused, then amplified his voice. "Go, number eleven!"

The second and third blobs reached the top of the rat-lines simultaneously, and both leaped onto the lubricated slide, squirting down at an alarming rate. Many of the spectators jumped out of their seats and screamed with excitement.

The two blobs tumbled next to each other, grappling with pseudopods and rolling. The steep, banked curve rose up in front of them like a wall.

"Oh, I can't watch!" Threepio said. "They're going to crash!"

The two blobs both struck the corner at the same instant and splattered into each other, forming one giant ball. The crowd roared with absolute delight.

"Total fusion!" the announcer cried.

The spectators continued to cheer. The two blobs had combined into one much larger mass, and they seemed to be working at cross purposes, trying to lumber over to the side of the track and out of the way of other oncoming blobs. Meanwhile, the amethyst blob increased its lead.

"Those two are out of the race," Lando muttered.

Artoo returned, bleeping with excitement. "Excuse me, sir," Threepio said, "but Artoo has located our man Tymmo. He has indeed come to the races and placed a very large bet. We have his seating assignment. We can go see him now if you wish."

Lando was startled to be interrupted during the race; then he jumped to his feet. "We found him already?"

"Yes, sir. And as I said, he has placed a very large bet, if you take my meaning, sir."

"Let me guess," Lando said. "On Blob Eleven, right?"

"Correct, sir."

"Looks like he's done it again," Lando said. "Let's go."

They pushed past other spectators who had not bothered to take seats, then emerged into the flagstoned halls. Lando allowed Artoo to lead, puttering down near-empty interior corridors. Lando was reluctant, wanting to see the outcome of the competition. "Hurry up, Artoo."

The little droid hummed downhill toward the lower levels of the sinkhole stadium. Through a graffiti-scrawled archway they passed into the section of least expensive seats filled with desperate-looking people, the ones who had staked everything on guessing the winner of just one race. Somehow Lando hadn't expected a winner as lucky as Tymmo to be in the low-rent section. Maybe he was trying to keep a low profile.

Though support pillars and debris screens crowded the view this far down in the crater, Lando could see that Blob 11 had increased its lead substantially, a full obstacle ahead of the remaining nine blobs. Farther back on the track two blobs lay motionless and rubbery in a bed of desiccant, too slow to cross the deadly obstacle before they suffered terminal dehydration.

The surviving blobs worked at stringing themselves through a sequence of metal rings dangling on ropes, each swaying and trying to extend a pseudopod to the next ring before the pendulum motion stretched it to the breaking point.

The amethyst blob had already crossed the desiccant trap and the rings and was now oozing precariously over a long bed of sharp spikes that continually poked through its outer membrane. Tireless, Blob 11 threw itself forward

with wild abandon, not heeding the spears jabbing through
its body.

Artoo whistled, and Threepio pointed to a man three
benches down. "General Calrissian, Artoo says this is the
man we want."

Lando squinted at Tymmo. Young and attractive, but
with a fidgety, furtive look, he had a disreputable air.
Though his blob was winning by a wide margin, he did
not seem elated. The other people around him cheered
or wailed, depending on where they had cast their bets,
but Tymmo just sat and waited, as if he already knew the
outcome.

Blob 11 dragged the last of itself off the bed of nails,
tugging to remove a few clinging strands from the spike
points. The nails had slowed it to a crawl just in front of
the next obstacle—a slowly turning propeller blade with
razor edges.

The amethyst blob poised itself but seemed too panicked to plan the best way through the spinning blades. It
squirted forward, elongating to gain speed, then shoved its
body into the gap between the whirring fan blades. About a
quarter of the blob made it through before the sharp edges
slashed through, bisecting it.

Mucus squirted but clung in one long, liquid thread
on the propeller blade. One segment of the blob waited
safely on the other side of the blobstacle. The remaining
three quarters hunched, then lunged through the next gap
in the blades. This time half of its mass passed successfully through, and the second segment oozed forward to
rejoin the first small mass. The rest of Blob 11 made
it through with only a nick in its posterior portion, but
as the fan blades spun around again, droplets of slime
on the edges congealed into a small lump and dropped
off, rolling to safety, where all the portions conjoined
once more.

The crowd cheered. Some of the losers in the lower levels began throwing drink containers against the guard mesh in front of them. Blue sparks flickered from the electrified wires. Tymmo hunched forward in his seat, keeping one hand in his pocket. Lando wondered if he carried some kind of weapon.

Tymmo looked around, blinking his eyes in alarm as if he suspected he was being watched. Lando winced, knowing that his fine clothes and rich cape made him appear painfully out of place in the lower levels. Tymmo noticed Lando and the two droids, tensed, then forced himself to watch the end of the race.

Blob 11 approached the final blobstacle, hauling pseudopods over the rungs of a ladder as it dripped down. It seemed burned to exhaustion, but still it pushed on as if demons were chasing it. Its bright amethyst tracings had faded to mere speckles.

Reaching the top of the ladder, the blob descended into an array of wide funnels that had exit holes of varying sizes, many of which were sealed shut. The amethyst blob thrust extensions of itself into various funnels, poking around until it found one with a large enough hole in the bottom.

Behind, the nearest other blob began negotiating the bed of nails in front of the whirling propeller.

Choosing an acceptable funnel, Blob 11 dumped itself into the cone and pushed. A pasty stream ribboned out the narrow end, rolling and piling on the ground as the blob re-collected itself. The thin strand of blob went on and on, coming out in spurts near the end until finally the tail plopped out of the funnel.

Blob 11's entire body shimmered as it trembled with exhaustion. It charged toward the finishing circle and looked as if it intended to keep going.

The crowd continued to cheer, but the race was clearly

over. Lando watched Tymmo. The other man adjusted something in his pocket.

Blob 11 came to a sudden halt in the finishing circle. Blob wranglers in coveralls rushed onto the track with wide shovels and a levitating barrow to scoop up the exhausted thing and return it to the blob pens for rehydration and a long rest. The audience then began to root for which blobs would place and show.

Tymmo slid out of his seat and flicked a quick glance from side to side, but Lando had already stepped behind a support pillar. Tymmo jostled the spectators still watching the rest of the race, making his way toward one of the cashiering stations where other winners had already queued up. Most of the winners jumped up and down, chattering with shared excitement; even the more reserved ones wore broad grins. Tymmo, though, showed only a metallic, unreadable expression. He seemed very nervous.

Lando and the two droids eased themselves into the line, butting through the crowd. Tymmo kept glancing back, but he did not see them again. Over the loudspeakers the announcer listed the order of winners in the blob race.

Lando pulled the cable jacks to the sheet-crystal Jedi detectors out of his sleeves and plugged them into the power pack on Artoo's body. He slid the flat paddles into the palms of his hands, ready for a chance when he could scan Tymmo to confirm whether or not he had the bluish aura of a possible trainee for Luke's academy.

Threepio seemed very excited. "Why don't we just go up to him and tell him the good news, General Calrissian?"

"Because something's fishy here," he said, "and I want to make sure before we get ourselves in too deep."

"Fishy?" Threepio asked, then looked around as if to locate any aquatic spectators at the blob races.

"His turn is next at the terminal. When he keys in his betting chit, it'll take a minute to process and cash in his winnings. He's effectively trapped until the transaction is done, unless he wants to throw away a lot of credits."

Of course, Lando remembered, cheating was punishable by death on Umgul, and Tymmo might be happy enough just to get away with his life. What had he been hiding in his pocket?

As Tymmo stepped up to the terminal and inserted his chit, the announcer broke through the background noise to remind everyone once again of the next week's races in honor of the visiting duchess from Dargul. Tymmo flinched visibly, but keyed in his ID code and inserted his account card to collect his winnings.

"Come on," Lando said, stepping out of line and moving toward the cashiering station. He flicked the power switch on the scanning pack; its warm-up hum vanished in the background noise.

Tymmo looked intently at the display on the cashiering station, punching in his access code and transferring his winnings as quickly as he could. Lando stepped up beside him and swept either side of the man with the detector paddles before Tymmo realized what was happening.

Tymmo looked up, saw Lando holding something that might have been a weapon, saw the two droids that might have been armed mechanical bodyguards, and panicked just as the terminal ejected his account card and called for the next customer. Tymmo snatched his card and fled, scattering a pack of Ugnaughts as he ran into the crowded stands.

"Hey, Tymmo, stop!" yelled Lando. The man was swallowed up in the surge of spectators exiting the stands after the race.

"Sir, aren't we going to follow him?" Threepio asked.

Other spectators had turned to stare. The next winner, grinning and oblivious, stepped up to the cashiering station.

"No." Lando shook his head. "We've got a reading for now. Let's check it out."

In a shadowed corner, not caring if anyone saw what they were doing since nobody would understand it anyway, Lando watched the power pack of the Imperial detector reconstruct a holographic aura mapping of Tymmo.

As Lando had unfortunately expected, Tymmo's reading showed a perfectly normal outline: no bluish haze of Jedi potential, nothing at all out of the ordinary. "He's a fraud."

Threepio seemed disappointed. "Can you be certain, sir? I should point out that many people were standing around, and they could have disturbed the readings. You also scanned him very quickly, and none too closely. Remember, too, that the detector itself is extremely old and may not be completely reliable."

Lando gave the protocol droid a skeptical frown, but Threepio's arguments did have some merit. He should take the trouble to be sure. Besides, Lando was enjoying himself on Umgul so far. "All right, we'll check him out a little further."

Relieved that the New Republic would pick up the tab, Lando relaxed in his spacious hotel accommodations. From the dispenser he ordered a cold punchlike drink popular on Umgul and went to the balcony to watch thick evening mists curl along the streets. He sipped the drink, unable to remove his perplexed frown or smooth his creased forehead.

"Could I get you anything else, sir, or shall I power down for the time being?" Threepio asked.

"Please do!" he said, realizing how nice it would be to keep the protocol droid quiet for a while. "But leave the circuit open in case Artoo tries to get back in touch."

"Certainly, sir."

Posing as a maintenance droid, Artoo had gone poking around the blob stables to see if he could uncover anything out of the ordinary. The little astromech droid had tuned his communication frequency to Lando's comlink so he could send a message.

Now with Threepio quiet Lando could finally think. He went over to the room's courtesy terminal and punched in a request for information. The screen automatically displayed a complete schedule for the next three weeks of blob racing, but Lando selected another menu.

The Umgullian Racing Commission was fanatical about being forthcoming with all information relating to the races and the blobs themselves. A sample of protoplasm was taken from each blob before and after any race, then subjected to rigorous analysis, the results of which were available to the public.

With help from the information assistant built into the terminal, Lando was able to collate the before-and-after tests for all of Tymmo's high-stakes winners. He didn't know what he was looking for, but he suspected some drug used to urge the blobs to greater speed, some incentive that would affect only the winners.

"Run a correlation," Lando said. "Is there anything unusual about these particular winners? Something found in these blobs, but not in the others?"

Tymmo bet only once in a while, and if his manipulation was subtle enough, Lando could imagine that the Umgullian racing commission might have missed a tiny modification. But Lando knew that one variable tied these particular winners together apart from the other blobs. Since hundreds of people bet and won on each race, the commission would have no reason to look at only those particular races where Tymmo had cashed in.

"One minor anomaly found in all cases," the information assistant said.

"What is it?"

"Faint traces of carbon, silicon, and copper in the postrace chemical tests of each winner in this subset."

"This wasn't noticed before?" Lando asked.

"Dismissed as irrelevant. Probable explanation: minor environmental contaminants from the blobstacles themselves."

"Hmmm, and these same traces show up on every one of the winners?"

"Yes."

"Do they show up on any of the other blob tests, winners or losers, in any race?"

"Checking." After a pause the terminal answered, "No, sir."

Lando looked at the test results. The amounts of contaminant were absolutely trivial, nothing that should have had any effect. "Speculation on what might have caused this?"

"None," the terminal answered.

"Thanks a lot," Lando said.

"You're welcome."

Threepio sat bolt upright, startled out of his recharging state. "General Calrissian! Artoo has just contacted me." Threepio bumped the comlink with his golden finger, and bleeping noises burst through the speaker. "Mr. Tymmo has appeared at the blob corrals, disguised as a blob wrangler. Artoo has verified his identification. What could he be doing there?"

"Let's go," Lando said. "I didn't expect him to try again so soon, but now we've got him, whatever he's doing."

Lando grabbed his cape and slung it over his shoulders

before he swept out of the room. Threepio raised his hands in alarm but shuffled off as fast as he could, his motivators whirring.

The two ran through the darkened, misty streets of Umgul City. Around them blockish limestone dwellings rose high, stacked upon each other like cracker boxes, lacquered to a high gloss with moisture sealants. Streetlights hung at the street intersections, shedding a pearly halo into the mist. Workers climbed on scaffolds, tearing down old banners that advertised the visit of one dignitary and putting up new ones welcoming the Duchess Mistal to Umgul City.

Lando sprinted up the cobblestoned streets with Threepio scurrying stiffly behind. Steep thoroughfares climbed the bluffs. Ahead and adjacent to the sinkhole arena, they could see a large lighted structure where the blobs were kept and monitored.

Lando ducked through a service entrance to the blob corrals, and Threepio followed. Strange smells, damp and musty, filled the air. Cleanup droids chugged through the halls, while others checked temperature controls for the blob pens. The lights had been dimmed for the evening, encouraging the blobs to rest.

"Threepio, do you know where we're going?"

"I believe I can locate Artoo, sir," Threepio said, and turned in slow circles before he pointed the way.

Down another level they reached a shadowy chamber cut into the limestone. The lights inside had been set to their lowest illumination, and moisture generators kept the room damp and clammy. "Artoo is in here, General Calrissian."

"Okay, be quiet. Let's see what's going on."

"Do you really think Mr. Tymmo could be cheating, sir? Even with the threat of capital punishment?"

Lando frowned at him. "No, I'm sure he has a perfectly

legitimate reason to be wearing a blob wrangler's uniform, slipping into the blob corral late at night, and skulking around in the darkness."

"What a relief, sir. I'm glad to hear he may yet be a Jedi candidate."

"Shut up, Threepio!"

They crept through the entrance into a room lined with blob pens. Banks of about twenty small enclosures blocked his line of sight in the shadowy room. Within each pen a gelatinous blob burbled and vibrated as it rested.

From the far side of the room came a rattling noise: a blob pen being eased open. Lando crept silently down the rows of blob enclosures, letting his eyes adjust to the dimness.

In the shadows of the far row of pens, Lando spotted a human form. He recognized Tymmo's build, his furtive movements, his lanky dark hair. Tymmo hunched over a cage, reaching inside, doing something to the blob in front of him.

Lando leaned close to Threepio and breathed words in the faintest of whispers, knowing he would not be overheard in the general stirring of the blobs. "Enhance your optical sensors so you can make out what he's doing, and record everything for later playback. We may need proof if we're going to get this guy."

Before the droid could answer, Lando clamped his hand over Threepio's mouth to keep him silent. Threepio nodded and turned to stare at the man in the shadows.

With a whirring sound Artoo-Detoo puttered down the walkway between the pens. Tymmo looked up, startled, but Artoo carried a cleaning attachment and scrubbed the floor under the pens. He whirred right by Tymmo, ignoring the man just as a cleaning droid would do. Lando nodded in admiration for the little astromech.

Tymmo turned back to his work, shaken by Artoo's

appearance and apparently wanting to be out of there as soon as possible.

"Sir!" Threepio cried. "He just implanted a small object in the protoplasm of that blob!"

Tymmo whirled and grabbed at one of the pockets of his jumpsuit. Lando didn't need greater illumination to recognize a blaster being drawn.

"Thanks a lot, Threepio!" he said as he tackled the droid. An instant later a blaster bolt sparked off the wall near where they had been standing a moment before. "Come on!"

He scrambled to his feet and ran over to where Tymmo had been hiding, ducking to take advantage of the cover the blob pens offered. Another blaster shot ricocheted through the dimness, missing them by a wide margin.

"Artoo!" Threepio wailed. "Sound the alarms! Call the guards! Alert the corral owner! Anybody!"

Tymmo shot at them again, and Threepio gasped as sparks erupted close to his head. "Oh, dear!"

Inside the corral the blobs awakened and stirred, rearing up against the bars of their pens.

He heard Tymmo crash into the corner of a cage. They reached the pen where Tymmo had been meddling. Lando kept his head low. "Threepio, see if you can tell what he planted in that blob."

"Do you really think that's wise right at the moment, sir?"

"Do it!" Lando had his own blaster drawn, scanning the shadows for Tymmo's form.

Ratcheting alarms rang out. "Good work, Artoo," Lando mumbled.

Seeing a hunched, moving form, Lando risked a shot on stun but missed. An indignant series of electronic noises told him he had almost deactivated Artoo. "Sorry about that."

By firing his blaster Lando had given away his position. Tymmo shot back, but his energy bolt spanged off the wall. Lando fired again, and as the stun beam expanded outward, he saw several blobs in its path curl up and condense sideways.

"A shoot-out at the blob corral," Lando said to himself. "Just the way I wanted to spend my vacation."

Threepio stood next to the pen trying to determine exactly what Tymmo had been doing. The blob itself, riled by the disturbance, reared up against the bars, leaning into the cage door. Dim light glinted off Threepio's polished body, offering a clear target; but this time when Tymmo fired, his blaster bolt incinerated the lock on the pen. With the pressing weight of the blob, the door flung open, and the entire gelatinous mass dumped onto Threepio's head, oozing down his body. The droid's muffled cries of panic came through the wet protoplasm.

Seeing Tymmo's form move through the shadows, Lando sprinted after him. The other man made for the archway exit as fast as he could move in the murkiness. "Tymmo! Hold it right there!"

Tymmo turned to glance in Lando's direction, then put on a burst of reckless speed. At that moment Artoo scuttled out of the shadows, placing himself directly in the running man's path. Tymmo crashed into the droid, somersaulted into the air, and landed on his back.

Lando pounced, grabbing Tymmo's blaster arm and yanking it behind his back until the weapon dropped free. "Good job, Artoo."

Tymmo thrashed and struggled as the alarms continued to sound. "Get away from me! I won't let you take me back to her!"

"Help me! Help!" Threepio cried. He waved his arms, frantically trying to wipe blob material from his outer shell.

Guard droids and human security officers scrambled into the grotto. Lights flared on as somebody upped the illumination. Tymmo fought more frantically.

"Over here!" Lando called.

The guard droids took possession of Tymmo, clamping their restraining arms around him. Another reached out to grasp Lando, and he suddenly realized he had no good reason to be in the blob corral either.

"What in the bleeping miasma is going on here!" a deep voice roared. A hirsute man who looked as if he had dressed hurriedly strode into the corral area. "And shut off those blasted alarms! They're upsetting my blobs, and they're giving me a headache."

"Over here, Mr. Fondine," one of the human guards answered.

The man came over to see Tymmo struggling in the guard droid's straitjacket grasp. Lando caught his attention. "I've uncovered a possible sabotage of the races, sir. This man here has been tinkering with the blobs."

The man gave Tymmo an acid glance, then turned back to Lando. "I'm Slish Fondine, owner of these stables. You'd better tell me who you are and why you're here."

Lando realized, with some surprise, that he had nothing to hide. "I'm General Calrissian, a representative of the New Republic. I have been investigating this man, Tymmo, as part of an entirely different mission, but I believe you will be very interested to study his track record of wins."

Tymmo glared at Lando. "You'll never take me back to her! I couldn't stand that—you don't know how she *is*. I'll die first."

Slish Fondine shushed him with a wave of his hand. "That can be arranged, if what the general says is true. On Umgul cheaters are executed." The alarm sirens finally fell silent.

"Will somebody please help me!" Threepio cried.

Fondine saw the droid struggling with the dripping greenish mass and rushed over to assist him. Brushing the protoplasm back up into the main mass, Fondine shushed and cooed the blob. "Easy now." He spoke to Threepio as well. "Stop struggling! The blob is as afraid of you as you are of it. Just be calm." He lowered his voice. "They can sense fear, you know."

Threepio tried to remain still as Fondine gently coerced the blob to reincorporate back toward its pen. Threepio suddenly grew excited again. "Sir! I've just found a near-microscopic electronic object inside this blob's protoplasm. Magnifying . . . it appears to be a micro-motivator!"

Lando suddenly understood what Tymmo had been doing. A micro-motivator implanted in the blob could send out a powerful internal stimulus, provoke a frantic flight response in any creature. If tuned properly, the micro-motivator could give a blob the speed born of absolute terror. The gadget was so tiny that Tymmo could self-destruct it after the blob had successfully won a race, leaving only minuscule traces of a few component elements in the blob tissue. And no one would ever know.

Slish Fondine glared daggers at Tymmo. "That is vile blasphemy against the whole spirit of blob racing."

Tymmo squirmed. "I had to have the money! I had to get off planet before she gets here."

In exasperation Lando said, "Who are you talking about? Who is *she*?" He freed himself from the guard droid's grip.

Tymmo's eyes goggled at Lando's question. "Didn't she send you to get me? I saw you spying on me at the races. You tried to catch me, but I escaped. I'll never go back to her."

"Who?!" both Lando and Slish Fondine bellowed in unison.

"The Duchess Mistal, of course. She clings to me every second, she blows in my ear, she won't let me out of her sight—and I couldn't stand it anymore. I had to get away."

Lando and Fondine looked at each other without comprehension, but Artoo trundled up, chittering an explanation. Threepio, extricated from the blob mass, stepped forward to translate.

"Artoo has run a check. The Duchess Mistal of Dargul has posted a million-credit reward for the safe return of her lost consort—apparently, he ran away from her. The man's official name is Dack, but his description precisely matches that of Mr. Tymmo here."

Tymmo hung his head in misery. Fondine crossed his arms over his chest. "Well? What have you got to say for yourself?"

"Yes, I'm Dack." He heaved a huge sigh. "The Duchess Mistal reached her age of marriage two years ago and decided to find the perfect consort. She advertised across the galaxy for likely candidates, and she received millions of applicants. I was one of them. Who wouldn't want the job? She was rich and young and beautiful. All the consort would have to do is live in total opulence and be doted upon by the duchess."

Tears sprang to Tymmo's eyes. "My particular talent was electronic wizardry. I built those micro-motivators from scratch. When I applied for the consort position, I knew my odds were small. But I succeeded in hacking into the central computer in Palace Dargul, sabotaging the other applicants, planting an algorithm so that the computer would spit out my name as the perfect choice."

Slish Fondine looked nauseated at the mere concept of cheating in such a heinous manner.

"The duchess and I were married, and everything seemed exactly as I had expected—at first. But the duchess was convinced I was her perfect match, fated to be with her forever. Every waking moment of the day she refused to let me move more than arm's length away from her. She would wake me up at all hours of the night, find me during her meal breaks. She would trap me in the gardens, in the libraries."

Tymmo's eyes grew wild, shining with panic. "I thought she would get tired of me—or at least *used* to having me around—but it went on for more than a year! I couldn't sleep, I jumped at shadows. I was a wreck, and that made her feel sorry for me . . . so she clung even tighter!

"And I couldn't leave! On Dargul they mate for life. Life! She'll never give up searching, and she'll never take another mate as long as I live." Tymmo looked as if a scream hovered on his lips. "I'll never be free of her! I had to escape."

"Well, it looks like you've finally found a way out," Slish Fondine said in an angry voice. "As an admitted scam artist, you'll be promptly executed under the laws of Umgul."

To Lando's surprise Tymmo didn't even try to defend himself. He seemed resigned to his fate.

But Lando wasn't so sure about the idea. "Let's think about this a minute, Mr. Fondine. Did you say there's a *million-credit* reward for his safe return to the duchess, Artoo?"

Artoo chirped an affirmative.

"Now, Mr. Fondine, think of what a wonderful gift of state this would be for the upcoming visit of the duchess, returning her consort in time to ease her loneliness."

Tymmo groaned in misery.

"On the other hand, if you were to execute him, *knowing* he is her missing consort, things could get very unpleasant between Umgul and your sister planet. Might even be cause for war."

Fondine's face darkened with the possibilities, but his honor had been so offended that the choice was not clear to him.

He sighed. "We will leave it up to the prisoner himself. Tymmo, or Dack, or whatever your name is—do you wish to be executed or returned to the Duchess Mistal?"

Tymmo swallowed hard. "How long do I have to think about it?"

"It's not a trick question!" Lando said.

Tymmo sighed. "Can I at least be allowed to rest until she gets here? I'm going to need all my strength."

The *Lady Luck* cruised out of the huge grotto of Umgul's spaceport, rising above the mists into the sky. Slish Fondine had insisted, out of fairness, that he would transfer half of the duchess's reward into Lando's account when she arrived.

No longer penniless, Lando would have seed money to invest in some new operation, some other scheme that could excite him. He had tried the molten metal mines on Nkllon, and the Tibanna gas mines on Bespin. He wondered what he might find next.

Though he had tried his best to track down a worthy candidate for Luke's Jedi academy, he hated to return empty-handed to Coruscant. But he knew there would be others.

Threepio remained uncharacteristically silent as the *Lady Luck* burst into hyperspace, heading home.

10

Images of starships whirled through space like pinpoints of fire around Coruscant. The holographic map of the system showed the locations of all vessels in range and plotted approved approach orbits on a huge spherical grid. Data terminals spewed information on vessel sizes and landing requirements, keeping track of anyone reporting impaired control. A scattering of red danger zones marked debris clouds of wrecked ships that had not yet been removed from the battle over Coruscant.

Dozens of space-traffic controllers stood at their stations around the 3-D map of the planet, pointing at images with light pens and drawing safe-approach vectors or prioritizing landing patterns. One of the war-damaged spaceports on the western end of Imperial City had just been brought back on-line in the last week, and much of the shuttle traffic was being rerouted there to ease the burden on landing platforms around the Imperial Palace.

Leia Organa Solo stood beside one of the traffic controllers. Seeing how busy the woman was directing space traffic, Leia tried not to ask too many questions, but she found it difficult to wait.

"There's something." The traffic controller reached up with the light pen to indicate a squarish violet icon used for *Small Starship—Type Unknown.* "Could that be the one you're waiting for, Minister Organa Solo? Just popped out of hyperspace. Unable to determine previous vector."

Leia felt a surge of excitement. "Yes, that's the one. Have they requested clearance yet?"

The traffic controller touched a receiver implant at her temple. "Coming in now. The pilot sends only her name. Sounds like some kind of code. Winter?"

Leia smiled. "No, that's her real name. Give her clearance to land on the top northside platform of the Imperial Palace, my authorization." She drew in a deep breath, feeling her heart pound faster. "I'll go meet her personally." She turned and took two quick steps away before she remembered to thank the traffic controller for her help. "Come on, Threepio," Leia said as she bustled past him.

The protocol droid snapped to attention, then hurried after her with his stiff-legged gait. He had returned to Coruscant with Artoo and Lando three days earlier and spent four hours in a luxurious lubricant-and-scrubber bath. Now he gleamed like new, with all traces of blob mucus removed from his finish.

Leia heard Threepio's motivators humming as he followed. She ignored him, lost in her own conflicting thoughts. Han should have been back from Kessel two days ago, but still she had heard no word from him. He'd probably fallen in with some of his old smuggling buddies, had too much to drink, gambled far into the late hours, and completely forgotten about his other obligations. It was a good thing Chewbacca had sworn a blood oath to protect him, because Han was going to have to face *her* when he got back, and he was going to need a Wookiee's protection. How dare he forget something like this?

For now, Leia would welcome her twin children home. Alone.

Standing on the top deck of the palace, Leia craned her neck and searched the hazy skies. Coruscant's aurora shimmered through the twilight, eclipsed by the complex matrix of the great orbiting shipyards.

"Threepio, tell me the minute you see them coming." The breeze tossed loose strands of hair in front of her eyes.

"Yes, Mistress Leia. I'm searching." In an imitation of a human gesture, Threepio cupped two golden hands around his optical sensors as if it would help him focus better. "Don't you think it would be wiser for us to step back slightly from the edge?"

Leia held her breath. Her children were coming home. They had not set foot on Coruscant for nearly two years, but now they would be back to stay. She could be a real mother to them, at last.

Just after their birth the twins had been sequestered on a secret planet uncovered by Luke and Admiral Ackbar. It was a world unrecorded on any chart, but habitable and protected. Luke and Ackbar had established a heavily guarded base there, leaving Leia's trusted servant Winter behind to watch over the Jedi children.

She suspected Luke had given the children a bit more than just Winter for protection, though.

During their protective isolation Leia had managed to visit Jacen, Jaina, and Anakin every few months, usually with Han in tow. At a prearranged time Winter would pop out of hyperspace in a long-distance shuttle. Without ever knowing their destination, Leia and Han would climb aboard the shuttle, be sealed in the back passenger compartment, and Winter would take them to the protected planet. The New Republic Senate was appalled at Leia's mysterious movements, but Luke and Ackbar had silenced their objections.

Leia hoped she would be able to find the time to visit her baby boy, little Anakin, now that she had the twins to watch over. It would be a tragedy if she had to be even less of a mother to the baby than she had been to these two.

"There it is, Mistress Leia!" Threepio pointed up at a flickering point of light that grew brighter every second. "A shuttle is coming down."

She felt a spasm of anxiety mixed with a thrill of excitement.

The shuttle approached, winking red and green lights in the twilight sky. It circled the former Imperial Palace, then activated its repulsorlifts to come down with a gentle sigh on the landing platform. Angular and buglike, the shuttle bore no markings, no indication of its planet of origin.

With a hiss of equalizing pressure, the hatch of the shuttle's passenger compartment split open, gently extending a ramp. Leia bit her lip and took a step forward, squinting into the sharp shadows. The shuttle blocked most of the breeze, leaving the area still and silent.

The young twins stepped out side by side and waited at the top of the ramp. Leia stared at Jacen and Jaina, both self-composed and dark-haired, with wide avid eyes and small faces that looked like the ghosts of Han and Leia.

After a second's hesitation Leia ran up the ramp, gathering the children in her arms. Both Jacen and Jaina hugged their mother. "Welcome home!" she said, whispering.

She sensed fear and reservation in them; Leia realized with a pang that she was a virtual stranger to them. Winter had been their nanny for as long as they could remember.

Leia had been just a visitor whenever she could find time in her duties. But she would make it up to them. She promised herself that much.

All the outstanding obligations rose up in her mind, haunting her with the specter of duty. She still had to deal with the Caridan ambassador and a thousand other delicate tasks to hold the New Republic together. Dozens of planetary systems were on the verge of joining the Republic if a skilled representative—Leia herself—showed good faith by making a visit of state. If Mon Mothma summoned Leia to help ratify a treaty, or to take her place at a state dinner, how could Leia refuse? The fate of the galaxy hung in the balance, clearly dependent on what she did.

How could mere children take precedence over that? And what kind of a mother did it make her even to think about it?

"Where's Daddy?" Jacen asked.

Anger went through Leia like a spear of ice. "He's not here right now."

Winter finally worked her way back from the pilot compartment. Leia looked up at her friend and confidante, and warm memories washed over her. Winter had had snow-white hair for as long as Leia could remember, a serene face that rarely allowed even a twinge of anger to show through. Noticing Han's absence, Winter raised her eyebrows, filling her face with questions, but she remained silent.

"Where's baby Anakin?" Jaina asked.

"He has to stay with me for a while longer," Winter said, nudging the two children down the ramp. "Come, now, we'll take you to your new home."

The two children dutifully marched ahead, with Leia following close beside them. Threepio didn't seem to know what he was expected to do during the reunion, so he just followed, waving his arms and making flustered exclamations.

"How long we stay here?" Jacen asked.

"Where's our room?" Jaina said.

Leia smiled at the questions and took a deep breath before answering them. From now on she had a feeling she would be hearing a lot of questions.

When Leia finally kissed the twins good night, Threepio couldn't decide whether mother or twins looked more exhausted. Leia pushed loose dark hair away from her eyes as she stood at the doorway to their room and blew another kiss.

After adjusting his servomotors to allow a little more flexibility in his joints, Threepio hunkered down between the twins' beds. He had already taken care of important details such as providing fresh cups of water for the children and installing small night-lights in the dark corners.

"You two be good for Threepio," Leia said. "He'll stay here until you go to sleep. You've had exciting things happen today, and we'll do a lot more tomorrow. I'm so glad to have you back." Leia flashed a heartfelt smile at them, showing joy even through the weariness on her face.

"I'm certain I can handle this, Mistress Leia," Threepio said. "I have reviewed most of the available child psychology databases, except for those recommended by the Emperor, of course."

Leia's answering look seemed to carry a bit of skepticism, which puzzled Threepio.

"Don't wanna go sleep," Jacen said, sitting up in bed.

Leia still smiled. "But you need your rest. Maybe Threepio will tell you a bedtime story if you're good."

She waved once more, then faded back into the main living area.

The children had indeed had a busy day. After their journey with Winter they had been taken on a quick tour of the Imperial Palace, then shown their new quarters. Even with her duties as Minister of State, Leia had managed to redecorate the twins' bedchamber in warm, soothing colors. Threepio would have offered his own assistance in the project, but at the time he had been with Lando Calrissian at the blob races. Thinking back, Threepio would have preferred the decorating chores.

Several times during the tour Leia was interrupted by insistent calls, documents that needed to be authorized, brief conversations that could not be delayed. Each time Leia looked guilty, as if realizing this was an indication of things to come.

The twins, though filled with excitement and wonder of the new things around them, grew cranky as they became tired. They had been overwhelmed by too much strangeness in one day, given a new home, and told to sleep in an unfamiliar room. According to the information Threepio had recently uploaded, it was perfectly normal for the children to cause minor difficulties.

"Don't wanna bedtime story," Jacen said, crossing his small hands over his chest and looking defiantly at Threepio.

"No story," Jaina echoed.

"Of course you do," Threepio insisted. "I have scoured the collected works of children's literature on thousands of planetary systems. I have selected what I believe will be a truly enjoyable story. It is called *The Little Lost Bantha Cub*, a classic that has been popular for generations with children of your age."

He had been looking forward to telling this story, recalling how much he had enjoyed telling the Ewoks of his adventures with Master Luke and Captain Solo. He had even selected some very exciting sound effects for appropriate points in the *Bantha Cub* story. Threepio had never actually been close to a live bantha during his time on Tatooine, but bantha riders—the Tusken Raiders—had dismantled him during their first attack on Master Luke. He supposed that gave him some small claim to expertise.

"Don't wanna story!" Jacen repeated. Both children had unruly dark hair, and the deep brown eyes of their mother. Right now the young boy had a determined and stubborn look on his face that Threepio had often seen on Han Solo.

Threepio realized that the issue at hand had very little to do with the actual story. According to his new information on young children, the twins were right now feeling displaced and helpless. With so many things out of their control, they needed to exert their power, to insist on some tiny spot of stability. Jacen needed to see that he could have some effect on his surroundings. Right now the boy was very upset; Jaina, picking up on her brother's distress, seemed on the verge of tears.

"Very well, young Master Jacen. I will tell you the story some other time."

Threepio knew just the trick to keep the twins happy and let them drift off to sleep. He was, after all, fluent in over six million forms of communication. He could sing lullabyes in any number of languages, any number of styles.

He selected a few that were guaranteed to please the twins. Jacen and Jaina would be asleep in no time. He began to sing.

"*Now* what are they crying about?" Leia said, sitting up sharply and looking toward the bedroom. "Maybe I should go and see."

Winter reached out to touch her wrist, stopping her. "It'll be all right. They're tired, they're frightened, they're anxious. Bear with them. And since you're new to them, they'll be testing your limits every moment, finding out how they can manipulate you. Don't teach them that you'll come running every time they make a sound. Children learn those sorts of things very quickly."

Leia sighed and looked at her personal servant. For years Winter had advised her in many things, and she was usually right. "Looks like *I'm* the one who needs to learn things quickly."

"Every part of it is a learning process. You must balance your love for them with their need for stability. That's what parenting is all about."

Leia scowled as hidden concern began to drown out her happiness at having the children back with her. "I might be doing this all by myself."

Winter's gaze seemed incisive, and she asked the question that had been on her mind for hours. "Where is Han?"

"He's not here—that's where he is!"

Not wanting Winter to see her flustered outrage, Leia stood up and turned her back. Over and over, she had imagined possibilities of Han hurt, lost, attacked . . . but she found it safer to believe other possibilities. "He's flying around in the *Falcon* with Chewbacca. He should have been back two days ago. He knew when the twins were coming home, but he couldn't bother to be here! It's bad enough we've been practically nonexistent as parents for the first two years of their lives, but he can't even spare the time to greet Jacen and Jaina when they finally come home."

Han had felt the razor of Leia's words many times, and her tongue had grown more precise with years of diplomatic practice. A small part of her was glad he was not here to bear the brunt of her anger. But then again, if he had been here, she would not have had cause for such anger.

"Where did he go?"

Leia waved her hand, trying to sound casual "Off to Kessel, to see if he could convince any of the old spice miners to join the New Republic. He hasn't bothered to call since he left."

Winter gazed at her, not blinking. Winter's intense periods of thought always unsettled Leia. "Let me tell you this, Leia. I think I'm right. If it were anyone else on a mission like this, two days overdue and no contact for a week or so, you would be concerned. Very concerned. With Han, you are making an assumption that he is just being irresponsible. What if something happened to him?"

"That's crazy." She turned away again, to keep Winter from seeing that the same worries had been plaguing her.

Winter's grave expression did not change. "According to the reports I have seen, Kessel is relatively hostile territory. Not only the spice mines, but the Imperial Correction Facility, with some powerful defenses in place to keep prisoners from escaping. The entire system has been out of contact with us for some time."

Winter paused, as if accessing other memories. "When Mara Jade and Talon Karrde unified some of the smugglers two years ago, Jade noted that Kessel might cause certain problems. Shouldn't you check with a diplomatic contact there to make certain nothing has happened to the *Millennium Falcon*?"

Leia blinked her eyes, annoyed at Winter's suggestion, though she had thought of it herself dozens of times. "Seems like overreacting, doesn't it?"

Winter regarded her calmly. "Or are you just unwilling to show your concern because it would embarrass you?"

•   •   •

The private communications chamber looked different in the bustle of a bright morning on Coruscant. The last time Leia had stood inside the room had been to contact the infuriating Caridan ambassador in the dead of night.

Now, as she looked out the mirrored walls, Leia watched minor functionaries hurrying to daily assignments, administrative and service personnel who had probably worked in Imperial City for years, caring little for what overall government ruled the galaxy.

Not long ago, Leia thought, the Alliance had been made up of the bravest and most dedicated fighters, those willing to die for their ideals. How could the New Republic degenerate into bureaucracy so quickly? She thought of heroes she had known, like Jek Porkins and Biggs Darklighter, who had died to destroy the first Death Star; she hoped their spirit still remained somewhere in the new government.

At the transmission console Winter made a small noise to attract Leia's attention. "This has been difficult, Leia, but I think I have a contact. The entire city of Kessendra seems to be abandoned, but I was able to obtain communications codes for the Imperial Correction Facility. With further inquiries I have tracked down a person who seems to be at least nominally in charge of what passes for a government there. His name is Moruth Doole, originally in the administration of the prison. Somehow he is now overseeing the spice-mining operations.

"There seems to be quite a bit of chaos there. My first contact was with the garrison station on Kessel's moon. Everyone seems quite alarmed at being contacted by the New Republic. I was bounced to several others before Moruth Doole finally agreed to speak with us. He is waiting for you now."

"Go ahead," Leia said. Winter checked her board, then

initiated contact. Leia stepped into the transmission field.

A small hologram of a froglike creature appeared above the dais. Static caused by poor transmission equipment on the Kessel end smeared Doole's coloring into yellowish green. His archaic waistcoat and bright-yellow cravat made him look a comical figure.

"You must be Minister Organa Solo?" Doole said. He spread his hands toward her image in a placating gesture. She noticed that he wore some sort of mechanical contraption, a focusing mechanism perhaps, over one of his lanternlike eyes. "I am extremely pleased to hear from a representative of the New Republic, and I apologize for any difficulty in getting in touch with me. We've had some social turmoil over the past couple of years, and I'm afraid we have not yet managed to quell all disturbances."

His fleshy amphibian lips stretched upward in what must have been meant as a smile. A long, sharp tongue flicked out as he spoke, but Doole talked so quickly that Leia could not get a word in edgewise. In her years of diplomatic service Leia had learned not to count too much on reading body language from nonhumans, but could this be a sign of nervousness?

"Now then, Minister, how can I help you? Believe me, we have been considering sending a representative to establish relations with the New Republic. I would like to extend an invitation for you to send an ambassador to our world, in the interests of maintaining harmony. On Kessel we like to think of the New Republic as our friends."

Doole stopped talking abruptly, as if he realized he had said too much. Leia frowned inwardly but controlled her expression. Moruth Doole was saying exactly what she wanted to hear, giving perfect political answers without her having to ask the questions. Odd. What was he thinking? "Actually, Mr. Doole—I'm afraid I don't know your proper title. How do you wish to be addressed?"

Doole stared with his one eye and fiddled with the mechanical lenses, as if he had never considered the question before. "Uh, Commissioner Doole will do nicely, I think."

"Commissioner Doole, I welcome your offer of openness and cooperation, and I hope we have not already acted prematurely. One of our representatives went to Kessel more than a week ago, but we have heard nothing from him. He was due to return three days ago. I am contacting you to see if you could verify that he did indeed arrive safely?"

Doole raised his long-fingered hands to his cheeks. "A representative, you say? Here? I am aware of no such arrival."

Leia kept her face placid, though her heart grew cold. "Could you check to see if his ship, the *Millennium Falcon* arrived? We had some difficulty tracking down a person in charge just moments ago. Perhaps he reported to someone other than yourself."

Doole sounded doubtful. "Well, of course I can check." He punched at a data terminal unseen beyond the fringe of the transmission field. Almost immediately—too fast, Leia thought—Doole straightened. "No, I am sorry, Minister. We have no record of a ship called the *Millennium Falcon* ever arriving in Kessel space. Who was piloting the ship?"

"His name is Han Solo. He is my husband."

Doole straightened in shock. "I'm terribly sorry to hear that. Is he a good pilot? As you may know, the black hole cluster near Kessel makes for extremely hazardous flying conditions, even in hyperspace. The Maw is one of the wonders of the galaxy, but if he was to take a wrong path through the cluster . . . I hope nothing happened to him!"

Leia leaned deeper into the transmission field. "Han is a very good pilot, Commissioner Doole."

"I'll muster a search team at once, Minister. Believe me, Kessel will offer whatever assistance we can in this matter. We'll scour the surface of the planet and the moon, and we'll search space for any disabled ship. I will inform you immediately of any progress we make."

Doole reached forward to the controls of his holotransmitter, then paused. "And of course we look forward to formally receiving any other ambassador you choose to send. I hope the next time we speak will be under happier circumstances, Minister Organa Solo."

As Moruth Doole's image fizzled into static, Leia let her stony expression fall into a scowl of confusion and suspicion.

Winter looked up from her controls. "I detected no outright contradictions of fact, but I am not convinced of the total truth of what he was saying."

Leia's gaze focused on something far away. Anxiety twisted her insides, and she felt very foolish for being angry with Han. "Something is definitely wrong here."

11

When Han Solo's temper finally snapped, he hauled off with a roundhouse punch that knocked the guard backward. Han leaped on the man, punching him again and again in the chest and stomach, cracking his knuckles on the scuffed stormtrooper armor.

The other guards in the muster room scrambled toward him, knocking Han to the floor. Behind the transparisteel observation cubicles, shift monitors sounded the alarm and summoned assistance. The door slid open from the communal areas, and four more guards charged in, drawing their weapons.

Chewbacca let out a thunderous Wookiee roar and waded through the other guards, yanking them off Han's back. His life debt to his partner took precedence over common sense.

Han continued to swing, yelling incoherently at his captors. Chewbacca smashed two of the guards' heads together and dropped their limp bodies. The reinforcements looked up at the Wookiee, and they goggled as they saw the wall of fur and muscle in front of them. They drew their weapons.

Young Kyp Durron bent low and dove into the knees of the closest armed guard, knocking him to the floor. Kyp scrambled out of the way, yanking at boots and legs, tripping two more men.

With nothing to lose, other prisoners joined in the brawl, indiscriminately punching anything nearby, guards or other prisoners. Many of the captive spice miners were themselves former prison guards who had been on the wrong side during Moruth Doole's rebellion—and the other prisoners hated them.

With a *whoop* of energy, blue arcs of a blaster set on stun lanced out and knocked Chewbacca flat on his back, where he coughed and groaned and tried to raise himself on his elbows.

The alarms kept ringing, a throbbing sound that increased the chaos in the muster room. More guards rushed out of the communal area. Blue stun bolts rippled through the air, mowing down the rioting prisoners and taking out other guards at the same time.

"Enough!" Boss Roke shouted into a microphone on his collar. The voice exploded through the muster-room speakers. "Stop it, or we'll stun you all and then *dissect* you to learn what's wrong with your brains!"

One more stun bolt was fired, dropping two struggling workers to the floor like sacks of gelatin.

Han yanked himself free of the guards and rubbed his split knuckles. Anger continued to seethe through his mind, and he had to work double time to calm himself so he wouldn't get shot.

"Everybody to the bunks! Now!" Boss Roke said. His lip curled; bluish-black stubble looked like a smear of dirty oil on his chin. His lumpy body seemed coiled and dangerous.

Kyp Durron lifted himself up, but as he caught Han's gaze, he flashed a smile. No matter what their punishment would be, Kyp had enjoyed lashing out.

Two very uneasy guards hauled Chewbacca to his feet, draping his hairy arms over their shoulders. Another guard wearing a battered old stormtrooper helmet trained his gun on the Wookiee. Chewbacca's arms and legs twitched as if still trying to struggle, but the stun bolt had thrown his nerve impulses into turmoil. The guards tossed him into one of the holding cells and activated the door before Chewbacca could engage his muscular control. He sagged to the ground in a flurry of mussed brown hair.

His eyes dark with anger, Han moved with taut readiness. He followed Kyp to the line of metal bunks. The guards brushed themselves off and glared at him. Han climbed into his uncomfortable sleeping pallet. Around him the metal rods holding the mattresses and bunks apart seemed like another cage.

Kyp climbed to the upper bunk and leaned down. "What was that all about?" he said. "What set you off?"

One of the guards rapped a stun stick against the side of the bunk. "Keep your head inside!"

Kyp's face popped back into his own area, but Han could still hear him moving. "Just touchy, I guess," Han mumbled. He felt a hollow sorrow inside. "I just realized that today is the day my kids are coming home. I wasn't there to be with them."

Before Kyp could acknowledge, Boss Roke flicked on the sleep-generating field that pulsed around the bunks and sent Han, still resisting, on an endless plunge into dull nightmares.

Standing outside the doorway of the spice-processing annex, Moruth Doole fitted an infrared attachment into place over his mechanical eye. He hissed in his own uneasiness, flicking his tongue in and out to taste the air, to keep himself safe.

The recent transmission from Solo's woman made him very nervous about what the New Republic might do to him. In the warm darkness of the spice-processing rooms, he could relax. Looking at the blind and helpless workers that did his bidding hour after hour made him feel stronger, more in control.

The heavy metal door thudded into place, sealing out the light. The secondary entrance slid open to a womblike vault that glowed in his IR attachment, warm and red from the body heat of the workers. Doole took a deep breath, sniffing the musty dankness of the gathered lifeforms.

He looked at the blurry orange images crouched over the processing line. They stirred, silently afraid of his presence. That made Doole feel good. He strode in among them, inspecting their work.

Hundreds of blind larvae, pale and wormlike with large sightless eyes, fumbled with four slender arms to handle the delicate spice crystals. They wrapped the fibrous segments in opaque paper and loaded them into special protective cases, which would then be ferried up to the shipyard and transfer base on Kessel's moon. With the larvae working comfortably in the total darkness necessary for spice processing, Doole's operation ran much more smoothly than it had under Imperial control.

The brief telepathic boost offered by glitterstim spice had made the substance a valuable commodity tightly controlled by the Empire. Other planets had a weaker form of spice, sometimes known as the mineral ryll, but Kessel was the only place where glitterstim could be found. The Empire had kept an iron fist around Kessel's spice production, keeping the glitterstim for espionage and interrogation purposes, as well as checks on loyalty and the granting of security clearances.

But there had always been a vast demand on the invisible market: lovers wanting to share an ephemeral telepathic link, creative artists seeking inspiration, investors trying to obtain inside information, scam operators wanting to dupe rich clients. Many smugglers delivered the spice to Jabba the Hutt and other gangster distributors.

But the Empire no longer controlled spice production. Doole had expected to have no further problems—until Solo came back.

Doole had been waiting for the call from Coruscant for days. He had rehearsed his answers over and over, knowing exactly what he should say. Perhaps he had rehearsed too much, coming up with snap answers that might make Minister Organa Solo suspicious.

Skynxnex told Doole he was overreacting, that they just needed to play their part. Solo and the Wookiee had been safely exiled to the spice mines. No one would ever find them. But there was always a chance something could go wrong. Maybe it would be best if he just ordered Solo killed and got rid of all the risks.

Doole walked along the rows of larval workers. His vision in the blurry infrared was not much worse than the normal eyesight from his mechanical eye. The caterpillarlike larvae bowed in silence, working slavishly. Doole had taken them from the egg sac and raised them here, centering their existence on processing spice. He was a god to them.

As Doole passed, one of the largest males reared up in a defensive posture, waving his frail arms as if to ward off Doole from his territory. To his shock Doole noticed that the male larva had nearly reached maturity. Had time gone by so quickly? This one would soon shed his skin and emerge as a strong adult.

Doole would have to kill him well before that. The last

thing he needed right now was competition—even if it did mean killing one of his own children.

Boss Roke stood in the muster room with hands on his hips, giving the workers a lumpy, appraising smile. "We lost another team yesterday. A guard and four workers, down in the deep new tunnels." He waited for that to sink in, but most of the prisoners had already noticed the missing workers.

"The samples brought up earlier show that this could be one of the richest strikes of spice we've found, and I'm not going to let incompetence and superstition cheat me out of a big payoff. I need some volunteers to go down with me to the lower tunnels and check it out—and if I don't get volunteers, I'll pick them anyway." Boss Roke waited. "Don't all volunteer at once."

He scanned the room. Watching him, Han knew that because of his part in the brawl the day before, he would be one of those picked. But he didn't mind—not if his suspicions were correct. Rather than give Roke the satisfaction of coercing him, Han stepped forward. "I'll volunteer. Beats another day of getting dirt under my fingernails."

Roke looked at him in surprise, then narrowed his eyes in suspicion.

"I'll go along, too." Kyp Durron stepped beside Han. Han felt a happy warmth swell up inside him, but he pushed it back. He didn't want to explain anything, not just yet.

Chewbacca yowled in surprise, then grunted a question about Han's sanity.

"What did he say?" Boss Roke asked.

"He's volunteering, too," Han said.

Chewie let out an uncomfortable snort of denial but made no further argument.

"One more volunteer," Roke said, then scanned the room. "You, Clorr." He pointed to a former prison worker who had done a lot of damage in Han's brawl. "I'm taking one guard and you four. Suit up. Let's go."

Roke didn't waste any time. By now Han had grown used to pulling on his thermal suit and adjusting the breath mask. He switched on the power pack to start warmth pulsating through his suit. Chewbacca looked ridiculous with his suit's empty third sleeve limp and taped flat against his torso.

Kyp and Chewbacca kept staring at Han, wondering what he had in mind. Han moved his hands slightly to quell their questions for the time being. Of course he had a plan.

One of the other guards, looking fidgety and uncomfortable, shifted a blaster rifle from shoulder to shoulder.

"Let's go!" Boss Roke said, and clapped his hands.

The four volunteers and the second guard lined up at the opening to the long metal chamber that housed the floating mine cars. They entered, and Boss Roke disengaged three cars from the long train. Roke and the guard sat up front, while the others crammed into the remaining two cars.

"Hey, how about some of those infrared goggles?" Han called. "If there really is something out there, we'll need to be able to see where to run."

Roke contemptuously put his own goggles over his eyes. "You're expendable." He activated the guidance system on the front car's controls. The lights went out, and the opposite door groaned open, flooding the compartment with cold, thin air.

"So much for that idea," Han said, then scrambled to put his breath mask in place.

The unenthusiastic prisoner, Clorr, groaned in dismay. Then the floating cars lurched into motion, gaining speed until they bulleted through the tunnels. The air whooshed as the car sped close to crumbling rock tubes from which generations of spice miners had peeled glitterstim deposits.

When the wind of their passage drowned out other noises, Kyp leaned closer to Han, speaking through his breath mask. "Okay, so tell me what we got ourselves into."

Han shrugged. "I have an idea, and if I'm right, we can all get out of this mess."

Chewbacca made a skeptical sound but ended in a question.

"Think about it, Chewie. People have been disappearing off and on from the same place—what if they found a way to escape? They've been working new tunnels, going into unexplored areas looking for spice, then suddenly a bunch of them don't come back. You and I know there are plenty of abandoned shafts from the illicit miners that slipped through Imperial security. This planet is honeycombed with entrances to the spice tunnels."

Han paused, hoping they had already figured it out. "Roke's teams usually have one guard and five blind prisoners. What if they came around the corner and suddenly found an opening to the surface, letting them see again. They could overpower the guard and make their way to freedom.

"Once Roke discovers the way out, though, he'll block it up and we won't have another chance. If we're ever going to get out, if I'm ever going to get back and see Leia and the kids, I've got to try. I thought maybe this desperate gamble would be worth it."

"Sounds like a good chance," Kyp said. "I've been down here so long, I'm willing to try anything."

Chewbacca agreed, but with somewhat less enthusiasm.

They plunged down and down, whipping around sharp corners. Several times Han thought the rocky walls brushed within a handbreadth of his head, and he tried to crouch down inside the car. He didn't want to imagine what would happen if Chewbacca's head struck an outcropping at the speed they were moving.

In the black spice mines Han rapidly lost all conception of time. He had no idea how long they traveled, how far they went, or how fast the floating cars moved through the tunnels. Boss Roke brought the vehicle to a stop and called for the prisoners to dismount. The guard noisily unshouldered his blaster rifle.

Han paid extra attention to the small noises he heard, building the best mental picture possible of where Boss Roke and the guard were standing at all times. That was something he would need to know if he had to make a quick escape. But they had gone down so deep now, he could not imagine finding a passage to the surface.

"Follow me," Boss Roke said. "I want one prisoner up front ahead of me and the guard taking the rear."

Han heard a shove and a gasp, then someone stumbled forward. Was it Kyp? No, from the unpleasant groan he determined that the point man would be Clorr, the former prison worker.

Boss Roke rustled in his pack, withdrawing some piece of equipment. Han heard an electronic clicking and pinging sound. It was some sort of detector. Han strained his ears, listening to the tones change as Roke moved the scanner from side to side.

"Spice all around us," Roke said. "Just as we thought, and the concentration seems even higher up ahead. Move forward."

Clorr stumbled into the blackness, followed by Boss Roke. Han walked blindly. He felt Kyp taking hold of his waist, and he heard Chewbacca's breath echoing behind his breath mask.

As they went farther, the tunnels grew colder and colder. Han's naked fingers crackled when he bent them. He turned up the heat in his suit, but the warmth comforted him little.

The electronic clicks from Roke's detector grew louder. "Concentration increasing," he said. "These are some of the densest, freshest veins of spice we've ever uncovered. There'll be a lot more work for you prisoners to do."

The detector clicked, and they shuffled ahead. Other than their own noises, the spice tunnel seemed a mouth of silence.

Han thought he heard a sudden scuttling noise farther down the passage, something massive that moved, stopped, moved again, then slowly began to come back, as if stalking. Up front Clorr muttered to himself, but Han heard Boss Roke shove him onward.

"The reading gets stronger right up around the corner." Boss Roke's gravelly voice carried a childlike hint of excitement. "I'm going to have to recalibrate this sensor."

Han heard the distant skittering sound again, but it seemed farther ahead. It wasn't a noise that anyone in their party had made. It sounded like sharp metal points ticking against glass.

The tenor of shuffling human footsteps changed as they turned the corner. "Spice reading is off the scale!" Boss Roke cried.

Suddenly Clorr screamed.

"Hey!" Roke said.

Clorr screamed again, but the sound came from much deeper in the tunnel, as if something had yanked him away and fled, carrying him to a secret lair.

"Where are—" Roke said, then he, too, gave a startled shout.

Han heard booted feet turning around, running back. Han nudged Kyp aside, back the way they had come. "Watch yourself!"

Boss Roke stumbled into Han, then fell backward. Han reeled against the rocky wall but kept his balance. Roke clawed at the floor, desperate to flee.

"Turn around!" Han shouted to Kyp, giving the young man a push toward the floating cars. "What is it?" he yelled to Boss Roke. He heard the pointy, ticking sound again, moving closer, skittering like many sharp legs that ended in stiletto claws.

Roke screamed, then gave an *oooof!* as the air was knocked out of him. Han heard a thud as the man hit the ground, but Roke clambered to his feet again, or at least to his knees, crawling forward.

As Han started to run, Roke grabbed his leg and held on. Han tried to jerk free, shouting, "Stop it! We've got to get out of here!"

But before Roke could let go, something behind him— something very large and very, very close—grabbed Roke and yanked him backward, breaking his grip. Roke's fingernails were like claws as he tried to grasp the slick fabric of Han's thermal suit, but with a quick whisking sound he was dragged away down the tunnel, still gurgling and crying out.

In the darkness Han could see nothing at all.

"Run!" Han shouted.

Chewbacca roared, then plowed like a demolition vehicle into the guard behind him. Kyp followed the Wookiee and leaped over the fallen man, but Han stumbled on him, sprawling flat on the broken rocky floor. Nobody could see anything.

The guard scrambled to his knees and started thrashing and pummeling as if Han were the enemy. But Han, blinded and desperate, grabbed for something else. He snatched at the infrared goggles on the guard's face and pulled them free.

The walls were closing in around him. The screams and sounds of panicked fleeing and the *tick tick* noise of the approaching monstrous thing made claustrophobic thunder around him.

The fallen guard's wail of sudden blindness and dismay was muffled by his breath mask. He clutched at Han, but Han knocked the breath mask free. The escaping oxygen made a whistling sound. The guard had to release Han to replace his mask.

Han scrabbled forward. He had to see. They needed to find the floating cars so they could get away. "Run, Chewie! Straight ahead! Make sure Kyp goes with you!"

He slapped the goggles over his head. He heard the scuttling, thumping sounds of the sharp, scampering legs again. Had an army of the things come to attack, or was it just one very large specimen with many legs?

Looking through the goggles, he could see the bright blob of the fallen guard's infrared signature and the fleeing brilliant shapes of Kyp and Chewbacca. He heard the thunder of hard, pointed legs coming back up the tunnel, stampeding down on them.

The guard moved, clambered to his feet, and began stumbling behind Han, but the man could not see. He weaved back and forth and struck the wall, smacking his head on a hard outcropping.

Running, monstrous feet came closer, like a patter of meteorites pelting the side of a ship. The guard screamed.

Han turned around to watch him, but he saw nothing else in the blackness of the tunnel, no shape, no signature, no body heat from any creature—*nothing* that was alive.

The guard suddenly froze, as if a giant invisible hand had grabbed him from behind. Then Han saw, to his horror, the *silhouette* of a long, spindly leg reaching around in front of the guard's waist and another one clipped over his shoulder, totally black, like a cutout from the infrared form of the guard. The man struggled and wailed.

The guard yanked at something—his blaster rifle. Han gasped as a brilliant lance erupted in the pitch darkness, striking against the multilegged thing, illuminating it for the shaved splinter of a heartbeat. Han saw what seemed to be a writhing mass of sharp twigs, a rat's nest of spindly legs and claws and fangs intermixed with eyes—many, many eyes. Then the creature absorbed all the light, plunging the tunnels back into opaque blindness.

The guard was lifted high in the air and turned around. Other shadows of the icicle legs wrapped around him. The glowing rectangle of the thermal suit's battery pack burned brilliantly in the infrared, but one of the sharp claws thrust into it like a stinger. Sparks flew into the darkness, leaving glimmers in front of Han's eyes.

As Han ran backward, stumbling and tripping, he saw the man's infrared outline grow dim as he became as cold as his surroundings. The creature, whatever it was, must be draining or feeding on energy, on body heat or anything it could find in the cold empty tunnels.

"Keep running!" Han yelled, now that he could see the forms ahead. He made out a dim glow of warmth still radiating from the floating mine transport. "The car's right in front of you, Chewie! Get on it!"

The Wookiee bumped into the metal side of the vehicle and dragged himself to a stop. Chewbacca reached over and grabbed Kyp, hauling him into the seat of the car.

Then Han heard the clacking, scrambling footsteps behind him again, charging down the tunnel. He was the next one in line. He dashed ahead, gasping, tripping on debris and bumping into walls he could not see. His blood had turned to ice water.

Chewbacca fumbled along the control panel of the floating mine car, trying to distinguish the buttons in the dark. Han kept running. The sounds of the sharp legs grew louder, rumbling.

Han risked a glance over his shoulder. Though he could hear the thing charging at top speed after him, he could see nothing in the darkness, nothing at all.

He reached the floating car and leaped in. "Just punch RETURN, Chewie! Hit anything!"

Chewbacca hit the start button, and the car pivoted on its axis to move back in the direction they had come.

The galloping sounds of the ice-pick-legged creature skittered faster and faster. The floating mine car picked up speed, but the creature kept coming behind it. Han still couldn't see it with the infrared goggles.

With a loud *spang* something struck the back car, rocking it sideways and slamming it against the side wall of the tunnel. Sparks flew as it scraped along the rocks, but the vehicle continued to accelerate.

Han heard a hollow roar behind them, and then they left the noises farther and farther away. The creature ceased chasing them. The darkness rolled ahead like a great black vacuum.

Han knew they were automatically heading back to the muster room. Chewbacca groaned and roared at him. Kyp sat panting in terror. "What did you see?" Kyp asked.

"I don't know," Han said. "Nothing like I've ever seen before."

Chewbacca chuffed in anger and annoyance and immense relief, and Han sighed. "I agree. This wasn't one of my smarter ideas."

12

Luke Skywalker showed Gantoris
the wonders of the universe. He took his passenger into
orbit in the modified shuttle, letting the man look down
on the doomed planet of Eol Sha. The too-close moon
hung above the world like a raised fist against a curtain
of stars.

Igniting the shuttle's sublight engines, Luke soared into
the blazing wonder of the Cauldron Nebula as Gantoris
stared out the viewports into the chaotic, glowing gases.
Then they plunged down the endless, other-dimensional
hole through hyperspace, shortcutting across the galaxy.

To Bespin.

During the uneventful trip Luke began telling Gantoris
about the Force, about the training the candidates would
undergo at the proposed Jedi academy. Now that he had
agreed to come along, Gantoris seemed willing and even
eager to understand the strange echoes and feelings that
had touched his mind throughout his life.

The hum of the shuttle's powerful engines and the giddy, abstract swirls of hyperspace were conducive to beginning a few exercises for awakening Gantoris's potential. Luke was surprised at the man's powers of concentration, at how he could close his eyes and sink into his mind undistracted. Luke had been an impatient young man during his own Jedi training; Gantoris had had a much harsher upbringing, making him grim and enduring.

"Reach out and feel your mind, feel your body, feel the universe surrounding you. The Force stretches around and through everything. Everything is a part of everything else."

Luke paid close attention to what he asked Gantoris to do. Obi-Wan Kenobi had spent some time training Luke, and Yoda had spent much more. But Luke had also undergone the abortive training of Joruus C'baoth as well as learning the powers of the dark side during his time with the resurrected Emperor.

Luke could not forget that Obi-Wan's training had also transformed Anakin Skywalker into Darth Vader. Would it be worth bringing back the Jedi Knights if the price was the creation of another Vader? Gantoris's ominous dreams of a "dark man" who would show him power and then destroy him made Luke very uneasy.

By the time Luke brought the shuttle out of hyperspace on an approach to Bespin, he thought Gantoris might be overwhelmed with new sights. But the stern man gawked out the viewports like a child, awed by the roiling gas planet where Lando Calrissian had once run Cloud City. The sight of the swirling planet suddenly brought back some of the greatest horrors in Luke's life. He squeezed his eyes shut as he felt the sting of those memories.

Gantoris, in the passenger compartment behind him, bent forward. "Is something wrong? I just sensed a strong flow of emotions from you."

Luke blinked. "You could detect that?"

Gantoris shrugged. "Now that you've taught me how to feel and how to listen, it came through very clearly. What's disturbing you? Are we in danger?"

Luke opened his eyes and looked out at Bespin again. He thought of his friend Han Solo kidnapped and frozen in carbonite for delivery to Jabba the Hutt; he thought of the duel with Darth Vader on the catwalks of Cloud City that had cost Luke his hand. And, worst of all, he recalled Vader's deep voice pronouncing his terrible message. "Luke, *I* am your father!"

Luke shuddered, but he turned to look back into Gantoris's dark eyes. "I have powerful memories of this place."

Gantoris kept his silence, asking no further questions.

Airborne mining installations rode Bespin's wind currents—floating automated refineries, storage tanks bobbing above the clouds, and facilities to scoop valuable gases from the cloud banks. Not all of these floating installations had proved profitable, though. The drifting colossus of Tibannopolis hung empty, a creaking ghost town in the sky.

Luke tracked the derelict floating city on his navigation screens. The construction hovered over the dark clouds as a storm gathered. The city tilted due to malfunctioning repulsorlift generators.

"Is that where we're going?" Gantoris said.

The roof, decks, and sides of Tibannopolis had been picked over by scavengers hauling away scrap metal. It looked like a skeleton of its former self, with buckled plates and twisted support girders in a broad hemisphere; dented ballast tanks hung below. Numerous antennae and weather vanes protruded from the joints.

"We're going to wait for someone here," Luke answered.

He brought the shuttle down on a primary landing deck that looked sturdy enough to support his ship. The criss-crossed structural beams were covered with scaled plating, but in some spots the seams had bent upward, popping their welds.

Luke emerged from the shuttle, and Gantoris joined him. The other man's long dark hair whipped around him like a mane, no longer braided, but he stood proudly in his hand-me-down pilot's outfit. His black eyes glittered with wonder.

The high wind gusting through the carcass of Tibannopolis made a moaning sound. The swaying metal groaned as rusted joints rubbed against each other. The wind had a bitter chemical tang from trace gases wafting to higher altitudes.

Black birdlike creatures with triangular heads clustered in the open gaps of buildings, nesting on stripped girders. As Luke and Gantoris moved forward, the flying creatures stirred and rustled leathery wings. Their mouths snapped open and closed with croaking sounds.

Below and around Tibannopolis, the clouds had turned the smoky gray of impending thunderstorms. Flashes of lightning rippled through the cloud bank below.

"What now?" Gantoris asked.

Luke sighed and gathered some inflatable blankets and a sleep roll from the passenger shuttle's storage compartments. "We've spent two days cooped up in the ship. I have no way of knowing when Streen might come back, and I think we should try to get a good rest."

"Streen?" Gantoris asked.

"The man we're waiting for."

The storm came through that night and rinsed off the exposed surfaces of Tibannopolis, causing fresh blooms of rust and patina on the construction alloys. Luke and Gantoris had found shelter in the decaying buildings of Tibannopolis, resting on the slanted floor because of the derelict city's tilt.

Awash in a Jedi trance more restful than sleep, Luke paid little attention to his surroundings but kept a small window open in his mind, ready to flick him back to wakefulness.

Gantoris surprised him. "Luke, I think someone's coming. I can sense it."

Luke became instantly awake and sat up from under the sheltered metal alcove, looking out at the washed-clean swirls of clouds. It took his mind only a moment to locate the approaching presence of a human—but he was impressed that Gantoris had been able to sense the distant stranger at all.

"I was practicing," Gantoris said, "reaching out and looking with my mind. There isn't much around here to distract me."

"Good work." Luke tried to keep the pleased expression from his face but failed. "This is the man we've been waiting for."

He used his sense to focus on a black shape approaching across the skyscape of rising gases. Luke saw an amazing cluster of lashed-together platforms and bulbous tanks held aloft by balloons and maneuvered with propellers that stuck out at all angles. The hodgepodge vehicle drifted toward them, riding the winds.

Luke smiled at the bizarre construction, while Gantoris stared in awe. They could make out the silhouette of a single man standing at the helm as buffeting breezes rippled trim sails at the sides of the main platform. Streen, the gas prospector, was returning home.

Luke and Gantoris made their way down to the landing platform to wait for him. As the collection of gas tanks, balloons, and flat walkways approached, Streen finally noticed them.

At the controls of his contraption he swerved and circled around the ruined city, as if frightened and reluctant to land. But somehow, seeing only the two of them waiting, he regained his nerve and rode the breezes in.

Streen did not land his vehicle, merely bringing it to the edge of the landing platform and lashing it to support posts mounted at the rail. Luke held on to the fiber-chains and helped Streen secure his vessel.

No one spoke. Streen kept surreptitiously slipping glances in their direction.

Luke sized him up. Streen was approaching old age, bearded, with brown hair so intermingled with strands of gray that it had turned to a creamy color. His skin bore a leathery look, as if the rough winds and harsh open air had sucked something essential out of his flesh. The prospector was clad in a well-worn jumpsuit studded with pockets, many of which bulged with hidden contents.

As Streen stepped onto the landing area, four of the black birdlike creatures fluttered up from roosts among the platforms, venting stacks, and gas tanks of Streen's vessel, returning to the jungle of construction frames in the floating city.

"Tibannopolis hasn't been inhabited for years," Streen said. "Why have you come here?"

Luke stood tall and faced the man. "We came to see *you*."

Gantoris stood patiently beside Luke Skywalker, feeling odd to be in a different position now. He had joined the Jedi to learn from him, swept up by his visions of a restored order of Jedi Knights and the powers they could tap through the Force.

This time Gantoris listened as Skywalker began to tell Streen of his plans for an academy, of his need for potential candidates who might have a talent for using the Force. He watched the skepticism on Streen's face, similar to what he himself must have shown at first. But unless Streen had suffered the same dark dreams or premonitions, this hermit on Bespin should be a more openminded listener than Gantoris himself had been.

Streen hunkered on the corroded surface of the landing platform and squinted into the sky before looking back to Skywalker. "But why me? Why did you come here?"

Skywalker turned instead to Gantoris. "There are many valuable substances dissolved in Bespin's atmosphere at various layers. The floating cities are huge mining operations that remain in place as they draw gas from below the cloud layers. But Streen is a cloud prospector. At certain times some storm or a deep atmospheric upheaval will make a cloud of volatiles belch up, waiting to be siphoned off. Streen goes out on the winds with his tanks, looking for the treasure.

"Bespin has computerized satellites to detect these outbursts and to dispatch company men—but Streen always gets there first. He somehow knows an upheaval is going to happen before it does. He is there waiting with his empty tanks to siphon off whatever comes bubbling up and sell it back to the independent refineries."

Skywalker squatted next to the hermit. "Tell me, Streen—how do you know when a gas layer is going to rise? Where do you get your information?"

Streen blinked and fidgeted. Now he looked even more frightened than when he had first seen the strangers waiting on the landing platform. "I just . . . know. I can't explain it."

Skywalker smiled. "Everyone can use the Force to some extent, but a few have a stronger innate talent. When I form my Jedi academy, I want to work most closely with those who already have the talent but don't know how to use it. Gantoris is one of my candidates. I think you should be another one."

"Come with us," Gantoris added. "If Skywalker is right, think of all the things we could accomplish!"

"How can you be sure about me?" Streen asked. "I always thought it was just luck."

"Let me touch your forehead," Skywalker said. When Streen did not move away, Skywalker tentatively reached forward with his fingers, brushing the man's temples. Gantoris couldn't figure out what Skywalker was doing until he remembered the test Luke had performed on him down in the lava chamber.

Skywalker's face looked blank and lost in concentration for a moment, then suddenly he jerked backward as if his body had been burned. "Now I'm sure, Streen. You do have the talent. There is nothing to fear."

But Streen still looked nervous. "I came out to this place because I need to be alone. I'm not comfortable around people. I feel them pressing in around me. I like people. I'm lonely, but . . . it's very difficult for me. It's all I can do to be around them just while I deliver my cargo. Then I have to run away.

"Seven or eight years ago, when the Empire took over Cloud City, everything got much worse. The people were agitated. Their thoughts were full of chaos." He looked up at Skywalker in dismay. "I haven't spent much time with people for eight years."

Gantoris could sense the man's emotions winding toward panic—and just when Gantoris felt certain Streen would refuse, Skywalker held up a hand. "Wait," he said. "Why not just watch us train for a while? Maybe you'll see what I'm talking about."

As if pleased at having an option that did not require

him to make an immediate decision, Streen nodded. He looked toward his floating platforms and gas tanks with a palpable stab of regret, as if wishing he had never come back to Tibannopolis. Gantoris could feel an echo of the other man's emotions, the yearning for freedom that Bespin's clouds offered, the solace of being alone.

"Show me your new Jedi exercises, Master. Teach me other things." Skywalker seemed to flinch at being called "Master," and Gantoris wondered what he had done wrong—was not Luke Skywalker a Jedi Master? How else should he be called?

Skywalker brushed aside the comment. He pointed to the thicket of girders and rusted metal bars in which flocks of the leathery black creatures made their homes, chittering and moving about in the afternoon. Far below, the clouds thickened into what could become another storm.

"Those flying creatures," Skywalker said. "We will use them."

Streen stiffened. His face grew dark and ruddy. "Hey, don't disturb my rawwks." Then he lowered his eyes, turning away as if embarrassed by his outburst. "They've been my only company all these years."

"We won't harm them," Skywalker said. "Just watch." He lowered his voice to speak as an instructor to Gantoris. "This city is a complex mechanism. Every girder, every metal plate, every life-form from those rawwks to the airborne algae sacks and everything around us, each has its own position in the Force. Size matters not. Tiny insects or entire floating cities, each is an integral part of the universe. You must feel it, sense it."

He nodded to the derelict structures around them. "I want you to look at this city, imagine how the pieces fit together, find the girders with your mind, tell me what you can sense and how one thing touches another. When you think you have found the intersection where a rawwk and girder touch, I want you to reach out and *push* with your mind. Make a little vibration."

Skywalker curled his forefinger around his thumb and stretched forward as he nodded toward a lone rawwk sitting on the end of a weather vane. He flicked out his finger, as if to shoo away a gnat, and Gantoris heard a distant *pinnngg*. Startled into the air, the rawwk flapped its wings and cried out in alarm.

Gantoris chuckled and, eager to try, flicked his own finger in imitation of what the Jedi had just done. He imagined seeing a whole flock of the rawwks take flight—but nothing happened.

"It is not that easy," Skywalker said. "You aren't concentrating. Think, feel yourself doing it, envision your success—then reach out with your mind."

More serious this time, Gantoris pursed his lips and squinted, looking for his target. He saw a delicate many-branched antenna on which five rawwks sat. He pictured the antenna, knowing his target, and stared. He took a deep breath and *pushed*. He still didn't quite know what he was doing, but he felt something happening in his mind, something working, some outside . . . *force* linking him and the antenna.

He watched as the antenna slowly swayed. The rawwks stirred but remained on their perches. Anyone else watching might have assumed the wind had shifted at that moment, but Gantoris knew he had done it.

"Good attempt. You have the right idea, but now close your eyes," Skywalker said. "You're letting your sight blind you. You *know* where the antenna is, you know where the rawwks are. You can sense their place in the Force. You don't need to see with your eyes. Tighten your focus. Feel it, know what you want to do."

Skeptical, Gantoris closed his eyes; but as he concentrated, he could indeed see vague outlines of what he had just looked at, tiny afterimages imprinted on the Force with tendrils reaching out and connecting them to everything else.

He reached out with his fingers to make the flicking gesture again but hesitated. He realized he did not need that either. Flicking the fingers was simply an example for Skywalker to make his point. Whatever actions he made, waving his hands or muttering spells were just so much mumbo jumbo. Understanding the Force was what allowed him to do what he needed.

Pleased with this sudden insight, Gantoris kept his eyes closed and folded his arms. He flicked out an imaginary finger, feeling the metal, picturing his fingernail striking the hard surface. In his head he heard the hollow *bong* as it struck, then opened his eyes to watch the five rawwks burst into flight, cawing at each other as if casting blame.

"Good!" Skywalker said. "I'm impressed. I thought this was going to be much more difficult." Still grinning, he looked at Streen, who had been watching them in silence. "Would you like to try it? You have the potential. I could show you how."

Streen balked. "No, I . . . I don't think I could do that."

"It isn't as difficult as it looks," Gantoris said. "You'll feel a different strength come into you."

"I don't want to," Streen said again, defensively. Then he lowered his eyes and patted his pockets, as if looking for something he didn't expect to find. Gantoris thought he was just making distracted movements.

The old man swallowed, then looked back at Skywalker. "If you teach me how to use this . . . sense I have—can you also teach me how to *switch it off*? I want to learn how *not* to feel the people around me, not to be bombarded by their moods and prying thoughts and sour ideas. I'm tired of having only rawwks for company. I'd very much like to be part of the human race again."

Skywalker clapped him on the shoulder. In his dark jumpsuit he looked like a benevolent god. "That much I can show you."

Luke watched as Streen cut loose the fiber-chains holding his floating hodgepodge ship to the Tibannopolis docking area. Standing on the docking platform, he gave his ship an unnecessary shove out into the breezes. The empty barge of platforms and balloons, propellers and gas storage tanks, drifted out to be caught up by swirling air currents.

Streen had emptied the pockets in his jumpsuit and now looked at Luke. "I know I'm not coming back. That old life is over."

The three of them climbed aboard Luke's passenger shuttle and made ready to depart Bespin. Luke felt a glowing satisfaction, not just to be leaving the gas planet that held so many dark memories, but to have both passenger seats filled, to have two new candidates for his Jedi academy.

He raised the shuttle off the landing platform, then began a steep climb toward orbit. Below them, in the opposite direction, Streen's abandoned platform continued drifting on its own, widening the gap between it and the derelict city.

Streen looked out the passenger window, staring with a bleak sadness that struck Luke's heart with pity. Below, the ghost town of Tibannopolis was truly empty again.

Then Luke watched something amazing happen. The city came alive with movement, swarming as tiny black figures took to the air. Thousands and thousands of rawwks that had made their home with Streen suddenly took flight, departing the abandoned metropolis in a huge flock that kept coming and coming and coming, spreading out among the clouds in a farewell salute to Streen.

Looking out the window and watching this, Streen smiled.

13

Skynxnex inserted a new charge pack into his double-blaster, smiled at the weapon, then thrust it into the holster. "Thank you, Moruth," he said. "You won't regret this."

Doole tapped his spongy fingers on the former warden's desk. One of the loose iridescent insects fluttered around the room, battering itself again and again on the wide landscape window.

"Just try not to make a mess of it," Doole said. "I want Solo gone and all traces removed. Nothing left. It's only a matter of time before the New Republic comes nosing around. We've got to be absolutely clean. Is the energy shield functional yet?"

"We're testing it this morning, and our engineers are confident it'll work. Solo and the Wookiee will be dead by then," Skynxnex said. "My personal guarantee."

Doole's lips curled like a rubbery gasket stretched out of shape. "Don't enjoy yourself too much."

Skynxnex smiled back at him and turned to leave. His

black eyes glittered. "Only as much as necessary," he said.

The mine car roared through the tunnels in total blackness. Han had no choice but to trust the computer guidance system.

Chewbacca had found the accelerator button and punched it repeatedly, trying to get farther away from the multilegged horror deep in the mines.

Han gripped the sides of the car with hands gone white from cold and terror. Each time they shot past a gaping side tunnel, his imagination heard noises of skittering legs and scythelike claws reaching out to pluck them from the passing car.

"Our course is taking us back to the muster room," Kyp said. "This could be our chance to escape."

"Where else should we go?" Han asked. He felt his heart pounding. Chewbacca groaned a question, and Han translated it. "Do you know any other way out of these tunnels?"

"I don't," Kyp said, "but maybe I could find one."

Han fought to contain a sudden fit of shudders. "I don't know about you, but I'm in no mood to go wandering through dark tunnels feeling for a way out—not with that thing chasing after us." The thought of a freezing death in the energy-draining fangs of the monster made the option of imprisonment in the spice mines seem not so terrible after all.

Before they could form some sort of alternative plan, the floating mine cars coasted to a halt in the long holding chamber. The metal door at the far end slammed shut behind them. With his infrared goggles, Han could see the activation controls on the wall next to an inner door.

His knees were weak; his hands trembled as he punched access for the muster room.

Light flooded around them, and the three survivors staggered inside, holding each other. Chewbacca used his hairy arms to keep both Han and Kyp on their feet.

Dazzled, Han cupped his hands over his eyes and let the infrared goggles dangle on his neck. "Boss Roke is dead," he croaked to no one in particular. "There's a monster in the tunnels. It attacked the guard. We barely got away."

"Han—" Kyp said.

Chewbacca sniffed, then roared in anger.

Han fought to focus his vision. He heard people rustling in the muster room. He saw only shadows in the glare. Finally, he could make out a tall, gangly form with dark hair and sunken eyes on a skull-like face.

"Glad you're back, Solo," Skynxnex said from the other side of the room. He drew the double-blaster at his hip.

Everything seemed to move slowly for Han. He had not yet come down from the boost of adrenaline caused by utter terror. Han saw the gun, saw Skynxnex, saw the man's cadaverous face. Doole had sent his henchman to kill them.

Han wasted no time, shoving Chewbacca backward. "Back in, Chewie! We've got to get out of here!" He yanked Kyp through the open doorway. Chewbacca let out a yowl and lunged into the dark chamber where the floating mine cars waited.

"Hey!" Skynxnex began to run in long, leaping strides that carried him across the muster room. Han sealed the door in his face, scrambling the lock mechanism.

"It'll take him a second to figure the access code. Get in the car, now!" Han leaped onto the swaying pilot seat.

"Looks like we're going to try one of those alternatives you wanted, Kyp."

He powered up the rocking vehicle. From the other side of the door came pounding and then the sounds of blasters striking the metal. Skynxnex was going to disintegrate his way through. They had to get to the relative safety of the tunnels right away.

Han punched up the computer guidance system and let the vehicle go. The great metal door on the far side of the long holding tunnel slid open with a grinding sound as the mine car accelerated back down the central tunnel from which they had just come.

"I hate to go back there," Han said. Chewbacca roared a comment, and Han nodded. "Yeah, I hate even worse to be blasted."

"Do you know Skynxnex?" Kyp asked, regaining his breath.

"We're old buddies," Han said. "That's why he wants to kill us."

The floating car rushed through the half-open metal gate just as the door from the muster room melted open, spilling a wedge of light into the tunnel.

"They're only going to be a minute behind us," Han said. With his infrared goggles he could see the pilot controls now—but none of the coordinates meant anything to him. The only exit he knew of was back through the muster room. "Any ideas, Kyp?"

"It's an automated course," Kyp said. "If I had time to think and get my bearings, I might be able to figure out something."

"We don't have that luxury right now."

The great metal door did not close behind them after they passed through. Wind whipped past their ears as Han kept his finger on the accelerator button. From behind they heard shouts, other people climbing into waiting mine cars. Han leaned over the controls, but the repulsorlifts could go only so fast.

Unable to see, and without any knowledge of the labyrinth of underground tunnels, Han did not dare fly the car manually. He would have to hope he could get far enough ahead so that Skynxnex could not follow . . . but then what? They would be lost in the cold, dark maze. How many other multilegged monsters waited for them in the shadows?

The sound of another mine car came roaring up behind them. Han had three cars linked together, hauling three riders with only one engine. If Skynxnex and the others took one car each, they would travel faster. They would be in blaster range within moments.

"Solo!" Skynxnex bellowed.

"Hold on!" Kyp said.

Han instinctively braced himself as the computer guidance system yanked them to the left-hand fork in an unseen tunnel, then plunged them steeply downward. Before Han could wonder if they had lost their pursuers, he heard the echoing whine of repulsorlift vehicles soaring down the tunnel after them.

"I'm open to suggestions," Han said. He looked behind them with his infrared goggles and saw the glowing target of Skynxnex and two other piloted vehicles. In the cold darkness his own body heat would be just as apparent to the pursuers.

Chewbacca held on to Kyp, pushing him down to safety in the second car. The Wookiee reached behind him, fumbling with the catch to the empty third car. Skynxnex and the two guards closed the gap. With a growl at the pursuers, Chewbacca decoupled the magnetic bearing from the third car.

Suddenly released, the empty car swung out behind them, dropping toward the ground. Skynxnex cried out

as he swerved up to avoid a collision. The other two
guards both curved to the left, battering into each other,
but somehow all three pursuers kept their balance. They
roared after Han.

"Nice try, Chewie," Han said.

Skynxnex pulled out his modified double-blaster, powered it on, and aimed. When he fired, the two barrels
sent their beams out at slight intersecting angles to each
other. A short distance beyond the muzzle, the two beams
coalesced and *phased*, forming a staccato series of bursts,
each one containing a brief impulse of power ten times
that of a single blaster beam. Though the weapon looked
impressive, it was almost impossible to aim, and most
other users—even hardened criminals—had dropped them
in favor of more reliable weapons.

The phased double beam poured out, striking the ceiling of the tunnel ahead of Han. The explosion of heat and
light blinded him through the infrared goggles. Somehow
Kyp reacted with molten speed and yanked the floating car
sideways. Miraculously, they swerved around the debris
that fell from above, struck only by the patter of small
pebbles.

"Everybody okay?" Han said.

Chewbacca grunted. "So far," Kyp said.

Han turned to look as Skynxnex zoomed safely through
the tiny avalanche he had caused. Falling rocks and debris
pelted the next car, though, making it spin out of control.
The car struck the rough tunnel wall in a shower of
sparks, then exploded, spewing shards of metal everywhere.

"One down," Kyp said.

Echoing sounds came from the open tunnel mouth ahead.
Through the infrared goggles Han could see other spots of
warmth, a caravan. They shot past the side tunnel just as
another train of floating mine cars emerged.

"They've got reinforcements!" Han said in dismay. But then he saw the cars were all linked together—another mining party on its way back to the muster room at the end of a shift.

Skynxnex and the other guard plowed right into them. Their accelerating cars rode up and over, knocking three hapless workers out of their seats and leaving them blind and lost in the tunnel. The driver of the work train slewed out of the way, ramming into the rocky wall of the tunnel.

Skynxnex spun in the air but somehow kept his seat. The second guard fared even better, pulling up beside Skynxnex as they zoomed away from the site of the wreck and the shouting work crew.

Han had no idea where they were going, but they were getting farther and farther away from anyplace good. With Skynxnex and his double-blaster behind them, they had no choice but to keep fleeing deeper into the tunnels.

Ahead in the inky blackness a sudden clump of pearlescent glitters sprang out of a bare rock wall, wavering in the air. Then the luminescence started traveling down the tunnel away from them, as if trying to outrun the approaching cars.

"Another bogey!" Kyp cried.

Their floating car followed the bogey, closing the gap. But as they neared, the swirling glowing thing accelerated, as if taunting them by flying ahead, whipping around curves just in front of them. By the faint glow Han could actually see the winding curves of rock.

Skynxnex and the other pursuer zoomed along in their wake.

"Uh-oh," Kyp said. "I think I just figured out what course we're on. All this feels very familiar."

"What?" Han said. "How can you tell?"

"The most recent set of destination coordinates in this

navigation computer was programmed by Boss Roke. We're going back down to where that monster was!"

The glowing bogey roiled ahead of them, dipping up and down but refusing to pop back into the spice-covered walls. As it rushed along, the bogey's bodily illumination activated threadlike veins of glitterstim, leaving a patchwork of blue sparks in their wake.

In a long, straight stretch of tunnel Skynxnex fired his double-blaster again.

As if he could sense the blast coming, Kyp rocked the car to one side as the intense pulsed bolt shot down the tube, passed through the bogey without harming it, and struck a distant wall. The impact blew open a huge aperture into another grotto.

Seeing an escape, the bogey ducked through the new opening.

"Put it on manual," Kyp said. "Let me fly it." By now their eyes had grown accustomed to the bogey's glow, and they could actually see where they were going.

"I don't want a free return trip to where that monster is waiting." Han relinquished the controls. Without a moment's pause Kyp launched the car into the wide-open section of wall that led to an unknown maze.

"This is the same series of tunnels," Kyp said.

As they plunged into the new grotto, something long and fibrous stung Han's face like a sharp wire whipping past him.

The bogey shot into the vast chamber, flying across the darkness to the far wall. Upon striking the rock face, though, it did not melt through and vanish as the first bogey had done days earlier. Instead, the glowing ball stuck on the rough rock surface. It glittered and spangled and pulsed, as if struggling.

Another whiplike strand struck Han's face as they flew through the air.

Around the bogey in the glow, wide veins of spice fizzled blue as the illumination activated them. The light crackled and spread outward in a network, geometrical crisscrossings along the wall. All of the spice in the chamber began to race around in long lines as the light increased in a chain reaction. The pattern looked familiar.

"Like a web!" Han said.

The bogey struggled frantically as the spice around it grew brighter and brighter. Han saw long fibers of free-hanging glitterstim draped through the open air of the grotto.

From behind them Skynxnex fired again in a long continuous blast that missed them in the wide space. The powerful pulsed beam struck the far ceiling of the chamber, making it erupt with hot broken stone that poured down from the roof of the tunnel. The images in Han's infrared goggles were blindingly bright.

The bogey stretched and struggled as parts of the spice web tore away in the avalanche, yanking portions of the glow with it.

Then Han saw the monstrous creature rise up from its lair on the grotto floor—a huge spider made of blown glass, all sharp edges, with a hundred legs and a thousand eyes. The bristling legs moved in a blur as it clambered up the debris toward the glowing bogey struggling in the spice web.

Han wrenched the floating car around, ready to plow his way out and away from the monster that had almost captured him in the tunnels—even if he had to fly right down Skynxnex's throat.

On the rocks below, tossed aside like wadded sheets of used paper, lay the crumbled forms of Boss Roke, Clorr, and the guard, frozen solid and drained of every drop of their bodily energy.

The creature must lay down deposits of spice as its

web to capture bogeys, Han thought, *or any other warm creature it can find down in these tunnels.* That was why light activated the glitterstim spice—to trigger the bogeys' capture in the trap.

Skynxnex and the pursuing guard roared into the grotto. The scarecrow fired again, paying little attention to where he was going. His blast ricocheted off the wall, activating more spice.

The spider-thing glowed a dull blue with electric arcs crawling up and down its needlelike limbs, as if the creature itself were made out of activated spice. Attracted to the approaching heat source, it reared up.

Skynxnex did not see it until he had driven his floating mine car nearly into the grappling-hook claws. In the last instant Skynxnex pointed his hot double-blaster down and fired at the voracious creature—but the energy spider absorbed the blaster's power and snatched out with a dozen limbs.

Skynxnex tried to leap out of the doomed car, but the spider thing speared him with a sharp leg, raising his scarecrow body higher. With the last of his strength, Skynxnex flailed his arms as his body grew cold.

The multilegged creature began to feed.

The pursuing guard rebounded sideways as he struck a thick mass of spice fibers dangling from the ceiling. The glitterstim sparked and glowed in the growing illumination. As the guard saw Skynxnex captured, saw the huge energy spider and the collapsing ceiling of the grotto, he whirled his floating mine car around and fled back out the cavern entrance as fast as he could go.

Han, though, saw an open passage in the ceiling and noticed a dim trickle of light coming from it. He wanted only to be out of there before the thing came scrambling after them, clawing its way up glasslike strands of glitterstim. . . .

"Up there!" Han urged.

Kyp plunged the car upward into the ceiling opening and suddenly came upon another network of tunnels. But these catacombs looked man-made. At last, one of the illicit mining shafts dug by spice smugglers searching to find active veins.

Han let out a whoop of delight. "This is it! We're out of here now!" Chewbacca clapped him on the back, nearly belting Han out of the pilot's seat.

They raced upward. The distant daylight pierced through the jagged obstacles of the passage. Han did not want to slow down. Kyp accelerated toward the light.

The floating car burst into the thin open air of Kessel, where watery light blinded them like a supernova. Blinking and struggling to see, Han yanked off his goggles and took back the pilot controls. He evened out their trajectory above the flat, desolate surface of the small planet.

Off to their right he saw the towering stack of an atmosphere factory gushing white steam and air vapor into the sky. "That way," Kyp said. "We'll be able to find a ship."

"Good idea," Han said.

As they approached the enormous construction, flying low enough to avoid notice, he kept an eye out. Moruth Doole would not know of their escape until the lone surviving guard returned to the muster room and made his report. Han, Kyp, and Chewbacca would have a few moments to get a head start, but not very long.

Adjacent to the atmosphere factory, Han did indeed see a broad landing pad with four craft on it. Two of the ships were local landskimmers and useless to them—but the others were small supply shuttles, spaceworthy enough, though they wouldn't go fast.

Holding the breath mask against his face, Han pointed with his other hand. "Down there. Get one of those ships and we're away from Kessel." He grabbed Kyp's shoulder. "We can go home."

14

When Luke returned to Corus-
cant, he had a joyous reunion with Han and Leia's two-
year-old children, whom he had not seen for some time,
not since he and Ackbar had set up the secret, protected
planet for them.

He waited in Leia's living quarters, playing with the
twins, tossing them in the air and juggling them using his
Jedi powers. Jacen and Jaina squealed in delight, giggling
and intuitively trusting that their Uncle Luke would never
let them fall.

Children were a wonder to him. Raised with his Uncle
Owen and Aunt Beru on the parched world of Tatooine,
Luke had had little time for playing with children because
the life of a moisture farmer was wrapped up in such
hard work.

When he left Tatooine with Ben Kenobi, Luke had joined
the Rebel Alliance, spending time as a fighter pilot and in
Jedi training with Yoda. He never had time or opportunity
to see children—and now he felt as much pleasure playing

with them, watching their wide-eyed innocence, as they seemed to enjoy having him around.

"Faster! Faster!" Jacen cried.

Instead, just to tease him, Luke stopped the boy cold in the air, letting him hang motionless as Luke orbited Jaina around him. The little girl squealed and stretched out her hand, trying to grab her brother's ear as she spun.

Tiring of that, Luke let Jaina drift into a cushioned seat while he reached out to catch Jacen as the boy descended, holding him in his arms. Jaina squirmed and reached her pudgy arms up, wanting to be held too.

Luke made faces at the little boy, puckering his lips and wiggling them back and forth. He spoke in a funny head-cold voice that sounded something like Yoda's. "The Force is strong in this little one, hmmmm? Yes!" But then Luke wrinkled his nose and noticed something he didn't need Jedi powers to understand. "Or maybe that's not the Force I sense. Leia, I think you need to perform a motherly duty." He held Jacen in front of him.

Threepio bustled into the room. "Allow me to take care of that, sir. I have been getting a great deal of practice in the past day or two."

Luke smiled at the thought of Threepio trying to manage squirming twins. He noticed the droid looked a bit scuffed and battered. "Was that part of your protocol programming?"

"My manual dexterity is sufficient to the task, Master Luke." Threepio flexed his golden motorized fingers, then took Jacen from Luke's grasp. "And believe me, I enjoy these duties much more than gallivanting through space, getting shot at by Imperial fighters, or getting lost in asteroid fields."

Leia came into the room. She forced a smile that Luke could tell was a mask. She looked very tired. It wasn't just the strain of combining her diplomatic duties with being a mother; something else deeply concerned her, but she hadn't said anything. Luke did not pry—he could have reached in and taken the secret from her mind, but he would not do that to his sister. And she might even have figured out how to block him by now. He would let her broach the subject in her own way.

"The prep unit will have the meal ready in just a few minutes," Leia said. "I'm very glad you're back, and the twins seem to be pleased too."

Luke realized that he hadn't seen Han since his return; but because of their busy schedules, seeing Han and Leia in the same place at the same time was a rare occurrence anyway. It was a wonder they had somehow managed to have three children! Could Han's absence have something to do with Leia's hidden concern?

Luke picked up Jaina with the Force again, raising her into the air. She giggled and began flailing her arms and legs as if swimming through the open spaces of the room.

"Leia, I need your help in a couple of bureaucratic matters," Luke said.

"Sure." She smiled wryly at him. "What can I do?"

"I still need to contact Mara Jade and a handful of other possible Jedi candidates. But now that I have two trainees here and waiting, I've got to find a place where we can begin our Jedi studies. And I have to find it soon.

"I've spoken with Streen and Gantoris, and it's clear to me that Coruscant is not appropriate. Streen doesn't like to be around people, and he's not going to be very comfortable anywhere in Imperial City. All of Coruscant is covered with metropolis, buildings on top of buildings.

"And—" He hesitated, but this was a private conversation with Leia; he could not hide any of his worries from her. "There is some danger about what we might do. Who am *I* to be teaching all these Jedi potentials?

I have no way of knowing what might trigger a disaster like one of the Emperor's Force storms. It would be better if we found someplace isolated, a place of solitude where we can conduct our training without interference."

"And in safety." Leia's dark eyes met his, and he knew that both of them were thinking of Darth Vader. "Yes, I agree. I'll try to find you an appropriate place."

"And while you're looking," Luke continued, "we also need to relocate all of the people on Eol Sha. There's only about fifty of them left on that outpost, but the planet is doomed. When I took Gantoris, I promised we would find a new home for the survivors. See what you can do."

"For a group of people that small, it shouldn't be difficult," Leia answered. "Anyplace sounds better than the planet they're leaving."

Luke laughed. "Or you could always have Han win another planet for them in a card game!"

She looked at him as if stung. *Yes indeed*, he thought. It was something to do with Han. He bounced Jaina up in the air again, touching her to the ceiling, then letting her fall back down.

Suddenly Lando Calrissian burst into the room unannounced. "Leia! Winter just told me that Han hasn't come back yet. Why haven't you talked to me about it?"

Startled, Luke let Jaina fall and barely managed to catch her in the air a handbreadth above the hard floor. Jaina giggled deliriously, confident that the whole thing had been planned.

Lando looked upset and angry as he glared at Leia, planting his hands on his hips, pushing back the cape to hang behind him. Then he noticed Luke standing in the room. "Luke, are you going to do anything about this?"

"I don't know what you're talking about—but I think Leia was just about to tell me."

Both men looked at her. She sighed and sat down. "Yes, Han is missing. He went off to Kessel about two weeks ago, but now he's four days late coming back. He never contacted me, so yesterday I got in touch with Kessel. I spoke to someone who seems to be in charge, a Rybet named Moruth Doole.

"Doole says that Han and Chewie never arrived. Kessel has no record of the *Millennium Falcon*. Doole suggested they might have gotten lost in the black hole cluster."

"Not Han!" Lando said. "And not in the *Falcon*. He knows how to fly that thing almost as well as I do."

Leia nodded. "All through the conversation I sensed something wrong with the way Doole was acting. His answers were too pat, and he seemed nervous. I had the distinct feeling he was expecting my call and had already made up appropriate excuses."

"I don't like that," Lando said.

"Well, if Han is missing and you knew since yesterday, why didn't you send out a fleet of New Republic scouts?" Luke said. "A formal search party? What if he *is* lost in the Maw somewhere?"

Leia sighed. "Think about it, Luke. If I mobilized an official force, I could create a galactic incident just when we're trying to get Kessel into the New Republic. And besides," she admitted, "you know Han. There's a very real chance he's just goofing around. He forgot his kids were coming back. Maybe he found a good game of sabacc or started talking old times with some of his spice-smuggler buddies—that's why he wanted to go on the mission in the first place."

"We'll go look for him ourselves," Lando said.

Luke could tell by the way Leia's face brightened that this was what she intended to ask all along. "We'll go snoop around," he said. "There won't be any official dispatch or record of our mission."

Lando said, "We'd better take the *Lady Luck*. She's just a privately owned yacht with some pretty good punch in her engines."

Leia stepped forward and plucked Jaina out of Luke's lap and cradled her. "I'll watch over Gantoris and Streen while you're gone."

Luke nodded and spread his hands wide. "You see, *that's* why you're a diplomat—you think of details like that. Just don't let the two of them get into any trouble."

"We should take Artoo with us," Lando said. "That little droid sure helped me out at the blob races."

Luke had heard of Lando's exploits with the scam artist Tymmo. "You can tell me all about it on our way there. Leia's waited long enough."

"Let's go to Kessel," Lando said.

15

They managed to steal the second shuttle.

Han and Chewbacca wasted precious time in the first cargo ship on the atmosphere factory's landing pad, trying to cross-circuit the controls as Kyp Durron kept watch in the open hatch. The air was cold on their exposed skin, and they didn't know how much stray radiation from the Maw actually penetrated the atmospheric shield; the sounds of breathing hissed behind their breath masks. No one had seen them. Yet.

After only a few minutes, Han accidentally triggered the shuttle's automatic lockout systems. He slammed his hand on the panel. "Should have known I couldn't beat the high-level security interlocks!"

Chewbacca pulled off an access plate and tossed it into the back compartment with the sound of a crashing landspeeder. Roaring in his Wookiee language, he began yanking wires out of the controls and jamming them into override ports, but the few lights still functioning on the panels continued to burn red.

"Forget it, Chewie. We'll try the other ship," Han said. "I think I know what I did wrong last time."

Kyp kept watch on the tiny doors of the atmosphere factory's massive stack. "Still no movement from inside. We're clear."

They raced across the open spaces of the landing field to the second cargo shuttle, an old Imperial model with scarred armor and long planar wings that made it look like a mechanical flying fish. Han and Chewbacca had flown a similar *Lambda*-class shuttle on their guerrilla mission to Endor; but this model looked even older. Prison facilities must have low priority for new equipment acquisitions, he thought.

Chewbacca opened the hatch, and Han ducked inside, moving straight to the controls. The Wookiee clambered after him as four guards marched into view around the perimeter of the atmosphere stack. The squad wore cobbled-together uniforms of old stormtrooper armor and thermal suits from the mines.

Kyp plastered himself to the wall just inside the open hatch. Looking across the landing field, he saw that they had forgotten to close the doorway on the first shuttle, and now their tampering was painfully obvious. He swallowed. "Better hurry, Han. We've got company, but they haven't seen us yet."

"If this doesn't work, we're in deep bantha dung," Han muttered, punching up the command screens and removing the access plate to the security override.

The squad of guards marched on what was probably a routine patrol. Han glanced up to see them through the shuttle's windowport, but the reflectorized transparisteel would prevent them from observing the pilot's compartment. He wondered how many times a day the guards walked around the circular perimeter of the atmosphere stack. He hoped they were sleepwalking by now.

He tried to fire up the shuttle's engines. The control panel gave him an ERROR message. "Bantha dung it is, then," he said. But he had one more thing to try.

The lead guard suddenly stopped and gestured toward the open hatch in the first shuttle. He tilted his head to speak into his helmet comlink, then went cautiously forward. He took another guard with him, while the remaining two drew their weapons and spread out, looking from side to side.

"Oh boy," Kyp said.

Han rewired the security circuit, feeding the password-checking mechanisms back into themselves; then he snapped the plate back on. "Let's try it. Kyp, get ready to close the hatch. If this works, those guards are going to be upset. If it doesn't work, *I'm* going to be upset."

The two guards poked their heads out of the first shuttle, gesturing wildly. They had seen the sabotage. The other two jabbered into their helmet radios, then sprinted toward the second shuttle, drawing their weapons.

Kyp slapped the button that slammed the hatch shut. All the guards began running, pointing their blasters at the shuttle.

Han punched the start controls. With a merciful whine and hum, the engines ignited. Power surged through the shuttle. Han gave a whoop of triumph, but Chewbacca knocked him back into the pilot's seat as he furiously worked the controls with his big hairy hands to lift them off the pad.

The guards fired blasters at the shuttle. Han heard the sizzling thumps as the beams struck, but the ship's armor could withstand attack from minor hand weapons.

At the base of the atmosphere stack, doors opened and an entire squad of guards boiled out like Anoat lizard-ants in mating season. One bright laser bolt splashed across the transparisteel directly in front of Han's eyes, dazzling him. "Time to leave this party," he said.

Chewbacca raised them off the ground, maneuvering the shuttle away from the other vehicles on the landing pad.

Two guards wrestled a blaster cannon into place, erecting it on its tripod and cranking up the aim point. Chewbacca growled, and Han took over the controls. "I know. That thing could be real trouble if we don't get some altitude fast."

A flurry of hand-blaster bolts pinged against the lower hull. Han flew the ship higher, adjacent to the gigantic stack, spiraling upward and using the curving walls as a shield. The guards managed to fire only one shot from the blaster-cannon, but the beam scattered wide as Han corkscrewed up, keeping the stack between him and the troops. Below, the guards ran around the perimeter to keep within firing range, but Han flew the shuttle beyond the reach of small weapons fire.

"We're out of here!" Han said. "Punch it, Chewie!"

Then the massive laser turrets mounted on the atmosphere tower began firing at them.

"What!" Han cried. "What are they doing with weapons on an atmosphere stack? It's a factory, not a garrison!"

One brilliant green bolt struck the starboard planar wing of the shuttle, sending the vessel into a roll. Han and Chewbacca grappled with the controls as they spun, and Kyp clung to the supports of the pilot's chair.

They careened into the gushing white updraft from the stack, knocked from side to side by manufactured air dumping into Kessel's atmosphere. "Hang on!" Han yelled. He did not want to crash on the planet again.

At the shuttle's top acceleration, he took them along the stream of air, roaring upward like a boat riding the rapids. Green blasts from the turret lasers continued to streak up, but by riding the center stream, Han kept the shuttle in the blind spot of their targeting mechanisms.

They zoomed toward the fringes of the atmosphere. Han looked at both Kyp and Chewbacca. "Well, so much for sneaking out of here. Now Moruth Doole is going to know we escaped."

As if on cue the shuttle's comm crackled, and they could hear Doole's croaking voice in the background. "Is this it? Did you get the right override channel this time?"

"Yes, Commissioner."

"Solo! Han Solo, can you hear me?"

"Why, it sounds like my old friend Moruth Doole!" Han said. "How are you doing, buddy? I hope you feel better than your assistant Skynxnex."

"Solo, you have caused me more grief than any other life-form in the galaxy—including Jabba the Hutt! I should have squashed you when I had you in my office."

Han rolled his eyes. "Well, you missed your chance, and I don't plan on giving you another one."

Doole chuckled, a hissing heh-heh-heh laugh like a fat man choking on sand. "You won't get away. I'll mobilize everything against you. Better start thinking about the afterlife now."

Kyp squinted out the port, as if deep in concentration. The atmosphere thinned around the fleeing ship at the far limit of where Kessel's gravity could keep hold. He saw Kessel's moon and suddenly shivered uncontrollably. He blinked in confusion.

Chewbacca bellowed into the speaker mesh. "You tell him, Chewie," Han said, then switched off the radio.

Kyp scrambled forward and grabbed the controls, activating the maneuvering rockets and making the shuttle lurch forward with enough force to slam Han and Chewbacca against their seats. Kyp tumbled backward, unable to keep his balance in the acceleration.

"What did you do that for?" Han demanded, glaring at Kyp.

But Chewbacca made an alarmed noise and dragged Han back to the console. Just below them the atmosphere shimmered and crinkled as an impenetrable ionized screen appeared, blanketing the planet.

"They've got their energy shield operational!" Han said. The workers on Kessel's moonbase had repaired the protective screen that blocked off the prison planet. If Kyp hadn't punched their acceleration exactly when he did, they would have been sizzled in the bath of power or trapped beneath the shield, unable to escape.

"How did you know?" Han said, looking over his shoulder at Kyp. Kyp picked himself up off the floor, shaking his head to clear his thoughts. "Never mind. Are you okay?"

"Yeah. Just get us away from Kessel."

Han spun around to the shuttle's controls. "Chewie, contact the New Republic. No waiting this time. They've got to learn what's going on here, just in case we don't make it back."

The Wookiee bent over the comm controls as Han struggled with the navicomputer. Han gawked at the task in front of him. "Damn! This thing's an old five-hundred-X model! Haven't seen one of these outside a museum. I hope they gave us a scratchpad to do backup calculations. That might be faster *and* more accurate!"

Chewbacca moaned and pounded his hairy fist on the console with enough force to buckle the panels. Han flashed a sidelong look at him. "What do you mean we're being jammed? Who's jamming us?"

Kyp turned to the side viewport, said in a low voice, "Here they come."

The garrison on Kessel's moon spewed fighters, dozens of rejuvenated battle craft, armored freighters, slim and heavily armed X-wings, and TIE fighters. Many of the ships must have been damaged during the recent war and then salvaged. Now Doole had also gotten his planetary defense shield running again. Kessel would be a veritable stronghold against any attack.

Streams of X-wings and Y-wings coursed out, flanked on either side by a squadron of TIE fighters. They roared through the wispy tail of atmosphere in Kessel's orbital wake, leaving a glowing window of ionized gas from their sublight engines.

"Strap yourselves in," Han said. "This is going to be a hell of a ride." He reached for the controls, preparing to fight, then felt a boulder drop in his stomach. "What? This ship is *unarmed*!" He frantically scanned the console. "Nothing! Not a single laser! Not even a slingshot!"

Kyp held the back of Han's pilot chair, bracing himself. "We stole a supply ship, not a fighter. What did you expect?"

"Chewie, pump everything into our shields—and I mean *everything*, including life support. We've got enough air in here to last longer than this ship is likely to hold. Boost shields until they're off the scale. We're going to have to outrun them."

The first wave of TIE fighters soared in, their Twin Ion Engines howling over the cockpit's feedback speakers. Laser spears shot out, pummeling the shuttle, but the shields held. X-wings attacked from the rear.

"Can't this ship go any faster?" Kyp asked. The lights dimmed as Chewbacca reinforced the shields.

"Like you said, kid, we stole a cargo shuttle. This isn't a racing ship, and it sure isn't the *Falcon*. Get ready for a jump to hyperspace as soon as this fossilized navicomputer gives an answer." He stared at the readout, then pounded on the panel. "It'll be another ten minutes before it coughs up a safe trajectory. Damn! The black hole cluster is screwing up the calculations."

Chewbacca interjected a loud, bleating comment.

"What did he say?" Kyp asked.

"He said our shields are going to fail in about two minutes. I wish I had weapons—I'd even settle for a rock to throw out the window!" His eyes were wide and suddenly empty of hope. "There's no way we can last long enough, and Doole sure won't take prisoners a second time. Sorry I got you into this, kid."

Kyp bit his lip, then turned to point out the front windowport. "Go there."

The Maw.

Swirling clouds of gas looped into the bottomless pits of black holes, making space look like a tangled skein of incandescent yarn. Gravity waited to tear apart any ship that came too close. The inexorable Maw cluster was destined to swallow up the Kessel system itself in only another thousand years—but Han didn't want to feed its appetite any sooner than that.

Chewbacca roared something that needed no translation. "Are you crazy?" Han asked.

"You said we're dead anyway."

Four Y-wings fired simultaneously on the port side of the shuttle, rocking it. A shower of sparks blasted from the comm unit, and Chewbacca struggled to reroute the circuits.

"There are supposed to be safe paths through it," Kyp said. "There must be."

"Yeah, and about a million paths that are sudden death!"

"It'll be flying a razor's edge all the way through." Kyp's young eyes looked immeasurably old as he stared at Han. "Do we have a better chance staying here and fighting?"

The enormous gravity wells of the Maw made a maze

of all the hyperspace and normal space paths through the cluster. Most of the routes were either dead ends or went right down the gullet of a black hole. "We'd never find the right course," Han said. "It'd be suicide."

Kyp gripped Han's shoulder. "I can show you the way."

"What? How?"

A TIE fighter looped overhead, rotating in flight and firing at the hijacked shuttle. Cruisers from the moonbase approached, closing the gap. Against the capital-ships' turbolasers, the escapees would be vaporized within moments. Chewbacca groaned as their rear shields weakened and failed.

Han scrambled with the controls; both he and Chewbacca tried to reinforce weak points by draining the stronger shields up front. Lights in the cabin dimmed as the shields gulped more power.

"I helped you navigate through the dark spice tunnels when we were running from Skynxnex, didn't I?" Kyp said. "I knew when Doole was going to switch on the energy shield! I can find the right path into the Maw."

"That still doesn't tell me *how*, kid!" Han shouted.

Kyp wore an embarrassed expression for a moment; then he spoke quickly. "This is going to sound like a hokey old religion—but it works! An old woman who spent part of her sentence in the spice tunnels told me I had some sort of tremendous potential. She showed me how to use something called 'the power' or 'the strength' or something."

"The Force!" Han cried in relief. He wanted to grab Kyp and hug him. "Why didn't you say so? Who was this woman?"

"Her name was Vima-Da-Boda. Down in the spice mines she taught me only a few things before the guards hauled her away. I never saw her again, but I've been practicing what she taught me. It's helped a few times, but I don't really understand how."

"Vima-Da-Boda!" Han said, remembering the withered fallen Jedi he and Leia had found on Nal Hutta. During her guilt-ridden hiding, Vima-Da-Boda had somehow spent time in the spice mines, long enough to train Kyp in a few essential skills. Han hoped that would be good enough.

"I don't like this," Han said. Another pair of fighters soared by, firing repeatedly. "But I like it better than our other options right now."

He altered course, swinging around and heading straight toward the seething cluster of black holes. He hoped the shuttle's weakened shields would last long enough to get them there.

The first of the capital ships reached them and fired, looping overhead, then returning, as if to ram them. The shape of the attacking freighter made Han's blood turn to water, and he stared in silent dismay for a full second before he managed to cry out. "That's the *Millennium Falcon!* That's my ship!"

The *Falcon* came straight at them, firing again and again as the shuttle's forward shields tried to compensate for the pummeling. At the last moment Han wrenched the stolen shuttle into a steep dive so the *Falcon* scraped by overhead. One of the shots passed through the wavering shields to scar the armor of the shuttle.

"That does it!" Han said. "Now I'm mad. Chewie, at my order drop shields and dump everything into thrust. Pump every last erg into our engines and take us straight into the Maw." He glanced down at his readouts. "Shields are failing in less than a minute anyway, and the navicomputer needs another six to finish its calculations. Blasted five-hundred-X models!"

Another wing of fighters strafed them, then roared by, leaving a gap to their rear as a huge Lancer frigate closed the distance. A wave of system-patrol craft and Carrack cruisers followed, ready to bring a full armada of turbo-lasers to bear. Moruth Doole was taking no chances this time.

"Go, Chewie!" Han said.

The Wookiee dropped shields and channeled all power to the sublight engines. The shuttle burst forward in an unexpected spurt of speed, startling the pursuing ships.

"Surprise is only going to help us for a few seconds," Han said. "Then we're on our own."

"By that time we should be in the grip of the Maw," Kyp whispered.

"If you're not right about this, kid, we'll never know it."

Curtains of incandescent gas blazed in front of them, swirling residue heated by friction as it spiraled in complex orbits through the Roche lobe of one black hole and down the gullet of another. Deadly x-rays filled space, forcing the transparisteel to dim itself to protect the eyes of the passengers.

"Only a complete idiot would try something like this," Han said. Chewbacca agreed.

The Kessel ships poured on additional acceleration, desperately trying to catch the escapees before Han could reach the Maw cluster. Han hunched over the controls, white-knuckled, as if to increase their speed by sheer force of will.

The fighters unleashed a laser firestorm, but the Maw's huge gravitational distortions spread out their focus and sent them on long arcs away from the target.

"Let's just hope these guys aren't idiots too!" Kyp said. Han drove toward the blazing shreds of hot gas.

The Kessel ships pursued until the last instant, then peeled off at full thrust with their maneuvering engines, letting their prey go to certain death.

Han's ship plunged into the gravitational jaws of the black hole cluster.

16

Leia suppressed a dignified smile as she led Gantoris into the projection chamber. The dark-haired man stared in his puppetlike way as he tried to gawk at everything at the same time.

Gantoris was resplendent in a new uniform, tailored to match the generations-old pilot suit he had worn as leader on Eol Sha. Leia had loaded a tailor droid with patterns from the archives and presented the uniform to Gantoris as a gift. He had been delighted, puffed with admiration.

Even after getting to know him, Leia felt uncomfortable around Gantoris. Though Luke assured her of the strong Jedi potential in the man, Leia did not like the thought of the deadly "tests" Gantoris had given Luke before he would agree to leave Eol Sha. Gantoris had lived a hellish life, she admitted, but he seemed too intense, his dark eyes fiery pits of contained fury. He had the look of a man accustomed to power suddenly shown how small he is in the grand scheme of things.

But the other side of Gantoris intrigued Leia. She watched him flick his eyes back and forth, craning his head to stare at the tall building spires rising to the fringes of Coruscant's atmosphere. He gaped in astonishment at the sparkling audience chambers, at the minor personal amenities in the quarters Luke had obtained for him. He had never before seen or even imagined things that Leia considered commonplace.

Now, as they entered the projection room, Gantoris stared at the giant windows that filled the walls with broad vistas of Coruscant and the centuries-old buildings that girdled the world. The two of them were not really high enough for such a view, Leia knew; the projection room was actually a deep internal chamber, and the "windows" were high-resolution screens displaying images from cameras mounted at the top of the Imperial Palace.

"What is this place?" Gantoris asked.

Leia smiled, folding her arms over her robe. "Right now this is just a room. In a moment, though, I'll give you a new world."

She stepped to the control dais in the middle of the room and called up images she had compiled from the archives, records left over from Old Republic surveys and the dossiers compiled during the Alliance occupation.

The window screens flickered, and the images changed, startling Gantoris. He whirled as the landscape suddenly showed a completely different planet. His eyes grew wide and panicked, as if Leia had just transported him across the galaxy.

"I'm showing you a new home. This is Dantooine, the place we have chosen for the people of Eol Sha."

Around them the window screens displayed vast plains of grassland and spiky trees. Purplish hills rolled across the distant horizon. A herd of small, hairy beasts roamed across the savanna; in the air a cluster of bright balloonlike things, either plants or rudimentary animals, drifted about; a few had snagged on pointed branches of the spiky trees. Two moons, one lavender and one greenish, soared overhead.

"We established one of our first Rebel bases on Dantooine. It has a mild climate, abundant life-forms, plenty of water. A few nomadic tribes roam up and down the coasts of the ocean, but for the most part the planet is uninhabited."

Leia had used Dantooine as a decoy when Grand Moff Tarkin interrogated her aboard the Death Star. To save her beloved planet of Alderaan, Leia had divulged the location of the old Rebel base on Dantooine rather than naming the real base on Yavin 4; but Tarkin destroyed Alderaan anyway, because Dantooine was too remote for an effective demonstration of the Death Star's power. Now, though, Dantooine could be put to use again, as a home for the refugees of Eol Sha.

"Do you think your people would like to live on a place like this?" Leia raised her eyebrows.

Gantoris, who had so far seen only his own blasted world, the gas planet of Bespin, and the city-covered surface of Coruscant, seemed impressed. "This looks like a paradise. No volcanoes? No earthquakes? Plenty to eat, and no sprawling cities?"

She nodded. Before Gantoris could say anything else, the door to the projection room opened. Leia turned, surprised to see the Chief of State, Mon Mothma, coming to join them.

The auburn-haired woman walked with a sure step that made her glide across the floor. The leader of the New Republic extended a hand to Gantoris. "You must be one of Luke Skywalker's first Jedi trainees. Please let me welcome you to Coruscant and wish you the best of success in becoming part of a new order of Jedi Knights."

Gantoris took Mon Mothma's hand and nodded to her with a slight bow; but Leia caught a fleeting impression that he considered himself a leader meeting an equal.

"Mon Mothma," Leia said, "I was just showing Gantoris some images of Dantooine. We are considering moving the refugees from Eol Sha to our old base there."

Mon Mothma smiled. "Good. I'm aware of the plight of your people, and I would like to see them safely on Dantooine. I always thought it was one of our most pleasant bases, not quite as rigorous as Hoth or Pinnacle Base, without the dense jungles of Yavin 4." She turned to Gantoris. "If this world meets with your approval, I'll direct Minister Organa Solo to begin the relocation work immediately."

Gantoris nodded. "If these are representative pictures, this place Dantooine would be a perfect new home for my people."

Leia felt a surge of relief. "I was thinking of putting Wedge . . . I mean General Antilles in charge of the relocation duties. He's been supervising the reconstruction of the lower city levels for months, and frankly, I think that's a waste of his talents."

"I agree," Mon Mothma said. Though buried under more diplomatic entanglements and bureaucratic decisions than Leia could imagine, Mon Mothma somehow maintained a calm energy. "Also, my calendar just reminded me that the Caridan ambassador will be arriving in two days. Are all the preparations going smoothly? Can I offer my assistance in any way?"

"Just plan to be there. That's the most I can ask of you. I have decided to move the reception to the Skydome Botanical Gardens, rather than holding it here in the Imperial Palace. Since Ambassador Furgan seems hostile to our cause, I didn't want to exacerbate his reactions by receiving him in the former seat of the Emperor's government. In fact, the ambassador is trying to disguise his mission here as a mere pilgrimage to visit the site of various Imperial landmarks."

Mon Mothma nodded slightly but gave a smile. "At least he's coming. That's the best signal of all."

"I suppose." Leia remained skeptical.

"By the way, I never received your report on Han's mission to Kessel. That was a brilliant idea to send him instead of a formal ambassador. Han can speak to those people in their own language, and reopening the spice channels away from the black market might do wonders for the new economy. Did he have any success?"

Feeling awkward, Leia dropped her gaze to the floor. "He has been delayed, Mon Mothma, so I don't have any information at the moment. I'll give you a full report as soon as he gets back. Let's hope his mission is a success."

"Agreed." Mon Mothma's expression hinted that she suspected there was more to Leia's story, but she asked no further questions. "I have to go debate with the Ugnaught representatives about salvage rights for the wrecked ships in orbit around Coruscant. I'm afraid it's going to be a long afternoon, and I just wanted to greet you while I had the chance. Gantoris, it was a pleasure."

Mon Mothma turned to go but flashed a glance back at Leia. "By the way, you're doing a fine job, Leia. Too often in government we get inundated by so many dissatisfied interest groups, so many complaints, that we forget the things we're doing right. You are doing a *lot* of things right."

Leia couldn't cover an embarrassed smile. If only she hadn't lost her husband, she might have been a lot happier.

• • •

The twins began bawling in unison as soon as Winter stepped onto the ramp of her unmarked shuttle. Leia's personal servant stopped, keeping her back turned to Jacen and Jaina, and then slowly faced them.

Leia gripped the shoulders of the two children, but they still treated their mother as a stranger, even after several days. She held on tightly, which she realized might not have been the best thing to do, but she felt suddenly possessive of the twins.

Winter's face was cold and impassive beneath her white hair. "Children, stop crying this instant."

Jacen snuffled. "We want you to stay, Winter."

Winter thrust out one hand, pointing her finger like a spear at Leia. "*That* is your mother. I was only taking care of you. You are big children now, and it's time for you to be at your own home. I have to go back and take care of your baby brother."

Leia kept herself from trembling. She had known Winter a long time; the woman had total recall of anything she had ever seen or heard, and she rarely showed any sort of emotion. Now Leia thought she could detect a sadness in her, a sense of loss as she finally gave over care of her two wards.

Leia knelt beside the twins. "You'll be staying with me now, both of you. And your daddy should be home soon. We'll have lots of fun together."

The twins turned to look at her; Winter took that moment to slip inside the shuttle. Before Jacen and Jaina noticed she had gone, Winter activated the doors, sealing herself inside.

Leia stood beside the children on the windswept landing pad. The shuttle's repulsorlifts whined, powering up. Leia stepped backward, nudging the twins with her. "Out of the way now. Back where it's safe." Jacen and Jaina still sniffled, on the verge of crying again. In her untrained way Leia tried to send them calm, loving thoughts.

She spoke into a comlink on the lapel of her robe. "Grant departure clearance to unmarked shuttle on top northside platform of the Palace, authority of Minister Organa Solo."

The orbital traffic controllers acknowledged, and Winter's shuttle rose from the platform, pivoted, then angled into the sky. Leia raised her hand in a farewell salute. "Wave to Winter," she said.

The twins flailed their pudgy arms in the air. Winter flashed the lights in the shuttle at them; then the orbital-burn rockets kicked in, and the vessel shot into the aurora-streaked distance.

"Come on, you two," Leia said to them. "I've got a lot of lost time to make up for."

Streen sat atop the ruined and abandoned skyscraper where he had made his home. When Luke brought him to the yammering mass of Imperial City, where millions of people covered the planet with all their thoughts and all their feelings, Streen had begged for a place where he could have some solitude until they moved off-planet to their Jedi training center. Luke showed him the abandoned parts of the city, and Streen had selected the tallest building. Being high up reminded him of the clouds of Bespin.

Now Leia brought the twins with her, keeping a firm grip on each of their hands as she led them into the barely functional lift, which took them to the rooftop. They walked out onto the upper platform where Streen sat alone on the edge. The old man dangled his feet over the sides, unperturbed by the unbroken kilometer drop below him.

He looked up and out at the unrelenting cityscape, the geometric spires of sprawling buildings. He watched the tiny shapes of hawk-bats riding thermals.

Leia walked across the rooftop. She had never been afraid of heights, although with the young children at hand she felt an altogether different kind of fear, a stomach-clenching paranoia of the millions of things that could bring danger to her children. Jacen and Jaina wanted to dash to the edge of the platform and look over, but she refused to release her grip.

Upon hearing them approach, Streen turned. Leia noted that he still wore his many-pocketed jumpsuit, not wanting to change into the warmer or more comfortable clothes she had offered him.

"We just came to check on you, Streen. With Luke gone I wanted to make sure there was nothing else you needed."

Streen paused a moment before answering. "What I'd like is solitude, but I fear there's no place I can have that on this entire planet. Even in the quietest places on Coruscant, I can still hear a constant hum of whispering thoughts and voices. It'll be very difficult for me here, until I learn how to block it out. The Jedi Master promised to teach me how to do that."

"Luke should be back shortly," Leia said.

They approached the edge, and Leia insisted on standing a safe distance away. But Jaina pulled forward to the full reach of Leia's arm, to where she could peer over the edge and gape all the way down. "That's far!" Jaina said.

"Too far to fall," Leia told her.

"I won't fall."

"Me neither," Jacen said. Then he insisted on straining forward to look over the edge as well.

Streen stared at them with a kind of wonder. "You're better than the others. The children's minds are simple and straightforward, and they don't bother me. It's only when thoughts are complex and filled with a thousand subtexts that it makes my head ache. And you, Minister Organa Solo, are quieter and more focused than most other people."

"Luke taught me how to control my own mind. I don't leak out the thoughts and feelings that bother you so much. I keep from broadcasting them to anyone else."

Streen gave a wan smile, then stared out at the vast sky. On various parabolic courses, blinking lights of incoming and departing diplomatic shuttles traveled across the sky.

"I hope all the Jedi trainees can learn to be as silent as you are, Minister. I'd very much like to be around other people, part of a community like yourself and the Jedi Master. How long will it be, do you think?"

He looked deeply into her eyes, and she pulled the children away from the edge. "Soon," Leia said. "As soon as possible."

She vowed that she would find a place for Luke's academy before he returned from Kessel. It had to be the right place, and she had to find it without delay.

Leia and Threepio insisted on giving the twins a warm ripple bath before bedtime. Leia ran the water as Threepio checked to make sure its temperature was perfect.

Leia shooed Jacen and Jaina toward the rippling water. Jacen balked. "Put bubbles in first!"

"I'll put the bubbles in while the water's still running. Now just get in."

"Winter puts bubbles in first," Jaina said.

"Well, this time we'll do it a little different," Leia explained a bit testily.

"I want bubbles now!" Jacen cried.

"Dear me! Perhaps we *had* better put the bubbles in, Mistress Leia," Threepio said.

But the twins' defiance had awakened Leia's own stubbornness. "No, I told you to get in the bath. I don't care how Winter did it. This is the place you live now. Sometimes we do things differently."

Jaina began to cry.

"It's all right!" Leia said. "It's still a nice bath. Look." She splashed her hand in the warm water. "It doesn't make any difference when you put the bubbles in."

"I put bubbles in?" Jaina asked.

"If you get in, you can add the bubbles."

Jaina promptly climbed into the water and held out her hands. Leia gave her an amber-colored sphere that would dissolve in the agitation of the ripples.

Jacen jumped into the ripple bath. "Now I put bubbles in!"

"Too late," Leia said. "Next time it'll be your turn."

"Perhaps we should let them add another sphere of bubbles?" Threepio said, bending over to situate the children in the water.

Jacen used both of his hands to fling water into the droid's face. "I want home!"

"This is home, Jacen. You live here now. I'm your mother."

"No. I want *home*!"

Leia began to wonder why her diplomatic skills were failing her now. The twins began splashing each other. It looked like light play at first, but suddenly—for no apparent reason—they both began to cry. Perhaps this would be good preparation for meeting the Caridan ambassador, Leia thought.

She squeezed her eyes shut as the two continued wailing. Threepio, growing more and more flustered, frantically tried to determine what the difficulty was.

Leia wished she knew where Han was.

17

The stolen shuttle plummeted into the Maw. Maelstroms of hot gas buffeted them from side to side as Kyp fought to guide Han along their tenuous course. The safe path was convoluted and treacherous where the gravitational singularities canceled each other out.

The Maw itself was one of the wonders of the galaxy. The very existence of a black hole cluster seemed astrophysically impossible and had led to much conjecture about its origin. Old Republic scientists cited probability arguments, that among the near-infinite stars in the universe, *something* like the Maw had to occur at least once. Other speculations, including those voiced by superstitious smugglers, suggested that the Maw had actually been *built*, assembled by a vastly powerful ancient race that had created the black holes in a barely stable configuration to open gateways into new dimensions.

At the moment, Han Solo cared only that the Maw was likely to be the cause of his death.

The shuttle's interior was dark and hot and stuffy. The wild colors and blazing light made psychedelic fireworks outside the ship and weird shadows inside. All lighting, life support, and temperature regulation had been shut down to increase power to the failing shields.

Han sweated in the pilot seat, watching the navigational controls he had relinquished to Kyp. Though he had been fighting for his life almost constantly during the past week, he missed Leia very much. She had no idea what had happened to him, and she must be terribly worried—but no doubt too proud to show it. Han hated even more to know that his children had finally returned from their sanctuary planet, and he hadn't been there to greet them.

But he would never see any of them again if the shuttle didn't survive passage through the Maw. Everything depended on Kyp Durron's mysterious abilities.

Kyp struggled with the controls, guiding the shuttle through some of the most delicate, most difficult maneuvers Han had ever seen—and Kyp kept his eyes closed! The young man seemed to be seeing through a different set of eyes, looking at some path not apparent with normal vision. Staring at the deadly black holes all around the shuttle, Han wanted to close his own eyes, too.

Kyp continued to negotiate the implacable obstacle course intuitively, threading through fragile points of stability. Chewbacca sat frozen with his own tension, afraid to disturb the young man's concentration.

Sparks flew on one of the far control panels as a shield gave out. Chewbacca growled as he jammed long fingers down on the controls, rerouting and spreading the remaining protection evenly around them. If a single gap appeared in the shields, the x-rays and fiery gases would tear them apart.

Kyp didn't flinch. "Coming up on the end of this ride," he said without opening his eyes. "There's a gravitationally safe island in the middle of the cluster, like the eye of a storm."

Han felt relief rush through him. "We'd better hide there for a while, recharge the power sources and make a few quick-and-dirty repairs." Chewbacca grunted his agreement.

"And take a good long rest," Kyp said. Han noticed a sheen of perspiration on his forehead. Despite his outward calm Kyp seemed to be concentrating enormously, straining his fledgling abilities. "We still have to find our way back out, you know."

The swirling ionized gases parted like a curtain thrown aside to reveal the gravitational oasis in the cluster's core, a safe haven for them to recuperate before returning to Coruscant.

"Made it!" Han said in a whisper.

But someone else had already found the hiding place.

Orbiting a small rocky island in the center of the Maw hung four gigantic Imperial Star Destroyers, bristling with weaponry.

Within a moment of their arrival swarms of TIE fighters poured out of the Star Destroyer hangar bays in a truly impressive show of force.

Han stared, unable to speak. They had just escaped execution at the hands of Skynxnex, the energy-spider attack in the spice mines, battle with the entire space fleet of Kessel, and destruction in the gravitational maze of the Maw. Now the shuttle's shields were failing, they had no weapons—and an Imperial armada had just been launched at them.

"The way things are going, we'll end up accidentally destroying the galaxy before suppertime," Han said. "Kick all the engines back on, Chewie! Let's turn this thing around. Kyp, find us another path out!"

"There aren't many paths to choose from," Kyp said.

The ship shuddered as if someone had kicked it from behind; then sparks sprayed out. Chewbacca groaned in dismay.

Han looked at the readouts. "All our shields just went out." He stared at the four Star Destroyers and the waves of TIE fighters and TIE Interceptors surging toward them. "I feel like we've got a big targeting cross painted right on our hull," Han said. "They can wipe us out with just a potshot." He glanced around, searching for something hard enough to kick; he found a bulkhead and lashed out at it.

The comm crackled, and for a moment Han expected another threatening message from Moruth Doole, but the ionized gases and distortions of the black holes would ruin any transmission passing through the outer shell of the Maw.

Gruff words spilled out of the speakers. "Imperial shuttle, welcome! It has been a long time since we received word from the outside. Please provide your security access code. Our TIE squadron is coming to escort you."

Han stiffened, remembering that they had stolen an old Imperial shuttle. They would have a few seconds before they were blown out of the sky. But a security access code? He had to think fast.

Han toggled the transmitter switch. "This is Imperial shuttle, uh . . . *Endor* coming in. We've, uh, had a rough ride through the Maw, and most of our computer systems are down. We request assistance." He paused, then swallowed. "Just how long has it been since you got news from the outside anyway?"

A loud click came from the other end. The TIE fighters continued toward them. Han squirmed, knowing his bluff couldn't work, that they were an unprotected target to be blown away by itchy Imperial trigger fingers.

The voice came back, gruffer and crisper this time. "Imperial shuttle *Endor*, we repeat—what is the security access code? Transmit immediately!"

Han turned to his copilot. "Chewie, how long until we get those shields?"

The Wookiee had removed the access panels on the side power compartments, yanking out masses of wires as he strung them through his fingers and tried to straighten the connections. Chewbacca sniffed to find burned circuits. It would be a long time before they had the systems even marginally functional again.

Han opened the transmitter circuit once more. "Uh, as I said, we've sustained substantial computer damage. We are unable to—"

"Unacceptable excuse! The code phrase is verbal."

"Just checking," Han said. "The code phrase is—" He looked to Kyp, desperately hoping that the young man would be able to pull the code out of the air, but even Luke Skywalker was unlikely to do something like that. Kyp could only shrug.

"Uh, the last code phrase we have is RJ-two stroke ZZ stroke eight thousand. Awaiting your confirmation." He clicked off, then looked at Chewbacca and Kyp, spreading his hands. "It was worth a try."

"Improper response," the gruff voice snapped.

"What a surprise," Han mumbled.

The transmission continued. "You have obviously not been sent by Grand Moff Tarkin. Shuttle *Endor*, you are to be taken prisoner immediately and brought aboard Imperial Star Destroyer *Gorgon* for deep interrogation. Any attempt at escape or resistance will result in your being destroyed."

Han wondered if he should bother to acknowledge, then decided against it. He was puzzled by the mention of Grand Moff Tarkin, the brutal governor who had built the first Death Star. Tarkin had been destroyed along with his doomsday weapon ten years before. Could these people have been out of touch for that long?

The shuttle lurched as if a giant invisible hand had grabbed it. Han could hear the metal plates groaning as pressure constricted the outer hull. "It's a tractor beam," he said.

The giant arrowhead shape of the flagship Star Destroyer loomed up at them. Chewbacca groaned something, and Han agreed. He had a bad feeling about this, too.

"Don't even bother, Chewie. We could never break that tractor beam, we could never run out of here fast enough, and we could never survive another passage through the Maw."

A squadron of TIE fighters surrounded the hijacked shuttle like a cocoon, making it impossible for them to deviate from the direct path of the tractor beam. The Star Destroyer *Gorgon* opened its huge receiving bay to swallow the prisoners. TIE fighters streaked up and into the cavernous metal mouth.

Han remembered being taken captive aboard the first Death Star in much the same way, flanked by Imperial starfighters, fighting against a powerful tractor beam. But that time he had been flying his own ship, and they had been able to hide in the *Falcon*'s secret storage compartments. Now they didn't even have uniforms to steal; they wore only the thermal prison suits used for working in the spice mines of Kessel.

"We're not going to make a very good impression," Kyp said.

The four Star Destroyers hovered over a cluster of interconnected rocky bodies at the very center of the Maw.

Other constructions and skeletal debris orbited low to the asteroid archipelago.

Han wondered again what all this was. A staging area? A secret base? Why would the Empire have squandered so much firepower to protect the little clump of rocks below?

The tractor beam lifted the shuttle into the *Gorgon*'s bay and hauled it over to an isolated landing area. As the shuttle came to rest, Han heard faint groaning and ticking sounds, like a chorus of mechanical sighs of relief from the battered ship. Armed stormtroopers hustled into position, running in regimented columns that showed they were still well drilled, still highly trained. They carried old-model blasters held at the ready.

"We'd better see what they want," Han said. "Any bright ideas?"

"Only dim ones," Kyp answered with a shake of his dark head.

Han sighed in resignation. "Let's go out together. Hands up and move very slowly."

Chewbacca grumbled that he had no particular aversion to dying while fighting, if they were going to be executed anyway.

"We don't know that," Han said. "Let's go."

Chewbacca, the most intimidating, took the central position while Han and the smaller form of Kyp Durron flanked him. They walked out and surrendered. The stormtroopers instantly directed their weapons toward the three. Han wondered how he could have earned himself such an unrelenting streak of bad luck.

At a signal for attention the back ranks of stormtroopers snapped erect, shouldering their weapons, while the front ranks held unwavering aim at the prisoners. Han watched as doors at the rear of the landing bay slid open and a tall woman strode through, accompanied by a bodyguard on each side.

She had a slender build and precise movements. She wore an olive-gray jumpsuit and black gloves. She marched forward, paying little attention to those around her, as if the troops were mere fixtures. She fastened her gaze on the prisoners.

Her most striking feature was a full head of hair that billowed around her shoulders and disappeared to some unknown length down her back. Her hair was the color of hot copper and seemed to crackle with an electric life of its own. Her eyes were green and piercing, like turbolaser bolts.

She walked straight toward them. Han saw the insignia at her collar and was taken aback to recognize the rank of a full admiral. Han had attended the Imperial academy himself when he was young and knew that a woman reaching the rank of admiral was unheard of. Emperor Palpatine had had a well-known prejudice against nonhumans, but he sustained more subtle discrimination against women, rarely promoting even those who passed the rigorous tests. For this woman to have the rank of full admiral—especially of a small fleet of Imperial-class Star Destroyers—was remarkable. Han put himself immediately on guard; this was no person to be trifled with.

She stopped at the foot of the ramp and looked stiffly up at them. Her features were as finely carved and as cold and rigid as a statue's. Her lips barely moved as she spoke.

"I am Admiral Daala, in charge of the fleet guarding Maw Installation." She flashed her green glance to each of them in turn. "You three are in a lot of trouble."

18

Luke and Artoo had little to do as Lando Calrissian piloted the *Lady Luck* toward Kessel. A nebulous haze of escaping atmosphere surrounded the potato-shaped rock, while the jagged garrison moon rode in its close orbit.

"Welcome to the garden spot of the galaxy," Lando said.

Luke thought of his home planet of Tatooine, the Dune Sea, the Great Pit of Carkoon, the Jundland Wastes. "I've seen worse," he said. Artoo bleeped in agreement.

Lando leaned closer to the viewports. "Yeah, well don't make any hasty judgments. We haven't looked at this place up close yet." He opened a comm channel. If Kessel had a good tracking network, the station should have pinpointed the *Lady Luck* the moment they came out of hyperspace. "Hello, Kessel! Is anybody listening? I'm looking for someone named Moruth Doole. I've got a business proposition for him. Please respond."

"Who is this?" a startled-sounding voice broke in. "Identify yourself."

"Name's Tymmo, and if you want any other information, have Doole ask me himself." Lando grinned at Luke. They thought using the fake name of the scam artist from the blob races added another bit of irony to their mission. "In the meantime my associate and I have some money to dispose of—half a million credits, to be exact—so run along and fetch Doole."

The speaker remained silent, evidently while the communications officer conferred with someone; then the answer came back. "We're transmitting parameters for a holding orbit, Mr., uh, Tymmo. Follow these instructions precisely. Our energy shield is currently operational and will disintegrate you if you make an unauthorized attempt to land. Do you understand?"

Luke looked at Lando, and they both shrugged. Lando spoke into the comm channel, "We'll wait right here for Doole to roll out the welcome mat. But if he takes too long, I'll go spend my cash somewhere else." He laced his fingers behind his head and leaned back in the pilot's chair. Below, Kessel filled the viewports. It was Lando's job to fast-talk them into places, while Luke would keep his eyes and Jedi senses open for any trace of Han.

Before leaving Coruscant they had doctored up false personal backgrounds for themselves, removing any mention of the New Republic but keeping enough hints at shady dealings and fast transactions to provide corroborating evidence. Luke would remain nameless, if at all possible.

A raspy voice finally burst out of the speakers. "Mr. Tymmo? This is Moruth Doole. Do I know you?"

"Not at the moment . . . but I've got a large and liquid credit account that says you might want to."

They heard a bubbling intake of breath. "And what might that mean? My communications officer said something about half a million credits?"

"I recently hit it big at the Umgullian blob races. I'm looking for a place to invest the credits, and I've always thought there was money to be made in spice mining. You willing to talk?"

Doole barely paused. "Half a million credits is certainly worth talking about. I'll send a flyer escort for you. They'll take you through a safe corridor in the energy shield."

"I look forward to meeting you face-to-face," Lando said.

Doole only made a hissing, froglike sound.

Lando left the *Lady Luck* on the landing pad of the Imperial Correction Facility, surrounded by scout vehicles, ground transports, and other ships that had been cannibalized for functional parts. He stood dressed in finery, smiling and bright-eyed. Beside him Luke wore a nondescript jumpsuit from which all insignia had been removed.

A squad dressed in hodgepodge stormtrooper armor and prison uniforms led Luke, Lando, and Artoo-Detoo toward the enormous trapezoidal edifice of the correction facility. The brooding mass of the prison seemed to throb with years of pain and punishment, working at Luke's enhanced senses. He remained silent, on guard. At least the escorts kept their weapons holstered and behaved in as welcoming a fashion as they could manage.

They rode the tube elevators that climbed the sloping front wall of the prison. Through the transparisteel Luke watched the wastelands of Kessel spread hopelessly in front of them.

When the elevators opened into the mirrored administrative substructure, the guards motioned them to follow. Clerks, bureaucrats, and seedy-looking functionaries bustled through the halls, looking busier than they wanted to be. Luke wondered if Doole had staged this activity as an impressive show for Lando; but the frantic scrambling seemed more chaotic than efficient.

Moruth Doole himself met them in one of the corridors. The squat amphibian rubbed his splayed hands together and bobbed his head at them. A mechanical contraption covering one eye focused and refocused itself.

"Welcome, Mr. Tymmo!" Doole said. "Let me apologize for our turmoil here. You haven't picked a very good time to visit. Yesterday I lost my right-hand man and my primary shift boss in a tunnel mishap. Please excuse me if I seem a bit . . . flustered."

"Quite all right," Lando said, shaking Doole's extended hand. "I've been administrator of several large mining operations myself. Sometimes the planet itself doesn't want to cooperate."

"Very true!" Doole said, opening and closing his mouth like a young rawwk begging for food. "Interesting way of looking at it."

"I hope the disaster didn't hurt your spice production too much?" Lando said.

"Oh, we'll be back up to full output in no time."

Lando gestured to Luke. "My associate is here to help me check out the details of spice mining and to advise me on its potential as an investment." He took a deep breath. "I know I must have taken you by surprise. Tell me, is there any part of your operation that I might invest in?"

Doole motioned for them to follow toward his office. His lizard-skin waistcoat rippled in the uncertain light of the corridors. "Come in, and we'll talk some more."

Doole waddled ahead, turning his head from side to side as if he had trouble seeing where he was going. Inside the former warden's office Doole indicated for them to take a seat. Artoo idled beside Luke.

Glancing around the office, Luke noticed the carbon-frozen man hanging on one wall; the life-support indicator lights on the control panel were all dark. "Friend of yours?" he asked.

Doole sputtered a hissing laugh. "A former rival. He used to be warden of the prison here, before our little revolution brought genuine capitalism to the spice-mining industry." He sat down heavily behind the desk. "May I offer you any refreshment?"

Once seated, Lando folded his hands in his lap. "I'd rather talk business first. If our negotiations look promising, maybe we can celebrate with a drink."

"Good policy," Doole said, rubbing his hands again. "Now then, I've been thinking ever since your transmission, and I may well have something that could be the perfect investment. It so happens that just before his demise, our shift boss uncovered an exceptionally rich deposit of glitterstim spice. It'll take a good amount of money and effort to make repairs in the collapsed tunnel and to exploit this resource, but the payoff can be greater than your wildest dreams."

"I have some pretty wild dreams," Lando said, flashing his broadest smile.

Luke interrupted with a stern, skeptical voice. "Those are extravagant claims, Mr. Doole. Would you allow our Artoo unit to tap into your network and inspect the profit/loss picture of your operations for, say, the past two years? That will give me hard data on which to make a recommendation to Mr. Tymmo."

Doole squirmed on being asked to open his records, but Lando pulled his credit-transfer card from his pocket. "I can assure you the droid will do no damage to your data system, and I'd be happy to give you a small deposit, if it would make you feel more comfortable. Say, five thousand?"

Doole was trapped between his own uneasy wish for

confidentiality and his need to appear aboveboard in front of a potential big investor—not to mention wanting the five thousand credits for its own sake.

"I suppose that would be all right. But I can give your droid access for only five minutes. It shouldn't need any more time than that to find the information."

Luke nodded. "That'll be fine, thank you." Artoo wouldn't waste effort checking out bogus profit/loss reports anyway. He would begin immediately trying to track down any record of Han Solo, Chewbacca, or the *Millennium Falcon*.

Humming forward, Artoo jacked into the terminal port beside Moruth Doole's desk. His data-link arm whirred as it accessed the information buried in the prison complex's computer.

While they waited, Lando continued his discussion with Doole. "I'd like to see all aspects of your spice mining and production. I'm sure you can arrange a tour immediately. Let us observe firsthand how the business works. *Including* these collapsed tunnels of yours—maybe I'd like to invest in repairs, if a good payoff seems likely."

"Uh," Doole said, looking behind him as if to find an excuse. "As I said, now is not a very good time. Perhaps we could arrange a more convenient time for you to come back—" Doole spread his squishy hands.

Lando shrugged eloquently and stood as if to leave. "I understand. If you're not interested, I can go someplace else. This money is burning a hole in my account. I want to do something with it, right *now*. There are other spice mines on other planets."

"Ah, but they are sources of ryll spice, not glitterstim—"

"They are still profitable."

Artoo withdrew and chittered to Luke. Though Luke only partially understood the droid's language, he heard enough to know that Artoo had not found Han, nor anything particularly incriminating as far as Doole was concerned. If the information banks had held any record of the *Falcon*, they had been wiped clean.

"Well, what's your droid's opinion?" Doole asked, hearing the bleeps.

"He finds nothing out of the ordinary," Luke said. He exchanged a dejected glance with Lando.

Doole stood up, beaming. "All right. I understand your concerns, Mr. Tymmo. Sometimes inconvenience must take precedence in business matters. I wouldn't want you to leave Kessel with any doubts. Come, I'll show you the spice-processing line, then we'll arrange a tour of the newly opened tunnels."

He burbled off, leading the way as they followed, still looking for any sign of Han.

A floater car took them across the surface to the entrance shaft of the collapsed tunnels. Luke and Lando ducked involuntarily as they sped into the narrow corkscrew passage.

"This was the site of an illegal mining operation back when the Imperial Correction Facility was in full control," Doole said, raising his voice above the sound of the speeding engines. "The perpetrators were caught, and this access shaft was sealed off until a recent avalanche opened everything up again."

Doole took them down into a wide grotto where part of the ceiling had fallen in. Wan light spilled down, illuminating the open areas. Workers had strung lights around the perimeter as they hammered and hauled broken rock. A crew of thirty or so milled around the chamber, shoring up walls and removing debris. The tunnels out of the grotto had been blocked by portable pneumatic doors that sealed the rest of the tunnels in blackness.

"This is a rare opportunity, Mr. Tymmo," Doole said. He had grown more and more loquacious after showing them the spice-processing rooms where the blind larvae packaged glitterstim. "Spice must be mined in total darkness, so we almost never get to see the tunnels in direct illumination. But the avalanche let in sunlight that spoiled all this glitterstim anyway. We sealed off the other shafts to preserve the rest."

"So what really happened here?" Lando asked, looking around.

"Tectonic disturbance," Doole said.

Luke could see the blackened marks where powerful blaster strikes had scored the stone walls, and he knew there was much more to this than simple seismic activity.

He felt a surge of startled fear from Lando. "What's that thing!" Lando pointed to the other side of the grotto.

Buried under a pile of jagged rubble, dozens of glassy spearlike legs protruded at all angles. Dim jewellike nodules dotted the spherical body core, eyes glazed in death. The rest of the body seemed to be made entirely of fangs. Falling chunks of rock had crushed it, and the creature's whiplike legs lay askew as if it had tried to flail the boulders aside.

Doole strutted over to the carcass. "That, my friends, seems to be the thing that creates the spice itself. It's the first such creature we've encountered, but there must be others deep in the tunnels. We're getting a xenobiologist to study it. The bulk of its body seems to be made of glitterstim itself, and the strands we pull from the tunnel walls are what it uses as a web." Doole stopped short of actually touching the fallen monster.

The guard in charge of dissection joined them. He nudged one of the sharp crystalline legs with his boot.

"We want to see if we can extract raw glitterstim from the web sac and spinnerets in the dead body."

Doole bobbed his head up and down. "Wouldn't that be something? Absolutely pure glitterstim!"

Lando nodded noncommittally. Luke, playing his part, fished around for more information. "So how does this affect your safety record? Did this creature prey on any of the miners?"

"Yes, it killed several, including the shift boss and my assistant—the ones I told you about. How many bodies have you found so far?" Doole asked the guard.

"Three fresh ones and two old ones, and we think it killed a bunch more. There's a big Wookiee and some other prisoners still unaccounted for."

Doole scowled at the guard, but quickly regained his false smile.

Luke felt cold upon hearing the news. Of course, there was no way of knowing whether the Wookiee in question was Chewbacca—the Empire had taken a great many slaves from the Wookiee homeworld of Kashyyyk, and many survivors could well have been shipped off to Kessel. Luke met Lando's gaze, and the other man shook his head ever so slightly. "Very interesting," Lando said.

"Come on, there's more to see," Doole said as he strode back to the floating cars. "I hope all this is impressing you."

"Certainly is," Lando said. "You have an amazing operation here, Moruth."

Luke remained silent. All day long he had been straining his senses, searching for some echo of Han or Chewbacca, but he had found nothing. Plenty of others wallowed in pain and misery here, but Luke found no hint of the ones he sought.

Han Solo might never have reached Kessel, and he was certainly no longer there. At least not alive.

19

The admiral's quarters on an im-
perial-class Star Destroyer were spacious and functional,
and they had been Daala's only home for more than a
decade.

Year after year she operated in a vacuum, alone as
always, following Tarkin's parting instructions with no
further input from the Grand Moff. The great distortion
of the Maw itself blacked out all external holonet trans-
missions. Her fleet had been isolated, and the crew on
her four Star Destroyers had fallen into a routine, but
Daala did not relax her grip. She was afraid to wonder
about events outside in the galaxy, confident at least that
she could count on the Empire with its unbending rules,
sometimes cruel but always clear-cut.

But now, in her turmoil, she was glad her quarters were
sealed and locked, quiet and empty, so no one could see
her like this. It would ruin her image entirely. Everything
had been cut-and-dried before the interrogation of the new
prisoners. . . .

Daala punched up the recording and watched it again, though she had already replayed the sequence a dozen times. She could mouth the words as the prisoner spoke them, but this tiny image could not convey the impact she had felt when watching him firsthand.

The man, Han Solo, sat strapped in a nightmarish, convoluted chair with steel tubes and wires and piping tangled around him. The gadgetry looked sharp and ominous—most of it served no purpose other than to increase the prisoner's terror, and in that it proved effective.

On the recording, Daala stood by Commander Kratas, the captain of her flagship, the *Gorgon*. She could smell the prisoner's fear, but his demeanor was full of bluster and sarcasm. He would crack easily.

"Tell us where you come from," Daala said. "Is the Rebel Alliance crushed yet? What has happened in the Empire?"

"Go kiss a Hutt!" Solo snapped.

Daala stared woodenly at him for a moment, then shrugged, nodding to Kratas. The commander punched a control pad, and one of the metal bars across the restraining chair hummed.

The muscles in Solo's left thigh began to spasm, jittering. His leg bounced up and down. The spasms grew worse. He had a puzzled, confused look on his face, as if he couldn't understand why his own body was suddenly behaving so strangely. The involuntary seizure clenched the muscles under his skin.

Daala smiled.

Kratas adjusted one of the controls, and Solo flinched as the muscles along the left side of his rib cage also began spasming, tightening his body, but the chair would not let him move. Solo fought back an outcry.

The seizures were not so painful as they were maddening. Daala had found that a most effective interrogation technique was simply to induce an unrelenting facial tick that made the eyes blink over and over and over again for hours without end.

"Tell us about the Empire," she said again.

"The Empire is in the garbage masher!" Solo said. Daala could see the whites of his eyes as Solo tried to look down at his rebellious leg muscles. "The Emperor is dead. He died in the explosion of the second Death Star."

Daala and Kratas both snapped their heads up. "Second Death Star? Tell me about it."

"No," Solo said.

"Yes," Daala said.

Kratas adjusted another button. The bars in the labyrinthine chair hummed, and Solo's right hand began twitching, his fingers scrabbling against the smooth metal, jittering and shaking. Solo tried to look everywhere at once.

"The second Death Star?" Daala asked again.

"It was still under construction when we set off a chain reaction in its core. Darth Vader and the Emperor were on board." Solo resisted, but he seemed to delight in telling the news.

"And what happened to the first Death Star?" Daala said.

Solo grinned. "The Alliance blew it up, too."

Daala was skeptical enough that she didn't believe him entirely. A prisoner would say anything, especially a defiant one like this. But in her gut she feared it might be true—because it explained other things, such as the years of silence.

"And what about Grand Moff Tarkin?"

"He's in a billion atoms scattered across the Yavin system. He burned with his Death Star. He paid for the lives of all the people on Alderaan, a planet he destroyed."

"Alderaan is destroyed?" Daala raised her eyebrows.

Kratas increased the power vibrating through the chair.

Tiny pearls of sweat appeared on his own forehead. Daala knew what the commander was thinking: during all these years of isolation they had been assuming the Emperor would maintain his iron grip, that the fleet of all-powerful Star Destroyers and the secret Death Star would cement Imperial rule across the galaxy. The Old Republic had lasted a thousand generations. And the Empire . . . could it have fallen in just a few decades?

"How long since the explosion of the second Death Star?"

"Seven years."

"What has happened since?" Daala finally sat down. "Tell me everything."

But Solo seemed to gain inner strength and clammed up. He glared with his dark, angry eyes. Daala sighed. It was like a rehearsed show they had to perform. Kratas adjusted the controls until Solo's entire body was a writhing, spasming mass of twitching muscles, as if a storm were happening inside his body.

Gradually, the prisoner spilled the entire story of the other battles, the civil war, Grand Admiral Thrawn, the resurrected Emperor, the truce at Bakura, the terrible conflicts in which the waning Empire had been defeated again and again—until finally she had Kratas release him. The loud humming of the chair suddenly stopped, and Han Solo slumped into exhausted bliss at being freed from the onslaught of his own muscles.

Daala motioned outside the door of the holding cell, summoning a glossy black interrogation droid that floated in with hypodermic needles glistening like spears in the dim reddish light. Solo tried to cringe back, and Daala could see the fear in his eyes.

"There," Daala said. "Now the interrogator droid will confirm everything you told us." She got up and left.

Later she had found out that Solo was indeed telling the truth in everything he said. Alone in her quarters, Admiral

Daala switched off the recording. Her head pounded with a gnawing, throbbing ache like dull fingernails scraping the inside of her skull.

One of the Maw Installation scientists, learning that the new prisoner had actually been on board the completed Death Star, demanded to speak with him. Daala would send the scientist this interrogation report—after she edited it, of course. Sometimes it was impossible to keep these prima donna scientists happy. They had such a narrow view of things.

Right now Daala had greater worries. She had to decide what to do with this new information.

In her quarters Daala stood between two full-length curved mirrors that projected a reflection of her body, head to toe. Her olive-gray uniform showed no wrinkle, only crisp creases and near-invisible seams. Through a strict regimen of exercises and drills, she had not added a fraction to her weight during her long assignment; her appearance, though older and harder now, still pleased her.

Daala wore her bright admiral's insignia proudly over her left breast: a row of six scarlet rectangles set above a row of blue rectangles. To her knowledge she was the only woman ever to wear such a rank in the Imperial Navy. It had been a special promotion, given directly by Grand Moff Tarkin himself, and it was possible the Emperor did not even know of it. He certainly did not know about the Maw Installation.

Her coppery hair flowed over her shoulders, rippled down her back to below her hips. More than a decade ago Daala had arrived at Maw Installation with her hair cropped short and bristly, part of the humiliation the Imperial military academy inflicted upon female candidates.

After being sealed inside the Maw, though, Daala was placed in charge by direct order from Tarkin. Asinine regulations-for-the-sake-of-regulations meant nothing to her anymore. She refused to cut her hair, as a gesture of her own independence: rank had its privileges. She felt Tarkin would have approved. But Tarkin was dead now.

Turning, she dimmed the lights, then activated the door. Outside, two bodyguards snapped to attention and continued staring ahead. Despite Maw Installation's isolation, Daala insisted on peak performance, regular drills, war-gaming sessions. She had been trained in the Imperial military mold; though the system had done its best to squash her ambitions, Daala followed its tenets.

Beneath their armor the two guards were well built and attractive; but Daala had not taken a lover since Grand Moff Tarkin. After him fantasizing had been enough.

"Escort me to the shuttle bay," she said, stepping into the corridor. "I'm going down to the Installation." She strode off, hearing the bodyguards march behind her, weapons ready. "Inform the duty commander that I have a meeting with Tol Sivron." One of the bodyguards muttered into his helmet comlink.

She strode down the corridors, pondering the complexity of her ship, the troops, the support personnel. In the Imperial fleet a single Star Destroyer housed thirty-seven thousand crew and ninety-seven hundred troops, but because of the secrecy of the Maw Installation, Tarkin had assigned her only a skeleton crew—people without families, without connections to the outside, some recruited from worlds devastated by the early battles of the Empire.

Even under rigid discipline, though, her crew had been trapped here for eleven years with no furloughs, no R and R other than the meager amusement facilities available on board. Her troops had grown weary of the entertainment libraries—restless, bored, and angry at being placed on standby alert for so long without word from the outside. They were well armed and itching to go out and *do* something—as was Daala herself.

At her fingertips Daala had the might of sixty turbolaser batteries, sixty ion cannons, and ten tractor-beam projectors, one of which had just been used to capture the battered Imperial shuttle. Inside the hangar bays the *Gorgon* alone carried six TIE fighter squadrons, two gamma-class assault shuttles, twenty AT-AT walkers, and thirty AT-ST scout walkers.

Three more identical ships, the *Manticore*, the *Basilisk*, and the *Hydra*, orbited Maw Installation, also under Daala's command. Years ago Moff Tarkin had taken Daala herself to the Kuat Drive Yards to watch her four Star Destroyers under construction.

Tarkin and Daala had flown a small inspection shuttle around the enormous superstructures being assembled in orbit. The two remained silent for the most part, staring at the enormity of the project. Around them in space the tiny lights of workers, transport vessels, rubble smelters, and girder extruders made a hive of activity.

Tarkin had placed a hand on her shoulders, squeezing with a grip made of steel cords. "Daala," he said, "I am giving you enough power to turn any planet to slag."

Now, aboard the Star Destroyer *Gorgon*, Admiral Daala entered a personnel lift that took her and her bodyguards from the command quarters below the bridge tower to one of the hangar bays. She did not announce her arrival when the doors slid open. Daala was pleased to see her troops bustling about the TIE fighters, the shuttles, and service vehicles. After so many years of boredom, her personnel kept every system functioning perfectly.

Only months after the completion of Maw Installation, Daala had noticed a malaise creeping through the personnel. Part of it was because of her, she was sure; commanded by the only female flag officer, assigned to baby-sit a bunch of scientists in the most protected spot in the galaxy, the troops had grown lax. But a few graphic executions and continual threats kept Daala's crew constantly on edge, honing their skills and making it inconceivable for them to shirk their duties.

That tactic had been one of Tarkin's prime lessons. *Command through the fear of force rather than force itself.* Daala had 180,000 people at her disposal, not counting the weapons designers in Maw Installation itself. She did not want to waste them.

She glanced up and down the hangar, her molten-metal hair trailing behind her. Inside an electromagnetic cage that shielded the entire vessel, technicians scoured the battered Imperial shuttle *Endor* that had been brought in by the new captives. *Endor*—what kind of name was that? She had never heard the term before. The technicians would be checking for service markings, locator beacons, and course-log files.

For a moment Daala considered taking the battered shuttle itself down to Tol Sivron, the chief scientist of Maw Installation; the effect would probably shock him into paying attention to her for once. But that would be a childish gesture. She let the technicians continue their work and chose instead the Imperial shuttle *Edict*.

"I can pilot this myself," she said to her bodyguards. "Leave me." On the flight down she wanted time alone. She knew what Sivron would say on hearing the news, but this time she would not let him get away with it.

The bodyguards dropped back and to the side as Daala stepped up the ramp into the shuttle. She moved with quick, habitual movements, powering up the engines, running through the automated checklist. She mounted the headset nodes to her temple and to her ear, listening to her course vector as she raised the *Edict* from its pad and arrowed it out through the magnetic shields that closed off the hangar bay from the vacuum of space.

Surrounding her was the colorful, deadly shell of gases

swirling into the endless gullets of black holes. Below hung Maw Installation itself, a cluster of planetoids crammed at the exact center of the gravitational island. The surfaces of the barren rocks touched in some places, grinding together. Immense bridges and bands held the asteroids in place. Access tubes and transit rails connected the cluster of drifting rocks.

Under Grand Moff Tarkin's direction Imperial constructors had ferried the rocks across space and through the obstacle course into the Maw. The insides of the asteroids were hollowed out into habitation chambers, laboratory areas, prototype assembly bays, and meeting halls.

If we present the citizens with a weapon so powerful, so immense as to defy all conceivable attack against it, a weapon invulnerable and invincible in battle, that shall become the symbol for the Empire. Daala had read a draft of the communiqué Tarkin had sent to the Emperor, urging the creation of superweapons. *We may need only a handful of these weapons to subjugate thousands of worlds, each containing millions upon millions of beings. Such a weapon must have force great enough to dispatch an entire system, and the fear it shall inspire will be great enough for you to rule the galaxy unchallenged.*

After getting permission for his scheme, Tarkin had used his new authority as Grand Moff to put together this supersecret think-tank installation, where he could isolate the most brilliant scientists and theoreticians, giving them orders to develop new weapons for the Emperor. Since Tarkin took credit for everything without citing his sources, the Emperor himself did not know of the installation's existence.

The workers and architects who built the place had boarded a return ship, thinking their job finished, but Daala had reprogrammed their navicomputers herself with an incorrect course out of the Maw. Instead of flying to their freedom, they had plunged straight into the mouth of a black hole. No loose ends.

The secret of Maw Installation had been protected. After Tol Sivron and his teams proved the initial concept of the Death Star, Grand Moff Tarkin had taken one of the Installation's top scientists, Bevel Lemelisk, to the Outer Rim to oversee actual construction of the first production-model Death Star.

Tarkin's last words to the Maw scientists had been a challenge: "Good. Now create an even more powerful weapon. Surpassing the Death Star may seem inconceivable, but we must maintain our superiority, we must maintain a sense of fear among the citizens of the Empire. The Death Star *is* terrible. Think of something worse. That is your reason for existence."

Tarkin gave them nine years to develop his next-generation ultimate weapon. And now, since Tarkin was dead and no one else knew Maw Installation even existed—Daala could make her own decisions, plan her own course of action.

Finally reaching the small gravity field of the central administrative asteroid, Daala secured the shuttle *Edict* in the docking bay. She stood beside her shuttle, breathing deeply of the dusty, exhaust-laden air and already wishing she could be back on the gleaming and sterile decks of the *Gorgon*. She would deal with Tol Sivron quickly, then return.

A contingent of stormtroopers assigned to ground duty bustled to assist her. "Follow me," she said. A show of force would smother any protests from the scientist administrator.

She did not announce her arrival but strode directly through the anterooms, startling the various clerks and administrative assistants. The stormtroopers stood at attention. The clerks stared at them, then slowly took their seats again and refrained from making any outbursts.

"Tol Sivron, I need to speak with you," Daala said, entering his office. "I have some important news."

The scientist administrator's office was cluttered, but with all the wrong things. More a bureaucrat than a scientist, Tol Sivron required the theoreticians and designers to build concept models and tiny prototypes of their ideas, which Sivron left on shelves, on furniture, in alcoves. Daala guessed that Sivron played with them as toys during dull moments.

Around the office lay piles of proposals, design studies, regular progress reports, charts of optimized parameters that the scientist administrator required in hardcopy. His clerks studied these reports, then wrote their own reports summarizing them and referencing still further documents. Daala didn't believe the administrator read any of them.

Tol Sivron swiveled his chair to look at her with a bored expression. "News? We haven't had any news in a decade."

Sivron was a Twi'lek, pasty-faced and hairless, with two whiplike head-tails that dangled from his skull. The tentacles fell over his shoulders like two skinless blood-eels sucking the back of his cranium. Sivron's close-set piglike eyes and mouthful of jagged teeth heightened Daala's disgust. Twi'leks were generally a disreputable lot, slinking around with smugglers and acting as henchmen for crime lords like Jabba the Hutt. Though Daala rarely questioned Grand Moff Tarkin's decisions, she didn't understand how Tol Sivron had obtained his position here.

"Well, we have news today. We captured three prisoners who blundered into the Maw in a stolen Imperial shuttle. We have put them all through deep questioning, and I see no reason to doubt the veracity of this information, as unpleasant as it may seem."

"So what is this unpleasant information?"

Daala kept her face absolutely rigid. "The Emperor is dead, the Rebels have won. A few warlords tried to put the Empire back together, but they merely caused years of civil war. A new Republic is now the primary government in the galaxy."

Sivron sat up in shock. In a nervous gesture his head-tails coiled behind his neck. "But how could that happen? With our Death Star design—"

"Grand Moff Tarkin built one Death Star, but the Rebels managed to steal the plans, and somehow they discovered a flaw, a thermal-exhaust port that allowed one small fighter access to the reactor core. The Rebels destroyed the Death Star and killed Tarkin."

"I'll assign a team to look over the plans so we can correct this flaw!" Sivron said, a matter of pride to him. "At once!"

"How is that going to help anything now?" Daala snapped. "Tarkin had Bevel Lemelisk with him on the outside. After the first Death Star was destroyed, the Emperor himself asked Lemelisk to design a larger model, this time eliminating the known flaw. The second Death Star was still under construction when the Rebels destroyed it."

Sivron scowled, as if trying to figure out how he could solve a problem already several years old. As the years stretched out with no word from outside, Sivron had sent self-destructing drones through the fiery walls of the Maw, carrying coded transmission bursts, updates for Tarkin. Daala had strict orders not to leave Maw Installation, and so they waited. And waited.

Daala's primary mistake had been overestimating the abilities of her mentor, Tarkin. She had graduated from the Imperial military academy on Carida, one of the toughest training grounds for military service in the Empire. She had excelled in every curriculum, defeated many warriors in single combat, used her strategic skills to wipe out entire armies in war games.

But because she was a woman, and because female officers were extremely rare in Imperial military service, the Caridan academy assigned Daala to difficult, thankless jobs, while they promoted the less talented men—men she herself had bested time and again—into positions of authority.

Out of frustration Daala had created a false persona in the computer networks, a pseudonym under which she could make suggestions that would be listened to. After a handful of these truly radical ideas paid off, Moff Tarkin had come to Carida to find this brilliant new tactician— but his detective work had uncovered Daala instead.

Luckily, Tarkin was more innovative and open-minded than the Emperor. He quietly reassigned Daala to his personal staff, took her to the Outer Rim territories on his fleet of Star Destroyers, and let her work with him.

They became lovers, two like minds, hard in spirit and unforgiving. Though he was older than she, Tarkin had a power and a charisma that Daala admired. Gaunt and tireless in his quiet viciousness, he had a self-confidence so great that he did not flinch even in the presence of Darth Vader.

To keep Daala hidden, Grand Moff Tarkin gave her four Star Destroyers and charged her with the task of guarding Maw Installation. But now that she had obtained new information from the captives, everything was changed. Everything.

Sivron stared at her with anger glowing in his eyes. "Where are these captives now?"

"In detention cells on board the *Gorgon*. They are recuperating from the . . . rigors of interrogation."

"What if someone comes looking for them?" He turned to glance out the transparisteel window on his office wall.

"They were escapees from the spice-mining operation on

Kessel. They had no idea where they were going. They'll be presumed lost in the Maw—I myself can't understand how they survived the passage through the cluster in the first place."

"Why didn't you just dispose of them?" Sivron asked.

Daala maintained her patience with an effort. This was yet another example of Twi'lek shortsightedness. "Because they are the only link with the outside we've had in a decade. Qwi Xux has already requested an interview with the prisoners to ask them for details about the actual Death Star. We may need to pump them for further information— before we decide what to do next."

Sivron blinked his piggish eyes. "What to do? What do you mean? What *is* there to do?"

She crossed her arms over her chest. "We can take the new Sun Crusher and destroy the New Republic system by system." She stared at him with her green eyes, not blinking.

The Twi'lek squirmed. "But the Sun Crusher isn't finished yet. We still have tests to run, reports to file—"

"You have been procrastinating for two years. You are behind schedule thanks to your bureaucracy and ineptness. Grand Moff Tarkin is not coming back, and you no longer have an excuse to delay. I need the weapon now, and I'm going to take it."

Her mind kept replaying the words Tarkin had told her while inspecting the Kuat Drive Yards. *I am giving you enough power to turn any planet to slag.* And with the newly designed Sun Crusher weapon, she could bring the New Republic to its knees.

"If Solo is telling the truth," Daala said, "then my fleet could be the most powerful remnant of the Imperial Navy." She picked up one of Tol Sivron's small models. "We can't just wait here any longer. Now it's our turn to show them what we can do."

20

The Caridan ambassador arrived
with his entourage on the recently repaired west landing
platform, far from the Imperial Palace. His diplomatic
shuttle looked like a glossy black beetle, bristling with
weapons that had been remotely neutralized before the
ship was allowed to approach Coruscant.

On the landing platform Leia waited to greet Ambassador Furgan with a full contingent of New Republic honor
guard. The wind picked up, blowing around the tall buildings, as if trying to push the Caridan delegation back in
the direction it had come. She wore her formal government
robes as well as rank insignia for the Alliance forces.

Carida, with its powerful military training center, was
one of the most important strongholds still loyal to the
Empire. If she could crack open negotiations with them,
her coup would not be soon forgotten. But the Caridan
system was going to be a tough jewel-fruit to crack, especially with a rude and icy ambassador like Furgan.

The shuttle's hatch hissed open as the denser air of

Carida rushed out. Two stormtroopers marched down the ramp, shouldering ceremonial blaster rifles equipped with bayonets. Their white armor gleamed from meticulous polishing. They moved like droids, walking off the ramp and stepping to either side, then freezing in position as a second pair of stormtroopers followed them down and waited at the end of the ramp.

Ambassador Furgan strode down, stubby-legged and self-important, as if to ceremonial music. His uniform was spattered with more badges, insignia, and ribbons than any person could possibly have earned in a lifetime.

After two more stormtrooper officers followed the ambassador down, Furgan drew a deep breath, looking into the distance and ignoring Leia. "Ah, the air of Imperial Center." He turned toward the waiting reception committee, beetling his thick brows. "Smells a bit sour now, though. The taint of rebellion."

Leia disregarded the comment. "Welcome to Coruscant, Ambassador Furgan. I am Minister of State Leia Organa Solo."

"Yes, yes," Furgan said impatiently. "After Mon Mothma's words about the extreme importance of Carida, I expected her to send more than a minor official to greet me. A slap in the face."

Leia had to fall back on some of Luke's temper-controlling exercises, a Jedi mind-blanking technique that allowed her to quell the surge of anger. "I see you have not taken the time to familiarize yourself with the structure of our government, Ambassador. Though Mon Mothma is the New Republic's Chief of State, the Cabinet is the actual governing body, of which the Minister of State and my subordinate diplomatic corps comprise perhaps the most important arm."

Leia stopped herself, angry with Furgan for goading her, and angry with herself for letting him manipulate her into petty games. Mon Mothma had instructed her to extend every diplomatic courtesy to the ambassador. She wished Han or Luke were there beside her.

"Mon Mothma has a great many other duties, but she has arranged for a brief face-to-face meeting with you later in the day," Leia said. "Until then, would you like me to show you to your quarters? Some refreshment, perhaps, after your journey?"

Furgan's eyes looked like small, overripe berries as he directed his gaze at her. "My bodyguards will go to my quarters first. They will sweep every inch of the rooms, every appliance, every wall and floor to remove hidden listening devices or assassination tools. The remaining guards will be with me at every moment. They will provide my food and drink from our own supplies to ensure against any possibility of poisoning."

Leia was appalled at his insinuation. She stopped herself from insisting that Furgan's actions were not necessary, since that would no doubt play directly into his hands. Instead, she showed him a small indulgent smile. "Of course, if such things make you feel more comfortable. . . ."

"In the meantime," Furgan said, "I would like an immediate tour of the Imperial Palace. Arrange one. I came on a pilgrimage to see my Emperor's home and to pay my respects."

Leia hesitated. "We hadn't planned on—"

Furgan held up a hand. Beside him the stormtroopers snapped even more stiffly to attention. The ambassador took one step closer to Leia, as if trying to look intimidating. "Nevertheless, you will arrange it."

That afternoon Mon Mothma stood in the dimmed audience chamber, waiting at the base of the holoprojector's controls. Though she had a thousand other duties to attend to, Carida seemed the likeliest flash point of resistance to New Republic stability. She had made it clear to Leia that she considered her sacrifice of time an investment to avert a possible war.

Without moving Mon Mothma seemed to fill the room with her quiet, commanding presence. Leia never ceased admiring her subtle but undeniable power, which Mon Mothma managed to exhibit even without Jedi training.

Leia followed Ambassador Furgan as he strode down the ramp to the base of the holoprojector. Grumpy, he looked behind him to where his stormtrooper bodyguards waited at the entrance to the chamber. Furgan had refused to leave them behind, and Mon Mothma had refused to let even disarmed Imperial stormtroopers near her. The power play had been brief and sharp, but in the end Mon Mothma allowed the stormtroopers to wait within sight of the ambassador, though outside the chamber.

But she had also won a seemingly minor concession. Mon Mothma required the stormtroopers to remove their helmets while they remained in her presence. The soldiers stood unmasked, holding the skull-like helmets under their arms, revealed to be humans, young cadets dressed in armor but with their anonymity taken away.

"Stand right there, Ambassador Furgan," she said without formally greeting him. "I would like to show you something."

The holoprojector shimmered, and the known galaxy filled the room, billions of star-specks flung in swirling arms throughout the enclosed chamber. The lights automatically dimmed as the sea-spray of stars came into focus. At the doorway the stormtroopers craned their necks to stare up at the huge image. On the chamber floor both Mon Mothma and Ambassador Furgan seemed insignificant.

"This is our galaxy," Mon Mothma said. "We have meticulously plotted every recorded system. These stars"—she waved her hand, and a wash of blue spangled across the arms of the galaxy—"have already sworn their allegiance to the New Republic. Others have remained neutral, though not unfriendly to our cause." A sprinkling of green appeared among the stars.

"The darkened area is what remains of the Ssi Ruuk Imperium." She indicated a splotch covering a portion of one spiral arm. "We have not yet fully explored their worlds, though it has been seven years since Imperial and Alliance forces joined hands at Bakura to drive out the invaders.

"Finally," Mon Mothma said, "we know of these systems that still remain loyal to the fallen Empire." A much smaller splash of red dusted the image, concentrated primarily toward the galactic core, from which the resurrected Emperor had launched his forces. "As you can see, your support is dwindling rapidly."

Furgan did not seem impressed. "Anyone can paint dots on a map."

Inwardly outraged, Leia marveled at the quiet way Mon Mothma handled the situation. Her voice did not grow louder; she merely looked at him with her calm, deep eyes. "You are welcome to speak to any of the ambassadors from these worlds to confirm their allegiances."

"Ambassadors can be bribed as easily as colors can be changed on a projection map."

This time Mon Mothma's voice grew just a bit brittle. "There are no bribes that can change the facts, Ambassador Furgan."

"If that is the case, then sometimes the facts themselves must be changed."

Leia could not keep herself from rolling her eyes. In a way this was amusing, but it seemed like a waste of time. Furgan was as unchangable as a man frozen in carbonite.

The entire planetary surface of Coruscant had been covered with layer upon layer of buildings, rebuilt, demolished, and rebuilt again. Galactic governments changed over the millennia, but Coruscant had always been the center of politics.

The complex construction patterns and towering metal and transparisteel pinnacles made weather difficult to predict. Occasionally, unexpected storms coalesced out of water evaporating from millions of exhaust vents, condensing and rising from the skyscraper forests, making small squalls that dumped rain down upon the hard surfaces of the buildings.

As the various diplomats gathered in the Skydome Botanical Gardens for Ambassador Furgan's reception, a sudden flurry of raindrops pattered down on the transparent panes, masking the bright curtains of Coruscant's aurora.

In the distance, near the horizon, the rebuilt Imperial Palace stood like a cobbled-together cathedral and pyramid, showing signs of many different eras. Leia had not wanted Furgan's reception to be held in any place that recalled the fallen Emperor's opulence and grandeur.

The Skydome Botanical Gardens rested on the level roof of an isolated skyscraper. Constructed by an Old Republic philanthropist who had grown rich by establishing the Galactic News Service, the giant terrarium was a carefully tended place with compartmentalized environments to house and display otherwise extinct or exotic flora from various systems in the galaxy.

Leia arrived with Threepio and her two children in tow just as the rain began to fall against the transparent ceiling. As Leia stepped through the door, she held herself defensively, her justifications on the tip of her tongue. She knew the presence of the twins might cause a stir at a stuffy diplomatic reception, but she did not care.

Throughout the day Furgan had pushed her around, complaining, demanding, acting generally rude. Leia had given up all of her time with the twins to be with the ambassador, and she decided that it was no longer worth the misery. She might be an important Cabinet member in the New Republic, but she was also a mother, still trying to adapt to the new demands on her time. In her quarters while changing clothes for the reception, Leia had felt her simmering resentment come to a boil. If she was going to be gone all the time anyway, she might as well have left Jacen and Jaina with Winter!

Besides, Threepio accompanied them, and he was a protocol droid. He could watch the twins and also help out with the fine points of the reception and translation if need be.

Since Han had disappeared, she was worried to the point of nausea much of the time. Luke and Lando had sent no word yet. She needed to have some stable point in her life. Leia almost hoped someone would challenge her about bringing the twins, so she could lash out.

When she passed through the door, Furgan's stormtrooper goons stopped her. The still-helmetless stormtroopers looked uncomfortable at meeting her eye to eye, but they stood firmly in her path. Behind them an equal number of New Republic guards stood at attention, watching the stormtroopers.

"What is the problem"—she glanced at the stormtrooper's insignia and deliberately misread it—"Lieutenant?"

"*Captain,*" he corrected. "We're checking everyone. A precaution against assassins."

"Assassins?" she said, deciding to be amused rather than upset. "I see."

One of the stormtroopers removed a handheld scanner and played it over Leia's body, testing for hidden weapons. Leia icily submitted to the scan. "This is for the ambassador's safety," he said. He looked disapprovingly at Jacen and Jaina. "We weren't informed there would be children attending."

"Are you afraid one of *them* is going to murder Ambassador Furgan?" Leia stared at the man's naked, pale face, scowling until he flinched. "That doesn't say much for your skills as a bodyguard, does it, Captain?" His flustered fidgeting was worth any amount of inconvenience he might cause her, Leia thought.

"Just routine precautions." The captain scanned Jacen and Jaina, showing visible discomfort at having to do so. When his task was complete, he still refused to move aside.

Leia crossed her arms over her chest. "Now what?"

"Your droid, Minister," the captain said. "We need to run a complete systems check. He could have assassin droid programming."

"Me, sir?" Threepio said. "Oh, my! You can't be serious."

Leia rolled her eyes at the mere thought of the prissy protocol droid being an assassin. "And how long will this complete systems check take?"

"Not long." The captain took a different scanner that trailed disconnected leads.

"Mistress Leia, I object!" Threepio's voice carried an edge of panic. "If you will recall, I have been maliciously reprogrammed in the past! I never want to trust a strange probe again."

Leia spoke to the droid but let her gaze bore into the

stormtrooper captain's eyes. "Let him do it Threepio. And if your programming is altered in the slightest, this man will be responsible for a galactic incident that could well lead to war—a war in which his own home system of Carida would be the prime target for the combined forces of the New Republic."

"I will be very careful, Minister," the stormtrooper said.

"Indeed, sir, you will!" Threepio insisted.

When they finally managed to get through to the reception area, the rainfall dwindled to a trickle. People wandered along the tour-paths to observe the brilliant and bizarre shapes of alien plant life. As the guests stepped through forcefield environmental barriers, the humidity and temperature changed drastically to provide proper growing conditions for various types of plants. Tiny placards displayed scientific names written in a dozen different alphabets.

Holding their mother's hands, Jacen and Jaina stared with amazement at the people garbed in diplomatic finery, the exotic plants from distant worlds.

In a bright desert scenario at the center of the chamber, a monstrously large tentacle-cactus served hors d'oeuvres, waving its thick stalks back and forth and displaying tiny sandwiches, fruit slices, sausages, and pastries stuck on its long spines. Guests snatched snacks from the spines whenever the tentacle-cactus waved in their direction.

Stocky Ambassador Furgan seemed the center of attention, but everyone looked at him from the corners of their eyes rather than speaking to him directly. Feeling her political obligations, Leia sighed and walked toward him, the children trotting beside her.

Furgan fixed his gaze on the twins and drained the drink he was holding. She watched as he held the empty glass to a pump flask at his right hip. Furgan depressed the button and squirted himself a new drink of honey-greenish liquid. *Of course,* she thought, *anyone paranoid about poisons would bring his own supply.* He wore an identical flask on his left hip.

"So, Minister Organa Solo, these are the famous Jedi twins? Jacen and Jaina, I believe you named them? Don't you have a third child as well, named Anakin?"

Leia blinked, unnerved that Furgan knew so much about her family. "Yes, the baby is elsewhere—safe and protected." She knew he could not possibly have uncovered the location of the sheltered planet, but a mother's instinct magnified her fear.

Furgan patted Jaina on the head. "I hope you protect these two as well. It would be a shame for such sweet children to become political pawns."

"They are very safe," Leia said, suddenly feeling helpless. Keeping an eye on the ambassador, she turned the twins around. "You two take Threepio and go play now."

"It will be a very educational experience for them, Mistress Leia," Threepio said, bustling the children off to look at the plant exhibits.

Furgan continued his conversation with Leia. "If you want my opinion, it's too bad the Emperor didn't manage to wipe out all of the Jedi. Incomplete tasks always end up causing trouble."

"And why are you so afraid of the Jedi Knights?" Leia said. Though she disliked this line of conversation, she might glean some information from Furgan.

The ambassador took a long sip from his drink. "My feeling is that with our sophisticated technology, we should not cringe in fear of sorcery and bizarre mental powers that belong only to a few random individuals. It seems elitist. Jedi Knights? They were like strongmen for a weak old government."

Leia took up the debate. "The Emperor whom you

revere so much was very powerful in the Force, as was Darth Vader. How are they so different?"

"The Emperor is *entitled* to special powers," Furgan said, as if stating the obvious. "After all, he's the Emperor. And Vader turned out to be a traitor in the end. As I understand it, he was the one who actually killed the Emperor. All the more reason to outlaw such powers."

Leia knew he must have seen Luke's widely broadcast speech to the Council. "Nevertheless, the Jedi *have* managed to survive, and the entire order of Jedi Knights will be restored. My brother will see to that. Within a few years the new Jedi Knights will fill the same role as the old, as protectors of the Republic."

"Too bad," Furgan said, turning away to seek other conversation, but no one seemed to want to talk to him.

Threepio lost track of the twins almost immediately, when they decided to play hide-and-seek among the flora exhibits, crawling under guardrails too low for Threepio to manage, then chasing each other around areas marked DO NOT ENTER. When the droid called for them to come back, Jacen and Jaina developed a selective hearing difficulty and continued to dash away.

He chased them through a grove of mucus trees that dripped yellow pollinated ooze all over his polished body shell; but at least the slime left a trail of footprints for him to follow. Threepio wailed in dismay when he saw the small footprints leading directly into the "Carnivorous Plants" area.

"Oh, my!" he said, imagining bloodthirsty shrubs already digesting pieces of the small children. Before he could sound an all-out alarm, though, Threepio heard Jacen's high-pitched giggles, joined by his sister's laughter. Using directional locators, Threepio bustled back to the center of the exhibit.

Sitting in the middle of the giant tentacle-cactus, the twins played with the waving fronds, oblivious to the thorns. Somehow they had blithely eased their way past the daggerlike points and made a pillow out of the central mass of fine new bristles.

"Master Jacen and Mistress Jaina, come out of there this instant!" Threepio said in a stern voice. "I must insist!" Instead, Jaina giggled and waved to him.

In a tizzy Threepio wondered how he could rescue the children from the great plant without dislodging any of the hors d'oeuvres.

A lull fell in the conversation, the type of pause that often occurs in forced social situations. During the quiet Ambassador Furgan made his move. "I require your attention!" he called.

Leia watched him suddenly step away from her. Not knowing what he might do, she tensed, ready for anything.

The few conversations stuttered to a halt. All eyes turned to the Caridan ambassador. Mon Mothma had been chatting with General Jan Dodonna, the aged tactician who had planned the strike on the first Death Star. Mon Mothma raised her eyebrows, curious at Furgan's call for silence. Jan Dodonna stopped telling his tale and held his hands in midgesture as he stared.

Furgan took his empty glass and dropped it to his hip, filling it from the left hip flask this time. Leia wondered if he had already emptied the right flask.

Raising his glass high, he took one step toward Mon Mothma, grinning. Leia watched in disbelief. Was the rude ambassador going to propose a toast?

Furgan looked around the enclosed Skydome, making

certain he had everyone's attention. Even the patchy rain had ceased. "To all gathered here, I wish to be heard. As ambassador of Carida, I have been empowered to speak for the Imperial military training center, my planet, and my entire system. Therefore, I must deliver a message to you all."

He raised his voice and raised his glass. "To Mon Mothma, who calls herself leader of the New Republic—" With a vicious sneer he hurled his drink into her face. The honey-green liquid splashed on her cheeks, her hair, her chest. She staggered back, appalled. Jan Dodonna caught her shoulders, steadying her; his mouth gaped open in astonishment.

The New Republic guards at the door immediately drew their weapons but somehow refrained from firing.

"—we denounce your foul rebellion of lawbreakers and murderers. You have tried to impress me with the number of other weak-minded systems that have joined your Alliance, but no amount of rabble can erase your crimes against the Empire."

He smashed his empty glass on the floor and ground the shards under his boot heel. "Carida will never surrender to your so-called New Republic."

With a flourish Furgan took his entourage and stormed off. At the doorway the gathered stormtroopers triumphantly placed the white helmets back on their heads, hiding their faces, and followed the ambassador out. The New Republic guards stared after them, weapons ready but not knowing what to do.

After a shocked silence the crowd erupted into a babble of outraged conversations. Leia ran to the Chief of State. Dodonna was already swabbing at Mon Mothma's damp robes.

The sticky drink drying on her face, Mon Mothma forced a smile for Leia. Into the rising hubbub of indignation she said, "Well, we didn't lose anything by trying, did we?"

In her disappointment Leia could not answer.

The tinny voice of Threepio burst over the background noise. "Excuse me, Mistress Leia?"

Leia frantically looked around for the twins, afraid Furgan had somehow kidnapped them during his diversion, but was relieved when she saw Jacen and Jaina standing with their faces pressed against the curved window looking out at the skyline of Imperial City.

Finally, from the corner of her eye, she noticed a golden arm flailing about in alarm. Somehow Threepio had gotten tangled in the tentacle-cactus exhibit; even from across the room Leia could see how badly scratched his plating had become. Hors d'oeuvres lay scattered about the floor.

"Could anyone assist me in getting free from this plant?" Threepio cried. "Please?"

21

an Solo seemed to be drowning in a syrup of nightmares. He could not escape the drugged and painful interrogation, as the hardened and porcelain-beautiful face of Admiral Daala stared at him and pummeled him with questions.

"Just put him over here," a woman's trilling voice said. Not Daala.

His body was being dragged like luggage across a floor.

"We have been ordered to stand guard," said a fuzzed voice filtered through a stormtrooper helmet.

"Stand guard, then, but do it outside my lab. I want to talk to him in peace." The woman's voice again.

"For your own protection—" the stormtrooper began. Han felt himself dropped to the floor. His limbs didn't seem to remember how to bend.

"Protection? What is he going to do—he doesn't seem to have the energy to sneeze. If you left any unscrambled memories in his head, I want to pick at them without any interference."

Han felt himself hauled upright again, his arms wrapped behind him. Cold, smooth stone pressed against his back. "Yes, yes," the woman's voice said, "chain him to the column. I'm sure I'll be safe. I promise to stay out of reach of his fangs."

He heard the marching boots of stormtroopers leaving the room. His mind became active long before his body figured out how to respond. He remembered parts of the interrogation, but not all of it. What had he told Admiral Daala? His heart began pounding harder. Had he divulged any crucial secrets? Did he even *know* any crucial secrets?

He was fairly certain he had told her the basic events about the fall of the Empire and the rise of the New Republic—but that caused no harm, and it might even lead to benefits. If Daala knew she had no chance, perhaps she would surrender. And if banthas had wings . . .

His eyes finally opened grudgingly, letting light slam inside. He flinched away from returning vision, but eventually his eyes focused. He found himself in a spacious room, some kind of laboratory or analysis center, not his detention cell on the *Gorgon*. He heard singing and the sound of flutes.

Han turned his head to see a willowy alien woman standing in front of a device that seemed to be a combination musical keyboard and data-entry pad. He had heard her voice arguing with the stormtrooper. She hummed a complex string of notes as her fingers played on the musical keys; in front of her a rotating blueprint of a three-dimensional triangular shape took form, like a shard of glass capped with a tetrahedron and some sort of energy pod dangling from the lower point. With each tone the woman processed, additional lines appeared on the complicated diagram.

Han worked his tongue around in his mouth and tried

to talk. He meant to say, "Who are you?" but his lips and vocal cords would not cooperate. The sounds came out more like "Whaaaaa yuuuurrrr?"

Startled, the female alien fluttered her slender hands around the 3-D geometrical image. Then she pranced over to where Han lay. She wore a badge on her smock, imprinted with her likeness and glittering holograms of the kind used for cipher-locks.

She was an attractive humanoid, tall and slender, with a bluish tint to her skin. Her gossamer hair seemed like strands of pearlescent feathers. When she spoke, her voice was high and reedy. Her eyes were wide and deep blue, carrying an expression of perpetual astonishment.

"I've been waiting for you to wake up!" she said. "I have so many questions to ask you. Is it true that you actually set foot on the first Death Star, and you got a look at the second one while it was under construction? Tell me what it was like. Anything you can remember. Every detail would be like a treasure trove to me."

The babbled questions came at him too quickly to assimilate. What did the Death Star have to do with anything? That was ten years ago!

Instead, Han focused his gaze past her. Pastel gases glowed on the other side of the broad window, swirling around the insatiable mouths of the black holes. He counted all four Star Destroyers in orbital formation high above. That meant he must be somewhere in the little cluster of planetoids in the center of the gravitational island.

And he was alone. Neither Kyp nor Chewbacca had ended up here with him. He hoped they had at least survived Daala's vicious interrogation. He worked his mouth, trying to form words again. "Who are you?"

The alien woman touched her badge with one of her long-fingered hands. "My name is Qwi Xux. And I know that you are Han Solo. I've read a hardcopy of the debriefing you gave Admiral Daala."

Debriefing? Did she mean the interrogation, the torture chair that made his entire body spasm?

Qwi Xux's entire demeanor seemed superficial and distracted, as if she were paying only a small amount of attention to details while she kept her mind preoccupied with something else. "Now then, please tell me about the Death Star. I'm very eager to hear what you remember. You're the first person I can talk to who was actually there."

Han wondered if the interrogation drugs were still muddling his brain, or if there really was a reason why someone should want him to talk about the defunct Death Star. And why should he tell this Imperial scientist anything anyway? Had he divulged anything important to Daala? What if she took her four Star Destroyers and attacked Coruscant?

"I've already been interrogated." He was pleased to hear his words come out clearly enough to be understood this time.

In one bluish hand Qwi held up a short printout. "I want your real impressions about it," she continued. "What did it sound like? What did it feel like when you walked down the corridors? Tell me everything you can remember." She wrung her hands in barely restrained excitement.

"No."

His response apparently shocked Qwi enough that she took a step backward and let out a startled musical squawk. "You have to! I'm one of the top scientists here." Her mouth hung partly open in confusion. She began to pace around the pillar where he had been bound, forcing Han to turn his head. The effort nearly made him pass out.

"What good does it do to withhold information?" Qwi asked. "Information is for everyone. We build on the knowledge we have, add to it, and leave a greater legacy for our successors."

Qwi struck him as being impossibly naive. Han wondered how long she had been sheltered in the middle of the black hole cluster. "Does that mean you share *your* information with anyone who asks?" he said.

Qwi bobbed her head. "That's the way Maw Installation works. It is the foundation of all our research."

Han barely managed a grin of triumph. "All right, then tell me where my friends are. I came in here with a young man and a Wookiee. Share that information with me, and I'll see what I can remember about the Death Star."

Qwi's uneasy reaction told him that she had never before considered anything but clear-cut cases. "I don't know if I can tell you that," she said. "You don't have a need to know."

Han managed a shrug. "Then I see how much your own code of ethics means to you."

Qwi glanced toward the door, as if contemplating whether to summon the stormtroopers after all. "It is in my charter here as a researcher that I have access to all the data I need. Why won't you answer my few simple questions?"

"Why won't you answer mine? I never signed your charter. I'm under no obligation to you."

Han waited, fixing his eyes on her as she fidgeted. Finally, Qwi pulled out her datapad and hummed as she keyed in a request.

She looked at him with wide deep-blue eyes that blinked rapidly. Her hair seemed like a glittering waterfall of fine down spilling to her shoulders. When she whistled again, the datapad gave a response.

"Your Wookiee companion has been assigned to a labor detail in the engine-maintenance sector. The physicist formerly in charge of concept development and implementation always swore by Wookiee laborers. He had about a hundred of them taken from Kashyyyk and brought to the Installation when it was formed. We don't have many left. It's hard and dangerous work there, you know."

Han shifted his position, still finding it difficult to move. He had heard rumors that Wookiee slaves had been put to work during the actual construction of the first Death Star. But Qwi spoke of these things with simple frankness.

"What about my other friend?" Han asked.

"Someone named Kyp Durron—is that him? He is still aboard the *Gorgon* in the detention area, high security. I don't see much of a report from his debriefing, so apparently he didn't have much to tell them."

Han frowned, trying to assess the information, but Qwi became animated again. "All right, I've shared the information you wanted. Now tell me about the Death Star!" She stepped closer to him but remained well out of reach.

Han rolled his eyes but saw no reason not to. The Death Star had been destroyed long ago, and the plans were safely locked inside the protected data core of the former Imperial Information Center.

Han told Qwi about the corridors, the noises. He knew the most about the hangar bay, the detention area, and the garbage masher, but she didn't seem much interested in those details.

"But did you see the core? The propulsion systems?"

"Sorry. I was just running interference while someone else knocked out the tractor-beam generators." Han pursed his lips. "Why are you so interested in all this anyway?"

She blinked her eyes. "Because I *designed* most of the Death Star!"

Before she could notice Han's shocked response, she trotted over to the near wall and worked a few controls that turned a section of the metal plating transparent. Suddenly a dizzying panorama replaced his narrow view of the bright gases. He could see the other clustered rocks that made up Maw Installation.

"In fact, we've still got the prototype Death Star right here at the Installation."

As Qwi spoke, a gigantic wire-frame sphere as large as any of the asteroids rose behind the shortened horizon of the nearest planetoid like a deadly sunrise. The prototype looked like a giant armillary sphere, circular rings connected at the poles and spread out for support. Nested in the framework and superstructure hung the enormous reactor core and the planet-destroying superlaser.

"This is just the functional part," Qwi said, staring out the window with admiration in her eyes. "The core, the superlaser, and the reactor, without a hyperdrive propulsion system. We didn't see any need to add the structural support and all the housing decks for troops and administrators."

Han found his voice again. "Does it work?"

Qwi smiled at him, her eyes sparkling. "Oh yes, it works beautifully!"

Kyp Durron felt like an animal trapped in a cage. He stared at the dull confining walls of the detention cell. Illumination came through slitted grills in the ceiling, too bright and too reddish to be comfortable on his eyes. He sat on his bunk, stared at the wall, and tried not to think.

Leftover pain still throbbed through his body. The interrogator droid had been vicious in finding the pain stimuli in his body, damping endorphins so the slightest scratch seemed like agony. The sharp hypodermic needles felt like spears as they plunged into his flesh; the will-breaking drugs flowed like lava through his veins.

He had begged his memories to divulge some detail the interrogators would find useful, if only to stop the questioning—but Kyp Durron was nobody, a hapless prisoner who had spent most of his life on Kessel. He didn't *know* anything to tell the Imperial monsters. In the end they had found him worthless.

Kyp stared at the self-making meal the door dispenser had given to him. By opening the lid of the pack, he spontaneously heated the textured protein main course and chilled the synthetic fruit dessert; after a short time the utensils themselves began to break down and could be eaten as snacks. But Kyp could find no spark of hunger inside him.

His thoughts drifted again to Han Solo's predicament. Unlike Kyp, Han knew a great deal about the New Republic and had many secrets to divulge. Han's interrogation would have been far more thorough than his own. And Admiral Daala's ministrations had been worse than anything Kyp had experienced during his years in the Imperial Correction Facility. At least down in the spice mines he knew how to avoid calling attention to himself.

Since the age of eight, Kyp had lived on Kessel, coping with the rules, the torturous work, the miserable conditions under the old Imperial rule or under the chain of usurpers and slave lords such as Moruth Doole. His parents were dead, his brother Zeth conscripted away to the stormtrooper academy, but Kyp had learned how to lie low, to survive, to endure.

Not until Han Solo's arrival, though, had he considered escape. Han showed that a small, determined group could break free of a prisoner's shackles. That they had stumbled into an even worse situation inside the Maw seemed irrelevant.

Piloting the stolen shuttle, Kyp had used his fledgling powers to steer them safely through the black hole cluster.

In the years since the withered Vima-Da-Boda had taught him the fundamentals of her Jedi skills, Kyp had made little use of his own affinity for the Force.

He remembered Vima-Da-Boda's face as shrunken and leprous; and she had a habit of huddling in corners, of pulling shadows around herself as if to hide from immense prying eyes. The fallen jedi had a guilty conscience that suffocated her like a blanket, but she had taken the time to teach Kyp a few things before the Imperials whisked her away. "You have great potential," she had told him in one of her last brief lessons.

Kyp had paid little attention to that, until now.

He stared fixedly at his untouched meal. Perhaps if he concentrated, focused his abilities on manipulating something, moving a tiny object, he could turn that skill into an escape.

Escape! The word rang through his heart, conjuring images of hope. He was not certain how he did what he did. Sensing the best route through darkened spice tunnels seemed perfectly natural to him. When flying the shuttle through the fiery gas clouds, he had listened to the mysterious whispering voice directing him. Kyp turned and altered course, spinning and whirling whenever it *seemed right*.

But now that he needed to make use of the Force, he didn't know where to begin.

He fixed his gaze on the flimsy foil covering of the instant meal, trying to bend it. He pushed with his mind, picturing the thin metal twisting and crumpling into a ball—but nothing happened. Kyp wondered how much of Vima-Da-Boda's ramblings had been simple superstition and craziness.

His parents had no special sort of powers. On the Deyer colony of the Anoat system, they had both been outspoken local politicians. Upon hearing of a growing rebellion against the Emperor's rigid policies, they decided to work from within, speaking out against Palpatine to make him more moderate rather than overthrow him entirely. They resoundingly protested the destruction of Alderaan—but their efforts had only gotten the two of them and their sons Zeth and Kyp arrested.

Kyp remembered that night-of terror, when the stormtroopers had melted down the door of the family dwelling even though it was unlocked. The armed soldiers marched into the living quarters, kicked over the fragile fiber-grown furniture. The stormtrooper captain read an arrest order through the filtered speaker in his helmet, accusing Kyp's parents of treason; then the stormtroopers drew their blasters and stunned the two astonished adults. Kyp's older brother Zeth had tried to protect them, so the troopers stunned him as well.

Kyp, with tears streaming down his face, could only stare in disbelief at the three crumpled forms as the stormtroopers linked stun-cuffs around his wrists. He still couldn't imagine how they had considered him a threat, since he had been only eight years old at the time.

Kyp and his parents were taken to Kessel, while fourteen-year-old Zeth was hauled off as a brainwashed recruit to the Imperial military academy in Carida. They had never heard from Zeth again.

After little more than a year Kessel went into enormous internal upheavals, with prison revolts, the Imperials overthrown, slave lords taking over. Kyp's parents had died during the commotion, executed for being on the wrong side at the wrong moment. Kyp himself had survived by hiding, becoming silent and invisible. He had rotted in the darkness of the tunnels for eight years, and now he had escaped.

Only to be captured again.

Somehow, it seemed, the Imperials were always there

to wreck his aspirations. On Deyer the stormtroopers had stolen him away from his home; on Kessel they had thrown him into the spice mines. Now that he and Han had finally escaped, the stormtroopers had clamped around him again.

Kyp's anger focused into a projectile, and he tried again to use his ability on the meal tray. He pushed, and a drop of sweat fell into his eyes, blurring his vision. Had the tray moved, jerked a little? He saw a small dent in the textured protein patty that formed the main course. Had he done that?

Perhaps anger was the key to focusing his latent energies.

He wished Vima-Da-Boda had spent more time instructing him down in the mines. He concentrated on the walls, on his narrow surroundings. He had to find some way of escaping—Han had already proved that it could be done.

Kyp vowed that if he did manage to get away, he would find someone to teach him how to use these mysterious powers. He never wanted to be left so helpless again.

Looking at the delicate, birdlike Qwi Xux, Han somehow could not imagine her as the developer of the Death Star. But she worked willingly in the Maw Installation, and she had admitted her role in a matter-of-fact way. "What's a nice girl like you doing in a place like this?" he finally said.

"This is what I do. This is what I'm best at." Qwi nodded her head absently, as if considering her answer. "Here I have a chance to grapple with the greatest mysteries of the cosmos, to solve problems that others have claimed are unsolvable. To see my wild ideas take shape. It's very thrilling."

Han still could not understand. "But how did this happen to you? Why are you here?"

"Oh, that!" Qwi said, as if suddenly understanding the question. "My home planet was Omwat, in the Outer Rim. Moff Tarkin took ten young Omwati children from various cities. He placed us in intense forced-education camps, trying to mold us into great designers and problem solvers. I was the best. I was the only one who made it through all the training. I was his prize, and he sent me here as a reward.

"At first I worked with Bevel Lemelisk to bring the Death Star to fruition. When we had the blueprints completed, Tarkin took Bevel away, leaving me to create newer and better concepts."

"Okay," Han said, "so I'll ask you again, *why* do you do this stuff?"

Qwi looked at him as if he had suddenly grown stupid. "It's the most interesting thing I can imagine. I have my pick of the challenges, and I'm usually successful. What more could I want?"

Han knew he wasn't getting through. "How can you enjoy working on things like this? It's horrible!"

Qwi took another step backward, looking baffled and hurt. "What do you mean by that? It's fascinating work, if you think about it. One of our concepts was to modify existing molecular furnace devices into autonomous 'World Devastators' that could strip raw materials from a planet's surface, feed it into huge automated onboard factories, and produce useful machines. We're quite proud of that idea. We transmitted the proposal off to Tarkin shortly after he took Bevel with him." Her voice trailed off. "I wonder what ever happened to that idea."

Han blinked in astonishment. The terrifying fleet of World Devastators had attacked Admiral Ackbar's home planet, laying waste part of the beautiful water world before the juggernauts were destroyed. "The World Devastators have already been built," Han mumbled, "and put to very efficient use."

Qwi's face lit up. "Oh, that's wonderful!"

"No, it isn't!" he shouted into her face. She sprang back. "Don't you know what your inventions are used for? Do you have any idea?"

Qwi backed off, straightening up again defensively. "Yes, of course. The Death Star was to be used to break up dead planets to allow direct mining of the heavy metals trapped in the core. The World Devastators would be autonomous factories combing asteroids or sterile worlds to produce a wide range of items without polluting inhabited planets."

Han snorted and rolled his eyes. "If you believe that, you'll believe anything. Listen to their names! *Death Star*, *World Devastator*—that doesn't sound like something for peacetime economic development, does it?"

Qwi scowled and turned her back on it. "Oh, what difference does it make?"

"The Death Star's first target was the planet Alderaan— my wife's home world! It murdered billions of innocent people. The World Devastators were turned loose on the *inhabited* world of Calamari. Hundreds of thousands of people died. Those efficient factories of yours manufactured TIE fighters and other weapons of destruction, nothing else."

"I don't believe you." Her voice did not sound confident.

"I was there! I flew through the rubble of Alderaan, I saw the devastation on Calamari. Didn't you read about it in my interrogation report? Admiral Daala pressed me over and over again for those details."

Qwi crossed her slender bluish arms over her chest. "No, that wasn't in your debriefing summary, which you so melodramatically call an 'interrogation.' "

"Then you didn't get the whole report," Han said.

"Nonsense. I'm entitled to all data." She stared at her feet. "Besides, I only develop the concepts. I make them work. If someone on the outside abuses my inventions, I can't be held responsible. That's beyond the scope of what I do."

Han made a noncommittal sound, simmering with anger. Her words sounded rehearsed, like something that had been drilled into her. She didn't even seem to think about what she was saying.

Qwi flitted back to her 3-D display panel, tapping on the musical keys and humming to sharpen the long, angular image she had been constructing when Han opened his eyes. "Would you like to see what I'm working on now?" Qwi asked, studiously avoiding any mention of the previous discussion.

"Sure," Han said, afraid that when she no longer needed to talk to him, Qwi would send him back to his detention cell.

She gestured to the image of the small craft. Four-sided and elongated, it looked like the long shard of a firefacet gem. From the diagram he could see a pilot's compartment with space enough for six people. Small lasers studded strategic areas; the bottom of the long point carried a strange toroidal transmitting dish.

"Right now we're working on enhancing the armor," Qwi said. "Though the craft is not much larger than a single-man fighter, we need it to be completely impervious to attack. By introducing quantum-crystalline armor, where only a few layers of atoms are stacked as densely as physics permits, laminated on top of another thin film just as tough but phase shifted, we can be confident that nothing will harm it. Not so much as a dent."

Han nodded to the laser emplacements; he couldn't see well from his vantage chained against a support pillar.

"Then why add the weaponry if the ship is indestructible?" He had visions of a fleet of these things replacing the TIE fighters; a small force of indestructible assault craft could fly into any New Republic fleet and carve the ships up at their leisure.

"This craft is highly maneuverable, and small enough not to be noticed on a systemwide scan, but they still might encounter some resistance. Remember, the Death Star was the size of a small moon. This accomplishes through finesse what the Death Star brought about through brute force."

With a cold fear inside Han did not want to know the answer to his next question. How could she compare this small ship to the Death Star? But he couldn't stop himself from asking, "And what is it? What does it do?"

Qwi looked at the image with awe, pride, and fear. "Well, we haven't actually tested it yet, but the first full-scale model is basically completed. We call this concept the Sun Crusher, tiny but immensely powerful. One small, impervious craft launches a modulated resonance projectile into a star, which triggers a chain reaction in the core, igniting a supernova even in low-mass stars. Straightforward and simple."

In his horror, Han could think of nothing to say. The Death Star destroyed planets, but the Sun Crusher could destroy whole solar systems.

22

Luke and Lando stood with Moruth Doole high inside one of Kessel's atmosphere stacks. They held the rusted guard railing at the edge of a catwalk, staring down the dizzying drop. Leaning into the stack, they breathed the manufactured air boiling into the sky; it reminded Luke of the great air shaft in Cloud City.

Doole shouted into the roaring background noise. "According to one old Imperial study, there's only enough raw material in Kessel's crust to keep the atmosphere in equilibrium for a century or two at our present rate of consumption." He shrugged, hunching his bumpy shoulders in a sort of seizure. "A few years ago the output was higher so that the slaves could walk around and breathe the air—but what's the point in allowing that?"

Lando nodded sagely, as if still interested, while Luke said nothing. Doole had been their tour guide for an entire day, talking more than even the long-winded senators on Coruscant. Doole wanted Lando's half million credits and went about extolling Kessel's virtues like a representative from the planetary chamber of commerce.

Wherever Doole took them, Luke strained his Jedi senses, reaching out to find some sign of Han or Chewbacca. But Luke could feel no tickle in the Force, no ripple of his friends' presence. Perhaps they were truly dead after all.

Lando continued his conversation with Doole, shouting into the rushing wind that rose through the stack. "A lot can change around here by the time the air runs out. What matters is what you accomplish during your own lifetime."

Doole's hissing laugh was swallowed by background noise. He reached up to lay a hand on Lando's shoulder. "We think alike, Mr. Tymmo. Who cares what happens after we're space dust? I'd rather squeeze Kessel dry while I've got it in my fist."

"You seem to have such an enormous operation. Why are you still running it solo?" Lando asked.

Doole flinched at the term "solo," and Luke knew Lando had chosen his word carefully; both of them caught the Rybet's reaction. "What do you mean?" Doole asked.

"Well, when the Imperial confiscation of spice ended, I would have thought you'd open all your markets, get a thousand representatives to spread the product. Jabba the Hutt is dead. Why didn't you link up with the unified smugglers under Talon Karrde and Mara Jade? That must have hurt your profits."

Doole pointed one gummy-ended finger at Lando. "Our profits are growing enormously, now that we get *all* the glitterstim, rather than just what we can steal from under Imperial noses. And after being so long under the yoke of the Empire, I didn't want to get into the same position with the New Republic. Everybody knows that Jade and Karrde are just puppets."

Seeing Lando's skepticism, Doole waved his hands. "Oh, but we are considering it, of course. In fact, I've already spoken with a minister from the New Republic, opening up a line of communication that may eventually lead to an alliance."

"Sounds like good news," Lando said in a noncommittal voice.

Doole led them back along the catwalk to the access doorway, where Artoo waited. Shutting the heavy door behind them, Doole paused a moment for their ears to adjust to the sudden silence. "As you can see, a great deal is changing around here. You, my friend, have chosen a good time to join in."

"*If* I decide to invest," Lando said firmly.

"Yes, yes, if you decide to invest. The truth is, this could be even more important, Mr. Tymmo. Since the death of Skynxnex, I'll be needing a new, er, *assistant* for running the spice mines."

Lando fluffed the cape behind him in a self-important gesture. "If I'm investing half a million credits, Doole, I'd expect to be more of a *partner* than an assistant."

Doole practically kowtowed. "Of course. Trivial details can be worked out. I'll also need a new shift boss. Maybe your companion here would be interested in the work?" He looked at Luke, squinting with his egg-white eye.

Luke met the Rybet's mechanical eye and stared into the focus-changing lenses, trying to pry some secrets from Doole's brain. Luke said, "I'll have to think about it."

Doole ignored him, focusing his attention back on Lando. "Now then, you've seen practically everything. Is there anything else I can show you?"

Lando looked to Luke, who pondered a moment. Thoughts of the jagged moon and its security base kept troubling him. If Han was not on Kessel itself, perhaps he was imprisoned on the moonbase.

"Aren't you worried about attack from remnants of the Empire?" Luke asked. "Or consolidation forces from the New Republic?"

Doole brushed aside the comment. "We have our own defenses. Don't worry."

But Luke persisted, trying to sound like a cautious business associate. "If we're going to invest, we should see these alleged defenses. We know about the energy shield left by the Imperial Correction Facility. But do you have a fleet of any sort?"

Doole began to sputter, but Lando took charge. "Moruth, if there's something you don't want us to see . . ."

"No, no, it's no trouble at all. I'll just have to arrange a shuttle up to the moonbase. I don't want you to think we have anything to hide!"

Doole bustled off to arrange for the shuttle, leaving Luke and Lando to exchange skeptical glances.

Lando did not like the idea of leaving the *Lady Luck* behind on the landing pad of the Imperial Correction Facility, but Doole continued to play the gracious host. Luke silently tried to console him as they lifted off in the short-range shuttle, but Lando kept looking out the small window as if he would never see his ship again.

Kessel's moon approached, looking like a hollowed sphere with most of the rock scooped out to house a large internal hangar and the enormous generators and transmitters that created the protective energy shield surrounding the planet.

After they landed, Moruth Doole strutted out of the shuttle, gesturing them to follow with an impatience that made Luke curious. Doole stood waiting for them as Artoo worked his way down the ramp and into the giant grotto. Behind a transparent atmosphere-containment screen,

Luke could see stars and the trailing wisps of gas looping around the black hole cluster.

Doole seemed prouder of his defensive fleet than he was of any other aspect of the Kessel operations. "Follow me."

He waddled across the rock floor of the hangar bay, leading them along rows and rows of fighter craft arranged in seemingly random order. They passed ships Luke found familiar and others so exotic he could not even identify them. He called on his knowledge as a fighter pilot to assess the fleet: X-wings, Y-wings, powerful Corellian Corvettes, a single B-wing, TIE fighters, TIE interceptors, four TIE bombers, several Skipray blastboats, gamma-class assault shuttles. In space, like prizes around the ragged opening of the moon, hovered larger attack ships—three Carrack cruisers, two big Lancer frigates, a single Loronar strike cruiser.

"After we drove out the Empire," Doole said, "I placed the highest priority on a defensive fleet. I bought every fighter I could find, no matter what its condition, and hired experienced mechanics from the Corellian sector of Nar Shaddaa."

He grinned with his amphibian lips. "We just got the energy shield operational again two days ago. I can heave a big sigh of relief now. With the shields finally up and our new fleet as a backup, Kessel is safe and independent. We can set glitterstim prices across the galaxy without interference from anybody."

"Sure is a lot of ships," Lando agreed. "I'm impressed."

Luke recalled how much trouble the New Republic had obtaining sufficient fighting ships during Admiral Thrawn's guerrilla campaigns. If Moruth Doole had been pulling all the strings he could to obtain every functional ship in the sector, no wonder supplies had been so limited.

"We should be able to defend against spice pirates, don't you think?" Doole said.

They kept walking along the rows of parked ships. Suddenly Lando froze, and Luke felt a surge of shocked emotion from him. Artoo began chittering wildly. Luke looked around until he saw one modified light freighter of Corellian manufacture—a ship that looked decidedly familiar.

"What is it?" Doole asked, looking down at the droid.

Lando took a moment to regain his composure. He rapped his knuckles on Artoo's top dome. "Stray cosmic ray, I suppose. Occasionally these old astromech units frazzle a circuit." He swallowed. "Could I speak with my assistant for a moment in private, Moruth?"

"Oh, uh, of course." Doole discreetly backed away. "I'll go make sure the mechanics are prepping the shuttle for our return to Kessel." He turned to Luke and forced humor into his tone. "Now, don't go talking your boss out of making an investment here!"

The moment Doole moved out of earshot, Lando nodded excitedly to the freighter. "That's the *Falcon*, Luke! I know her like a krabbex knows its shell!"

Luke looked at the ship, recognizing it himself but wanting more proof. "You positive?"

"It's the *Falcon*, Luke. I owned her, remember, before Han stole her from me in a sabacc game. If you look, you can see the streaking scar on top where I knocked off the subspace antenna dish trying to zip away from the Death Star."

Luke also noticed scorch marks from a recent space combat. "They could have changed the markings, wiped the memory core. Is there any other way we can prove it?"

"Just get me inside the cockpit. Han's made some modifications to the ship nobody else would know about."

When Doole returned, Lando said, "My assistant wants to be sure you've been doing thorough maintenance on these ships. If you're not taking care of them, they don't make much of a defensive fleet. Let's take a look inside one at random . . . say, that Corellian ship over there."

Doole seemed taken by surprise, glancing at the *Falcon*. "That one? Uh, we have plenty of top-notch fighters you can check out. That one is something of a . . . piece of junk."

Lando waggled his finger. "If *you* choose the ship for us, Moruth, that contradicts the whole point of a random inspection, doesn't it? Open this one up. Go on."

Reluctantly, Doole worked the external controls that dropped the *Falcon*'s ramp. Lando took the lead, followed by Luke, while Artoo puttered so closely behind Doole that he nearly ran over the Rybet's heels.

Inside, Lando strode to the cockpit, ostensibly to check out the systems. Running his fingers lovingly over the stained, worn surfaces, he flicked a few switches. "Ion-flux stabilizer checks out as optimal, so does the stasis-field generator. Should we go back and check out the power converter? Those things are notorious for breaking down in Corellian freighters."

Lando backed down the narrow corridor leading from the cockpit to the central living section of the ship. Turning left toward the entry ramp, he stepped carefully on the main deck plates. From the control panels he had unlatched the hidden locks, and when he stomped on the appropriate plates with his boot heel, they popped up, revealing the seven secret compartments Han had personally installed as spice-smuggling bins beneath the floor.

"Caught you, Doole, you bastard!" Lando grabbed him by the yellow cravat at his throat. "What have you done with Han and Chewbacca?"

Doole seemed completely astonished, flailing his splayed hands in the air. "What are you talking about?" he croaked. As Lando glared down into the Rybet's huge eyes, Doole slipped one of his hands into his waistcoat and yanked free a small "hold-out" blaster pistol. Luke saw it and reacted instantly, shoving with his mind and using the Force to hurl Moruth Doole away from Lando.

The blaster went off, sending a deadly beam ricocheting around the *Falcon*'s corridor. Doole fell backward, then scrambled to his feet. He fired at them again, but his mechanical eye had no time to focus, and the beam went wide. Doole dove down the ramp, bellowing for the guards. His mechanical eye fell off, clanging and rolling across the floor. He scrambled after it in a panic, feeling blindly with his hands.

Luke smacked the door controls, raising the ramp and sealing the hatch, "We should have kept him as a hostage," he said. "Now it's going to be a lot more difficult to get out of here."

Outside, Doole raised the alarm. Guards scrambled through the parked ships, drawing blasters, fastening their armor.

"Artoo, get to the computer!" Luke said.

Lando jumped into the chair behind the controls. "I doubt we can do anything for Han anymore. We need to get back and tell Leia. She can bring a full-scale occupation force to Kessel. We'll go over this place with a high-res scanner."

"If we get out of here alive," Luke said.

"Artoo," Lando called, "jack into the copilot's computer and tie into the hangar controls." The astromech droid chittered his willingness to help and rolled toward the navicomp console.

Outside in the hangar, security horns sounded. People ran around every which direction, not knowing where to go. Luke saw immediately that these mercenaries had far less experience working together than the sloppiest Imperial regiment. But the moment Lando lifted the ship off the landing-pad floor, everyone had an unmistakable target.

"Artoo, get that door field down!" Lando shouted.

Using maneuvering thrusters, he edged the ship forward, picking up speed as they rose over the other parked fighters. Pilots scrambled into their ships, ready for a space battle. In orbit around the moon, the capital ships did not yet seem aware of the situation.

Lando accelerated toward the wide hangar opening to space. They could not see the invisible shield. Artoo bleeped and whistled, but the sounds were not positive. "Get the shield down!" Lando insisted.

Artoo's interface jack whirred as he worked with the hangar bay's computer, trying to skirt the password controls.

"We need the shield down *now*, Artoo!" Luke said.

The *Falcon*'s rear thrusters kicked in and they lurched forward, gaining speed. "Come on," Lando said to the ship. "You can do it. Do it one last time for Han."

Artoo bleeped in triumph a moment before they shot through the opening. Luke flinched, but the shield dropped just in time.

Alert lights began to wink on in the big battleships riding in orbit. Weapons systems warmed up, targeting modules locked on to aimpoints.

The *Millennium Falcon* soared into open space as, behind them, the Kessel forces scrambled in pursuit.

23

Hunched in his dark robes, Tol Sivron came to visit Qwi Xux in her research room. He drew in a long, hissing breath, and his head-tails twitched with uneasiness as he stared at her setup. The Twi'lek administrator gave the impression of never having set foot inside an actual laboratory before—which seemed odd to Qwi, since he was in charge of the entire installation.

Qwi stopped her musical calculation with an atonal squawk. "Director Sivron! What can I do for you?"

Tol Sivron demanded regular written reports, feasibility studies, and progress summaries; he hosted a weekly meeting among the scientists to share their ideas and their work in a frank and stimulating exchange.

But Tol Sivron did not make a habit of *visiting*.

He shuffled around the room, poking at things, kneading his knuckles, and looking at the standard equipment as if deeply interested. He brushed his clawed fingertips over the calibration gauge of a weld-stress analyzer, muttering,

"Mmm hmmm, good work!" as if Qwi herself had invented the common instrument.

"I just came to commend you for your consistently fine efforts, Dr. Xux." Sivron stroked one of the vermiform head-tails draped around his neck; then his voice grew stern. "But I hope you are about finished with your endless iterations on the Sun Crusher project. We're past Grand Moff Tarkin's target date, you know, and we must move soon. I insist you write your final report and get all the documentation in order. Submit it to my office as soon as possible."

Qwi blinked at him in annoyance. She had submitted five separate "final" reports already, but each time Sivron had asked her to rerun a particular simulation or to retest the structural welds in the Sun Crusher's quantum armor. He never gave any reasons, and Qwi got the impression that he never read the reports anyway. If it had been up to her, the Sun Crusher would have been ready for deployment two years ago. She was getting bored with it, wanting to move on to a new design she could start from scratch and get back to the enjoyable, imaginative work again.

"You'll have the report by this evening, Director Sivron!" She would just send a repeat of the last one.

"Good, good," Sivron said, stroking his head-tail again. "I just wanted to make sure everything is in order."

For what? Qwi thought. *We're not going anywhere.* She hated it when the administrators and the military types kept sticking their noses in her work. Without another word Tol Sivron left.

Qwi stared after him, then activated the rarely used privacy lock on her door. Returning to her imaging terminal, she continued trying to crack the wall of passwords in front of her. She did like challenges, after all.

Qwi could not stop thinking about what Han Solo had told her. At first it was a new puzzle to solve, but then she finally began paying attention. To her all the prototypes she developed were abstract concepts turned into reality through mathematical music and brilliant intuitions. She kept telling herself that she did not know, or care, what her inventions were used for. She could certainly guess, but she tried not to. She didn't want to know! She blocked those thoughts before they could surface. But Qwi Xux wasn't stupid.

The Death Star was supposed to be used to break apart depleted, dead planets to provide access to raw materials deep in the core. Right! Had she thought up that excuse afterward? The World Devastators were supposed to be immense wandering factories taking useless rubble and fabricating scores of valuable industrial components. Right! Tarkin had been with her during the immense pressure of her original training. She knew what the man was capable of.

And the new Sun Crusher was—"What?" Han had said, raising his voice so that it hurt her fragile ears. "What in all the galaxy could the Sun Crusher be used for *other than to completely wipe out all life in systems the Imperials don't like?* You don't even have a bogus excuse like rubble mining. The Sun Crusher has one purpose only: to bring death to countless innocent people. Nothing more."

But Qwi could not possibly have the responsibility for lives on her hands. That wasn't part of her job. She just drew up blueprints, toyed with designs, solved equations. It exhilarated her to discover something previously considered impossible.

On the other hand, she was perfectly aware of what she was doing . . . though feigned naïveté provided such a nice excuse, such a perfect shield against her own conscience.

In the Maw databanks Qwi had discovered the complete "debriefing" of Han Solo—protected by a password she had easily broken—full video instead of just a transcription. Sivron and Daala had indeed kept much of it from her—but why?

As Qwi watched the entire torture session, she could not believe her eyes. She had never suspected the information had been taken from him in that manner! The words on paper seemed so cool and cooperative.

But on a deeper, professional level she was outraged at Admiral Daala. Access to data was supposedly open to all Maw scientists. She had never been denied a single information request in twelve years inside the black hole cluster! But this was even worse. She hadn't just been denied access to the full report—she had been *deceived* into thinking Han's debriefing held no more data.

But information is meant to be shared! Qwi thought. *How can I do my work if I don't have the pertinent data?*

Qwi had little trouble breaking through the various passwords. Apparently, no one had expected her to bother looking. She read the full report with sickened astonishment: the destruction of Alderaan, the attack on Yavin 4, the ambush of the Rebel fleet over Endor, the huge hospital ship and personnel carriers blown into micrometeoroids by the second Death Star's superlaser.

"What did you think they were going to be used for?" Han had said. Qwi closed her eyes to the thought.

Focus on the problem. It had been a mantra of her childhood. Be distracted by nothing else. Solving the problem was the only important thing. Solving the problem meant survival itself. . . .

As a child she remembered spending two years in the sterile, silent environment of the orbital education sphere above her homeworld of Omwat. Qwi had been ten standard years old, the same age as her other nine companions, each selected from different Omwati honeycomb settlements. From orbit the orange and green continents looked surreal, blurred by clouds and dimpled with canyons, blemished by upthrust mountains—nothing like the clean maps she had seen before.

But beside Qwi's educational sphere orbited Moff Tarkin's personal Star Destroyer. It had been a mere Victory class ship, but powerful enough to rain death and ruin down on Omwat if the students should fail.

For two years life for Qwi had been an endless succession of training, testing, training, testing, with no other purpose than to cram the total knowledge of engineering disciplines into pliable young Omwati minds—or to burst their brains in the process. Tarkin's research had shown that Omwati children were capable of amazing mental feats, if pushed properly and sufficiently. Most of the young minds would collapse under the pressure, but some emerged like precious jewels, brilliant and creative. Moff Tarkin had wanted to test that possibility.

The gaunt, steel-hard man had stood in his dress uniform during important examinations, staring at the surviving Omwati children as they wrestled with problems that had stymied the Empire's best designers. Qwi remembered how alarmed they had been when one of her classmates, a young male named Pillik, suddenly fell to the floor in some kind of seizure, grasping his head and screaming. He managed to climb to his knees, weeping, before the guards grabbed him. He still grasped for his examination paper as they hauled him away, yelling that he wanted to finish his work.

In silence Qwi and her three surviving classmates went to the window of the educational sphere so they could watch as turbolasers from the Victory-class Star Destroyer obliterated Pillik's honeycomb settlement in punishment for his failure.

Qwi could not be distracted by consequences. If her concentration faltered, everyone would die. She had to lock away all caring. Problems were pure, and safe, to be solved for their own sake. She could not allow herself to think beyond the abstract challenge at hand.

In the end Qwi had been the only one of her group who made it through the training. She received no instruction in biological sciences, saving her memory space for more physics, mathematics, and engineering. Tarkin had whisked her off to the new Maw Installation and placed her under the tutelage of the great engineer Bevel Lemelisk. Qwi had been in the Maw ever since.

Problems had to be solved for their own sake. If she allowed herself to be distracted by feelings, terrible things would happen. She remembered images of burning Omwati cities winking like faraway campfires from orbit, the laser-ignited wildfires that swept across the savannas of her world—but she had too many calculations to finish, too many designs to modify.

Qwi had salved her conscience by laying the responsibility on others. But the truth was, she created devices that had directly caused the deaths of entire civilizations, the destruction of whole worlds. With the Sun Crusher she could wipe out solar systems with the push of a button.

Qwi Xux had a lot of thinking to do, but she didn't know how to go about this kind of pondering. This was an entirely new and different type of problem to solve.

Chewbacca stood like a statue, refusing to move and daring the keeper to use his power-lash again.

The keeper did.

Chewbacca roared at the pain lancing across his skin; his nerves writhed in the aftermath of the charge. He raised his hairy arms, seething with the desire to rip the fat, placid man's limbs from his spherical torso.

Fourteen stormtroopers leveled their blasters at him.

"Are you going back to work, Wookiee, or do I have to nudge the power setting up a couple more notches?" The keeper tapped the handle of the power-lash against his palm, gazing at Chewbacca with a bland expression. His complexion was dusty-looking and bloodless, as if no hint of life had ever passed beneath the skin.

"Any other time I might have enjoyed the challenge of breaking you, Wookiee. I've been here fourteen standard years with an entire crew of Wookiee slaves. We lost a few during the process, but I cracked them all, and now they follow orders and do their work. But Admiral Daala insists that everything be in top-notch condition for mobilization by tomorrow."

He flicked the sizzling green tip of the lash in the air in front of Chewbacca's face, singeing some of the fur. Chewbacca peeled back his black lips and growled.

"I don't have time to play games right now," the keeper said. "If I have to waste any more time disciplining you, I'm going to dump you out into space. Do you understand?"

Chewbacca considered roaring in his face, but the keeper looked serious. At the very least Chewbacca had to survive long enough to find out what had happened to Han. A long time ago Han had rescued Chewbacca from other enslavers, and he still owed the man a life debt. He gave a low grunt of acquiescence.

"Good, now get back to that assault shuttle!"

Chewbacca wore gray work coveralls with pockets to hold engine diagnostic tools and hydrospanners. None of the tools could be used as a weapon; Chewbacca had already checked that much out.

The gamma-class assault shuttle took up a good portion of the *Gorgon*'s lower hangar bay. Chewbacca had a small databoard listing the configurations for the tractor-beam projector and the deflector-shield generators. He had worked on other ships before, and he knew the *Falcon* inside out thanks to the many on-the-spot repairs he and Han had been forced to make. With the specs on the databoard he could easily service decades-old Imperial technology.

On the rear of the assault shuttle Chewbacca checked the exhaust nozzles of the thrust reactors and grudgingly tested the blaster-cannon mountings. In the front of the vessel a convenient boarding hatch allowed access for the command crew, but Chewbacca opted for the more rigorous method of popping open and climbing through one of the foldaway launch doors used to disgorge zero-G stormtroopers during a space assault.

Inside, he had access to the engineering level, where he tinkered with the power modulators and the life-support systems. He restrained his urge to rip out circuits and damage the equipment—the keeper would execute him immediately, and such a minor sabotage would accomplish nothing. Even subtle damage was likely to be discovered in the initial checkout procedure.

The assault shuttle's spartan passenger section held only benches for its complement of spacetroopers, as well as power-coupled storage compartments for their bulky zero-G armor. Up front Chewbacca powered up and checked out the command console, did a test run of the twin-tandem flight computers . . . and thought about uprooting the chairs on which the five members of the command crew would sit.

Outside in the *Gorgon*'s hangar bay the fat keeper shouted and lashed at the air. Chewbacca felt a surge of anger upon hearing cries of agony from the other cowed Wookiee slaves. He knew nothing about his fellow captives; he had been held in a separate cell, and they were not allowed to speak to each other. Chewbacca wondered how long it had been since these exhausted slaves had touched the branches of their home trees.

"Get working!" the keeper yelled. "We have a lot that needs to be done today! Three hundred ships on the *Gorgon* alone!" And Chewbacca knew the three other star destroyers had an equal number of TIE fighters, blastboats, and assault shuttles.

Chewbacca clenched his fist around an upraised storage lid, bending it noticeably. He wanted to know why Admiral Daala insisted on such desperate speed.

Qwi Xux did not like to be muscled around by stormtroopers. In her years at the Maw Installation, she had learned to ignore the rigid troopers marching around the corridors in white armor, in endless robotic training and formations that made no sense at all. Did they all have faulty memories, or what? Once she learned something, she didn't need to keep drilling, drilling, drilling. Qwi paid little attention to them anymore—until a squad marched into her laboratory and insisted that she follow them.

Only moments earlier Qwi had shut down her illicit database searches, and she had disengaged the privacy lock on her lab's entryway. She had no reason to think the stormtroopers suspected anything, but she still felt unreasoning terror.

The troopers folded around her in a protective bubble as they marched her along the tiled corridors. "Where are you taking me?" Qwi finally managed to ask.

"Admiral Daala wishes to see you," the captain said through the filtered speaker on his helmet.

"Oh. Why?"

"She'll have to tell you that herself."

Qwi swallowed a cold lump in her throat and put a haughty tone in her voice. "Why couldn't she come to me herself?"

"Because Admiral Daala is a busy person."

"I'm a busy person, too."

"She is our commanding officer. You aren't."

Qwi asked no further questions but followed in silence as they took her across an access tube to another asteroid in the main conglomeration, then aboard a small shuttle in the landing bay.

When they arrived aboard the Star Destroyer *Gorgon*, Qwi could not keep herself from staring in wide-eyed fascination. Though the enormous ships had hung in the sky above Maw Installation for as long as she could remember, Qwi rarely had an opportunity to board them. Her stormtrooper escorts took her directly to the *Gorgon*'s bridge.

The trapezoidal command tower rose high above the arrowhead-shaped main body, giving a panoramic view overlooking the vast landscape of the ship. Qwi stood and stared out the front viewport toward the cobbled-together collection of rocks that made up Maw Installation. For a moment she remembered watching from the orbiting educational sphere as Moff Tarkin obliterated Omwati cities far below. . . .

Command crew bustled about their stations, intent on their work as if in the middle of an important drill. In the corridors stormtroopers marched by at a brisk pace. Overlapping intercom messages peppered the air. Qwi wondered how the troops could be so busy after a decade of doing nothing.

Admiral Daala stood by her command console, staring at the deadly swirling gases that blocked her from the outside. Qwi saw her trim, perfect figure masked by an aurora of chestnut hair that flowed like a living blanket down her back. When Daala turned to face her, some of the hair remained where it hung, wrapping around her waist while other strands arced behind her.

"You wanted to see me?" Qwi asked. Her reedy voice quavered despite her efforts to control her nervousness.

Daala looked at her for a moment, and Qwi had the impression of being placed under a magnifying lens in preparation for dissection. Then Daala suddenly seemed to recognize her. "Ah! You are Qwi Xux, in charge of the Sun Crusher project?"

"Yes, Admiral." She paused a moment, then blurted, "Have I done something wrong?"

"I don't know. Have you?" Daala answered, then turned back to the broad window, staring out at her other ships. "I can't get any straight information out of Tol Sivron, so I'll tell you directly. If you have any further work to do on your Sun Crusher, finish it now. We are mobilizing the fleet."

Daala misinterpreted Qwi's shocked silence. "Don't worry—I'll authorize whatever assistance you need, but everything must be done within a day. You've had two years longer than Grand Moff Tarkin gave you. It is time to put the Sun Crusher to use."

Qwi took a deep breath, trying to keep her thoughts from spinning. "But why now? Why such a rush?"

Daala whirled back at her, wearing a sour expression. "We have received new information. The Empire lies wounded and vulnerable on the outside, and we can't just sit here and wait. We have four Star Destroyers, a full fleet the Rebellion knows nothing about. Since the Death Star prototype is not capable of hyperspace travel, it is useless to us in this operation—but we will have the Sun Crusher. Your beautiful Sun Crusher." The lights of the fiery gases outside glimmered in Daala's eyes. "With it we can destroy the New Republic, system by system."

All of Han's warnings echoed as loud as screams in Qwi's head. He had been right about everything.

Daala dismissed her, and Qwi stumbled as the storm-troopers escorted her back toward the waiting shuttle. Qwi would have to make her decision sooner than she had expected.

In her own quarters images of planets scrolled in front of Leia's eyes. Statistics, populations, resources—cold data that she had to absorb and assess to make her decision. She rejected most of the worlds out of hand; others she marked as possibilities. So far nothing had jumped out at her as the *perfect* place for Luke to establish his Jedi academy.

It hadn't seemed like such a difficult request, since the New Republic encompassed so many possible planets. She had found Dantooine as a new home for the survivors from Eol Sha—why was an academy site causing her so much trouble?

After meeting Luke's first two trainees and seeing how *unusual* they were, Leia suspected the Jedi studies would require complete isolation. She had spoken again to Gantoris and Streen in the past day and was discouraged to find both of them feeling miserable and abandoned. If only Luke would come back soon—with Han!

As she thought of other places, Leia pondered how

Yoda had trained Luke on the swampy planet of Dagobah, a place completely devoid of other intelligent life. Her brother would want someplace similar for his own trainees.

Okay, what about Dagobah itself? she thought, putting a fingertip on her lower lip. The swamps had hidden Yoda for centuries, and it was certainly isolated from the mainstream of galactic traffic . . . but Dagobah had no appropriate facilities either. They would have to erect an academy from scratch. Mobilizing the New Republic construction forces, Leia could get the job done in short order—but she wasn't sure that was the right answer. Somehow she felt the right site would jump out at her. Because the restoration of the Jedi Knights meant so much, Luke would be very selective about the proper site. She just hadn't found it yet.

The message center buzzed. Again. Though it was barely midmorning, she had already lost count of the interruptions. With a sigh Leia answered it, seeing the image of another minor functionary take shape in the central focus.

"Minister Organa Solo," the functionary said, "I'm sorry to call you at home, but we need you to decide on a meal selection for the Bimmini banquet. The deadline is today. The choices are grazer fillets with tart sauce, nerf medallions with sweet fungi, broiled dewback—"

"I'll take the nerf medallions. Thank you!" She switched off the receiver, then calmed herself before returning to the images of the planets.

In the bedchambers Jacen burst into loud sobs, joined in a moment by his sister. Threepio cooed sounds of consolation, then began another one of his lullabies, which set them to crying louder. Part of Leia wanted to hurry into the children's room to see what was the matter, while another part of her just wanted to seal their door so she could have a little more quiet.

On the morning after the reception at the Skydome
Botanical Gardens, both children had come down with a
cold. Slight fever, congestion, and general crankiness—
the type of frequent minor illness the twins would no doubt
suffer for another few years—but Leia didn't want to just
abandon them to the care of Threepio.

After some refresher programming, the protocol droid
had proved himself capable of caring for the two-year-olds.
But Leia felt a defensiveness in herself. She was their
mother; while it was a new set of responsibilities for her,
Leia did not want a droid to watch them all the time, no
matter how competent his programming. The children had
already spent so much of their lives with Winter that Leia
wanted to make up for lost time—if her political duties
would only give her the chance!

Before she could call up the file on another planet
to consider, the message center buzzed again. "What is
it?" she said, mustering every scrap of civility she still
possessed. She did not recognize the alien administrator
in the image.

"Ah, Minister Organa Solo, I am calling from the office
of the deputy assistant minister of industry. I was told you
might be able to offer a suggestion about a type of music
that would be appropriate to play during the arrival of the
Ishi Tib delegate?"

For a moment Leia reconsidered her time as a prisoner
of Jabba the Hutt. At least the sluglike crime lord had not
required her to do anything more than sit there and look
beautiful. . . .

Before she finished signing off, a message came in
from Admiral Ackbar. Though she liked the Calamarian
admiral, she found it difficult to keep her temper from
boiling. How was she supposed to get anything done with
all these interruptions?

"Hello, Admiral—can I help you quickly? I'm in the middle of a rather large project right now."

Ackbar nodded graciously, swiveling his big fish eyes to the front in a gesture of courtesy. "Of course, Leia. I apologize for the interruption, but I'd like to solicit your comments on the speech I have just written. As you remember, I am giving it before the Cabinet tomorrow, and you agreed to provide me with data on the rezoning of embassy sectors in the devastated areas of Imperial City. I did write the speech without your input, but I need to have the information before tomorrow. I've marked clearly where you need to add your thoughts. Would it be possible—"

"Of course, Admiral. I'm sorry I haven't been more attentive. Please send it to my personal network address, and I'll get to it right away. I promise."

Ackbar nodded his salmon-colored head. "Thank you, and I apologize again for the interruption. I'll let you get back to work."

When he signed off, Leia could do no more than sit with her eyes closed, hoping for a few moments of silence. In quiet times, though, she began to worry too much about Han. . . .

The door chime sounded. Leia almost screamed.

Mon Mothma stood at the doorway in her flowing white robes. "Hello, Leia. Do you mind if I come in?"

Leia stuttered, trying to regain her composure. "Uh, please!" Mon Mothma had never come visiting, never shown the slightest inclination to make any sort of social call. Though calm and quietly charismatic, the Chief of State had always distanced herself from anyone else.

During the early days of the Rebellion, Mon Mothma had sparred with Leia's father Bail Organa on the floor of the Senate. Mon Mothma was a new senator then, a fire-brand insisting on rapid and sweeping changes that dis-

mayed the seasoned and cynical Bail Organa. Eventually,
though, they joined forces to oppose Senator Palpatine
in his quest to become President; when they failed and
Palpatine proclaimed himself "Emperor," Mon Mothma
began to speak of open rebellion. A horrified Bail Organa
had not seen the need until after the Ghorman Massacre,
when he finally realized that the Republic he had served
for so long was truly dead.

The death of Bail Organa and the destruction of Alderaan
had affected Mon Mothma deeply. But she had never hinted
that she wished to become friends with the daughter of her
old rival. "What can I do for you, Mon Mothma?" Leia
asked.

Mon Mothma looked around the private quarters, fixing
her gaze on the sweeping landscapes of Alderaan mounted
on the walls, the grasslands, the organic-looking tower
cities, the underground settlements. The faintest sheen of
tears seemed to film her eyes.

"I learned that your children are sick, and I wanted to
offer my consolations." She fixed a sharp gaze on Leia.
"And I have also learned that Han and Chewbacca never
returned from their Kessel mission. I wish you hadn't tried
to hide that from me. Is there anything I can do?"

Leia looked down. "No. Lando Calrissian and my brother Luke have already gone to see what they can find. I
hope they bring back news soon."

Mon Mothma nodded. "And I also wanted to commend
you on the job you are doing. Or perhaps *console* you is
the better word."

Leia could not hide her surprise. "The reception for
Ambassador Furgan was a disaster!"

Mon Mothma shrugged. "And do you think anyone
could have performed better than you did? You did a
perfectly adequate job with the Caridans. Some battles

simply cannot be won. Given the Caridans' potential for galactic mayhem, I think getting a drink thrown in my face is a relatively minor debacle."

With a faint smile Leia had to admit that the Chief of State was right. "Now, if only I could find a place to house Luke's Jedi academy, I'd feel like I'm making some progress through this whole morass."

Mon Mothma smiled. "I've been thinking about that too, ever since Luke made his speech. I believe I have a suggestion."

Leia's dark eyes widened in surprise. "Please!"

Mon Mothma indicated the data terminal in Leia's living chamber. "May I?"

Leia gestured for her to use the system. Though a lifelong politician, Mon Mothma set to work on the database; she was obviously no stranger to doing her own research.

When images of the new planet crystallized in the projection zone, Leia felt the tingle of excitement creep through her. The confident feeling that this was the *right* place grew in her heart. She wondered how she had overlooked something so obvious.

"Consider," Mon Mothma said, smiling. "It has everything he could possibly need—privacy, good climate, facilities already in place."

"It's perfect! I don't know why I didn't think of it myself."

The message center buzzed again.

"What?" Leia barked at the caller. She realized she should have been more restrained, but she had reached the end of her fuse. Mon Mothma remained at the data terminal, watching from outside the field of view.

The caller also dispensed with tact. "We need your report right now, Minister Organa Solo. The orbital debris committee is deliberating on the disposition of wreckage around Coruscant. You were supposed to attend our discussions this morning—"

Leia recognized the functionary as Andur, the vice-chairman of the committee. "My aide has already canceled my appointments for today. I'm sorry I was unable to attend."

"We received your cancellation, but we didn't receive your report. You agreed to write a summary and distribute it to us at this session. It's past due! Sick children do not make the New Republic stop functioning."

Seeing red, Leia remembered standing in Jabba's palace, holding the pulsing thermal detonator in her hand, waiting for it to explode and kill them all. Five, four, three, two . . .

Somehow she restrained herself. Perhaps spending a day with Ambassador Furgan had toughened her calluses. "I may be the Minister of State, Mr. Andur, but I am also a mother. I have to do both jobs—I can't sacrifice one for the sake of the other. My children need me now. The committee can wait."

Miffed, the vice-chairman raised his voice. "It would have been much easier to complete our deliberations if you had been here rather than home playing nurse—couldn't you hire a medical droid to take care of your kids' runny noses? This is an important issue we're dealing with, affecting the fate of all space traffic approaching and leaving Coruscant!"

Leia stiffened. "This is an important issue I'm dealing with here, too! How can you expect me to care about the whole galaxy if I don't even care for my own family? If you wanted mindless devotion to duty without caring about people, then you should have stayed with the old Empire!" She reached for the controls. "My report will be issued to you *in due time*, Mr. Andur." She switched him off before he could say another word.

At the end of her outburst, Leia slumped into her self-conforming chair, suddenly remembering her guest. Her face turned scarlet with embarrassment.

"That committee meets weekly, and there's no reason why they couldn't have waited until next time," she said in a simmering, defensive voice. "I'm really not going to let any important negotiations go down the drain. I know my duty."

Mon Mothma nodded, sharing one of her placid, heartfelt smiles. "Of course you won't, Leia. I understand. Don't worry about it." The Chief of State looked at Leia with what seemed to be a new and surprising respect.

Leia sighed and stared at the planetary image on the data terminal. "Maybe I should go off and spend a few months at the Jedi academy myself as soon as Luke gets it under way—though I know that'll never happen. Taking a vacation from Imperial City is about as easy as walking away from a black hole. Affairs of state swallow up my entire day."

She caught herself complaining and quickly added, "But of course restoring the order of the Jedi Knights is very important. I have the potential to use the Force and so do the twins. But thorough training will take a lot of time and concentration—two commodities I don't seem to have."

Mon Mothma looked at her gravely, then squeezed Leia's shoulder. "Don't worry too much. You have other important things in store for you."

25

Han rolled over with a groan in the detention cell. The hard ridges on the surface of his bunk—Han thought of them as "discomfort stripes"—made sleep itself a nightmare.

He awoke from a dream about Leia, perhaps the only enjoyment he had experienced in three weeks. The dim reddish light filtered down, hurting his eyes without providing useful illumination.

He blinked his eyes open, hearing people move outside his cell door, the clank of stormtrooper boots on the floor gratings, muffled voices. The cyberlock clicked as someone activated the password code.

He sat up, suddenly alert. His body ached, his mind still buzzed from the interrogation drugs, but he tensed as the door opened. He had no idea what this was, but he felt certain he wouldn't like it.

Corridor light flooded in, and Qwi Xux stood beside an armed stormtrooper. She looked battered and abused by her own thoughts, which gave Han a smug grin. He hoped she had lost a lot of sleep after learning of the devastating use to which her inventions had been put. She might be able to fool herself, but she couldn't fool him.

"What, have you come back to discuss a few more moral issues, Doc? Am I supposed to be your conscience?"

Qwi crossed her pale-bluish arms over her chest. "Admiral Daala has given me permission to interrogate you again," she said coldly, though her body language did not match her tone. She turned to the guard, her pearlescent hair sparkling in the dim corridor. "Would you accompany me inside for the interrogation, Lieutenant? I'm afraid the prisoner might not cooperate."

"Yes, Dr. Xux," the guard said, following her into the cell. He slid the door partially closed behind him.

While his back was turned, Qwi withdrew a blaster from the utility pocket on her smock, pointed it at the guard, and fired a stun blast. Rippling arcs of blue fire surrounded him, then faded as he crumpled to the floor.

Han leaped to his feet. "What are you doing!"

Qwi stepped over the fallen stormtrooper. The previous day she had seemed more fragile; the Imperial-issue heavy blaster pistol looked huge in her delicate hand. "Admiral Daala is mobilizing this entire fleet in less than a day. She plans to take the Sun Crusher and her four Star Destroyers to wipe out the New Republic. Your friend Kyp Durron is also scheduled for termination this afternoon." She raised her feathery eyebrows. "Does that add up to enough of an excuse to escape as soon as we can?"

Han's mind reeled. At the moment all he could think of was seeing Kyp and Chewbacca again, then getting back to Coruscant so he could be reunited with Leia and the twins. "I don't have any appointments I couldn't be persuaded to cancel."

"Good," Qwi said. "Any questions?"

Han smirked as he began to pull on his disguise of stormtrooper armor. "No, I'm used to doing this sort of thing."

Kyp could sense the difference in the air—his first indication that his efforts to focus the Force were actually accomplishing something. He studied every slight change in air currents, in the sluggish odors around the cell, the myriad tiny sounds that echoed through the metal walls.

Stretching his mind through invisible webs of the Force, Kyp could feel a *surge* from the guards when they walked past his cell. He could sense a *twinge* each time someone dispensed the food tray through the door. But their attitudes had changed. Over the whole ship he could catch faint ripples of activity, tension, growing anxiety.

Something was about to happen.

Closer at hand, he understood a deeper gut-wrenching truth. The emotions had been so clear in the guard stationed beside his door the previous sleep period. Kyp Durron was not to be part of whatever activity the Star Destroyers were preparing. A young man from the spice mines of Kessel could provide no useful information; they had no reason to keep him alive.

Admiral Daala had already scheduled Kyp's termination. He had not much longer to live. His lips curled back in an angry snarl. The Empire had been trying to destroy him all his life, and now they were about to succeed.

When he heard voices outside his door, he sensed the barrage of their uneasiness, the curdling plans of violence behind the forefront of their minds. He had no way to defend himself! Despairing, Kyp slid his head against the cool metal wall of the door, trying to pick out a few select words of the conversation.

"—scheduled for execution this afternoon."

" . . . know that. We are . . . take him. Admiral . . .
authorization right here."

" . . . irregular. Why . . . want him?"

"Weapons test . . . target . . . new concept . . . vital to
the fleet's new armaments . . . right away!"

" . . . need specific . . . only a general authorization."

"No . . . good enough!"

The voices rose, but Kyp couldn't make out more of
the words. He tried to decipher three voices talking all
at once.

Kyp made ready to lash out the moment the door slid
open. He knew he would be cut down by blaster fire in
no time—but at least it would be over, and he would be
shot on his own terms, not the Empire's.

" . . . check with . . . first. Wait—"

Suddenly Kyp heard a thump and a muffled blast. A
heavy object smashed against the doorway. Kyp flinched
back as the door whisked open.

The dead stormtrooper guard sprawled backward into
his cell with a clatter of white armor. A smoking hole
oozed steam from the waist joint in the brittle uniform.

Another stormtrooper stepped inside holding the still-
warm blaster pistol. Beside him stood a willowy alien
woman, looking delicate but outraged at the same time.

"I hope *that* was sufficient authorization," the stormtrooper said, then pulled off his helmet.

"Han!" Kyp cried.

"I really hate red tape," Han said, nudging the dead
guard with his foot. "Think you can fit into that uniform, kid?"

"No, I don't want one of the slow old ones!" Qwi snapped
at the keeper of the Wookiee work detail. Through the

narrowed field of view in his stormtrooper helmet, Han watched the delicate woman play the part of a tough, impatient researcher.

The rotund man glanced at his hairy charges, unintimidated as if he were accustomed to being shouted at by prima donna scientists. The keeper's face looked like _le, wet clay.

Han fidgeted, sweating in the cramped uniform. The helmet had nose filters, but the suit still smelled of body odor from its former owner. The stormtroopers at Maw Installation lived in their uniforms and likely disinfected the interiors much less often than they polished the exteriors.

The keeper shrugged, as if Qwi's impatience did not concern him. "These Wookiees have been worked hard for over a decade. What do you expect from them? They're all slow and worthless."

Han could see that most of the other Wookiees wandering around the hangar bay had patchy fur and stooped shoulders, bringing them almost to the height of a human. These slaves looked as if their will had been crushed over years of harsh servitude.

"I don't want to hear your excuses," Qwi said. She tossed her head, making the feathery pearls of her hair shimmer. "We've been ordered to get a lot of work done before the fleet departs, and I need a Wookiee with some energy. Give me that new prisoner you have. He'll do the work."

"Not a good idea," the keeper said, wrinkling his pasty forehead. "He's unruly, and you'd have to double-check his work. Can't trust him not to try sabotage."

"I don't care how unruly he can get!" Qwi snapped. "At least he won't fall asleep on the job."

On the far side of the bay a tall Wookiee stepped out of

a gamma-class assault shuttle. He straightened from the cramped quarters and looked around the bay. Han had to force himself not to yank off his helmet and call out Chewbacca's name. The Wookiee seemed ready to strike, barely restraining himself from flying into a suicidal rage. With his bare hands Chewbacca could dismantle five or six TIE fighters before the stormtroopers took him down. The keeper glanced at Chewbacca, as if considering.

"I have authorization from Admiral Daala herself," Qwi said, holding out a curled hardcopy bearing Daala's seal. Han glanced at the other stormtroopers standing guard in the engine pool. He could not invoke the same violent "authorization" he had used to spring Kyp Durron from his cell.

Beside Qwi Xux, Kyp—wearing the smaller of the two stolen stormtrooper uniforms—stood stock-still. Han knew the kid must be terrified, but Kyp had snapped to attention and done everything Han suggested. Han felt a rush of warmth inside, and he hoped Kyp could get out of here to the normal life he deserved.

"All right, but you take him at your own risk," the keeper finally said. "I won't be responsible if he ruins whatever you have him working on." He whistled and motioned for a pair of stormtroopers to bring Chewbacca over.

The Wookiee growled in anger, glaring around with hard, dark eyes. He did not recognize Han, nor did he know Qwi Xux. Chewbacca glared at them, resenting another assignment.

"A little more cooperation!" the keeper yelled, then struck out with his energy lash, burning a smoking welt across Chewbacca's shoulder blades.

The Wookiee howled and snarled but somehow restrained himself as the other stormtroopers hauled out their blasters, ready to stun him if he went wild. Han tensed, clenching his fists as much as the armored gloves would allow. More than anything he wanted to shove the generating handle of the energy-lash down the keeper's throat and switch it on full power.

But instead Han stood at attention, doing nothing, saying nothing. Like a good stormtrooper.

The four of them marched out of the hangar bay. The keeper ignored them as he strode to the other captive Wookiees and began to strike left and right with his energy-lash, venting his anger. Han felt his stomach knotting.

Chewbacca kept looking from side to side, as if searching for his chance to escape. Han just hoped they could get someplace private before the big Wookiee decided to tear them all apart.

The doors closed, leaving them in a harshly lit white corridor. "Chewie!" Han said, pulling off his stormtrooper helmet. After breathing through the sour nose filters, even the musky scent of a Wookiee smelled sweet to him.

Chewbacca bleated in delighted surprise and grabbed Han in a huge hug, wrapping hairy arms around him and lifting him off the floor. Han gasped for breath, grateful for the protection of the armor. "Put me down!" he said, trying to stop himself from chuckling. "If somebody sees you, they'll think you're killing me! Wouldn't that be a stupid reason to get blasted?"

Chewbacca agreed and lowered him back to the floor.

"Now what?" Han asked Qwi.

"If you can pilot us out of here, we can escape," Qwi said.

Han grinned. "If that's our only problem, we're home free. I can pilot any ship—just give me the chance."

"Then let's get out of here," she said. "Time is running out."

• • •

When they boarded the shuttle back down to Maw Installation, Han could ask no further questions. Surrounded by other stormtroopers rigidly minding their own business, neither he nor Kyp could speak with Qwi. Casual conversation seemed forbidden.

Qwi fidgeted, looking at the shuttle walls, the narrow windows showing the deadly barrier of the Maw itself with its secret pathways—if they could escape.

Han desperately wanted to see Leia and the twins again. They filled his thoughts more and more, preoccupying him at times when he should have fixed every iota of attention on the peril around him. He ached to hold Leia again—but thinking of her while he wore a stormtrooper uniform seemed to taint the emotion.

Beside him sat Kyp, unreadable behind a stormtrooper mask. But the eyeholes of the helmet continued to turn toward Han, as if seeking reassurance. Han wished he had more to offer—but he did not know Qwi's plan.

Why were they returning to Maw Installation, rather than just stealing a ship and racing off into space? It would be a breakneck run, no matter when they started—and Admiral Daala's attack preparations grew more complete with each hour.

Han had to warn the New Republic of the disaster about to befall it. First, he had been concerned about the concentration of space power around Kessel—but the fleet of four Star Destroyers and the Maw Installation's secret weapons looked infinitely worse than whatever Moruth Doole had pieced together from the scrap heap.

Chewbacca wore mechanic's overalls, looking like a worker assigned to perform maintenance on some piece of equipment down in one of the laboratories. He made grunting sounds to himself, content to be reunited with his friends but anxious for action.

Qwi remained uncommunicative, keeping her thin bluish hands folded in her lap. Han wondered if he had gone too far in his accusations of her naïveté and the evil nature of her work. He wished he knew what she was thinking.

When the shuttle landed in one of the Installation's asteroids and the stormtroopers disembarked, Qwi led Han, Kyp, and Chewbacca away from the rocky hangar through a tunnel high enough to allow the movement of ships. "This way," she said.

Han did not recognize where she was taking them. "Aren't we going back to your lab, Doc?"

Qwi froze in midstep before turning to him. "No, never again." Then she moved on.

When they reached a tall metal doorway guarded by two stormtroopers standing at attention, Qwi took out her badge again, flashing the imprinted holograms in the light. The stormtroopers straightened to attention.

"Open up for me," Qwi said.

"Yes, Dr. Xux," the head guard said. "Your badge, please?"

She handed him her badge with a barely controlled smile. Han began to grow uneasy. These guards recognized Qwi by sight, and she seemed more comfortable now than she had been during other parts of their escape. Was this some kind of treachery? But to what purpose? He and Kyp turned toward each other, but the stormtrooper helmets kept their expressions unreadable.

"The Wookiee is here to do heavy maintenance on the engines—a complete coolant overhaul before tomorrow's deployment of the fleet," Qwi said. "These two guards are specially trained to prevent him from acting up. This Wookiee has caused some damage before, and we can't afford delays." Han tried not to cringe. Qwi was talking too quickly, letting her nervousness show through.

"Just give me the proper authorizations," the guard said. "You know the routine." He slid her badge through a scanner to log Qwi in, then handed it back to her. The stormtrooper seemed unconcerned, as if glad to be posted here rather than in the middle of frantic preparations for deployment.

Qwi went to the door's data terminal and punched up a request, then she handed him the hardcopy printout of Admiral Daala's permission again. Han wondered how many times she was going to use the same piece of paper!

"There, you'll see the approved work request for the Wookiee with a notation for special handlers. It's been authorized by Tol Sivron himself."

The guard shrugged. "As usual. Let me scan the service numbers of these two troopers. Then you're free to go in." He entered Han's and Kyp's numbers, then worked the door controls.

The great steelcrete doors ground to each side, revealing a hangar lit by levitating globes of light. Overhead, wide rectangular skylights let in the eerie glow of swirling gases around the Maw. Qwi stepped inside the chamber, and her whole demeanor changed, as if she had suddenly turned breathless. Han, Kyp, and Chewbacca followed.

The guard worked his controls, and the doors slid closed, sealing them inside. Qwi visibly relaxed.

Han stared up at a ship like none he had ever seen before. Smaller than the *Millennium Falcon*, this craft was oblong and faceted, like a long shard of crystal. Its own repulsorlifts kept it upright, with an actual ladder leading to the open hatch. Defensive lasers bristled from the corners of its facets.

The armor plating was multicolored and shimmering, like a constantly changing pool of oil and molten metal. At the lower vertex hung the oddly fuzzy torus of an immensely powerful resonance-torpedo transmitter. Though not much larger than a fighter craft, the Sun Crusher hummed with deadly potential.

"We're going to steal that?" Han cried.

"Of course," Qwi Xux said. "It's the greatest weapon ever devised, and I've spent eight years of my life designing it. You didn't expect me to leave it here for Admiral Daala, did you?"

26

The *Millennium Falcon's* sub-space engines flared white hot as the ship blasted away from Kessel's garrison moon. A swarm of fighters streamed after it, peppering space with multicolored blaster fire. Large capital ships began to nose into the *Falcon*'s flight-path like sleeping giants roused by stinging insects.

Lando Calrissian did his best to dodge the concentrated blaster fire. "The sublight engines are still optimal. Either Han's been maintaining her with a real mechanic for a change, or Doole reconditioned her for his fleet," he said. "Let's see how well the weapons systems work."

A pair of wasplike Z-95 Headhunters streaked after them, shooting fire-linked banks of triple blasters; close behind followed three battered Y-wing long-range fighters.

Luke spun around and whistled in surprise. "Headhunters! I didn't think anybody used those anymore!"

"Doole couldn't be choosy, I guess," Lando said.

The *Falcon* rocked with several direct blaster hits;

the fresh and fully charged shields held, though, for the moment.

Lando dropped the blaster cannon through its ventral hatch, then fired back at the pursuers. After five prolonged shots, Lando managed to hit the exhaust nacelle of a Y-wing, forcing it to break formation and peel off for repairs.

"One down—only about a thousand more to go," Lando said.

The Z-95 Headhunters pummeled them with repeated blaster fire, as if to punish the *Falcon*.

"Go down close to the planet and skim the atmosphere," Luke said. "Let's burn them up in the energy shield."

Lando set course for the lumpy world of Kessel as he voiced his complaints. "We can't detect that energy shield either. How do you know we won't get disintegrated ourselves?"

"We've got better reactions than they do."

Lando didn't seem convinced. "I've already almost flown into an energy shield once during our attack on the Death Star. I'm not anxious to repeat the process."

"Trust me," Luke said.

Kessel swelled in front of them, pockmarked and wreathed in a cottony halo of escaping air. "We're getting close."

Luke held the back of the pilot chair, his eyes half-closed. He breathed regularly, reaching out, sensing the pulsing power generated as a protective blanket by the garrison moon.

"Don't fall asleep on me, Luke!"

"Keep flying."

The Headhunters swooped after, flanked by the remaining pair of Y-wings.

"The aft deflector shield is starting to feel the pounding," Lando said. "If these guys get any closer, they're going to fly up my exhaust ports!"

"Get ready," Luke said.

Kessel filled their entire viewport now, boiling with its turbulent thin-air storms, tiny plumes from the numerous atmosphere factories tracing lines above the landscape.

"I'm ready, I'm ready! Just say the word and I—"

"Pull up, now!"

Lando's tension helped him react like a spring-loaded catapult. He hauled up on the controls, ripping the *Falcon* straight up in a tight cartwheel. Taken by surprise, all four of the attacking ships splattered into clouds of ignited fuel and ionized metal as they slammed into the invisible energy shield.

"Missed it by a couple of meters at least," Luke said. "Relax, Lando."

Artoo bleeped, and Luke answered him after looking at the expression on Lando's face. "No, Artoo, I don't think he's interested in an exact measurement."

They soared just above the atmosphere on a tight orbit that took them around Kessel's poles. The curtain of stars rolled out from the edge of the planet as the landscape sped beneath them; then they looped back into space in a mad dash to escape.

They ran straight into the wave of fighters belching out of the garrison moon.

Yelling in surprise, Lando launched a pair of Arkayd concussion missiles from the front tubes. The density of approaching ships was so great that even the wild shots scored twice, taking out a TIE fighter and a blast boat, while the hot debris cloud destroyed a heavily armed B-wing.

"Let's not get cocky because we took care of a couple of ships. I've got only six more missiles."

"We will not surrender now," Luke said.

"No, I just mean we're running, not fighting. At least the engines are in tip-top condition," Lando said. "The *Falcon* hasn't been this pampered since *I* owned her."

"How fast can we get out of here?" Luke asked.

Jacked next to the copilot's chair, Artoo chittered and bleeped. Luke glanced down and saw rows of flickering red lights on the navigation panel. "Uh oh."

"What is he saying?" Lando said. He flicked his gaze from the ships swarming by the front viewport to the little astromech droid. "What's wrong with him?"

"The navicomp's not working," Luke said.

"Well, fix it!"

Luke had already dashed around the bend in the corridor to pry off the access panel to the *Falcon's* navicomputer. He glanced at the boards, feeling his heart sink into a black hole as deep as the Maw. "They've pulled the coordinate module. It's not here."

Lando groaned. "Now what are we going to do?"

In response to Lando's concussion missiles, the Kessel fighters formed into tighter battle groups, striking at the *Falcon* with a firestorm of blaster bolts. Luke had to shield his eyes from the blinding flashes of near misses and deflected hits.

"I don't know, but we'd better do it as fast as we can."

"They're from the New Republic!" Moruth Doole fumed in his rage, stomping up and down. "They'll go back and report everything!" He straightened his mussed yellow cravat to regain his composure, but it didn't work. He wanted to squash the escapees like a pair of bugs to eat. Spies and traitors! They had led him along, lied to him, taunted him.

"Send out every ship we have!" he screamed into the

open channel that broadcast to his forces. He had managed to make it to the command center on the garrison moon. "Surround them, crush them, smash into them. I don't care what it takes!"

"Sending out every ship might not be a good strategy," responded one of the captains. "The pilots don't know the formations, and they'll just get in each other's way."

Doole's mechanical eye lay in pieces scattered about the top of the console, and he could not see well enough to put it back together. With the blurry focus of his one half-blind eye, Doole could not identify the dissenting mercenary.

"I don't care! I don't want to lose these like we lost Han Solo!" He pounded his soft fist on the console, jarring the pieces of his mechanical eye. The primary lens bounced, then slid off the edge to shatter on the floor.

The *Falcon* ran straight toward the Maw, leaving Kessel behind.

"We'll be all right," Luke said. "I can use the Force to guide us through on a safe path."

"If there *is* a safe path," Lando muttered.

Sweat stood out on Luke's forehead. "What other choice do we have? We can't hide anyplace else, we can't outrun all those fighters, and we can't go into hyperspace without a navicomp."

"What a great selection of options," Lando said.

Finally mobilized, the capital ships came after them, firing ion cannon blasts powerful enough to clear a path through an asteroid field. The two big Lancer frigates made a deadly web in front of the *Falcon* with their twenty quad-firing laser cannons; but the Lancers were sluggish, and the *Falcon* increased its lead.

Somehow the other capital ships anticipated their run

to the black hole cluster and converged ahead of them as Lando pushed the *Falcon*'s engines. "Come on, come on! Just squeeze a little more speed out."

Ten system patrol craft, originally designed for maximum speed to combat smugglers and pirates, surged past the *Falcon* and lined up in a blockade. But in the three-dimensional vastness of space, Lando managed to slip under their grasp. Laser blasts erupted all around them.

"Our shields are edging the redlines," Lando said.

Three *Carrack*-class light cruisers—midway in size between the Lancer frigates and the larger Dreadnaughts such as the ones in Bel Iblis's lost *Dark Force*—formed a triple-pronged pincer, right, left, and top.

In hot pursuit behind the *Falcon* came the jagged ovoid of a Loronar strike cruiser, the largest ship in the Kessel fleet. As the chase plowed through the net of system patrol craft, the strike cruiser harmlessly took stray fire meant for the *Falcon*.

Lando stared out the viewport windows at the horrifying spectacle of the Maw and the giant battleships moving to meet them. Artoo bleeped something that even Luke could not translate.

"Only a complete idiot would go into a place like that," Lando said. He squeezed his eyes shut.

"Then let's just hope they're not idiots, too," Luke said.

27

Admiral Daala stood in the bridge tower of the Star Destroyer *Gorgon*, looking out at her fleet and feeling the energy build inside her. The time was at hand! The Empire might have fallen, but with it went all the people who had squashed her. Now she could show her worth. Daala could fight her own battle.

She gazed at the misty colors of the Maw and the clump of strung-together rocks that had spawned the weapons for her assault. In formation the *Hydra*, the *Basilisk*, and the *Manticore* powered up, waiting to spring out upon the galaxy with swift and deadly precision. The New Republic would fall to its knees.

She had no interest in ruling the former Empire herself—Daala never had any such aspirations. Her main intent right now was just to cause them pain. She licked her lips, and her hair hung heavy down her back, serpentine like the demon for whom her flagship had been named. Grand Moff Tarkin would have been proud.

Commander Kratas, the man who ran the subsystems of the *Gorgon*, spoke to her from a communication terminal. "Admiral Daala, I have a priority message from the detention level!"

"Detention level? What is it?"

"The prisoners Han Solo and Kyp Durron have escaped! One guard was found stunned in Solo's detention chamber, and another is dead in Durron's cell. Both were stripped of their armor. We are attempting to question the survivor now."

Daala felt a jolt of anger disrupt the eagerness singing through her veins. She drew herself up taller, raising her eyebrows and focusing intently on Kratas. "Track the service numbers of the stolen uniforms. Maybe they've logged in somewhere." Her orders came like staccato laser blasts.

Kratas consulted his terminal, spoke into the comlink. Daala clasped her hands behind her back and paced, barking orders to the bridge personnel. "Put together a search party immediately. We'll comb every deck of the *Gorgon*. They can't have gotten off the ship. There's no place else they could have gone."

"Admiral!" Commander Kratas said. "The surviving guard claims that one of the scientists from the Installation came to see Solo. Qwi Xux. The guard insists that Dr. Xux had an authorization directly from you."

Daala's jaw dropped; then she clamped her lips together in a bloodless, iron line. "Check on the Wookiee! See what's happened to him."

Kratas queried the database. "The keeper says that the new Wookiee prisoner has been requisitioned and taken to a higher-priority assignment." He swallowed. "Qwi Xux was the one who requisitioned him. She used your authorization code again."

Daala's nostrils flared, but then another thought struck

her like a crashing asteroid. "Oh no!" she said. "They're after the Sun Crusher!"

Alone in the guarded hangar holding the Sun Crusher, Han clambered into the hatch. "Can't remember the last time I had to use a *ladder* to get inside a ship! Pretty primitive for such a sophisticated weapon."

"It works." Qwi hauled herself up the rungs behind him. "The sophistication is inside. All the rest is just window dressing."

Han sat down in the pilot's chair in the cockpit and looked at the controls. "Everything seems to be labeled the way it should be, though the placement is a little odd. What's this for? Wait a minute, I'll figure it out."

Kyp reached the top of the ladder, paused, then pulled off his stormtrooper helmet. "Those mask filters stink!" he said, then with obvious pleasure tossed the skull-like helmet to the floor of the chamber. It clattered and bounced like a severed head. Kyp's dark hair was curled with sweat and mussed from the confining helmet, but his face shone with a grin.

Chewbacca swung into the compartment, ducking his head and squeezing through the narrow hatch. He looked at the skylights in the chamber's ceiling, then growled at the shape of a Star Destroyer orbiting overhead.

Han dropped his own helmet to the floor of the cockpit. Kyp kicked it under the seat and out of the way. Han touched the Sun Crusher's navicomp, switching it on. "This thing is in better shape than the Imperial shuttle we stole. Are all the coordinates burned into the database, Doc?"

Qwi nodded, sitting down primly and strapping herself

into her seat. "The Sun Crusher has been ready to go for years. We've just been waiting for orders from the Empire. Good thing nobody came back, right?"

Han pursed his lips, scanning the controls. "Everything here looks pretty standard," he said. "I won't have much time for practice."

Chewbacca gave an ear-splitting Wookiee bellow of challenge. Below, Han heard the heavy armored door grind open and then clattering footsteps as a squad of stormtroopers charged into the chamber.

Standing at the door, Kyp stuck his head out of the narrow hatch. "Here they come!"

"Seal that hatch, kid," Han shouted. "We're in here for the duration now! Chewie, have you found the weapons controls yet?"

In the copilot's chair, Chewbacca ran his huge hands over the buttons and dials. Finally finding what he wanted, he let out a yowl. Defensive laser cannons mounted at different targeting angles swiveled as he tested the aiming mechanisms.

Small thuds banged against the Sun Crusher's hull as the stormtroopers fired their blaster rifles, causing no damage. Han looked at Qwi. "We don't even have the shields on!"

"This armor will hold against anything they can throw against us," she said with a smug smile. "It was designed to."

Han grinned and cracked his knuckles. "Well, in that case let's take an extra few seconds and do this right!" He worked the controls, activating the repulsorlift engines. The interior of the Sun Crusher wobbled as the entire craft rose into the air, floating on its repulsor cushion. Outside they could hear the faint screeching of an alarm.

"Chewie, point those laser cannons straight up. Let's

give ourselves a twenty-one-gun salute—right through the roof!"

The Wookiee roared to himself; then, without waiting for Han to give the order, he fired all of the Sun Crusher's weaponry at once. Kyp scrambled for his seat, strapping himself in. Qwi stared at the roof of the cockpit with wide eyes.

The ceiling of the hangar chamber blasted outward under the barrage of laser energy. Some of the larger chunks of rubble fell downward, clanging against the Sun Crusher's hull, but most of the skylights burst into space with the outrushing of contained air that spewed into the Maw.

Stormtroopers, flailing their arms and legs, were sucked out through the breach, flotsam among the rock and transparisteel debris in low orbit around the clustered rocks. Their armor might protect them against massive decompression for a few minutes, but every one of them was doomed.

Han raised the Sun Crusher up, accelerating through the escape hole they had blown through the top of the chamber. They shot into open space, and Han felt an exhilaration he had not felt since they had first arrived at Kessel.

"Here goes nothing!" he said. "Now for the fun part."

Staring down at the Installation from the *Gorgon*'s bridge, Admiral Daala felt her stomach knot. For years her entire duty had been to protect that small clump of planetoids, to pamper the scientists. Grand Moff Tarkin had said these people held the future security of the Empire, and she had believed him.

Daala had been stepped on, abused, taken advantage of at the Caridan military academy. Tarkin had rescued her from that. He had given her the responsibility and the power she had earned through her own abilities. She owed Tarkin everything.

She would avenge him by destroying the New Republic as she caused their star systems to go supernova one by one. They could hide nowhere. At the same time, she would make her mark on the history of the galaxy, a warlord who had succeeded where an entire Empire had failed. The thought made Daala's pale lips curl upward in a grim smile.

As she watched, Daala saw the puff of an explosion on one of the rocks of Maw Installation. Then the tiny form of the Sun Crusher streaked by, a characteristically angular speck fleeing the confines of the planetoid containing it.

"Red alert!" she shouted. "Mobilize all forces. They have the Sun Crusher, and we can't let them take it away. That is our most valuable weapon!"

"But . . . Admiral," Commander Kratas said, "if the technical reports are correct, nothing can harm the Sun Crusher."

"We must find some way to capture them. Mobilize the other Star Destroyers. We'll try to blockade them, cut off their escape. Release enough small fighters to overwhelm them."

She fixed Kratas with her gaze. Her hair seemed to rise by itself, as if threatening to become a garrote for his throat. "Make certain you understand this, Commander. I don't care how many losses we take, we cannot forfeit the Sun Crusher. That one weapon is worth more to me than all six TIE fighter squadrons onboard this Star Destroyer. Retrieve it at all costs."

Three Star Destroyers closed in behind the stolen Sun Crusher.

"Didn't take them long to figure something was up," Han said.

Clouds of TIE fighters spewed out of the launching bays of the *Manticore* and the *Gorgon*, swarming toward them in formations so dense that Han could not see through them. Flashing, splattering laser bolts struck like pelting raindrops on the viewscreen.

"I always wanted to see if I could fly blindfolded," Han said.

"What are they doing? Trying to smother us or just confuse us?" Qwi said.

The Sun Crusher, undamaged, rocked left and right from the pummeling of blaster strikes. "No, but they can wipe out our external weaponry—in fact, they already have," Han said, checking the readouts. "Every one of our lasers is offline."

"We just have to outrun them then," Kyp said.

Another Star Destroyer, the *Basilisk*, unleashed its squadrons of TIE fighters in wave after wave out of the launching bay.

"Those ships are going to clog space so we can't even move!" Han wrenched the Sun Crusher's controls, trying to dodge but just squeezing his eyes shut most of the time. "Whoever heard of a traffic jam in the middle of a black hole cluster?"

Kyp grabbed his shoulder. "Watch out, Han."

The fourth and last Star Destroyer reared up between them and the outside universe, blocking their passage. The *Hydra* lanced out with its enormous turbolaser cannons, aiming concentrated firepower at the single small ship. The remaining three Star Destroyers pressed in from behind to cut off their escape through the maze of the black hole cluster.

"Now what?" Kyp asked. The great arrowhead shape of the *Hydra* filled space in front of them.

"Qwi, you said this armor could take anything, didn't you?" Han asked.

"Everything I could test it with."

"All right, hold on. Time to accelerate for whatever this fancy toy is worth." He jammed the control levers back. The sudden force shoved the four escapees back into their seats as the Sun Crusher surged forward, straight toward the *Hydra*.

The huge battleship grew larger and larger, filling their entire field of view, and still expanding. Great green turbolaser bolts shot out at them, but the cannons could not refocus their aimpoints fast enough to compensate for the ship streaking directly at them.

"Han, what are you doing?" Kyp cried.

"Trust me," Han said. "Or actually, trust *her*." He nodded toward Qwi. "If she messed up her test measurements, we're all going to be one big organic pancake!"

The *Hydra*'s trapezoidal bridge tower rushed toward them, directly in their path. One suicidal TIE fighter rammed into the Sun Crusher to deflect its course, but merely exploded upon hitting the invincible quantum armor. Han had no trouble compensating for the error in trajectory.

"Look out!" Qwi yelled.

Details of the bridge tower filled their view now as they screamed toward the Imperial battleship. Han could actually see the windows of the bridge, the tiny figures of the command crew, some of them paralyzed in horror, others fleeing madly.

"Han!" Qwi and Kyp screamed in unison. Chewbacca gave a wordless roar.

"Right down their throat!" Han said.

The armored Sun Crusher tore through the *Hydra*'s control bridge like a bullet. Flying debris sprayed in their wake. The ship shot out the other side, shredding the superstructure on its way out.

The impact, the inferno, and a sound like a thousand gongs knocked them into a temporary stupor. Han finally whooped. "We made it!" Behind them the great battleship erupted in flames.

"You're crazy!" Qwi said.

"Don't thank me yet, Doc," Han said.

Burning, out of control, the decapitated *Hydra* wheeled backward, drifting helplessly toward the gravitational trap of one of the black holes. A flurry of escape pods shot out of the crew decks, but the low-power lifeboat engines could not generate sufficient acceleration to take them free of the black holes, and their trajectories began to spiral in.

The lower decks and the immense hyperdrive engines of the doomed Star Destroyer began to explode as it toppled into the unstable trap of the Maw cluster. Clouds of belching flames stretched out and elongated, mingling with the swirling gas as the *Hydra* began its infinite plunge into the singularity.

"We're not home free by a long shot," Han said as he soared into the soup of ionized gas. "Okay, Kyp," he said. "Now it's your turn to take the controls. Get us out of here."

Moments later the other three Star Destroyers rallied behind them in howling pursuit.

28

On the *Gorgon's* bridge, Admiral Daala watched in horror as the *Hydra* crumpled into destruction, its command bridge blown apart from the impact of the Sun Crusher. The battleship's only survivors would be the fighters in the six TIE squadrons; otherwise, all hands would be lost.

Though her expression was carved in ice, hot tears burned unshed in Daala's eyes. Thousands of people crashed to their deaths as the *Hydra* fell like a great slain dragon into the black whirlpool.

Glinting with its maddening invincibility, the Sun Crusher streaked through the wreckage, arrowing for the outer wall of the Maw.

"After them!" Daala snapped. "Full pursuit."

Failure crashed down on her like an anvil. She had been hiding in the Maw for too long, drilling her troops, putting them through practice exercises and dress rehearsals—but that had not been enough. In her first actual battle Daala had lost a quarter of her command—against *four* escaped prisoners!

Grand Moff Tarkin would have struck her sharply across the face and relieved her of her rank. Daala's cheeks stung with the imaginary blow. "They will regret the day they ever unleashed us!" she whispered.

But without the Sun Crusher, her plans to spread havoc among the New Republic would fall apart. She took a deep, sharp breath. No time to panic now. Think fast. Make decisions. Salvage the situation.

The communications dais shimmered, and an image of Tol Sivron appeared. The transmission flickered with staticky disruptions caused by the laser blasts flashing around them. "Admiral Daala! If you intend to deploy your fleet, I insist that you take the scientists of Maw Installation with you."

Not bothering to turn and look at the image of the Twi'lek, Daala continued to watch the *Hydra*'s fiery death. She thought of all the run-ins she'd had with the administrator—Sivron's incompetence, his delays, his excuses, his insistence on reports and tests ad nauseum. "You're on your own, Tol Sivron. It is time we do our duty as Imperial soldiers."

Tol Sivron flicked his head-tails straight out behind him in agitation. "Are you just going to leave us undefended? What about the orders Grand Moff Tarkin gave you? You are supposed to protect us! At least leave one of your Star Destroyers behind."

Daala shook her head, making coppery hair stream around her. "Tarkin is dead, and I'm making all the decisions now. I need every ounce of firepower to deal a fatal blow to the New Republic."

"Admiral Daala, I must insist—"

Daala yanked out the blaster pistol at her hip and pointed it at Sivron's image on the communications dais.

If the Twi'lek had been on the bridge in person, she would have killed him; but she would not destroy valuable equipment in a fit of anger. Keeping the blaster pointed directly into Tol Sivron's image, as if to threaten him, she strode forward. "Request *denied*, Director Sivron," Daala said, then disconnected the dais. She turned back to watch her fleet, undisturbed.

"Commander Kratas, we are going to leave the Maw in pursuit of the Sun Crusher. Recall all TIE fighter squadrons, now!"

Kratas gave the order, and she watched as the tiny ships streamed back toward their bays. Daala fidgeted, hating the delay. "Have all three Star Destroyers link into the same course computer. I will call up the specific coordinates from my own personal records, coded to my password."

The last time anyone had left Maw Installation, it had been the construction engineers—and they had been given the wrong course, dooming them to fall into one of the black holes. This time, though, Admiral Daala and all the firepower at her disposal would spring out upon the unwary galaxy, ready to take it back.

The Sun Crusher vibrated from a thousand stresses as it rode the razor's edge of gravity through the maelstrom of the Maw.

Kyp Durron sat at the simplified controls, next to the watchful eyes of Han Solo, but Han didn't dream of interfering with Kyp's intuition, no matter how nightmarish the path ahead seemed.

Kyp half closed his eyes as he looked through a mental vision of the perilous maze to safety. He jerked the ship to starboard, then plunged down, frantically avoiding unseen obstacles. Han kept a firm, reassuring pressure on the kid's shoulder. Hot gas blazed around them like hell's furnace.

Qwi Xux stared at Kyp and his blind piloting, her dark-blue eyes wide and her face transfixed with terror.

"Don't worry," Han said. "The kid knows what he's doing. He'll get us through, if anybody can."

"But how is he doing it?" Qwi's voice sounded flutey, like high-pitched notes played by an amateur performer.

"Not in any way your science can explain. I'm not sure I understand the Force myself, but I don't question it. I used to think it was a hokey religion, but not anymore."

Abruptly the curtains of gas parted in front of them, peeling away to reveal the black infinity of open space. At last they were free of the Maw!

In their mad run away from the forces of Kessel, Luke and Lando tried to push through the clustered capital ships. They winced simultaneously every time a bolt impacted the *Falcon*'s shields.

The mammoth form of the Loronar strike cruiser lay directly across their path, cutting them off from a dubious escape into the Maw. The ten ion cannons mounted in front of the strike cruiser belched destruction at them.

One bolt struck the *Millennium Falcon* dead on, and their systems flickered as sparks flew out of the control panels. Lando grabbed at the overrides and yelled to Luke, "Our shields are failing, and these guys don't want to take prisoners."

"Just get us into the Maw," Luke said. "It's our only chance."

"I never thought I'd be keeping my fingers crossed for *that* to happen!" Lando hunched over the controls. "Artoo, see if you can pump up the front shields. We're going to take quite a pounding from that strike cruiser when we pass by. One good hit and we're fried."

"Wait," Luke said, squinting at the swirling gases ahead of them. "Something's coming *out*!"

The thornlike form of the Sun Crusher streaked away from the cluster, leaving a trail of hot gases. A few moments later three fully armed Imperial-class Star Destroyers charged out of the Maw like banthas on fire.

Han's sigh of relief turned into an exclamation of dismay as he saw the array of Kessel's battle fleet massed in front of them, weapons already blazing. "Where did all those ships come from! They can't still be waiting for us!"

Exhausted from his piloting ordeal, Kyp said, "Han, why is it that every time we escape, we end up in a worse situation than the one we left?"

"Just good timing, kid." He slammed his fist down on the armored controls. "This isn't fair! They should have given us up for dead days ago!"

Chewbacca yowled and jabbed his hairy finger at the viewport, pointing to a ship at the vanguard of the gathered attack forces. The *Millennium Falcon*.

Han's lip curled downward. "I'm going to get that slime merchant who's flying my ship. Don't we have *any* of our laser cannons still operational?"

After rechecking the banks of instruments, Chewbacca grunted a negative.

"Then we'll ram them like we did that Star Destroyer."

"Han," Kyp said, "it looks to me like those other ships are *chasing* the *Falcon*. They're shooting at it."

Han leaned forward to take a closer look. Qwi agreed with Kyp's assessment. "That light freighter doesn't appear to be part of the attacking fleet."

Green turbolaser bolts streaked toward the *Falcon* from the system patrol craft, the big strike cruiser, and the Carrack-class light cruisers. Han's expression changed immediately. "Hey, what's going on here? They better not blow up my ship!"

Then Daala's Star Destroyers emerged behind them, plowing their way out of the clutches of the Maw.

"Look on the rear screens, Han!" Kyp said.

The Star Destroyers *Gorgon, Basilisk,* and *Manticore* burst out like monsters leaping from a closet, giant demons loaded with destructive weaponry from the fallen Empire.

The pell-mell mercenary forces of Kessel, already firing their laser cannons at the *Falcon,* ran headlong into the Imperial fleet. Some peeled sideways, turning to flee back toward the sanctuary of Kessel. Others panicked and opened fire on the Star Destroyers.

Admiral Daala tried to control the actions of her entire fleet from a single station on the bridge. Encountering the strange warships on the other side of the Maw shocked her, but she reacted quickly. "Shields up! This was a trap. The Rebels had their forces here waiting."

How had Han Solo deceived her interrogation droid? Had the Rebels somehow found out about the Installation and sent Solo inside with a cooked-up story to lure Daala's fleet out where they could be destroyed?

She saw the enemy fleet opening fire on her ships, but they were no match for her firepower. After all, Grand Moff Tarkin had given her enough weaponry to slag whole planets.

"Battle stations! Let's mop up this rabble once and for all." She pointed to the conglomeration of fighters swarming across her path. "Open fire!"

•   •   •

Luke and Lando spared a moment to glance at each other as the crossfire erupted around them. "This could be our chance to get out of here!" Lando said.

"Yeah, they might not even notice us leaving," Luke said.

"But where in the universe did those Star Destroyers come from?"

Suddenly a beep sounded from the *Falcon*'s comm-channels, distinctive because it sounded so innocent amid the warning tones of overloading systems and failing shields. Artoo whistled, calling attention to it. Lando looked down.

"We're getting a message over the *Falcon*'s private comm frequency." Lando frowned. "How would anybody know to transmit that? How would anybody even *know* the *Falcon*'s private code?"

Then Han Solo's angry voice burst over the speaker. "Whoever is on the *Falcon* better have a damned good reason for flying my ship!"

"Han! Is that you?" Lando said. A sudden thrill surged through Luke.

"Lando?" Han said after a pause. Over the speakers Chewbacca's roar drowned out Han's own exclamation. "What are you doing here?"

In space around them, blinding lances of light flashed as the weapons of two fleets were brought to bear. Like rival krayt dragons in mating season, the Kessel and Imperial forces slammed into each other in a total free-for-all space brawl.

"Han, listen to me. Luke is here, too," Lando said. "We've got to get away from Kessel, but the *Falcon*'s navicomputer is disabled. We can't make the jump into hyperspace."

An explosion rocked them from the starboard side, but

most of the Kessel fighters concentrated their firepower on the much larger threat of Daala's Imperial fleet. Though hopelessly outmatched, the three Carrack cruisers lined up and began to blast the *Basilisk*.

Over the private comm channel Han spoke to someone else behind him, then answered Lando. "We can dump the coordinates to your navicomp, and we'll fly tandem back to Coruscant."

Lando checked the computer, saw the numbers scrolling through, and raised a fist in triumph. "Got it! Artoo, get ready to go."

"You'd better keep my ship safe, Lando," Han said. "On my signal."

"You have my word, Han." Lando's hands flew over the *Falcon*'s familiar controls.

"Ready to enter hyperspace!" Han said.

The Kessel forces flanked and attacked the far larger Star Destroyers, pummeling the Imperial ships with blasts from their ion cannons and turbolaser banks. But the Star Destroyers disgorged their own squadrons of TIE fighters to butcher the unregimented forces from Kessel.

"On your mark, Han!"

"Punch it!"

The last thing they saw was Kessel's massive Loronar strike cruiser exploding under the concerted fire from the *Manticore* and the *Gorgon*. They watched the flaming hulk reel and ram into the Star Destroyer *Basilisk*, causing the bottom of the arrowhead hull to buckle and burn.

Then the universe filled with starlines.

29

The reunion was everything Han had imagined. He had spent a lot of time thinking about it during the long hyperspace flight back to Coruscant.

Leia and the twins met him the moment the Sun Crusher and the *Millennium Falcon* touched down side by side at the high landing platform. Han backed out of the Sun Crusher's hatch and began climbing down the ladder, but Leia ran forward and hugged him before he managed to get all the way down.

"Glad I'm back?" he asked.

"I missed you!" she said, kissing him.

"I know," he said with a roguish smile.

She put her hands on her hips. "What? You didn't miss me?"

Han turned away sheepishly. "Well, first we crashed on Kessel, then we were stuck in the spice mines, then we got captured by a bunch of Imperials in the middle of a black hole cluster. I really didn't have a whole lot of—"

When Leia looked as if she were going to punch him,

Han reacted with a grin. "But even through all that I don't remember more than about two seconds when I didn't miss you with all my heart."

Leia kissed him again.

Artoo trundled down the *Falcon*'s ramp, and Threepio bustled to greet him. "Artoo-Detoo! I'm so glad you're back. You wouldn't believe the difficulties I've had while you were gone!"

Artoo bleeped something nobody bothered to translate.

Kyp Durron and Qwi Xux climbed down from the Sun Crusher and stared out at the endless spires and towers of Imperial City, the metropolis of glinting transparisteel and alloy that stretched to the horizon. Above them the tiny lights of shuttles winked across the sky. "Now *that's* a city!" Kyp said with a sigh.

Qwi looked overwhelmed. The Sun Crusher would be transferred to a high-security hangar for study by the scientists of the New Republic. Qwi did not like abandoning it, but she had no choice.

Han strode over to his two children, bending his knees and gathering Jacen and Jaina into his arms. "Hey, kids! Do you remember your daddy? It's been a long time, huh?"

He mussed their hair and stared down at them with the wide-eyed astonishment he always felt when seeing how much they had grown between the visits Winter arranged to the hidden planet of Anoth. Now, though, Jacen and Jaina's two years of isolation and protection were over, and the children were home to stay, leaving only baby Anakin in need of special protection.

Jacen nodded; then a moment later Jaina nodded as well. Han wasn't sure he believed their answer, but he hugged them anyway. "Well, if you don't remember me, I'll try to make it up to you from now on."

● ● ●

A puffed-up official wearing the bright uniform of an offworld administrative office finally cornered Lando in a high-brow diplomatic lounge. The official held an armored briefcase similar to the type credit investigators carried, and he had the same pinch-faced demeanor of a person being given a mission whose importance he drastically overestimated.

"Are you Lando Calrissian?" the official said. "I have been attempting to locate you for several days. You've made my job most difficult." He bustled forward.

Lando saw that he could not slip out the back entrance of the lounge. Beside him at the table Han raised his eyebrows. Both of them had gone to the lounge to relax and settle down after their long debriefings by the Alliance High Command. Unfortunately, the lounge catered to bureaucrats and political functionaries, and served only cloyingly sweet drinks. Han and Lando sipped theirs slowly, trying to keep from grimacing.

Lando had heard rumors about an investigator trying to track him down and had managed to avoid him thus far. He feared some debtor coming after him, or a complaint regarding the tibanna gas mining operations he had abandoned on Bespin or the hot metal mines he had recently lost on Nkllon.

"Yes, you finally caught me," Lando said with a sigh. "What do you want? I can get the best legal representation in the galaxy here in Imperial City."

"That won't be necessary," the investigator said, heaving his armored briefcase onto the table, then fiddling with the cyberlock. "I'll be glad to be rid of this."

He lifted the lid of his case, and glittering light sparkled out. Other people in the lounge turned to gape.

The briefcase brimmed with carefully sorted packets of firefacet gems and shimmering chrysopaz.

"I am from the planet Dargul, and this is the reward owed to you by the Duchess Mistal for the safe return of her beloved consort Dack. You can have them appraised, but I am told these jewels are valued at approximately one million credits. Plus the briefcase, which is worth another forty."

Lando stared, hunched over the briefcase and dazzled by its contents. "A *million*?" he said.

"A million, plus forty for the briefcase."

"But I was only supposed to get half of the reward."

The investigator reached into his pocket. "I neglected to give you this. It is a message wafer for you from Slish Fondine, the owner of the blob stables where you assisted apprehending our consort Dack." He handed Lando a small rectangular object.

Lando turned it over in his hand, frowning, then ran his fingernail along the crease in its center. He cracked the message wafer open, then folded the two halves back to stand it upright on their small table.

An image of the blob-stable owner wafted up. "Greetings, Lando Calrissian. Since you are listening to this message, I will assume you've received your reward. I'm happy to say that your suggestion of not executing the criminal Tymmo has proved advantageous to all concerned. Duchess Mistal was so delighted to receive her consort back that she insisted on paying you the full reward, as well as offering to build a subsidiary blobstacle course for me in the main stadium on Umgul. We are already hiring creative engineers to design even tougher blobstacles for the new course, which, at the Duchess Mistal's request, will be called the 'Dack Track.'

"I am forwarding these firefacet and chrysopaz gems to you and hope you will spend the reward wisely. Why not come to Umgul and do some gambling? I'd be happy to be your host."

As the message dissolved into wisps of light, Lando could do little more than stare open-mouthed at his fortune.

Han laughed, then gestured for the short investigator to sit down. "Join us for a drink. In fact, here—you can have mine! It's too sweet for me anyway."

The investigator shook his head, the hard expression remaining on his face. "No, thank you. I don't think I would enjoy that. I'd rather get back to my work." With that the investigator left the lounge.

Han clapped Lando on the shoulder. "What are you going to do with all that money? Still thinking of investing it in spice mining?"

Lando came back to reality with a streak of defensiveness. "I hate to say this, but when Moruth Doole showed us around, I *was* rather impressed by the potential there. Spice has plenty of good uses, too—perfectly legitimate alternatives in psychological therapy, criminal investigation, communication with alien races, even artistic inspiration and entertainment. You knew that, Han, or you wouldn't have run spice yourself in the old days."

"You've got a point, Lando."

But Lando's imagination kept working on the problem. "I don't see why the spice mines have to be run as some sort of slave-lord operation. A lot of that could be automated. Even if there are more of those energy spiders running around, we could just use supercooled droids down in the deeper tunnels. No big investment. I don't see what the problem is."

Han looked at him skeptically, took a gulp of his sweet drink, then puckered his lips. "Uh-huh."

"Besides," Lando said, "I'm in the market for a new ship. I had to leave the *Lady Luck* stranded on Kessel. I may never get her back. What am I supposed to do for the time being?"

Seeing the eager stares from the others in the lounge, Lando snapped shut the lid of the armored briefcase. "Well, anyway, it's wonderful just to be solvent again!"

"Everybody in!" Wedge Antilles called inside the echoing Imperial City spaceport. "Let's get ready to go."

The last of the New Republic colonization specialists, sociologists, and survival instructors hauled their personal packs up the ramp of the medium transport. The ninety-meter-long ship occupied the better part of an entire bay in the supply sector, but the group needed a transport large enough to haul the Eol Sha survivors and their meager possessions, as well as the supplies necessary to set up a new home on Dantooine.

Wedge kept track of the final details of the operation, skimming a checklist on his datapad. At least this was a better assignment than knocking down ruined buildings—for the time being. He was glad to be flying again, even if it was only a sluggish transport carrier instead of a fighter.

But he knew tougher assignments lay in the near future. Admiral Daala and her three Imperial Star Destroyers had devastated the Kessel system, then vanished into hyperspace. The New Republic had sent its best trackers to find where she had gone to hide. Han insisted she was bound to make destructive guerrilla strikes, popping out of hyperspace and blasting a random planet. A loose cannon like Daala would not follow a predictable overall strategy. The entire New Republic had to be on its guard.

Chewbacca insisted that a New Republic occupation force head out to the Maw Installation to free the other Wookiee slaves. The Alliance High Command also wanted to get their hands on any other plans and prototypes remaining in the secret weapons lab. *So much for relaxing and picking up pieces*, Wedge thought. *Things are going to get a lot more interesting.*

But right now his assignment was to get the people of Eol Sha to safety on their new homeworld.

When everything checked out onboard, Wedge noticed Gantoris standing alone beside supply containers piled next to the wall. The displaced colony leader looked tall and powerful, but didn't seem to know how to react to seeing the relocation ship leave.

"Don't worry," Wedge called, "we'll take your people to their new home. After living with volcanoes and earthquakes all their lives, Dantooine will seem like a paradise to them."

Gantoris nodded, furrowing his smooth forehead. "Give them my greetings."

Wedge waved to him. "You just go and become the best of the new Jedi Knights."

Luke looked deep into the eyes of Kyp Durron, searching for the core of a Jedi. The younger man flinched but continued to meet Luke's gaze.

"Are you nervous, Kyp?" Luke asked.

"A little. Should I be?"

Luke smiled as he remembered boasting to Yoda that he wasn't afraid of his impending Jedi training. "You will be," Yoda had said, "you *will* be!"

Han interrupted them, clapping his hand on Kyp's shoulder. "You should have been there to watch him zipping through the dark spice tunnels. And he navigated us right through the Maw with his eyes closed! This kid has a lot of potential, Luke."

Luke nodded. "I was about to do that trick in the Maw myself. I know how difficult it must have been."

"Does that mean you'll take me for your Jedi academy?" Kyp asked. "I want to know how to use this power I have. While I was sitting in a cell on the Star Destroyer, I vowed never to be helpless again."

Luke withdrew the power pack and sheet-crystal sensor paddles from the old Imperial scanner that had once been used to detect Jedi descendants. "Let's try this scanner first." Untangling the cords, Luke stretched out the sheet-crystal paddles on either side of Kyp. "This won't hurt or anything. It just maps the potential of your senses."

He tripped the scan switch on the control pack, and a narrow line of coppery light traveled down Kyp's body as a smaller image of the copper scan-line reappeared in reverse motion in front of them, digitizing its analysis of Kyp Durron.

Kyp's reproduction hung in the air, bathed with the pale-blue corona Luke had found on the others with genuine Jedi potential. But the aura waxed and waned, knotting itself, turning darker, growing brighter, streaked with red, then becoming tangled.

"What does that mean?" Kyp said.

"He's okay, isn't he?" Han seemed eager to have his protegé accepted.

Luke wondered at the anomalous mapping, disturbed because he didn't know how to interpret it. The shimmer could be a result of faulty scanning equipment, since the instrument had been roughly treated and could no longer be calibrated—or it could be that because of the strain and pressure on Kyp for so many years, he hadn't quite sprung back to his full potential yet.

"I see a lot of power there. A lot," Luke said, and Kyp sighed at the reassurance. "Let me try one other test."

Luke stretched out his hands to touch the curly black

hair on Kyp's head. "Let him do what he needs to," Han whispered to the young man. "Trust him."

Luke closed his eyes and sent a tendril of thought to the back of Kyp's mind where the deep primal memories hid, leaving little room for conscious thought. Luke touched inward to the isolated nub in his subconscious. He pushed—

—and suddenly found himself hurled backward, tossed aside like a piece of fluff in a Bespin wind storm. He landed flat on his back on the other side of the room, gasping.

Han and Kyp ran toward him as he struggled to prop himself up on his elbows. Luke shook the daze from his head.

"I'm sorry!" Kyp said. "I don't know what I did! I didn't try to. Honest!"

"What happened?" Han said. "What does that mean for Kyp?"

Luke blinked, then smiled at the others. "Don't worry about me. I triggered that myself." He shook his head. "Kyp, you have *amazing* power!"

Luke stood up and gripped the young man's hand. "You're definitely welcome to train at my academy. I just hope I know how to handle it when you come into full control of your abilities!"

EPILOGUE

Luke Skywalker, Jedi Master, stood atop the Great Temple on the fourth moon of Yavin.

Below his feet lay the empty throne room and grand audience chamber with skylights open to the sun. Garbed in a new Jedi cloak, wearing his lightsaber at his side, Luke felt warmth bathing him. Spicy, lingering scents rose as steam from the lush rain forest below.

The ancient ruins left behind by the vanished Massassi race sprawled out in great geometrical edifices, now overgrown by voracious jungles. Luke stood on top of the ziggurat that had once been a towering lookout station when the Rebel base had been housed on Yavin 4.

In the sky a swollen sphere of pale orange filled most of his view, the looming planet Yavin. The bloated gas giant had been a shield for the Rebel base as the first Death Star orbited into position to fire with its planet-destroying superlaser. The Yavin base had been abandoned by the Rebels years before. But many of the broken stone structures were still serviceable.

With the unleashed might of the Maw fleet, and the expected depredations of Admiral Daala, the New Republic desperately needed a strong force beyond pure military might, a group of guardians to maintain order in the galaxy.

Luke intended to bring together everyone he could, immediately—not just Gantoris and Streen, but also Kyp Durron, Mara Jade, several of the witches of Dathomir, Kam Solusar, and others he had encountered since the Battle of Endor. And the search for new people with Jedi potential would have to be intensified. He needed candidates, as many as possible.

The top levels of some of the flat-roofed Massassi structures had been clear enough for Luke to land his ship. On the broad courtyard once used as a launching pad by the Alliance, Luke's old X-wing fighter lay cooling in the rising mists from the Yavin jungles.

When Mon Mothma and Leia had offered Luke the abandoned Rebel base, he had jumped at the chance.

To begin his actual training, Luke tried to recreate all the exercises Yoda had taught him on Dagobah, as well as the practice sessions Obi-Wan Kenobi had begun. Luke also had the ancient Jedi Holocron, the visual historical database Leia had taken from the resurrected Emperor's stronghold. He had studied the information from the hidden repository of Jedi knowledge on Dathomir. He had many tools, and his students carried inside themselves doorways to great power.

But again Luke worried. If one of his trainees—or more than one!—fell to the dark side, would he himself have the power to bring him back? And who was this "dark man" who haunted Gantoris's dreams with prophesies of destruction?

As Luke looked across the sweeping vista of dense wilderness, he saw wide burned scars where fires had ravaged the rain forests. But the ecology of the moon struck back with a vengeance, healing itself. Dense clusters of sharp-smelling blueleaf shrubs, Massassi trees, and climbing ferns clogged the ground in an impenetrable mesh that stretched as far as he could see, broken only by scattered temple ruins poking through the greensward.

The alien constructions left behind by the Massassi seemed filled with secrets and knowledge of their own. Luke blinked his eyes and felt the power of the place around him, the wonder, the mystery of it all. He could not wait to begin bringing his students here.

It was the perfect place to train a new order of Jedi Knights.

About the Author

For some years KEVIN J. ANDERSON has worked as a technical editor and writer at the large government research lab, Lawrence Livermore National Laboratory . . . which he insists has nothing to do with the large Imperial research lab, Maw Installation, in JEDI SEARCH. He is also the author of 18 science fiction or fantasy books, including three co-written with Doug Beason—LIFELINE, THE TRINITY PARADOX, and ASSEMBLERS OF INFINITY. His works have appeared on numerous Best of the Year lists, as well as preliminary or final ballots for the Nebula and Bram Stoker Awards. In addition to the three novels in the "Jedi Academy" trilogy, he has worked on various STAR WARS projects, including THE ILLUSTRATED STAR WARS UNIVERSE, an art book featuring 25 new paintings by artist Ralph McQuarrie showing daily life on the planets in the STAR WARS universe. He has edited three anthologies of short stories, the first of which—TALES FROM THE STAR WARS CANTINA—tells the stories of all the bizarre characters from the Cantina scene.

Here is an excerpt from

Dark Apprentice

by Kevin J. Anderson

A Bantam Paperback

In the second exciting novel in the Jedi Academy Trilogy, Luke Skywalker will begin to train his students—only to find the most brilliant of them delving dangerously into the dark side of the Force. Meanwhile, Admiral Daala is using her Imperial fleet to conduct guerrilla warfare on peaceful worlds—and will soon threaten the watery homeworld of Admiral Ackbar.

In the following excerpt, from early in *Dark Apprentice*, Ackbar and Leia Organa-Solo are headed for the planet Vortex on a diplomatic mission to attend the Concert of the Winds, a rare and beautiful event in Vor culture that is about to be marred by tragedy.

Fidgeting from the long voyage
in the expanded B-wing fighter, Leia Organa-Solo rode
in silence beside Admiral Ackbar. The two of them sat
in the cramped, metallic-smelling cockpit as the ship
plunged through hyperspace.

Being Minister of State for the New Republic kept
Leia on the move, shuttling from diplomatic event to
ambassadorial reception to political emergency. Dutifully, she hopped across the galaxy, putting out fires
and helping Mon Mothma hold together a fragile alliance in the vacuum left by the fall of the Empire.

Leia had already reviewed the background holos of
the planet Vortex dozens of times, but she could not
keep her mind on the upcoming Concert of the Winds.
Diplomatic duties took her away from her family far too
often, and she used quiet moments to think about her
husband, Han, and her twin children, Jacen and Jaina.
It had been too long since she had held her youngest

baby, Anakin, still isolated and protected on the secret planet Anoth.

It seemed that every time Leia tried to spend a weekend, a day, even an *hour* alone with her family, something interrupted. She seethed inside each time, unable to show her feelings because she had to wear a calm political mask.

In her younger days Leia had devoted her life to the Rebellion; she had worked behind the scenes as a princess of Alderaan, as Senator Bail Organa's daughter; she had fought against Darth Vader and the Emperor and more recently Grand Admiral Thrawn.

Now, though, she felt torn between her duties as Minister of State, as Han Solo's wife, and as a mother to three children. Despite her guilt, she had allowed the New Republic to come first. This time. Again.

Beside her in the cockpit Admiral Ackbar moved his amphibious hands quickly, fluidly, as he pulled several control levers. "Dropping out of hyperspace now," he said in his gravelly voice.

The salmon-colored alien seemed perfectly comfortable in his shining white uniform. Ackbar swiveled his gigantic glassy eyes from side to side, as if to take in every detail of his craft. Through the hours of their journey Leia had not seen him fidget once.

He and the other inhabitants of the watery world Calamari had suffered much under the Empire's iron grip. They had learned how to be quiet yet listen to every detail, how to make their own decisions, and how to act upon them. Working as a loyal member of the Rebellion, Ackbar himself had been instrumental in developing the B-wing class of starfighters, which had taken a huge toll on Imperial TIE fighters.

As Leia watched him pilot the stretched-out, cumbersome-looking fighter, Ackbar seemed an integral part of the gangly craft that appeared to be all wings and turbolaser turrets mounted around a dual cockpit. Ackbar's crew of fishlike Calamarians, led by his chief starship mechanic Terpfen, had expanded the former one-man craft into Ackbar's personal diplomatic shuttle, adding a single passenger seat.

Through the curved dome of the cockpit windows Leia watched multicolored knots of hyperspace evaporate into a star-spotted panorama. The sublight engines kicked in, and the B-wing streaked toward the planet Vortex.

"It's beautiful," Leia said, peering over the plasteel lip of the viewport at the planet directly beneath them. The blue and metallic-gray ball hung alone in space, moonless. Its atmosphere showed complex embroideries of cloud banks and storm systems, swirls and spirals of clouds that raced in horrendous gales.

Leia remembered her astronomical briefings on Vortex: the planet's axis tottered at a high tilt, which produced extremely sharp and severe seasonal changes. At the onset of winter a vast polar cap formed rapidly, freezing out atmospheric gases like a great flood going down a drain. The sudden drop in pressure caused immense air currents; clouds and vapor streamed southward in a battering ram to fill the empty zone where the atmosphere had solidified.

The Vors, hollow-boned humanoids with a rack of

lacy wings on their backs, went to ground during storm season, taking shelter in half-buried hummock dwellings. To celebrate the winds, though, the Vors had established a cultural festival renowned throughout the galaxy.

Leia's dress uniform felt damp and clinging, and she tried to adjust the folds of slick white fabric to make herself more comfortable. As Ackbar concentrated on the approach to Vortex, Leia pulled out her pocket holopad, laying the flat silvery plate on her lap.

Deciding to review the details one more time before they landed and the diplomatic reception began, she touched the icons etched into the synthetic marble frame. It would not do for the Minister of State to make a political faux pas.

A translucent image shimmered and grew out of the silvery holoscreen, rising up in a miniaturized projection of the Cathedral of Winds. Defying the hurricane gales that thrashed through their atmosphere, the Vors had built a tall ethereal structure that had resisted the fierce storm winds for centuries. Delicate and incredibly intricate, the Cathedral of Winds rose like a castle made of eggshell-thin crystal. Thousands of passageways wound through hollow chambers and turrets and spires. Sunlight glittered on the transparent walls, reflecting the rippling fields of windblown grasses that sprawled across the surrounding plains.

At the beginning of storm season gusts of wind would blow through thousands of different-sized openings in the hollow walls, whipping up a reverberating, mournful music that whistled through pipes of various diameters.

The music of the winds was never the same twice, and the Vors allowed their cathedral to play only once each year. During the concert thousands of Vors flew into or climbed through the various spires and wind-pipes, opening and closing air passages to mold the music into a sculpture, a work of art created by the weather systems of the storm planet and the Vor people.

On the holopad Leia scrolled to the next files, skimming. The music of the winds had not been heard for decades, not since Senator Palpatine had announced his New Order and declared himself Emperor. In horror at the excesses of the Empire, the Vors had sealed the holes in their cathedral and refused to let the music play for anyone.

But this season the Vors had invited representatives from the New Republic to listen.

Ackbar opened a comm channel and pushed his fishlike face closer to the voice pickup. Leia watched the bristly feelers around his mouth jiggle as he spoke. "Vortex Cathedral landing pad, this is Admiral Ackbar. We are in orbit and approaching your position."

A Vor voice crackled back over the speaker sounding like two dry twigs rattling together. "New Republic shuttle, we are transmitting landing coordinates. They take into account wind shear and storm systems along your descent. Our atmospheric turbulence is quite unpredictable and dangerous. Please follow precisely."

"Understood." Ackbar settled back into his seat, rubbing broad shoulder blades against the ridged back of the chair. He pulled several black strands in a web across the white chest of his uniform. "You'd better strap in, Leia," Ackbar said. "It's going to be a bumpy ride."

Leia switched off her holopad and tucked it beside her seat, wiggling it until the slick surface slid between the other debris crammed there. She strapped in, confined by the restraints, and took a deep breath of the stale recycled air. The faintest fishy undertone suggested Calamarian anxiety.

Staring intently ahead, Ackbar took his B-wing down into the swirling atmosphere of Vortex, straight toward the storm systems.

Ackbar knew that humans could not read expressions on the broad alien faces of the Mon Calamari. He hoped Leia did not realize how uneasy he felt flying the shuttle through the hellish weather patterns.

Leia did not know that Ackbar had volunteered to pilot the mission because he trusted no other person to take someone as important as the Minister of State, and he trusted no other vehicle more than his personal B-wing fighter.

He turned both of his large brown eyes forward to watch the approaching cloud layers. The ship cut through the outer layers of atmosphere, zooming into buffeting turbulence. The sharp wings of the starfighter sliced through the air, curling wind in a rippling wake. The edges of the craft's prong wings glowed cherry red from the screaming descent.

Ackbar gripped the controls with his finlike hands, forcing his concentration into fast reactions, split-second decisions, making sure everything worked just right—because there would be no room for error. He cocked his right eye down to scan the landing coordinates the Vor technician had transmitted.

The craft began to rattle and jitter. His stomach lurched as a sudden updraft knocked them several hundred meters higher and then let them fall in a deep plunge until he managed to wrestle control back.

Ackbar rechecked the landing coordinates as blurry fists of high-rising clouds smacked into the transparisteel viewports, leaving trails of condensed moisture that fanned out and evaporated.

Ackbar tracked from side to side across the panels with his left eye, verifying all the readouts. No red lights. His right eye cocked back to catch a glimpse of Leia sitting rigid and silent, held in place by black restraint cords. Her dark eyes seemed almost as wide as a Mon Calamarian's, but her lips were pressed together in a thin white line. She seemed afraid, but afraid to show it, trusting in his ability. Leia said no word to distract him.

The B-wing headed down in a spiral, skirting an immense cyclonic disturbance. The wind hooked onto the rattling wings of the fighter, knocking the craft from side to side. Ackbar wrestled with the controls, deploying the secondary aileron struts in an attempt to regain stability, then he retracted the turbolaser turrets to minimize wind resistance.

"New Republic shuttle, we show you off course!" The

brittle twiglike voice of the Vor controller came over the speaker, muffled by the roaring sound of the wind.

Ackbar turned his left eye to double-check the coordinate display and saw that the starfighter had indeed veered from its course. Calm and focused, he tried to lurch the craft back onto the appropriate vector. He couldn't believe he had gone so far astray, unless he had misread the coordinates in the first place.

As he yanked the B-wing toward the wall of spiraling clouds, a blast of gale-force winds hammered them into a roll, and Ackbar slammed against his pilot seat. The fighter spun end over end, knocked and battered by the wind storm.

Leia let out a small scream before clamping her mouth shut and closing her eyes. Ackbar hauled with all his strength upon the levers, firing stabilizer jets in a counterclockwise maneuver to counteract the spin.

The B-wing responded, finally slowing its crazed descent. Ackbar looked up to see himself surrounded by a cottony whirlwind of mist. He had no idea which direction was up. He accordioned out the craft's set of perpendicular wings and locked them into a more stable cruising position. His fighter responded sluggishly, but his cockpit panels told him that the wings were in place.

"New Republic shuttle! New Republic shuttle! Please respond."

Ackbar finally got the B-wing upright and flying again but found he had missed his coordinates once more. He angled back into them as easily as he could. His mouth felt dessicated as he checked the altitude panels and saw with alarm how far they had dropped.

The metal hull plates on the fighter craft smoked and glowed orange with the heat of tearing through the atmosphere. Lightning slashed on all sides. Blue balls of discharge electricity flared from the tips of the wings.

His readouts scrambled with racing curls of static, then came back on again. The rest of the cockpit power systems dimmed, then brightened as reserve power kicked in.

Ackbar risked another glance at Leia and saw her fighting with fear and helplessness. He knew she was a woman of action and would do anything to help him out—but there was nothing she could do. If he had to, Ackbar could eject her to safety—but he did not dare risk losing his B-wing yet. He could still pull off a desperate but intact landing.

Suddenly the clouds peeled away like a wet rag ripped from his eyes. The wind-whipped plains of Vortex spread out below, furred with golden-brown and purple grasses. The grasslands rippled as the wind combed invisible fingers through the blades. Concentric circles of bunkerlike Vor shelters surrounded the center of their civilization.

He heard Leia gasp in a deep wonder that sliced through even her numbing terror. The enormous Cathedral of Winds glinted with light and swirled with oily shadows as clouds and storm systems marched overhead. The high lacy structure seemed far too delicate to withstand the storms of Vortex.

Winged creatures swarmed up and down the sides of

the fluted chambers, opening passages for the wind to blow through and create the famous music.

Ackbar looked at his vector again, scrambling for control.

"New Republic shuttle, you are on the wrong course! This is an emergency. You must abort your landing."

With a shock Ackbar saw that the displayed coordinates had changed again from the first numbers he had seen. The B-wing did not respond as he fought the controls. The Cathedral of Winds grew larger every second.

Cocking an eye to look through the upper rim of the domed viewport, Ackbar saw that one of the perpendicular wings had jammed at an atrocious angle, yielding the worst control and maximum wind resistance. The angled wing slapped against the turbulence and jerked the starfighter to the left.

His cockpit panels insisted that both wings had deployed properly, yet his own vision told him otherwise.

Ackbar jabbed the controls again, trying to straighten the wing to regain control. The bottom half of his body felt cold and tingly as his reserves of energy went into his mind and his hands on the control levers.

"Something is very wrong here," he said.

Leia stared out the viewport. "We're heading straight for the cathedral!"

One of the aileron struts buckled and snapped from the plasteel hull, dragging power cables as it tore free. Sparks flew, and more hull plates ripped up.

Ackbar strangled an outcry. Suddenly the control

lights flickered and dimmed. He heard the grinding hum as his main cockpit panels went dead. He had to hit the second auxiliary backup he had personally designed into the modified B-wing.

"I don't understand it," Ackbar said. His voice sounded loud and guttural in the confines of the cockpit. "This ship was just reconditioned. My own Mon Calamari mechanics were the only ones who touched it."

"New Republic shuttle!" the voice on the radio insisted.

On the crystalline Cathedral of Winds multicolored Vors scrambled down the sides, fleeing as they saw the craft hurtling toward them. Some of the creatures took flight, while others stared in horror. Thousands of them packed the immense glassy structure.

Ackbar hauled the control to the right or left, anything to make the craft swerve—but nothing responded. All the power had died.

He couldn't raise or lower the ship's wings. He was in a large deadweight falling straight toward the huge cathedral. Desperately he hit the full battery reserves, knowing they could do nothing for the mechanical subsystems, but at least he could lock in a full-power crash shield around the B-wing.

And before that, he could break Leia free to safety.

"I'm sorry, Leia," Ackbar said. "Tell them all I am sorry."

He punched the button on the control panel that cracked open the right side of the cockpit, splitting open the hull and blasting free the tacked-on passenger seat.

As it shot Leia into the clawlike winds, Ackbar heard the wind screech at him through the open cockpit. The crash shield hummed faintly as he hurtled toward the great crystalline structure. The fighter's engine smoldered and smoked but did not respond.

Ackbar stared straight ahead until the end, not blinking his huge Calamarian eyes.

Leia found herself flying through the air. The blast of the ejection seat had knocked the breath out of her.

She couldn't even shout as the wind caught and spun her chair. The seat's safety repulsorlifts held her like a gentle hand and slowly lowered her toward the whiplike strands of pale-hued grasses below.

She looked up to see Ackbar's B-wing shuttle in the last instant before the crash. The starfighter smoked and whined as it plunged like a metal filing into a powerful magnet.

In a frozen moment she heard the loud, mournful fluting of winds whistling through thousands of crystalline chambers. The breeze picked up with a gust, making the music sound like a sudden high-pitched gasp of terror. The winged Vors scrambled and attempted to flee, but most could not move quickly enough.

Ackbar's B-wing plowed into the lower levels of the Cathedral of Winds like a meteor exploding the brittle crystal. The booming impact made the crystalline towers detonate into razor-edged spears that flew in all directions like a gigantic shrapnel bomb.

The sound of tinkling glass, the roar of sharp broken pieces falling in an avalanche, the shriek of the wind, the screams of the Vors sliced to ribbons—all combined into the most agonizing sound Leia had ever heard.

The entire glasslike structure seemed to take forever to collapse. Tower after tower fell in upon itself.

The winds kept blowing, making somber noises through the hollow columns, changing pitch. The music became a thinner and thinner wail, leaving only a handful of intact wind tubes lying on their sides on the ground.

As Leia wept with great sobs that seemed to tear her apart, the automatic escape chair gently drifted to the ground and settled in the whispering grasses.

STAR WARS – JEDI SEARCH
Volume I of the Jedi Academy Trilogy
by Kevin J. Anderson

As the war between the Republic and the scattered remnants of the Empire continues, two children – the Jedi twins – will come into their powers in a universe on the brink of vast changes and challenges. In this time of turmoil and discovery, an extraordinary new *Star Wars* saga begins . . .

While Luke Skywalker takes the first step toward setting up an academy to train a new order of Jedi Knights, Han Solo and Chewbacca are taken prisoner on the planet Kessel and forced to work in the fathomless depths of a spice mine. But when Han and Chewie break away, they flee desperately to a secret imperial research laboratory surrounded by a cluster of black holes – and go from one danger to a far greater one . . .

A Bantam Paperback
0 553 40808 9

STAR WARS – CHAMPIONS OF THE FORCE
Volume III of the Jedi Academy Trilogy
by Kevin J. Anderson

Suspended helplessly between life and death, Luke Skywalker lies in state at the Jedi academy. But on the spirit plane, Luke fights desperately for survival, reaching out psychically to the Jedi twins. At the same time, Leia is on a life-and-death mission of her own, a race against Imperial agents hoping to destroy a third Jedi child – Leia and Han's baby Anakin – hidden on the planet Anoth. Meanwhile, Luke's former protegé Kyp Durron has pirated the deadly Sun Crusher on an apocalyptic mission of mass destruction, convinced he is fighting for a just cause. Hunting down the rogue warrior, Han must persuade Kyp to renounce his dark crusade and regain his lost honour. To do it, Kyp must take the Sun Crusher on a suicide mission against the awesome Death Star prototype – a battle Han knows they may be unable to win . . . even with Luke Skywalker at their side!

A Bantam Paperback
0 553 40810 0

STAR WARS – HEIR TO THE EMPIRE
Volume 1 of the Empire Trilogy
by Timothy Zahn

The Adventure Continues!

A long time ago in a galaxy far, far away . . .

It is a time of renewal, five years after the destruction of the Death
Star and the defeat of Darth Vader and the Empire.

But with the war seemingly won, strains are now beginning to
show in the rebel alliance. New challenges to galactic peace have
arisen, and Luke Skywalker hears a voice from his past, a voice
with a warning.

Beware the Dark Side . . .

Heir To The Empire is the first volume in the authorised sequel to
the most popular series in movie history.

A Bantam Paperback
0 553 40471 7

STAR WARS – DARK FORCE RISING
Volume 2 of the Empire Trilogy
by Timothy Zahn

Five years after the *Return of the Jedi*, the fragile Republic that was born with the defeat of Darth Vader, the Emperor, and the infamous *Death Star* stands threatened from within and without. The dying Empire's most cunning and ruthless warlord – Grand Admiral Thrawn – has taken command of the remnants of the Imperial fleet and launched a massive campaign aimed at the Republic's destruction. With the aid of unimaginable weapons Thrawn plans to overwhelm the New Republic, and impose his iron will throughout the Galaxy.

Meanwhile, dissension and personal ambition threaten to tear the Republic apart. As Princess Leia – pregnant with Jedi twins – risks her life to bring a proud and lethal alien race into alliance with the Republic. Han and Lando Calrissian race against time to find proof of treason inside the highest Republic Council.

But most dangerous of all is a new Dark Jedi, risen from the ashes of a shrouded past, consumed by bitterness, and thoroughly, utterly insane . . .

A Bantam Paperback
0 553 40442 3

STAR WARS – THE LAST COMMAND
Volume 3 of the Empire Trilogy
by Timothy Zahn

It is five years after the events of the *Return of the Jedi*. The fragile New Republic reels from the attacks of Grand Admiral Thrawn, who has not only rallied the remaining Imperial forces but has driven the rebels back with an abominable new technology: clone soldiers.

Hopes are dim as Thrawn mounts a final siege against the Republic. While Han and Chewbacca struggle to form a wary alliance of smugglers in a last-ditch attack against the Empire, Leia keeps the Alliance together and prepares for the birth of her Jedi twins. But the Empire has too many ships and too many clones to combat. The Republic's only hope lies in sending a small force, led by Luke, into the very stronghold that houses Thrawn's terrible cloning machines.

There a final danger awaits. The dark Jedi C'baoth schemes in his secret fortress, directing the battle against the rebels, nursing his insanity, and building his strength to finish what he had already started – the destruction of Luke Skywalker.

An odyssey of fast-paced action, stunning revelation, and final confrontation, *The Last Command* spans a galaxy in flames – a tale that will conclude in this third and last instalment as Good and Evil battle 'a long time ago, in a galaxy far, far away . . .'

A Bantam Paperback
0 553 40443 1

A SELECTION OF STAR WARS TITLES
AVAILABLE FROM BANTAM BOOKS

☐ 40808 9	STAR WARS: Jedi Search		Kevin J. Anderson	£5.99
☐ 40809 7	STAR WARS: Dark Apprentice		Kevin J. Anderson	£5.99
☐ 40810 0	STAR WARS: Champions of the Force		Kevin J. Anderson	£5.99
☐ 40971 9	STAR WARS: Tales from the Mos Eisley Cantina	Kevin J. Anderson (ed.)	£5.99
☐ 50413 4	STAR WARS: Tales from Jabba's Palace	Kevin J. Anderson (ed.)	£5.99
☐ 50471 1	STAR WARS: Tales of the Bounty Hunters	Kevin J. Anderson (ed.)	£5.99
☐ 40880 1	STAR WARS: Darksaber		Kevin J. Anderson	£5.99
☐ 50546 7	STAR WARS: The Paradise Snare		A. C. Crispin	£5.99
☐ 50547 5	STAR WARS: The Hutt Gambit		A. C. Crispin	£5.99
☐ 50548 3	STAR WARS: Rebel Dawn		A. C. Crispin	£5.99
☐ 40926 3	STAR WARS X-Wing 1: Rogue Squadron		Michael A. Stackpole	£5.99
☐ 40923 9	STAR WARS X-Wing 2: Wedge's Gamble		Michael A. Stackpole	£5.99
☐ 40925 5	STAR WARS X-Wing 3: The Krytos Trap		Michael A. Stackpole	£5.99
☐ 40924 7	STAR WARS X-Wing 4: The Bacta War		Michael A. Stackpole	£5.99
☐ 50599 8	STAR WARS X-Wing 5: Wraith Squadron		Aaron Allston	£5.99
☐ 50600 5	STAR WARS X-Wing 6: Iron Fist		Aaron Allston	£5.99
☐ 50605 6	STAR WARS X-Wing 7: Solo Command		Aaron Allston	£5.99
☐ 50688 9	STAR WARS X-Wing 8: Isard's Revenge		Michael A. Stackpole	£5.99
☐ 81271 8	STAR WARS X-Wing 9: Starfighters of Adumar		Aaron Allston	£5.99
☐ 50431 2	STAR WARS: Before the Storm		Michael P. Kube-McDowell	£5.99
☐ 50479 7	STAR WARS: Shield of Lies		Michael P. Kube-McDowell	£5.99
☐ 50480 0	STAR WARS: Tyrant's Test		Michael P. Kube-McDowell	£5.99
☐ 40881 X	STAR WARS: Ambush at Corellia		Roger MacBride Allen	£5.99
☐ 40882 8	STAR WARS: Assault at Selonia		Roger MacBride Allen	£5.99
☐ 40883 6	STAR WARS: Showdown at Centerpoint		Roger MacBride Allen	£5.99
☐ 40878 X	STAR WARS: The Crystal Star		Vonda McIntyre	£5.99
☐ 50472 X	STAR WARS: Shadows of the Empire		Steve Perry	£5.99
☐ 50497 5	STAR WARS: The New Rebellion		Kristine K. Rusch	£5.99
☐ 40758 9	STAR WARS: The Truce at Bakura		Kathy Tyers	£4.99
☐ 40807 0	STAR WARS: The Courtship of Princess Leia		Dave Wolverton	£4.99
☐ 40471 7	STAR WARS: Heir to the Empire		Timothy Zahn	£5.99
☐ 40442 3	STAR WARS: Dark Force Rising		Timothy Zahn	£5.99
☐ 40443 1	STAR WARS: The Last Command		Timothy Zahn	£5.99
☐ 40879 8	STAR WARS: Children of the Jedi		Barbara Hambly	£5.99
☐ 50529 7	STAR WARS: Planet of Twilight		Barbara Hambly	£5.99
☐ 50417 7	STAR WARS: Specter of the Past		Timothy Zahn	£5.99
☐ 50690 0	STAR WARS: Vision of the Future		Timothy Zahn	£5.99
☐ 50686 2	STAR WARS: Tales from the Empire	Peter Schweighofer (ed.)	£5.99
☐ 50601 3	STAR WARS: The Mandalorian Armor		K. W. Jeter	£5.99
☐ 50603 X	STAR WARS: Slaveship		K. W. Jeter	£5.99
☐ 50687 0	STAR WARS: Hard Merchandise		K. W. Jeter	£5.99
☐ 50665 X	STAR WARS: The Illustrated Star Wars Universe	Kevin J. Anderson	£12.99
☐ 50705 2	STAR WARS: The Magic of Myth		Mary Henderson	£14.99